Praise for *Commune of Women*:

"*Commune of Women* is a riveting read. The characters are diverse and their stories will find a place in your heart. From Betty's fascination with fake flowers to Pearl's horrifying and tragic life, there is something uplifting in how each found the strength to carry on. In a nightmare situation...the women came out stronger than when it began, with compassion and the will to survive. *Commune of Women* is a captivating read that I highly recommend!"
– Minding Spot

"I very highly recommend this book. The writing is outstanding and the story is compelling, with characters that are real and easy to relate to...It's entertaining, touching, and inspirational. It is full of drama, suspense, mystery, and even romance. This was the first book I have read by Suzan Still and I am definitely a fan!"
– Life in Review

"*Commune of Women* is one book you do not want to miss... It is an incredible tale that will stay with you long after you read the last word. Pick up *Commune of Women* and be prepared to laugh, cry and gasp."
– Single Titles

"Wonderfully written...All in all, *Commune of Women* was extremely satisfying to read and I am honored to have been able to review this book."
– Simply Stacie

COMMUNE OF WOMEN

COMMUNE OF WOMEN

Suzan Still

THE
STORY PLANT

The Story Plant
Studio Digital CT, LLC
P.O. Box 4331
Stamford, CT 06907

Jacket design by Barbara Aronica Buck
Author photo © 2011 by Robert White

Print ISBN-13: 978-1-61188-110-3
E-book ISBN-13: 978-1-61188-111-0

Visit our website at www.TheStoryPlant.com
Visit the author's website at www.SuzanStill.com

First Fiction Studio printing: July 2011
First Story Plant printing: September 2013

To David,
love of my life.

And to all beings who crave freedom.
May your hunger be peacefully and completely filled.

Day One

Los Angeles International Airport
Los Angeles, California
Monday, 8:37 AM

Erika

The noise as Erika steps out of the cab is deafening. She's screaming at Amelia, "Just call Dallas and tell them..." and the fucking phone cuts out. She spins around, hoping to pick up the signal again, but Amelia's gone.

Erika imagines her sitting at her desk, yelling into the phone, "Ms. Reiner? Ms. Reiner?" like an idiot – like she's never had Erika's phone cut out before. It'll take her ten minutes to settle down and remember that she already knows what she's supposed to tell the Dallas office. They went over it yesterday. *Christ!*

The cabby's on Mexican time. He's taking her bag out of the trunk like he's doing it underwater. She's got 40 minutes to dash through the terminal, get through fucking Homeland Security, and catch the flight to Berlin.

Come on!

No one tells you when you crash through the glass ceiling, that one of your job descriptions will be sprinting through airports in three-inch heels, pulling a carry-on. Another place where men have the distinct advantage.

Every loser in Creation is in her way. Why do most people look like genetic throwbacks? They mope along, looking dazed – no sense of direction; no focus. How do they manage to feed and clothe themselves? What must their sex lives be like?

She's like a shark among guppies. If she has to, she'll *bite* her way through this sea of zombies!

Heddi

The thing Heddi always hates about LAX is the frantic pace. Hotel airporters, taxis, police, breakneck Ninja motorcycles and private cars like theirs all swarm around entrances, exits and parking spaces like bees around a disturbed hive. Once she's run that gauntlet, dealing with the mess inside the terminals is a piece of cake – relatively speaking.

Thank God Betty insisted on driving her today. It made it so much easier this morning to lock up the house and set out. The thing with Hal has her so upset! And this Wellbutrin's so strong she wouldn't trust her life or anyone else's with her own driving right now. But Betty – big and solid as a navy-and-red mountain, her grip on the wheel like a strangler's; her jaw, lost in a pudding-like sack of triple chins, firmly clenched in determination – is navigating the commute traffic like one of the Norns clutching the reins of the Car of Fate.

For the population of the L.A. basin, it's business as usual, Heddi notes vaguely. Shopping malls are opening their doors and their parking lots are filling rapidly. School security officers scanning truants for weaponry at the gates must be relieved that, soon, they can grab some coffee in the staff room. Office buildings divided into hive-like cubicles should already be humming with the electronic honey-making that is business. Heddi watches it all slip by like water flowing past.

She usually doesn't indulge her patients like this. And of course, neither one can know that the other *is* her patient.

As a Jungian analyst, confidentiality is primary for her. She's never let a patient drive her anywhere before and this is the first time she's ever come to the airport to pick one up. (She did, once, early in her practice, deliver one to a jet that was taking him far, far away, much to her relief – but that's another story!)

But Heddi has a special spot in her heart for this arrival. According to her own analyst, Dr. Copeland, Ondine represents some part of Heddi's shadow – which is why Heddi always finds her so marvelously aggravating.

"Offer her particular hospitality," Dr. Copeland advised her. "She has much to teach you."

How would Ondine feel, Heddi wonders, if she knew she's paying 200 dollars an hour, so *she* can teach *Heddi?* Analytic psychology, she's found over the years, really initiates one into paradox and irony.

Hospitality is one of the buzz words of depth psychology. It doesn't mean putting Ondine up while she's here, or feeding her well, or even doing what she's doing now – which is fighting her way upstream like a salmon toward the reception area of the International Terminal through a clotted rapids of arrivals flooding out of Customs.

Hospitality means remaining open and receptive to the field of energy generated between them. Not to let it constellate her own complexes, which is what a good analyst is supposed to do, anyway. Except there's always that damned countertransference!

The digital read-out of Arrivals says Flight 3742 from Paris is on time, probably taxiing up to Gate 34 at this very moment. Which means she has at least half an hour to use the loo and then read a few pages of the murder mystery that's got her hooked – if she can hold Betty at bay – before she even has to start looking for Ondine in this mob.

And to make herself suitably hospitable, whatever that might entail.

Betty

Betty never thought she'd be the kind of person who'd go to a shrink. She's as normal as apple pie. Dish water. Laundry soap. Whatever.

But things happen to you in this life; things you don't expect and that are painful. That was a surprise. She grew up so normal and still that was no proof against suffering.

During their last session, Heddi said that Betty survived her normality by staying unconscious – not, like, out cold, but by not really thinking about the things that were wrong. That's why things got so crazy – because Betty wasn't bringing any of the stuff to consciousness.

Betty steals a sidelong glance at Heddi, so cool and aloof in her short blond do and pale blue silk pencil skirt that glints like surgical steel, so slender and self-contained, and she feels a shudder run through her. She's not sure if it's from pleasure at being of service to such a svelte, sophisticated creature, or from pure terror of her.

At their last session, Heddi also said that Betty has made a fetish out of plastic flowers. She says Betty is living in a very primitive state of religiosity. That *religio* is the root word, meaning *careful consideration* of the dangers.

"What dangers?" Betty asks.

"The gods," Heddi says. "The gods will have their way with us."

"Gods? I don't believe in them."

"It doesn't matter. They believe in you."

"So, what *is* a flower fetish, anyway?"

Betty watches Heddi, who's always so classy, take a sip of her Pellegrino water and set the glass carefully back on the coaster that protects the pristine embossed leather of her French desk. "Primitive people make fetishes – of mud, feathers, bones, blood, whatever. Then they project the energy of the gods into the fetishes and believe that it is these things hanging around in their houses that have all the power. You've done that with your flowers: you've projected religious power into them and forgotten about the living gods."

Betty doesn't get it. She's new at this. If her friend, Em, hadn't sworn that this was the best thing for her to do right now to save her sanity, she'd quit.

Maybe Heddi's right – Betty just doesn't know. She says Betty's adorned her house with amulets like some ancient goatherd. She asks these impossible questions: was Betty trying to ward off the evil eye of neighbors? Trying to bind her family to herself with some substitute for love?

It's all a mystery to Betty, but at least she's up out of the BarcaLounger and doing something positive – if navigating L.A. traffic, especially LAX traffic, can be considered positive. It does kind of perk her up, getting her adrenaline going like this. And Heddi's surely in no shape to drive. Betty's never seen her so somber. Maybe it's this mystery person who's arriving that she's thinking about.

It doesn't matter if Heddi doesn't even say a word to her. Betty doesn't expect her to use this time to give her extra therapy.

All Betty wanted was to get out of her house before she took a butcher knife and drove it straight through her own heart.

Pearl

Ever since she lost her spot in front a Pop's Diner, Pearl's been a gypsy. She tried settin up at the pier, but either the wind was too sharp or the sun got ta her. Then she tried a couple a blocks back from the ocean, by the Safeway. But people was too busy, bustlin in, bustlin out. Nobody paid her no nevermind.

She went from a good, solid twenty-dollar day at Pop's ta almost nothin.

It's been two weeks an Pearl purdy near starved ta death, til José come along, him an his cab.

"Pearl, I been looking for you," he says. "All over town."

José was one of Pop's regulars, an he never stiffed her. Ever single time he put somethin in her can – sometimes a dollar, sometimes two, or even five. Always with a smile an a *"Buenos dias, Madre."*

Madre! Callin the laks a Pearl *Mother!* Well, if that don't beat Hell!

"What you are doing, now, Pearl? Where you are sitting?"

"José, I ain't got no spot no more. Since Pop up an died on me, I'm double homeless. Ain't got no home an also ain't got no business establishment."

"Dis is *turriblay*." He rattled off them r's lak he'd got a chill. "Terrible, Pearl. You got to come wit me."

"Whar we goin?"

"I don' know. You get in. We theenk about it."

"What bout mah chariot? Cain't leave mah cart behind."

"You get in, Pearl. I poot eet een de trronk." Pearl smiles at how these Mesicans can mangle the language.

And sure enough, he hefts that damn thing in thar lak it warn't nothin, an off they go.

"Whar you takin me, José?"

"I don' know, Pearl. We got to theenk. How about de pier?"

"Tried that. Most froze mah tush off."

"How about de shelter?"

"Nope. Ain't goin ta no shelter. If'n I gots ta sleep in the sand on the beach, I'll do that. But I ain't goin inta no shelter."

By now, theys out on the freeway. Don't ax her which one, cuz she ain't never drove a car in her life. She barely done rode in one.

José is real quiet an Pearl's thinkin he's regrettin takin her up. But then he shouts, "I got it! Pearl, I know where you got to go! You have good business there."

"Whar?"

"De airport!"

"Now how the Hell am I gonna get ta the airport?"

"I take you."

"Now listen, young man. I don't need no one-day gig. I gots ta do this ever day."

"Jes. Jes, I understand. I take you every day."

"Are you *crazy?*"

"No. Listen, Pearl. I got to go to de airport every day, anyways. That's where most of my fares come from. I take you in de morning and pick you up, my last run at night."

Well, Pearl argued a piece, but José was so enthusiastic, she finally done give in an said she'd give it a try. It's illegal as Hell, she's sure. But the amazin part is, she's made more in the first hour then she usually makes all day.

She's keepin a low profile – stashed her cart with José and jes kept her pack. Hangin out mostly in the bathrooms. She cain't ratly believe how many a them suckers they is. They gots more bathrooms then a pig's got poop.

Pearl figgered out rat away that she could take a paper towel an wipe the counter an the bowl, fore a lady washes her hands. She knows they laks ta plunk they purses down – an them wet spots jes gives em the shivers.

Some jes brushes her off, but more often then not, they'll dig in a pocket or a purse an hand her some change, or even a bill.

Pearl cain't hardly believe her good fortune. Only trouble is, she cain't smoke her pipe. She's gonna have ta do what them office workers do, lak she's seen downtown – step out and have her a smoke, now and then.

Other then that, thins is lookin real good.

Ondine

When you lift off from Orly and climb above Paris, you can see the inner ring – the *Périphérique,* the freeway that follows the ancient fortifications of the city. It makes a huge mandala in the midst of the urban sprawl and confirms Ondine's deeply held conviction that Paris *is* the Center of the Universe. And at its beating heart, on the tail of the *Île de la Cité,* the Great Mother is enthroned – Notre Dame Cathedral. That view never fails to bring tears to her eyes.

Flying in over L.A., on the other hand, brings a different kind of tears to her eyes. It doesn't matter that the full name of the city is *La Ciudad de la Madre de Los Angeles.* Somehow Our Lady, Mother of the Angels, has gotten squeezed out of the center of things – or asphyxiated by smog.

Ondine gropes for her seat belt, as the jet angles down steeply over the web of freeways in final approach. She drags her maroon leather hobo bag from beneath the seat and rummages for her cosmetic bag, refreshes her lipstick, flicks pretzel crumbs off her pristine aqua lapel, pushes the usual errant lock of auburn hair back from her face and glances again out the window.

There *is* no center here. No *there* out there, as they say. She's diving down into an eye-smarting jumble. Into chaos

Sophia

Sophia had a dream last night, on the eve of her departure for Los Angeles. She dreamed she was flying. No plane around her; just her arms outstretched and the wind rushing over her. She simply rose up from her mountain cabin until she was up high enough to see the Pacific Ocean on her right and the white phalanx of the Sierra crest on her left. Her plaid flannel shirt and blue jeans flapped in the wind and her scuffed Red Wing work boots trailed behind her, weightlessly. Her hair arced out around her like long, gray wings. She just flew and flew. It was exhilarating.

Which is a good thing because in actual fact she hates to fly. It raises her blood pressure until she thinks blood will squirt from her ears. So it wasn't a bad thing to take a little preliminary trip and discover flying from a different perspective.

She hates Southern California even more than she hates flying. She loves the Earth. She loves all the creations of the Goddess, right down to the humblest nematode. But Southern California's a wasteland, with all natural life suppressed under asphalt and buildings. If the conference on goddess cultures wasn't too good to miss, she'd never have come.

She had another dream a few days ago that said it all: in the middle of a brand new road, with a freshly painted bright yellow line running right over the center of her, the figure of a huge woman of mythic proportions was completely paved-over in pristine black asphalt.

That's how this civilization treats the *Goddess*.

Sophia does like air terminals, though. She loves seeing the people arriving from foreign flights, especially: the women in saris, the men in turbans, the Africans with deep ritual scarifications on their cheeks, and the little huge-eyed children.

Since her bus for Pasadena doesn't leave for an hour, she's decided to come over to the international terminal and get a dose of the exotic that simply never penetrates into the hills where she lives.

She settles her denim derrière in a molded plastic chair and watches what must be a tour from China coming at her – several dozen Chinese, all talking too loudly in that nasally singsong and dragging their suitcases on rollers behind them. They're perfectly dressed; perfectly coiffed. How do they do that, after hours in the air? Maybe it's genetic.

And here comes a Muslim couple. He's in a well-cut business suit. She's in *chador*, walking three steps behind him. A stair-step covey of brown-eyed children gathers in their wake, dutiful and subdued.

The last time a woman in Sophia's neck of the woods covered her head, it was raining. What must it be like, walking around in a black tent all your life?

One thing's for sure – they don't look like terrorists. But then, what does a terrorist look like? On general principles, everyone's supposed to be hating these people. But they look like a nice couple to her. Their kids are neat, well fed, and well behaved. He doesn't look unkind or demented.

Who knows what *she* looks like? Sophia wonders how Homeland Security handles the fact that three people could be hiding under such a copious garment? Do they shoot first, and ask questions later? Do they make her lift her skirts and peer underneath with a flashlight?

That poor woman is a walking international incident in the making!

She keeps repeating to herself this mantra: *Violence is power; power is violence.*

She will not let her mind think any other thing.

Violence is power; power is violence.

Violence is power; power is violence.

The van's windows are blacked out, and the Brothers have duct taped a curtain between the driver's seat and the back where they are all sitting. At first, she is able to imagine the turns and stops: the potholes on their narrow, weed-lined street that lacks sidewalks and dead-ends under a freeway overpass, the stop sign at the other end, the right turn onto the wider street, the sounds of increasing traffic.

Did anyone notice them, a dozen people all in black, emerging from the dilapidated stucco apartment building, abandoned long ago to its fate as student housing? Or see them wedge themselves and their gear into a battered Tradesman van and pull the side door shut, without ever speaking a word? In this big city, does anyone really notice anything – or care, if they do? Certainly, no one would notice – or care – that they are all male, except for one young woman, who has had a demotion. The men have taken away her name and call her, simply, *X*.

She has lost all idea, now, of where they are, or how close to their goal. She could be in a rocket ship speeding to the moon, for all she knows.

Jamal is next to her, which is a comfort, even though he will not look at her, or speak.

So far, everything is going as planned. Only her bowels do not seem to understand the necessity of discipline. They, and her heart, which is racing so fast she feels like it will explode.

Violence is power; power is violence.

Violence is power; power is violence.

The van leans into a curve and she hears Ibrahim say softly, "Only two or three minutes, now."

Jamal cracks her ribs with the stock of his gun. She is careful not to hit him in the chin with the barrel of hers, as she raises it from the floor and tucks the stock into her right armpit.

There is rustling all through the darkness, as the others make similar preparations. She pulls down the rolled balaclava from her forehead and settles its holes over her nose and mouth.

Then they are all thrown forward as the van slams to a stop. Suddenly, the side door is thrown open and Ibraham is standing in the blinding glare, shouting "GO! GO! GO!"

They all scramble out and run.

Violence is power; power is violence.
Violence is power; power is violence.

Pearl

More good luck! A cleanin lady come inta the bathroom an Pearl thunk, *Oh Hell! I'm busted.*

But turns out, she's José's cousin or somethin. She cain't speak even as good as José. She come ta Pearl an says, "You Berl?"

"Yes," Pearl says, "I am." Feeling kinda feisty, thinkin she's gonna get thrown out. Maybe Pearl's on her turf.

"I Maria, *la prima de José*...his cowsin."

Well, that perked Pearl rat up! "Howdeedo?" she says. "Glad ta meetcha."

"José say, go you for rest."

"Rest? I don't need no rest."

"You come." Maria grabs Pearl's pack in one hand an her elbow in t'other, an steers her toward the door.

"Wait a minute..."

But theys outside in the big hallway, now. Maria don't have enough words fer Pearl ta protest with.

She kinda drags Pearl along, through the crowd, ta this door. No sign on it. Jes blonde wood, all kinda smeary an dirty lookin. She opens it with a key from a big ring of em an steers Pearl inside.

"Dis worker room. You rest here."

She points ta a saggin sofa against the wall an angles Pearl over thar. Pearl's startin ta feel lak a ol mule you gotta wrestle down the road.

Maria lowers her down, pretty firm, an Pearl kinda topples back onta the sofa. One good swoop an Maria gots these strong, wiry arms under Pearl's legs, an flops her down flat an props her head with some pillers.

"You rest."

Ain't no arguin with that!

Theys some vendin machines against the wall an Maria goes over an puts in some coins. Pearl smells coffee, hot an acidy black, soundin lak it's peein inta the cup. She feels the saliver start ta work back in her jaws.

"Is for you." Maria hands her the cup. "I go. You be here. I come."

Without waitin fer no back talk, she's gone, slammin the door behind her.

Truth be told, it don't feel half bad, layin thar.

The coffee tastes lak a cup a heaven. Pearl drinks it down an sets the cup on the floor.

Fore she knows it, her eyes is rollin back in her head.

She ain't rested her bones on anythin this soft fer a hunert years! Ain't gonna hurt nothin fer her ta jes snooze fer awhile...

Heddi

The reception area is ahead, obscured in a mist of moving humanity, so she has no clear sighting of it – at least not yet. She shifts her trajectory to bring her out of the concourse to the left of Customs, near the ladies' restroom. One well manicured hand smoothes her pencil skirt, as she walks.

What's that? Popping noises.

Some Chinese kids must have brought firecrackers to welcome Grandma from the Old Country. That'll make Homeland Security pee their collective pants!

More pops.

Screaming!

The loose mist of bodies is starting to aggregate and move in her direction, like a gathering storm cloud. It looks like a stampede coming at her! Everyone's screaming!

What's happening? What's happening?

She feels her entire body jerked sideways so violently that she almost falls. She staggers, tethered by her left arm, through a doorway.

Betty

Betty's trailing along behind Heddi, as they thread their way through the crowd to where they're meeting Heddi's friend. She's never been to the international terminal before. She was only here at LAX once and that was at the domestic terminal to pick up Larry's cousin, Patty, when she visited one summer from Tucson. She didn't want to do it, but Larry had to work.

She thought she'd have a heart attack. Coming in off the freeway, the exit immediately branched: *Arrivals* or *Departures*. And she's thinking, *Am I the Arrival, or is Patty? Or is Patty Departing the airport? Don't we both Arrive, and then both Depart?*

Then there's the *Long Term Parking* one, the *Short Term Parking* one, the *Rental Car* one, and a couple more she can't remember. In the meantime, she's in traffic going a gazillion miles an hour, with everyone cutting lanes to get to the exit they need.

She had to go around three times before she got the right exit. When she finally got to her, Patty asked if Betty had Parkinson's, she was shaking so bad.

This time isn't so traumatic because Heddi knows exactly which lane to be in and where to park. She's been here a hundred times. She goes to Zurich to the Jung Institute every summer. Plus who knows where on her vacations? Betty thinks that she...

What's that? She hears something! Sounds like gunshots! People are starting to scream somewhere up ahead!

The crowd's stopped their forward surge. They're milling.

Now they're turning around! They've got the same look on their faces as the people running out of 9-11 as the buildings were coming down.

My God! What's happening?

Heddi's just up ahead, still moving forward. She doesn't seem to know anything's wrong, yet.

Betty takes two big strides, leans forward and catches Heddi by the upper arm. There's a door to her left. She grabs the knob and – *thank you, God!* – it opens!

She gives a huge heave and basically slings Heddi through the door, crack-the-whip style. She lets her go and turns to slam the door behind them. She can hear people out in the hall, screaming louder now. And over that, she thinks she hears more gunshots.

When she turns into the room, she almost trips over Heddi, who's sprawled on the floor.

Oh, my God! She's shot!

Heddi

Betty looms over her, a dark cloud of royal blue polyester trimmed in red streak lightning.

"Are you okay?"

Heddi stares up at her from the floor.

Is she okay? She has no idea.

"What the Hell was that all about?" She means it to sound bitchy, but it comes out quavery; squeaky. She's never heard herself sound like that before.

"I don't know!" Betty is sounding squeaky, too. "I think those were gunshots!"

Erika

Erika's sprinting down the concourse, her designer heels clattering, toward Gate 28. Most of the foot traffic is heading the other way, so she's making good time. If Security isn't too crowded, she should just be able to make her flight. Mentally, she's ticking off the things she told Amelia yesterday, at the office...

Something's happening up ahead.

There's some kind of disturbance in the traffic flow. People are milling.

No! People are running! Running this way! What's going on?

My God! It sounds like gunfire!

Something spins her around to the left and knocks her right off her feet. A tremendous tearing pain in her left shoulder takes her breath away. She wants to scream but no sound will come.

Ondine

Ondine is so glad Heddi's picking her up. Technically, the flight from Paris is only eleven hours, but once you add having to get to the airport early for security clearance it's been 15 hours since she set out from her hotel on Rue de Sévigné.

Even flying first class on Air France, which is a very luxurious experience, that's a long time. She's exhausted. Her legs are actually wobbly.

She's instantly aware of the change in air, too. It's hot and dry and tinged with that metallic taste of smog. She feels her lungs constrict, and her long auburn hair, always a kind of sensor, feels dry and flyaway.

She learned a long time ago not to check baggage. She always just takes a little rolling carry-on and stuffs anything left over into her hobo bag. So she breezes right through Customs. The reception area is jam-packed and she starts scanning the crowd for Heddi, who said she'd be to the left, in the seating nearest the restrooms.

The place is like one of those computer-generated animations of subatomic particles in an accelerator. People are rushing in every direction, totally randomly.

She dodges a little pod of Japanese tourists, as she tacks left, and then some Americans. She can tell by the huge suitcases they're hauling. American travelers always think they have to pack their entire closet with them. Then, there's an African couple in marvelous, brightly dyed fabrics, their faces glowing like oiled rosewood. And...*oh my God!*

Oh my God!

She can't breathe.

Adrenaline shoots through her in one pure bolt of lightning.

Men in black ski masks! Guns!

Oh my God!

She turns to her right and pushes through the crowd, blindly.

Sophia

Sophia's getting a little worried about missing her bus. She thinks she'll just start ambling out of the terminal toward the bus stop. Maybe grab a *latté* at Starbucks on the way out.

This place certainly hasn't lost its fascination for her. Maybe she's been living in the hills too long! A couple just passed her, speaking a language that's so foreign that she can't place it anywhere in the world. Could it be some form of Slavic? Mayan? Malay? It's impossible to tell by looking where the two of them are from. They're that wonderful *café-au-lait* color that could be from anywhere or everywhere.

They also seem to be in love. They're holding hands, smiling that certain smile.

Oh! One of them fell down! The man. She's bending to help him and...

Goddess!

The young woman's blown backwards and crumples at Sophia's feet and a squall of blood droplets peppers her face!

People are screaming all around her.

She's standing there like a goose. What the hell is happening?

Then, she hears it.

POP! POP!

My God! Someone's shooting inside the terminal!

Immediately, Sophia hunkers down, wiping the girl's blood from her face with the back of her wrist. All around her, people are scattering.

Through a break in the crowd, she sees the opening to the concourse, just a few feet to her right.

She makes a break for it, running full out, her Red Wing boots really taking flight.

She passes people squatting in the hallway, hands to their faces.

Sorry folks...that won't save you!

She leaps over a body that's sprawling across the floor, then another one.

In her peripheral vision, she can see clots of plaster spurting out of the walls. She's running through a hail of bullets.

Just ahead, two people are disappearing through a doorway. If she can just get there, she'll take cover in there, too.

Her back seems to have eyes – looking for the bullet that's going to paste her, dead through her spine.

Somehow, she gets to the door and slams into the doorframe, wrenching the knob, twisting to get through.

Just as she's crashing forward, a body hurtles into her arms; a young black woman with blank eyes and a twisted mouth. What seems to be a red rose corsage proves to be blood gushing from her shoulder. Sophia heaves her into the doorway and shoves forward.

Then, something hits her from behind with tremendous force.

Ondine

Now there are shots, just steps behind Ondine, and people screaming.

She sees the looming tunnel of the concourse, breaks free from the crowd in Reception and runs for it.

She pounds down the hallway, pushing people out of her way, her powerful dancer's legs pumping, her long auburn hair flapping about her like panicked wings.

More shots and the steady rattle of automatic weapons. Screams.

Ahead of her, a door magically opens. Some people are trying to fit through, all jammed together. She hits the back of the snarl like an NFL tackle and they all pop through the door like a cork flying out of a bottle of champagne.

Erika

Erika's listing diagonally, caught in a web of arms and backs and shoulders, all being carried sideways. Feet are trampling her feet. Someone's hard sole grazes her ankle, knocking off her shoe. It's excruciating and she screams out in pain.

She's in a cyclone of body parts and gravity is having its way with them. Together, they're toppling into a heap.

The pain in her left shoulder is unbearable. Everything goes black.

Sophia

Sophia topples through the door, enmeshed in arms and legs, dragging the injured woman with her. They stagger and stumble forward. Someone's on the floor and she trips over her legs. Then, as one body, they collapse into a heap.

Ondine

She can't get her feet under her. She's leaning into all of them.

Forward momentum carries them a few steps and then they all go down like dominos.

Betty

Before she can get Heddi up off the floor to see if she's been shot, the door blows open and a knot of people falls through. They topple in a mass and fall – right on top of Heddi!

Heddi

Betty's reaching down to help her off the floor when the door flies open and a snarl of people crashes in, all tangled up in each other. One of them trips over Heddi. They all fall. She feels like she's being crushed in a landslide.

Someone is screaming – and Heddi suspects it may be she.

Pearl

Pearl's just driftin off when, next thin she knows, theys a big ruckus. She sets up jes in time ta see bout a half dozen folks, layin in a heap on the floor, thrashin around, screamin.

Now, what the Hell do you make a *that?*

An theys this great, fat gal, lak a blue an red ball, bouncin round the heap. Fatty slams the door shut, squints at the knob, an pushes the little button in. They's people startin ta hammer on the outside a the door, but the lock holds.

X feels triumphant exhilaration, as her black-clothed group races into the terminal, shooting as they run. At first, she knows Jamal is by her side, but then she becomes unsure. The ski masks make the Brothers unrecognizable, even to her, and the crowd is chaotic. Despite the gunfire and the maelstrom of screaming people, a strange quiet settles inside her brain, then, punctuated by wails and the steady pop of automatic weaponry that are eerily distant. Bodies topple over like puppets tossed down by careless children after play. She observes it all in slow motion, as if from a great distance.

Just beyond the reception area, a fat man steps through a doorway, straight into the path of the oncoming Brothers and, shot, is blown backward, staggering back a few feet into his room.

Apparently, one glance tells Ibrahim the importance of this little room because, without hesitation, he grabs X by the arm and slings her in, shouting, "You stay here and monitor things until we return. *Do not leave!*"

With a wave of his arm, he summons the others onward.

X stares wild-eyed at the small room where Ibrahim has flung her. An entire wall gazes back at her from the cold blue eyes of banked video monitors. She takes in the uniformed man, bleeding from a gaping wound directly through the center of his back and slumped on the counter-like desk beneath him. She slowly turns to take in the remainder of the cramped little space, with its rolling chair, small metal desk, beige file cabinet and large wall-hung map of the facility. With a hand still stiff from clutching her weapon, she slowly and deliberately closes the door and locks it.

They did it! They are in!

She expected to die, but she did not.

She does not mind dying for an ideal. This she committed herself to do. It is just that the body is like some balky animal being dragged down a chute to the depths of an *abattoir*. It resists what the mind accepts.

Palpitations and sweat assailed her, loose bowels, panting, and shakes so severe she could not aim her gun. She just had to shoot scatter-shot method and hope she hit something...someone.

So, the Brothers have put her in here to monitor things, while they go charging off to glory! This is supposed to be libratory, this day. Why does she suddenly feel that she is just a female – nothing but a bothersome weakling, a girl, at this moment of triumph?

Maybe she cannot shoot an AK-47, but she is very good with computers. It does not take her very much time to figure out how this entire airport terminal is monitored with cameras, or how each screen relates to a geographic spot on the airport map.

The biggest problem is reaching the computers because X is only five-two and this very fat dead man – along with an enormous lunch box open by his side – makes about three of her. She thinks she may throw her back out, dragging his huge body and his monster food box out of here into the hallway.

The screens show the carnage. Passageways are filled with bodies; waiting areas are running with blood. People are crawling, or flapping like birds with their feathers ripped out. People hold each other like lovers, but bent at odd angles and unnaturally still.

She knew there would be death; hers, theirs. She just did not expect it to be so...agonized. Thank Allah-God there is no sound accompanying these images. She can see by the contorted faces of the still-living that there are sounds being uttered that no ear should have to hear.

She must give credit to the Brothers. They are very efficient. On one screen, she can see a little group of the enemy, huddling behind a bank of chairs. Then, suddenly, some of the Brothers rush up and take aim. The people go into odd postures. They shrivel up like banana slugs sprinkled with salt. Their arms go up to shield their faces. And then the guns jerk and the people go limp. It's strange how fast it happens − like a plug is pulled and the machine just stops dead.

She stares and stares at that frame, long after the Brothers move on. From the corner of her eye, she sees them flickering across the wall of monitors. They stop. They shoot. They move on, popping up on another screen, and then another. But she keeps staring at that first one, as if something more would happen. But nothing does. They just lie there. There is not the flutter of an eyelid or the tremor of a finger. They just lie there, like trash blown into a corner by the wind.

Where did that line come from: "For once, then, something." Wordsworth? Robert Frost? Something from an English class? She cannot remember. But this day, this now, is *something*. It redeems a thousand yesterdays of uselessness and helplessness.

For once, then, I am.

Betty

Since Betty's the only one left standing, she's going to have to be the one to sort this heap of humanity out, like so many pick-up sticks.

There are several legs kicking, none of which seems to belong to a pair. Also, none that looks like Heddi's.

On top of the heap, already wiggling off to the floor on the right, is a slender woman in a beautiful aquamarine pants suit. She has long reddish hair that seems to have come undone from an up-do. Half of it is hanging across her face and chest. The other half is still rolled up at the back of her neck.

Anyway, she seems to be doing fine on her own, so Betty bends to the next person, who's got a big, broad, jeans-clad butt in the air. Her feet are kicking but she can't get a purchase on the floor because of everyone else underneath her.

"Wait!" Betty says. "Wait. Let me help you."

She pushes aside a leg that she doesn't recognize, in snagged taupe nylons and no shoe, with a huge purple bruise on the ankle bone. She makes a place for the big woman's knee. Then, she runs around to the front and supports her elbow, while she slides backward off the pile onto her knees.

Betty helps lift her, as she staggers onto her feet. She can't believe her eyes. This woman's a giant! She's not fat, just large – well over six feet tall, with shoulders like Paul Bunyan.

She looks at Betty, wild-eyed, and rasps, "Thanks. Thanks for your help." She looks down, then, and sees the mess still writhing on the floor. "Oh my! Let's get these others up."

Together, they reach for the next person, the one with the bruise – a pencil thin black woman in a perfectly cut navy suit and with close-cropped hair. When they turn her over, two things are clear: she's ravishingly beautiful and she's out cold.

The reason for that is plain enough. There's blood streaming from her left shoulder. This woman's been hit!

The giant lifts her off the heap and carries her over to a sofa that sits against the wall, with Betty trailing along, ineffectually supporting the uninjured ankle.

There, they find another surprise – a wizened little person like an apple doll, staring up at them like they're aliens that just landed from Mars.

"Lady, you'll have to get up," the giant says through her teeth, because she's straining. "This woman needs to lie down."

There's a flurry of what looks like gray rags and a movement that's ferret-like in its quickness. And there she is, standing beside them, saying, "It's all yers," in a voice like ravens croaking.

The giant deposits her unconscious burden onto the couch, careful to place her outside leg, which dangles onto the floor, beside her, before turning back to the others.

Only there's just one more – Heddi. She's lying there, groaning. She looks like a flower that's been trampled – all crumpled and bruised. The redhead is squatting beside her, holding her hand.

The giant and Betty take Heddi by both armpits and hoist her to her feet. There's an orange Naugahyde armchair next to the couch, so they guide her over to it and lower her into it. She's dazed and mutters, over and over, "Oh my God! Oh my God!" The redhead comes to hover, so Betty turns away and takes a look around.

They're in a small, beige-painted room. Vending machines line the wall near the door. There's a Formica table against the back wall with two molded plastic chairs around it – one green and one white – the sofa, the orange chair, and nothing more, except another door opposite from the one they all just crashed through.

She goes to investigate and finds a little restroom with the toilet jammed in the corner next to the sink. It's about the size of a coat closet.

Nevertheless, it offers sanctuary for a second. She closes the door and locks it. She rests her hands on the edge of the sink and stares into a tiny mirror that's duct taped to the wall, slightly out of plumb.

She scarcely recognizes the face that stares back at her. Her pupils are dilated. Her hair's sticking out from her head in weird tufts. And her face is smeared with blood.

Sophia

What should she do next?

Everything's bedlam. People are hammering on the door, but if she opens it, she may let in the shooters.

She doesn't know who's out there.

The door seems to bulge with the assaults from outside. The knob doesn't look very strong. It could give at any moment.

Sophia needs something to barricade the door. But what? The sofa isn't heavy enough. The only other thing is one of these vending machines.

The pounding and screaming is growing more intense. She leaps to the first machine, inserts her fingers into the gap between it and the next one, and leans with all her might into it. It's heavy as hell.

She takes a new purchase in the little crack that's opened up, slides her whole hand in and puts her shoulder to the edge of the machine. She pushes like she had her truck stuck in mud, with night coming on; pushes until her eyes feel like they're bulging out.

At last, with a shrieking scrape, the machine lurches sideways and almost topples over.

Someone screams, and the fat woman in blue who's just coming out of what must be a bathroom, sees what's happening and dashes over to help.

She wraps her arms around the machine, Sumo wrestler style. Sophia pushes, while Fatty stabilizes. Sophia sees that the reason they're having so much trouble is that the weight of the machine is tearing up the linoleum, instead of sliding over it.

They decide to walk it, instead. They rock it and then swing it forward. Inch by inch, they get it into position and at last, slam it against the doorframe. It would take a bulldozer coming through to push it aside. They stare at each other in shocked relief. And they're not a moment too soon.

The screaming in the hall outside intensifies. There is a thunder of banging on the door – and then gunshots, right outside.

The glass front of the vending machine blows out.

They're shooting right through the door!

"*Get down!*" Sophia screams.

They all hit the floor.

There's a rattle of gunfire and the back wall erupts in little fountains of plaster.

To her left, someone is shrieking hysterically.

Then, the gunfire moves off down the concourse. There is no more screaming and no more banging.

Instead, an unholy silence descends outside.

Heddi

There's a deadly quiet outside. It's both a relief and a horror.

Heddi's afraid to look up, for fear of what she'll see.

She hears someone moving to her left and as they do, shattered glass crunching.

She's still in the chair but doubled over. She looks down at her body – is it all there? She seems to be intact but who knows, really, at a time like this?

When she finally looks around, it's as if everyone is frozen in space like bugs in amber. Bodies are crouched in odd positions all over the room. The giant is closest to the door, ducked down behind the vending machine she moved.

Moving a vending machine, for God's sake! Who *is* she?

On an ugly coffee-stain-colored couch to Heddi's left is a young black woman, covered in blood. Miraculously, between her chair and the couch, Ondine is face down on the floor. At least, it seems to be Ondine, by the long auburn hair and the slight figure. Betty is wedged into the corner to the left of the door, her eyes huge, her polyester suit coat smeared with blood, sobbing uncontrollably.

And then, off to her right, there's this vision straight from Bruegel; one of those ragged, lice-infested crones you see in the background of his paintings, lugging huge loads of firewood or lurking in the darkened doorway of a hovel. She's a vision in gray – ashen face, grizzled hair, faded clothing. She wavers, ghostly, staring toward the door where the shot-up vending machine is bleeding its canned and bottled bodily fluids onto the floor.

"Shee-it!" says the Bruegel. "All them drinks goin ta waste!"

No thought, apparently, for what else might be wasted, just on the other side of that door.

Ondine

Ondine's afraid to look up.

What in God's name has happened?

Are they still barricaded, or did the terrorists get into the room?

She lies still and listens, barely daring to breathe.

Then there's a voice like a parrot's, rough and raucous, saying something about wasted drinks. No gunfire afterward. They must be safe.

She lifts her head to look around. She's on the floor, at eye level with the dirty, worn skirt of a shabby couch. The fabric is faded brown, patterned with stylized flowers in beige and teal. The floor beneath her is white linoleum, streaked with gray – and none too clean.

Ondine rolls to her left to pull herself up by the front of the couch. Slipping her hand onto the seat cushion, she feels something sticky and wet, just as the smell hits her – that briny, metallic smell of blood. She remembers it from the morgue, still fresh on Jackie's body.

She pulls herself up and discovers its source, a beautiful young black woman, with blood seeping – no, more like pouring – from her left shoulder.

Ondine lets out a shriek. "My God! I've never seen any-one bleed like this! Someone...*help!*"

A calm, firm voice comes from behind her. She realizes through the fog of shock that it's giving her instructions.

"Find something you can use to apply pressure," it's say-ing. "You, with the long hair. Yes, you. Use your jacket."

Ondine turns uncomprehending eyes toward the door. The voice is issuing from a huge woman who, neverthe-less, has a voice like melted butter, fluid and sweet. Ondine shakes her head at her. She has no idea what she wants.

The big woman rises from a crouched position next to the vending machine barricade and hunches towards Ondine, keeping her head down. Ondine feels instant re-lief. Somehow, this woman exudes confidence, even in this madhouse.

"Who's got something cotton?" the giant asks, her eyes sweeping the room. "You there, in the blue suit. Give me that scarf... Yes, that one. Quick!"

A fat woman in an atrocious, shiny polyester suit comes wobbling out of the corner, untying her neck scarf and hic-cupping as she comes. Her face is smeared with blood that's already drying and that doesn't seem to have issued from her own person, as far as Ondine can tell.

The giant woman grabs the scarf from the fat woman in one quick, definitive pluck and turns without hesitation to the woman on the couch. "Help me get her coat off," she says to Ondine, not gruffly, just very authoritatively. Ondine kneels down in front of the couch and struggles feebly with buttons on the black woman's suit jacket. The injured woman groans, as if the smallest touch pains her even in unconsciousness.

"Here, let me," says the big woman. She reaches into her jeans and comes out with a pocketknife. She flicks open a blade and, in one deft slice, cuts the sleeve of the black woman's jacket from wrist to shoulder. Then, she works the blade through the neckline, cuts outward through the thickness of fabric at the shoulder and peels the jacket off, as if it were a banana skin.

There's a thin white blouse beneath, saturated in blood. Ondine can only tell it's white by the very top of the shoulder that has somehow remained pristine. The big woman wields her knife like an expert. In one quick movement, she cuts through the blouse and bra strap, too, leaving the wound fully exposed.

It's a nasty, ragged round hole from which blood pours as if it were overflowing from a drainpipe. Then, in an instant, it disappears, as the big woman slaps the wadded scarf onto it and says in a commanding voice, "Here. Hold pressure right here." Ondine moves to do so, as if in a dream. Everything has a floating, unmoored quality to it.

As soon as she's got the scarf in hand and has pressed down sufficiently, the big woman slides a hand behind the black woman's shoulder and flips her forward, putting additional pressure onto the wound and making Ondine feel more efficient.

The big woman is peeling clothes from the injured woman's back now, and probing around. "Thank the Goddess,"
she breathes. "There's an exit wound, too. No bullet to dig
out," she says by way of explanation, meeting Ondine's eyes.
"If we can find some materials, we can stitch her up and stop
some of this bleeding."

She turns to the room in general. "Who has a needle?"
And then, "Someone look around...under the sink there,
or in the bathroom. There might be a first aid kit in here,
somewhere."

She pushes up from the couch and goes to look for
herself because everyone is still moving like their bodies
are suspended in water. Ondine is left holding pressure. It
comes as a real surprise to her to find that she is crying in
silent, wrenching sobs.

She feels a hand on her shoulder and turns to find Heddi
bending toward her from a chair.

"Ondine? Oh, thank God! It *is* you. You're crying. Is it
too much? Too much like..."

She doesn't dare say "...Jackie?" Ondine realizes. This is
hardly the quiet, therapeutic confines of her office where
such a question could be broached after half a session of
gentle lead-up. Here, Ondine is raw, shocked and vulnerable.
Heddi must be in a quandary.

"It's okay, Heddi," Ondine gulps. "I can do this. I'm
okay."

Heddi gives Ondine her famous long look, but it's not
really the same because her eyes are dilated, her face is set
in a harrowed startle and her short-cropped blonde hair is
standing on end. She looks like someone who was in the
bathtub when the hair dryer fell in.

"Really, Heddi," Ondine says again, "I'm fine. I can do
this." With that, Heddi settles back in her chair and closes
her eyes, as if she's fallen into an exhausted sleep.

Pearl

Well, Pearl's seen a lotta damn thins in this life, but this here beats all! Looks lak she done fell inta one a them Civil War stories her Granpap use ter tell, all bout folks shootin one t'other, an cannonades an fusillades, an arms blown off, an legs sawed off, an who knows what else kinda wickedness thunk up by the mind a man.

Good Lord!

They be blood an glass an tarnation everwhar. Theys women cryin an women settin lak theys plum dazed, an women bleedin. An theys this one great tall woman, lak a tree, doin all the work.

Pearl's seen it a hunert times in this long life – everone settin on they tush an but one woman doin it all. Most times, that one was Pearl.

So Pearl up an says ta her, "*I* gots a needle." An she starts diggin round in her bosom, cuz that's whar she keeps the thins she needs most – money, needle an thread, her pipe an tobaccy. The thread she has is good an strong, too. She uses it fer everthin – her dress, her shoes. Even flosses her teeth with it. Picks it up down at the discount store, five spools fer a dollar.

By now, the giant's rootin round under the sink. Out come a sponge, all curlt up. A open package a more sponges. A box a cleanser. Rubber gloves; some used, some new. A squirt bottle a window cleaner.

"No first aid kit." She comes outta thar, lookin darkly.

Without another word, she whips inta the bathroom an starts the same thin in thar. Rolls a toilet paper. More cleanser. A plastic bag a clean rags. Not much more.

Pearl's kinda follerin along behind, jes ta be companionable. She's backin outta that cabinet when Pearl axes her, "Is this here what yer lookin fer?" An she grabs a red box with a big white cross down from the wall.

"Where'd that come from?" the giant asks, amazed.

"Rat thar," says Pearl, pointin. "Rat in front a our noses." Pearl laughs an the giant gots the good grace ta laugh, too.

She reaches out an Pearl thinks it's fer the box, so she hands it ta her. She takes it, puts it t'other hand an holds out her hand again. Then Pearl sees she means ta shake hands.

"Sophia," says the giant, smilin.

Well, Pearl cain't remember if'n anybody *ever* done shook her hand. Maybe the preacher did, back when she done married Abel Johns. But that was a long time ago an she espects he done it in a spirit a irony.

So Pearl's a bit slow, but when she gets round ta it, she puts her whole strength inta it.

"Pearl," she says. "Name's Pearl Johns. Pleased ta meetcha."

Erika

Everything's hazy. There seems to be a big commotion, but Erika can't make out what it is. She hears screaming from someone near her, then it goes quiet. She hears that noise again, like fireworks, off in the distance.

She's floating in a space that's not unpleasant, but her mind keeps trying to kick start itself, to rev up some semblance of alarm over something. But she resists it.

Then, there are people bending over her, pulling at her. They're hurting her! She tries to tell them to fuck off, but all that comes out is a groan. She can't find her tongue. It's sort of stuck somewhere in her mouth, lying useless.

God! Fucking cows!

They're pulling her clothes off!

They're flopping her around like a rag doll. Like one of those two black babies, a boy and a girl, her Gramma sewed for her, with the long, lank legs and arms. Jerry Huff tried to pull one away from her in third grade, calling it a *nigger doll*, and the legs were so long he seemed to be a yard away when the leg finally tore off.

Erika cried, then. She might be crying now. She can't tell.

They're talking and it's too loud, and she still can't make out a word – just the note of urgency. A weight like a pile driver descends on her shoulder and she distinctly hears the word *pressure*.

Something silver flashes near her face.

My God! They're knifing her!

Her clothes rip.

She wants to run, but she can't move.

She's twelve again and it's her father with his big K-Bar in hand, hissing, "You kick me again, you little bitch, and I'll cut your nose off!"

She wants to fight, but instead she sinks down into herself, like always. She turns into the blackness like it was an old friend.

Heddi

Heddi just wants to sit here quietly and calm herself. Then, when she opens her eyes, she's sure – she believes with all her heart – that this will all have gone away. She'll be lying in her bed. The light off the Pacific will be flat and white, making little rippling, shadowy lines of the ocean's wave pattern pass over the ceiling.

It's this medication Dr. Copeland prescribed. It's too strong. She knew it the first time she took it, but she kind of liked the fuzzy state it put her in.

But this is too much. Dreams like this show a severe disruption in the psyche. Instead of helping her, these meds are pushing her to nervous collapse.

Heddi focuses on her breathing, the way she teaches her patients to do it when they're upset – ten long counts in, hold for five, five long counts out, over and over.

But she keeps being disrupted by voices; voices coming from nearby – all around her.

Two women are laughing. One sounds like a file drawn over raw metal. Closer, to her left, she's sure she hears Ondine. How did Ondine get here? She never found her in Reception. Did she? She's confused.

Then she hears the unmistakable voice of Betty. She's asking, "Has anyone seen a broom?" and a voice Heddi now recognizes as the giant's answers, "There's one in the bathroom, behind the door...and a mop, too."

Heddi decides at least to pretend that these are hallucinations, although by now she's onto herself. Denial has always been one of her best defenses. It's starting to look like this will be one of those times when it will be completely ineffectual against circumstances.

Sophia

The room's beginning to reanimate. Women are moving, all around, looking white and shaky but otherwise fit. There seems to be consensus that, for the moment at least, danger has passed them by – although Sophia cautions them to speak very softly.

She looks around to see what needs doing next and what materials she's got to do it with.

Her eyes meet with the fat woman's with the broom. "Is there a way to boil some water?"

"There's a microwave by the sink."

"See if you can find some way to get me hot water. Then bring me that package of clean sponges and those rags that are in the bathroom.

"Is there any sugar here?" she asks to the room in general.

Pearl whips over to the table at the back of the room like a crow dive-bombing a dead gopher. She lashes out with one claw and from among a motley assortment of instant coffee and creamer jars, napkin holders and salt-and-peppers, pulls the little white plastic cubic box ubiquitous to all public places, with its hoard of sweetener packets.

"Rat here. I gots it rat here," she caws victoriously.

"Look and see if there's any sugar in it. We can't use sweetener. Only sugar."

A look of consternation flies across Pearl's face. She moves toward Sophia, proffering the box, saying, "You better look fer yersef."

But Sophia's already turning away toward the couch, where her patient is still unconscious. "Just give me the sugar," she says again over her shoulder, "and leave the rest."

The woman with the long auburn hair is still at her post, holding pressure front and back, weeping soundlessly. She's in an awkward position and Sophia knows that she's probably already exhausted by it. She puts her hand on her shoulder, saying, "You can stop now. I'll need to be where you are for awhile."

The woman rolls to the right without hesitation and crouches there, watching Sophia's every movement – either too stunned to move, or waiting to see what further service she can provide.

Sophia peels the blood-saturated scarf from the wound. Edema has already set in. What was a round, ragged hole minutes ago is already swelling and puckering like a pursed and bruised mouth. The blood flow, front and back, has eased to a slow seeping.

"I'll need that water, as soon as possible," she calls over her shoulder.

"It's heating. Just 30 seconds more."

She uses the time to assess her patient's vitals: the pulse is weak and fast, but steady. If Sophia can get her patched up, she's pretty sure she'll make it.

A fat white hand reaches over her left shoulder, holding a Pyrex bowl of steaming water.

"Dip one of those clean rags in it," Sophia says.

She hears her set the bowl on the floor, a tussling of plastic as she rips open the bag of cleaning cloths, and a splash of water being wrung out. Then, the fat white hand is there again, holding a steaming cloth.

"I'll need another." Sophia bends closely over the patient and begins wiping away the blood, clearing the field of operations. When the rag is saturated, she throws it on the floor and reaches for another – and then another. They go through five rags before she's satisfied.

"Now, tear off pea-sized pellets of clean sponge and dip them in water. Then, sprinkle them heavily with sugar."

Sophia turns to watch her tear the sponge. "No, too big. Here...like this. This size. Dip it. And then... where's that sugar? Pearl? Where's the sugar?"

Pearl approaches like a frightened vizier before a potentate, bowing and proffering as she comes. The cube of sweetener packets is in her wizened hands.

"Just give me the sugar," Sophia says again, annoyed this time.

Pearl advances, just to the right of the fat woman, extending the holder. Sophia gives her a real scowl this time. There's no time to waste here.

"The sugar, Pearl!"

A look close to desperation clutches Pearl's withered face into even deeper gouges and ravines. Then, in the voice of a terrified and ashamed child, she whispers, "Ye'll have ta find it, yersel. I cain't read."

Ondine

Ondine doesn't know who this giantess is, but she's absolutely awed by her composure. She seems to know just what to do.

Some quality utterly lacking in Ondine – and in most women she knows – comes effortlessly to her. Ondine would have to call it command. She's in command of herself, and not afraid to command the rest of them, either!

As she watches her minister to the injured woman, Ondine sees no hesitation, no self-doubt, just the forward momentum of self-assuredness.

She's so fascinated by what she's doing that it's almost too late when Ondine looks at her assistant. This poor woman must be a hundred pounds overweight, and wearing a royal blue polyester suit so hideous that Ondine wouldn't even use it as a Halloween costume. But she's been hanging in there, right at the giantess's shoulder.

Right until she hands her the first sugar-dipped sponge, that is. When the giantess turns and shoves the sponge straight into the wound and blood spurts out and the patient shrieks, Ondine looks over just in time to see the fat woman swooning. Her face has gone the color and waxy consistency of library paste, and she sits back on her big bottom with a plop.

Ondine jumps up and dashes to her. "Are you okay? Can I help you?"

The fat woman shakes her head and Ondine can see that if she opens her mouth to speak, she'll vomit.

"Here. Take my hand. I'll help you up. You need to go to the bathroom and splash some cold water on your face. I'll take over, here."

She's dense as iron. It feels like it'll take a fifty-ton crane to winch her up from the floor. But Pearl comes forward and hefts an elbow, and between them they get her up.

The giantess seems oblivious to all of this. She's reaching her hand over her shoulder, calling for another sponge. Ondine slips into the fat woman's place, tears off a bit of sponge, dips it in water and then sugar before handing it to her. The transition is almost seamless.

The big woman packs the entrance and exit wounds as deeply as possible with the little sponges, and then says, "I'll need another of those clean rags in hot water."

As Ondine hands it to her, she says, "Thanks for taking over. I could tell that other one wasn't up to it. Some people just can't take the sight of blood."

"I'm glad I can help."

"Do you know what I'm doing?"

"Well, my husband's a doctor. My ex-husband. I know a little. You're packing the wound. But I don't know why you're using the sugar. Won't that cause sepsis? Isn't it a medium for bacteria?"

"No," she says, wiping up around the wounds. "Just the opposite. Sugar's an end product, metabolically. It's clinically sterile and the body recognizes it as something of its own. It's used as an emergency field dressing in combat zones."

She wipes the wounds clean again.

"Are you a nurse?"

"No."

"Then, how..."

"Now, where's that needle and thread? Can you thread it for me?"

Ondine struggles just to break the thread off from the spool. It's thick and brown and very tough. Without a word, the giantess whips her knife toward her, blade up. Ondine cuts the thread against it and threads the needle.

Without hesitation, the giantess turns to the wound and runs the needle directly into the ragged skin. For an instant, Ondine feels light-headed. It's the other woman's voice that keeps her focused.

"I've learned the proper suture stitches," she says, mat-ter-of-factly, "but I still prefer the buttonhole stitch. It's quick and strong." She makes the familiar looping, over-and-under stitch, deftly. She works neither slowly nor quickly. Time is not the measure here, but patience, exactness and care.

"We're so lucky she's still out cold. Otherwise, I don't know how we'd get this done. It would be brutal, having to hold her down. And the shock might kill her."

"You must be a surgeon?"

The big woman doesn't answer.

Finally, she finishes. The wound is neatly sutured and there's scarcely any blood still seeping from it. Then, she pulls the woman forward to reach the exit wound. "Can you hold her, like this?"

Ondine nods and reaches to support the unconscious weight.

"Good. This exit wound is nasty. See how the skin is more ragged? This will take some time. Can you do it?" Ondine doesn't even waste the energy on words, just nods, and the big woman bends to her task.

At last, it's done. She cleans the wounds to her satisfaction, and says, "Now, hand me a couple of those clean sponges, whole. Wet and sugar them first." Ondine does and the woman slaps them over the wounds.

"Now, open that first aid box and get out the gauze."

When she has the gauze in hand, she says, "Hold this end here, on the top of her shoulder." Then, she begins expertly winding the bandage in a diagonal, cross-woven fashion, trapping the patient's arm to her side in the process.

"Got to have it good and tight, but not too tight." She glances over her shoulder. "I need a sling," she says to the room in general.

But no one responds. From the bathroom, they can hear retching, accompanied by the caws of Pearl, meant, they are sure, to be soothing.

The only one not occupied is Heddi.

"Heddi?" Ondine says gently. She's got her head down and her eyes closed and Ondine hates to disturb her. "Heddi?"

Nothing.

"*Heddi!*" The giantess snaps, like a pistol going off.

Heddi's head jerks up.

"I need your scarf for a sling!"

Heddi stares at Sophia dully, and then with dawning realization. "But..." she finally manages to stammer, "this is *Hermes!*"

Sophia turns to squint at her in astonishment. "*So?*"

"So...I bought it in *Paris.* I mean...I can't just..."

"Take that scarf that's lying on the floor then, and wash it out. *Now!* I need it." She turns back to her patient with a look in her eye that makes Ondine draw back.

Heddi pushes out of her chair like a sleepwalker and comes to rummage in the pile of bloody rags. She finds Betty's scarf and wanders off with it, her face blank.

The giantess sits back on her heels and surveys her work with satisfaction, then turns to Ondine and says, "My name's Sophia. Thanks so much for your help."

"I'm Ondine. I'd shake your hand, but I'm pretty sure that's forbidden in operating rooms."

Sophia smiles a big, radiant, warm smile — totally unexpected from someone who's just performed a medical miracle.

"Aren't you exhausted?"

"Me? No. All in a day's work. There's still a lot to be done. I'll be tired tomorrow. Or next week. Whenever we finally get out of here."

"Do you really think we will?"

"Oh, yeah. I think we will. If we can keep our wits about us and the door barricaded. Sooner or later, the Powers That Be will prevail and they'll come for us. Our job's to survive until they can."

Heddi wafts back, clean scarf in hand. She's even managed to dry it in the microwave.

"Thanks, Heddi. Sorry I was so gruff. I'm Sophia." She smiles up at Heddi, then turns to fold and apply the sling.

Heddi looks at her as if observing her with field glasses from a mile away. She nods slightly, then turns, sinking back down in her chair without a murmur.

Betty

Well, Betty can't remember being that sick in her entire life – ever.

It felt like all the bile in her liver, plus all the toxins she's ever inhaled or ingested as a resident of the bedeviled City of Angels, just came out in one swell foop.

Pearl was a brick, right there every minute, wiping Betty's face and pounding her on the back when she choked. Chattering the whole time, raucous and coarse as a magpie.

Sitting here, with her back to the wall, the smell of her own vomit rank around the toilet, Betty's just trying to gather her wits. Some part of her can't believe what's just happened, while another part knows full well they're all in deep doodoo.

She's shaking like a leaf. She's *got* to collect herself.

What to do? What to do?

Her mother used to say, *When in doubt, clean*.

So she pulls herself up by the sink, grabs a handful of paper towels, wets them and commences mopping up after herself.

The door opens a crack but the room's so small that the doorknob whacks her in the rump. Pearl's claw, like a hand from the grave, reaches through holding a mug that reads, *SANTA MONICA* in big red letters and is emblazoned with a lurid decal of Pacific Ocean Park with its ancient rollercoaster.

"Here. Water. Drink it. Ye'll feel better."

Betty takes the mug in trembling hands. The surface of the water is agitated, as if by an earthquake. She manages to get some into her mouth, swishes it around and spits. Then, she sips some – and it actually tastes good to her, despite its overburden of chlorine and salt.

Slowly, methodically, she cleans around the base of the stool. She wipes down the walls. She gets fresh towels and cleans the seat. Finally, she feels there's nothing left to do and she's left with the same dilemma: what to do? What to do?

She needs to empty the wastebasket, but where? Into a bigger one in the other room, where the stink will infect everything? There's nowhere else. Maybe there are some garbage bags under the sink in the other room.

That means she has to go out there.

She doesn't want to go out there.

It's got nothing to do with the other women, her fellow captives. Going out there means facing their situation: seeing them all trapped in a tiny little room full of shattered glass and pooled Coke, with bullet holes in the walls – and in at least one of *them*, too. It means facing the full devastation of their situation.

Pearl

Well, Fatty, in thar – her name's Betty, Pearl found out – she's in a bad way. Cain't stand the sat a blood. But Pearl reckons it's more'n that. She's scairt shitless. Which jes goes ta show she's a reasonable gal. Anyone who ain't scairt rat now gots ta be plum nuts.

Now it ain't that Pearl ain't been in some bad sitchiations in her life. Livin with Abel Johns warn't much removed from bein attacked by tearists. Din't a day go by, but she done thunk it mat be her last.

But this here is somethin else. Ain't nowhar ta run ta. Got no woods ta hide in. No kinfolk ta shelter em. Not even a axe in the woodshed, as last resort.

What they gots here is *all* they gots – and it ain't much.

Now thar's one thin Pearl knows fer sure: when you ain't got much, you takes care a what you do got. An thar's lots a thins goin ta waste this very minute. So, she'd better tend ta em, cuz it don't look lak nobody else is goin ta.

Take that vendin machine, thar, fer instance. She's gotta sweep up all that glass, ta get ta it. Then, she's gotta save as much a them drinks that's in thar as she cain. Some is jes layin on they sides, dribblin through bullet holes. If she cain find somethin big – a bucket or a dishpan – she cain pour em all in thar. Kinda lak Skip-an-Go-Naked Punch they use ter make, down at the Grange hall when she was a girl. Whatever anybody done brung got poured in the pot.

Whoo-ee!

Heddi

Heddi has *got* to pull herself together! Two of these women are her patients, for God's sake! She's got to find her professional cloak that, unfortunately, seems to be shredded with bullet holes and soaked in blood – metaphorically speaking.

If ever there were a time when breeding and training should come to the fore, this would surely be it. My God! She's a direct descendent of Robert E. Lee! She was reared to believe that chivalry – Hal Merriweather notwithstanding – is not dead! At Miss Pryor's School, they were taught that the courage of Southern women sustained the Confederacy!

All that must count for something. Surely, she can rally herself and offer something besides dead weight.

The trouble with depth psychology – she sees very clearly at this moment – is that it takes place within the sacred precinct of The Room. Tranquil and beautiful surroundings. Gentle probings. Years to burn, sorting through the psyche. No one ever trains you for triage. It's a profession for peacetime, not the battleground.

In L.A., you see these idiots driving around with *WWJD* bumper stickers: *What Would Jesus Do?* Every time Heddi sees one, she laughs, because *WWJD* turns to *What Would Jung Do?* in her perverse mind.

Well, what *would* Jung do? Right here? Right now?

He was a medical doctor, which she is not. Or rather, she is, but she's never practiced. Psychiatry is hardly training for a medic. It's been more than forty years since she did her surgical residency.

Besides, the giant seems to have the physical end of things sewed up – quite literally, as it turns out. Heddi watched her close those wounds with an exactness that would shame some surgeons. She's an interesting case. Heddi wonders what her typology is? Strong in Sensation, she's guessing.

So if the medical end is covered, there's still the wounded psyche. These women have been through Hell. And Heddi's quite sure they're all aware that Hell may not be through with *them*, yet.

In times of trauma, it's best to restore routine and order as quickly as possible. That's why Jung had people draw mandalas – to center themselves in an orderly universe and soothe their psyches. But they'd think her mad if she tried to get them to draw mandalas right now.

The Bruegel has swept up. Now she's mopping. So the housekeeping end is covered.

What can she offer? All she really knows how to do is talking therapy, and they're too scattered, yet, to think about doing a group debriefing.

Then it comes to her! She knows what *she* wants! She bets the others do, too.

When she stands up, she's surprised how weak and shaky her legs are. In a voice that's not as commanding or compassionate as she expected, she asks, "Who wants a cup of coffee? If the machine's still working, I'm buying."

Sophia

The patient's still out cold, so Sophia can start thinking about what else needs doing now.

Pearl's dug a plastic dishpan from under the sink and she's pouring liquid from the wounded cans and bottles into it. They'll have to screen it through something. Don't need anyone swallowing glass or metal shards.

But Pearl's got the right idea. No telling how long they'll have to be in here. They have to consider the basic functions: eating, sleeping, elimination. As long as they've got water and can defend the door, they can hold out for weeks, if necessary.

Goddess! Tell me we won't have to do that!

A situation like this turns you on to what plumbing is all about, Sophia notes grimly. Without water, they can't last more than a few days. These people are already shocky. If they get dehydrated, they'll start keeling over on her. Not to mention what happens to a toilet in short order, without water.

Their only food is in those machines and it's the lowest quality – processed cheese with denatured crackers, candy bars that are pure sugar, chips of various kinds, stale nuts. Not much to recommend it, but it's all they've got.

They'll have to work out a system of equal distribution. Can't have anyone raiding the machines and taking more than their fair share. Fatty over there looks like she could eat everything in there and look for more.

And they still have their patient to think about. She's going to wake up soon and she'll be in howling pain. The drink machines must have ice. Can it be accessed, without destroying the machine? Ice would keep the swelling down and give her a lot of relief. Sophia will have to work on that.

And there's one more critical factor: the bodies outside the door. She knows without looking that there are at least eight out there. She can feel them. In very short order – a matter of hours – decomposition will set in, and the stench will become unbearable.

Much as she hates to think about it, they're going to have to go out and move those bodies. She's thought about it every way she can and it all leads to that. If they wait, they'll only be harder to handle and the smell will make it unbearable.

And who knows what's on the other side of that door? Are the terrorists still out there? She heard them run off but that doesn't mean they haven't snuck back, or posted a guard somewhere along the concourse, waiting for just this kind of thing – people sneaking out of their hidey-holes, thinking everything's clear.

Once she removes the barricade, they're vulnerable until they know what's outside. But there's no way around it. If they don't move those bodies, they'll be so miserable that they'll wish they were among them.

Ondine

Ondine just feels exhausted. She had jet lag before all this, but now...

The other women seem to be rallying. They're moving about, doing this and that. Heddi just bought them all coffee, which was an inspiration. Amazing how the smell of even this rankest of brews is heartening.

Sophia is moving around, introducing herself to everyone. She stops and talks to each one, shakes her hand and moves on. She's a natural leader. Thank God they've got her. They wouldn't have survived that first assault, without her.

Now Sophia moves to the center of the room and holds up her hands for silence. "Ladies, could I have your attention, please? We have some important issues to discuss." She's still speaking softly, aware, as they all are, that there could be listening ears outside the door.

"First, I'd like you each to put all the change you have in a pile there on the table. We'll use it to buy food for ourselves. I think it would be best if we eat at regular intervals and share everything equally. Are we agreed on that?"

There's a general nodding of heads.

"Second, if any of you has any pain medication of any kind, prescription or over-the-counter, please put that in a pile on the table, too. We're going to have our patient waking up any minute now and she's going to be in terrible pain. We need everything we've got to keep her comfortable. Not to mention that, if she starts screaming, she could draw the terrorists back to us. We have to avoid that, at all costs."

The women begin shuffling around the room, collecting purses. Miraculously, all of them still have them. It must be a reflex reaction to clutch your purse in an emergency. When Ondine travels, she always takes her hobo bag, with a strap that crosses her chest, so no one can slip it off her shoulder in a crowd. She never expected it to have to survive a terrorist attack, but that's what it's done.

She has a big bulge of coins in there but most of them are French. There's also a tube of Advil and a few prescription sleeping pills left over from the flight. She adds them to the growing pile.

"That's great!" Sophia says. "Now, I want to warn you about the liquid Pearl's collected. She was absolutely right in doing it. We have to conserve every resource we've got because they're so scarce. But we have to strain it before we drink it, in case there are splinters of glass or metal in it."

Ondine has an idea. "I know! The patient has pantyhose. She'd be better off without them anyway, wouldn't she? Better circulation. Let's use hers."

"Good idea. You're right. She would be better off. We'll have to be very careful, though. We don't want to wake her up with a start or it'll get her bleeding again. Maybe we'll wait until she's awake. Just nobody drink from the dishpan until we can strain it."

The fat lady raises her hand.

"Betty...isn't it?"

"Yes, Betty. Listen, I've got knee-high's on. I'll wash them out and we can use them."

"Okay. Good, Betty. That's settled." Sophia flashes her amazing smile and continues. "Now, we have no idea what the infrastructure situation is. I mean, right now, we have water, but what if they turn it off for some reason? Or if we're running off an auxiliary tank, already? I think we should fill the bucket and any other large container while we can, as an emergency supply. And then, only flush the toilet if you need to."

"Meaning...?" It's Heddi, needing precise information, as always.

"Meaning, as we used to say during drought times in the mountains...*If it's yellow, let it mellow. If it's brown, flush it down.*"

"Thank you. That clarifies it nicely." Heddi sounds unusually cranky.

"Also, we have no idea if the electricity will stay on. The police might turn it off in order to mount a sneak attack on the terrorists. Does anyone smoke? Do any of you have matches?"

The bag lady nearly does a dance. "Matches? I gots matches! I even gots candles! Rat thar in mah pack! I even gots a flashlat an batt'ries."

"That's astonishing!" says Heddi, the totally urban woman, whose envelope purses bulge in unsightly fashion, just carrying lipstick and a credit card. She's staring at Pearl as if she were some rare species that's just been dredged up from immense depths in the ocean – an albino fish or mammoth squid.

"Thank you, Pearl. You're the winner of the *Who Would You Want To Be Stranded On A Desert Island With? Award*." Sophia bestows an incandescent smile on her that threatens to set the old bag of tinder on fire.

"Now...here's the hard one. I don't know how to say this gently... There are dead bodies outside our door."

A communal rustling sigh passes around the rough ring they've formed, like a sudden gust through dry woods. Heads drop or shake and eyes close or roll. The little haven of sanity they've so tentatively established seems suddenly gashed and vulnerable. Silence descends like the herald of Death.

Sophia honors the moment before she continues.

"In a matter of days, if we're lucky, or hours, if we're not, those corpses will begin to stink. Once they do, this room will become unbearable...not to say dangerous. The gases emitted can be lethal, especially methane."

She looks around the group, taking the measure of each one of them.

"Sooner or later...and I personally would vote for sooner...we're going to have to move those bodies, or we won't be able to breathe."

The silence grows deeper. It's the first time they've balked at instantly doing her bidding. Finally, it's the fat woman, Betty, who voices what must be a universal concern. "You mean, you don't think we'll be rescued, before... before..."

"Before the corpses begin to decompose? There's no way to know. But good judgment would suggest that we act as if we're here for the long haul."

The silence only deepens. Each of them seems cast into a personal Inferno, where their worst fears are materializing in the mind's eye.

"Has anyone tried the phone?" Betty asks meekly. She nods toward the back wall where, to her astonishment, Ondine sees a beige wall phone. How could she have missed it?

Ondine whips to the back of the room and picks up the receiver. The line is dead. She jiggles the hook, the way she's seen people do it in movies. She has no idea why. It never seems to work for them and it doesn't work this time, either. "It's dead."

"What about cell phones?" Betty persists. "Have you tried your cell phones?" They rummage in their bags. Several minutes of punching buttons and futile listening, while spinning to all points of the compass, ensue.

"Dead," Ondine says, at last.

"Mine, too."

"Mine, too."

Sophia has the wisdom to let this moment of deepened discouragement pass without adding to it.

"We can talk about this later. We have time." She glances up at the round institutional wall clock above the door. "It's 12:34. We've been in here approximately four hours. That's barely time for the police to send an e-mail to the FBI." She smiles at her little exaggeration. "Let's not worry about what's outside the door right now. Let's just get ourselves as comfortable as we can, for the time being...and as quietly as possible."

Heddi is about to say something when an eerie sound interrupts her – the high-pitched anguish of their awakening patient. They all rush to her as a body, until Sophia warns them off.

"Ladies, let me handle this. Just go about your business. There's plenty to do. Get yourselves cleaned up. Strain the drinks. See what else you can dig out of the cupboards..."

She turns away to attend to the patient. The rest of them stare at one another like lost sheep.

It's Heddi who rallies them. "As I was about to say, let's introduce ourselves, and then see what we can do to get this place livable."

Betty

They're taking turns in the bathroom. Each woman goes in looking like an extra from a Hollywood horror film and comes out, in due course, looking fairly normal – blood washed off, hair combed, clothes straightened, lipstick applied. It's funny that even under the worst of circumstances women use their lipstick.

Sort of like Nero, fiddling while Rome burned. Or Betty, arranging flowers while her family all moved out.

There are just some things the mind fixes on as necessary or pleasurable, even if they're absurd, or even destructive.

But even as they're moving around, restoring themselves and organizing things, Betty's feeling a growing sense of unease. Heddi's been trying to train her to listen to her feelings. She says Betty just represses them, which allows the unconscious obsessions free reign. Something like that.

When Betty really stops to think about it, though, it's pretty simple. She's missing her routine. At home, it's time for the soaps. She'd put her feet up, have a cup of coffee and watch the afternoon sun lighting up the arrangement in the west window – autumn leaves and chrysanthemums, this month. Maybe have some buttered toast, or a cookie or three.

Before, it would have been the time just before the kids got home from school, the calm before the storm. Since the mass exodus, it's just been a time to blot out her mind.

It's funny, realizing that no one in her family will even know she's in this mess. Larry will probably even talk with his friends over a beer about the big terrorist standoff at LAX, without even realizing she's out here. Sam calls her every day, sweet boy, but if he doesn't get her he won't worry about it. And Serena...well, if she knew, she'd probably be glad.

Another thing that's bothering her is being in a room without windows. She's so used to the light. Not her view, particularly, since it just looks out into shrubbery and asphalt. But the light comes in and spotlights her arrangements – and there's a sense of depth, too. Like there really is more life out there, if she wanted to go and find it.

But in here, with the blank walls, she feels like there's no future, no prospect to look out on or even imagine. There are a couple of travel posters pushpinned to the walls. One shows a sunny beach, palm trees and a serene blue ocean, and the other must be some place in Europe. There are half-timbered houses and a gray, grudging-looking sky not made any more pleasant by being peppered with bullet holes.

The posters don't help. They make her feel even more trapped. She's even had the sensation that the room is getting smaller, as if the walls are actually squeezing in on her.

She never realized that the simple light of the sun was so important to her. Even if she never really wanted to go out into it, it was always there as a potential.

What's her potential now, she wonders?

Will she survive to sit in her living room and feel lonely, ever again?

Even loneliness would be a pleasure, compared to this sense of sitting inside a trap. It's the frightened animal in her – that's what she'd tell Heddi if they ever got to have a session again.

She's sitting here and what she's feeling is something inside that doesn't want to die – but that is aware of death, very near.

For a gal whose biggest excitement is finding plastic daffodils on sale at K-Mart, this new sensitivity could almost be thrilling, if it weren't just flatly paralyzing her.

X

No one has come back for her.

On the monitors, she can see where the Brothers are. They have rounded up a few dozen hostages in the food and shop area back near the gates. It is a smart idea because they can eat and stay there for a long time.

As for her, she is starving. Her stomach is grumbling. She wants to urinate and then eat, in that order. And she wants to do it now.

This is very silly, considering that a few hours ago she expected to die. And now, all her idealism is reduced to animal cravings by a full bladder and an empty stomach. She wonders if philosophers and theologians ever consider that in their revolutionary theories?

The monitors are very boring. Dead bodies do not do much.

She did see one body move, throw off a leg that was wrapped around it and begin to crawl. She could not tell if it was a man or a woman. It crawled right off the screen and has not reappeared on any of the others. She can see the patrols moving along from screen to screen on a regular basis, though. So she expects they will find this survivor before long and shoot it.

On the monitors there are a few pockets of survivors, mostly out in the gate areas beyond the food court. She does not think the Brothers care if they get to them or not. They have what they want – hostages and an opportunity to make the world listen.

Other than that, it is just quiet – very quiet, the way a city never is. She keeps thinking the police will charge in at any second, or that Jamal will come back to tell her to join them.

Or maybe, the door will creep open and that crawling thing will crawl in here with her and she will have to shoot it.

Allah-God, it has been a long day! She has been making sit-ups and jumping jacks to awaken herself.

It took her almost two hours, with so many monitors, before she realized that there is a television set over on the left. So now, she is watching the news, which is being broadcast live from where, but LAX! So she is learning what the world is thinking about them and what they do.

Making the news is a pretty blonde with a microphone in her hand, looking concerned. It is strange how America wants to be fed its television news by attractive blondes. And how these women try to look intellectual and as if their emotions are involved.

Part of the reeducation of the American people needs to be focused on this: could you bear to have your news delivered by an ugly, older woman? Someone with dark hair and an accent? Someone with a brain?

It would seem that nobody really cares if she sleeps or not. The "Brothers" – *ha!* – have not checked in with her once. They've forgotten all about her – even Jamal, apparently.

She could go and find them but that is forbidden. She was ordered to stay here.

Too bad for them! If the cell phones worked or if they would just come by to see her, she could tell them all that is happening – of which there is plenty.

Some things she can see on her monitors, and some on the television. All of it is relevant to them, if anyone were interested.

"By now, the entire world has seen the amateur video taken at the time of the attack: a camera trained on happily departing vacationers recorded the moment when, suddenly, the doors behind them are filled with terrified, running, shoving people," the newswoman begins. X watches as the footage is replayed again. At first, the human flood is silent but urgent. Then, a second wave emerges, screaming, their faces contorted in terror. And finally comes a third wave, bloodied, limping, staggering, their faces blank with shock and their mouths opened for screams that will not come.

Only by seeing what is written in those faces can anyone comprehend what has happened. The reporter's words just slither in one side of the brain and out the other, but those faces speak a language any human can understand: their eyes have looked upon the face of Death.

"Security cameras, too, have captured the initial assault. However, as the assailants are masked, it will take some time to establish their identity. The van in which the terrorists arrived, and which they left abandoned at the curb, has been determined to be stolen. The FBI is presently disassembling it on the spot, in an effort to find the smallest clue.

"One hopeful note: the possible identity of the assailants may be linked to a scrap of paper found trampled in the gutter near the van, with the printed heading *UCLA Kultur Klub*."

X feels as if the blonde woman has just reached straight through the screen and punched her in the stomach. How could they have been so careless? And if the police know about the Klub, what will happen to Father Christopher and the Iman? She reaches for the wastebasket, just in time to capture a stream of vomit.

As the afternoon progresses, she watches the rescue of three groups of people – all of them out at the international gates ready to board when the attack came. To be rescued, they simply come down the covered ramps and then, down roll-away stairways, the kind in front of shiny airplanes in old movies.

Of course, there is more to it than that because there are helicopters hovering and SWAT teams behind barricades, and armored trucks making an avenue for the people to escape. The blonde newswoman is obviously thrilled with the drama of it all.

X expected, then, that the police would invade the terminal – but still, nothing.

The authorities have tried several things, however. They have shouted through the front doors with a bullhorn, demanding the release of hostages and the immediate surrender of their group. They have sent in robotic drones, but they could not get through the tangled bodies in the halls. They even sent in a negotiator, but he lost his nerve halfway down the concourse and retreated. Twice, SWAT teams have swept the front lobby, removing bodies but have gone no further.

Then, the negotiator came back. On the monitor, she watched the way he moved. He was clearly badly frightened. But then, who would not be? He made it all the way back to where the hostages are – and the Brothers took him hostage. They did not even listen to him. In fact, they gagged him and sat him on the floor against a counter.

She thought the approach of the police would be far more aggressive. *Is* it the hostages? Or is there some other reason they hesitate?

She also has seen both the Imam and Father Christopher interviewed on the television early in the evening. Both of them looked very frightened. Father Chris had a large blue bruise over his right eye. Did they abuse him, when they questioned him?

It's the eleven o'clock news now, and she is sure they will show them again. Yes, here's Father Chris now, the same clip, saying, "We started the Kultur Klub in an attempt to bring warring factions together. We hoped that, on the basis of their shared tragedies, these young people would begin a dialogue that would aid, in some small way, in overcoming fundamentalist prejudices and in bringing peace to the Middle East and other parts of the world."

The Imam looks even worse. Because he is Islamic, she is sure that the questioning has been far more severe for him. He looks haggard. There are big blue circles around his eyes. Under his brown skin, he appears pale and bloodless.

"These young men" – he does not mention X, the woman among them, a typical Islamic prejudice against the female – "have experienced terrible losses in their lives. My only hope in bringing them together was to replace with love the bitterness and hatred they carried in their hearts towards other religious and ethnic groups."

She believes the Imam and Father Christopher had good intentions in founding their Klub. What the Klub became was not their fault. In fact, they would have known horror at what the Brothers were planning – and they must be very discouraged now.

This much is sure – they succeeded to help all of them bridge their bigotry towards each other. The individual stories in group sessions, the oral reports on the situations of each of their peoples – these aided their mutual understandings. They began to see that they are not the enemy to one another. They understand, now, with Ibrahim's guidance, that they have but one common enemy.

At first, this frightened them. And it repelled them, that they were being carried in the bosom of their enemy. Then, through days and nights at discussion and planning, they began to see this as a tremendous advantage. They came to understand that Allah-God, as they call Him now to please all their religions, has placed them strategically.

They realized that He has given them a mission that they must carry out. At first, they had no idea what the mission might be.

They all realized that ideology without action is hypocritical and cowardly. They understood that the political is personal – this they knew from most painful individual experiences. What they did not know, and what took the longest time and the most argument, was the nature of their action.

When finally they decided, the men tried to discourage her from participating. "A woman has no place in violent action," they said.

"Tell that to my dead mother and Aunty," she would respond. "Or to your own."

At first, she was torn between her emerging feminist understandings and her allegiance to the men's cause – even though it seemed too violent and sexist to her. But the men did not want her to participate; a prejudice that spurred her to insist on inclusion.

Finally, she won the right to join them in training. Thank Allah-God that she is strong and could keep up with them. They certainly did not cut her the slack, as the Americans say.

But with the guns, she is hopeless. They say she is too small for the rifles. With the handguns, the explosion so close to her ear is painful. "You keep squeezing your eyes shut and the trigger at the same time," Hansi jeers. Even with one hand cut off, he is doing better than she is.

She feels like a failure, but she refuses to quit.

The Brothers stop calling her by her name and tease her by calling her "X." "You are the unknown factor in this operation, so from now on you will be called X." A further humiliation.

At the bomb making, she is better. Her fingers are small and delicate. Once she understands the principles, she becomes the best at twisting the circuit wires and soldering the parts. She handles the dynamite sticks in their paper skins and the blocks of C-4, as if they were her firstborn child. She feels a certain love for her creations.

On the other hand, she is secretly beginning to loathe some of the Brothers. She admires their love of risk, their skill and their power. She loves what they are able to manifest – this action glorifying Allah-God. But personally, they become loathsome to her – all, except Jamal.

They are everything Women's Studies teaches – hierarchical, misogynistic, sexually depraved and simply messy. They expect her to clean up after them. They deliberately do not help her. Every day they deliver the message that she is second-class, inferior.

Still, she envies their confidence that they deserve power. They are convinced of their superiority. She personally never has experienced this.

But with the gun in her hand, or the bomb, she begins to feel powerful. It is intoxicating.

At the same time, she is terrified. When she thinks of their plan, she wants to leap up and make it happen *now*. That is because she expects to die. If she is going to die, she wants to complete this ordeal immediately. She does not want to live with the fear of it, which makes her vomit. Her chest is so constricted with fear, she begins to pant, as if she cannot draw breath fully.

But she keeps on because she will not let down the females. If she is going to die, let it be as a martyr. Death is the ultimate way to prove that women can manipulate political power. If she dies for their cause, how then could these men feel superior to her? Dead, she is beyond criticism.

They write a Manifesto: *We are a multi-national and religiously diverse group assembled for the purpose of affirming international brotherhood* (they would not include *sisterhood*, despite her many arguments) *and to wage war on the American military-industrial complex, and to protest that unquestioning obedience to multinational corporate interests is not patriotic, but idiotic. In defense of the downtrodden peoples of the world, and of their resources and their labor that ought to belong to them and not be stolen by corporate greed, and in the name of Allah-God, we call for a universal uprising against the forces of oppression, and give our lives willingly as martyrs to this cause.*

They labor over this statement for weeks, nearly warring among themselves.

One night, she goes to the restroom and when she comes back, the men tell her to leave.

"After all this time, you are dismissing me?" She is almost too outraged to speak. Her voice is shrill.

"No, no," they assure her. "We have someone coming who will only deal with us men. It is secret – and very important. Our mission depends on it. You must trust us."

So, reluctantly, she goes. But she does not leave. She hides. She sneaks into the next room, puts her ear to the furnace grate, and listens. She hears a man's voice. He is offering their group money to aid the fight. He is saying that they must negotiate, using hostages, and make the government fly them to the Middle East. There, they will be safe to continue the struggle.

She wants very much to go into the meeting room and see this man, but does not dare. His voice goes on and on, promising so many things – guns, training camps, money, access to top leadership. Where have the Brothers found such a powerful man? Why does one with such power interest himself in them? She sits on the floor and feels even sicker and more anxious.

After that, there is no stopping the Brothers. The rhetoric of violence intensifies. They feel they are indomitable.

This is her weakest moment. She is nearly overwhelmed with temptation to tell them that she cannot join them. That they are correct. She is the weak link. She is the one who will make an otherwise successful operation come to grief.

It is a supreme act of will not to falter. She accomplishes this by saying nothing. She sits like a stone and accepts their dictates. She fears that if she speaks, it will come out as a whimper. This, she cannot tolerate in herself. She chews a hole inside her lower lip, but she manages to stay silent.

And now, here they are. Here *she* is. They, the Brothers, are elsewhere. But they are all here in the Los Angeles International Airport international terminal.

To their credit, they have made a tremendous victory. Bodies lie heaped in the corridors. They have vanquished the enemy.

To their discredit, they have murdered a few hundred unarmed innocents. Bodies lie heaped in the corridors. In what way are they distinguished from the enemy they hope to vanquish?

Pearl

Well, one good thin bout this here sitchiation is, Pearl ain't gots ta figger out a place ta sleep. By the looks a thins, ain't none of em a-goin nowhar.

Pearl never had much use fer other women. That's why she cain't go ta the shelter. All them women. They fuss bout this an nag bout that. Worse then a swarm a hornets. She'd rather set down on a anthill then go ta that damn shelter.

So Pearl cain't quite get the jist a these here gals. Theys a different breed a cat. Theys so nice an proper an polite, one t'other, you'd think they was at a church social. Or a meetin a the Golden Star.

Not that Pearl's ever been ta either, but she's seen it often enough – ladies all dolled up, wearin heels an hats, carryin cake plates, sayin, *Oh, Howdy-do? Oh, how pretty you look! Oh mah, ain't it a lovely day?*

But that ain't even quite rat. These gals ain't simperin. Theys more lak folks bein real gingerly, tryin ta keep thins in balance, goin over the falls together in a big barrel. Alls it takes is one panickin an the whole she-bang gonna flop over an they'll all be kilt.

Her Granny use ter say, *Thems cain't work together, fails together.* From the look a this crowd here, ain't no one plannin on failin.

Lak, at dinnertime, everone gots a paper plate from the stack on the microwave. Sophia passed a pen an everone put they name on they own. Pearl made a *X* on hers.

Then they parceled out the food. Ever one of em gots ta choose somethin. Pearl chose peanuts. Nothin keeps yer stomach from growling lak peanuts!

But the machine don't deliver but a little tiny sack an then she gots ta divvy it five ways. Nothin fer the nigger gal. She don't get nothin but water, says Sophia.

Then Betty, she chooses cookies. Thar warn't but four a them. She breaks em, so everbody gots roughly they share.

Now the one called Onion or somethin lak that, she looks an looks inta that machine, lak all of a sudden a fried fish is gonna appear in thar, or a cherry tart. She chooses crackers an cheese, after the chef turnt up missin. That split up purdy good.

Sophia come next. She takes some corn chips, rat smart. No waitin around. Pearl laks a gal knows her own mind.

Then Heady. She's as bad as the Onion. Worse. She whines bout this an sniffs bout that, an Pearl's bout fed up. It's almost as bad as the shelter. But then, Heady gots a smile full a whimsy an says, "I know! I'll buy dessert!" an pops fer a Payday. Sophia saws it up lak a log with her knife an that's how Pearl gots some of her peanuts back!

By the time theys finished parcelin stuff out, the plate's almost full. Shoot! Been many a nat Pearl ain't et this good!

Don't seem lak time's passed much, but all of a sudden, it's going on 11:00. Everbody's sayin how tared they is.

Ain't no way fer a body ta get comfortable here. Floor's hard as a straw boss's heart. The ladies is beddin down, best they cain. Everbody gots issued a roll a toilet paper fer a piller.

Pearl, she gots her pack. Never lets hersef be parted from it. She gots a blanket an a piller made from a sack stuffed with plastic bags – latweight ta carry, but nice an soft under her head.

Sophia turnt out the lats, hours ago. She was scairt the lat'd go through the bullet holes in the door an out inta the hall an attract the tearists. Ain't nothin but the lats in the machines, an them kinda purrin ta theirselves, keepin thins cold.

Lots a gruntin an groanin as the gals settle in – especially from that nigger gal. Sophia's layin next ta her, by the sofa. She reaches up an takes the gal's hand.

Lord knows what tomorrow'll bring – ain't a one a them does, Pearl's certain. That be the joy a it, she s'poses, from His perspective.

Ain't none of em gonna take it fer granit, an that's fer sure!

Erika

All day, the women's voices are like the hum of bees. Sometimes, Erika hears it. Sometimes, she drowses and dreams she's in a meadow full of flowers with the bees buzzing through them.

Then, the pain shoots through her and she wakes herself, moaning.

This big woman, Sophia, is always there when she opens her eyes. She's got a nice way with her, firm but gentle.

She keeps getting Erika to take tiny sips of water. She's swallowed she doesn't know how many pills. Each time they take effect, the voices of the women fade and she's in that meadow again. It's not bad, really.

Sophia says she was shot by terrorists. That would make Erika laugh, if it didn't hurt too much. That's what they say about women over 40: that they have a better chance of being shot by terrorists than of finding a husband – and her, only 34!

That's our little Erika – always exceeding the norm. Ever the over-achiever.

If they survive – and Sophia thinks they will – she'll enjoy telling that one over lunch.

With the lights out, everything's quiet – except for someone's snoring over by the vending machines.

In a few hours, she would have been in Berlin in that Bauhaus hotel with the impossible name. All those clean lines and minimal furniture. Hot, hot shower. Duvet a foot deep in goose down. Dining room, featuring an impossible number of ways to cook *schnitzel*. Nothing like a steamed vegetable or garden salad within the national borders of Germany.

She would have been tired, hungry, and bitchy at having to eat such heavy food.

Albert was right. Everything's relative.

Instead, she's opted for a life-threatening wound and a steady diet of water and assorted meds, while lying in deep pain in a hacked-up thousand-dollar Donna Karan suit on a blood-crusted couch. Apparently, one half of an eight hundred dollar pair of heels is lying out in the hall under a pile of dead people.

Another stellar career move brought to you by *Black Girl Makes Good Productions.*

X

An army has been steadily amassing all around the perimeter of LAX's international terminal. X watches it all with growing alarm on the television news.

"From the first frantic police responders in the morning to the black vans of SWAT teams rolling in from surrounding areas all afternoon," the blonde reporter intones, "to the early evening arrival of a convoy of Elands and Bradley Fighting Vehicles, armored personnel carriers from the local National Guard Armory, an exotic Armada of high-tech and imperviously armored gadgetry is being assembled."

The television shows the view from the helicopters that continually circle the building, their searchlights strobing through the darkness. "The surrounding area is a sea of flashing red lights, a conglomeration of Police, Sheriff, FBI, FEMA, Red Cross, and OES vehicles, fire trucks and ambulances, all throbbing in the perennial starless dusk that is an L.A. night."

The reporter announces that the LAPD relinquished control before noon to the highest-ranking FEMA official in the L.A. area. He is shown conferring with a man from the Office of Emergency Services. Until late into the evening, it is reported, they are giving orders and organizing the fleet of vans arriving with everything from sensitive snooping devices – their antennae and broad dishes giving them a vaguely insect-like creepiness – to catered sandwiches. A second wave consisting of more and more media trucks and vans is fulminating at a distance.

Finally, close to midnight, a black helicopter beats swiftly across the parking area and descends, all TV cameras trained on it. A tall man emerges from it, wearing black jeans and sneakers and a black jacket with *FBI* emblazoned across the shoulders in white. He is followed by a shorter man who looks like a box freezer in his chunky jacket of the same white on black design.

Handshakes go around the small group assembled to greet the two men just arriving from Washington D.C. The tall man is introduced to the public as the incident's Director of Operations, the number one spot, and the shorter one is number two, the On-Site Commander.

By now, the commanders from FEMA and OES look exhausted and irritable, as if they are trying to disguise that they are out of their league. With evident relief, they relinquish control to the FBI command staff who immediately duck into a nearby tent to confer with various agency commanders and captains. X wonders sleepily how these new arrivals will affect her fate.

Despite her exhaustion, she is impressed by the efficiency of these men. FBI technicians have strung up phone lines, erected radio repeaters and gotten encryption devices on line. The Tactical Operations Center has seen to it that there is a free flow of information to the command, while Special Agents in Charge storm around the various operations looking resolute and making sure that everyone can now talk to everyone else. She learns all this from the newswoman who, at the end of this long day, is also looking exhausted and disheveled.

"Information *is* flowing," the reporter enthuses, one hand holding her blonde hair back from her face in the rising night wind. "There are now some revelations on the identity of the terrorists, hunted down by investigative agents who, with the help of Interpol, have tirelessly chased leads, worked timelines and scoured the intelligence logs.

"Negotiators are huddled with psychologists, talking through scripts and plotting strategy, while the FBI's Hostage Rescue Team is primed for the assault they've trained so long to perform. The sniper commander has placed his best shots in prime strategic positions. All is in readiness! What will the next move be?"

The TV screen suddenly fills with an advertisement for a gigantic car lot. X shakes her head in aggravation. All that blonde woman needed to say was, "Tune in tomorrow for the next episode of *Terrorists in L.A.!*" She treats the entire incident as if it were entertainment. X can scarcely contain her disgust.

The news returns to the screen. They are signing off for the night. The camera pans away from the blonde woman. Only a few hundred yards further out from the throbbing ring of emergency lights is the steady river of headlights, the never-ceasing traffic on L.A.'s freeways, flowing on and on, sounding like falling water. Only a few miles further, X imagines, the Pacific Ocean rocks in its vast basin like a cauldron of molten tar. The shore lights of the city reach feebly into its bottomless blackness and then, a hundred yards from shore are lost, drowning in the fathomless dark.

Day Two

Heddi

Heddi's quite sure she's never spent a more miserable night in her entire life. Not even in that fleabag motel up on the Big Sur coast, where the mattress sloped 30 degrees and she slept hanging on to the edge all night to keep from rolling downhill into Hal. Who, of course, slept like a baby.

She rubs the bruises from yesterday's pile-up gingerly. Her watch says its 5:14, but you'd never know if that was morning or afternoon in here. Isn't there a law against building rooms without windows – some fire code, or something?

She was more awake than asleep, all night. She didn't hear a sound outside in the concourse and she had this funny thought that it was all a mistake. That this morning some worker would unlock the door and here they'd all be, all over the floor, their heads balanced on rolls of toilet paper. And the people in the concourse, with their rolling suitcases and suiters over their arms, would look in here and frown and wonder what the hell was going on.

That struck her as hilarious. She started to giggle and had to throw an arm over her mouth to keep from waking the others – something she definitely does *not* want to do.

Pretty soon, these women are going to be waking up, anyway, and Heddi dreads it. She wishes they could all just lie here, absolutely still, until the police come for them. Being caged up with all these women and their anxieties today is going to be like running the group therapy session from hell.

Already, she hears someone moving over by the machines. She opens her eyes just a slit, not letting on she's awake...

Oh, it's the Bruegel. Look at that old sneak!

She tiptoes over to the table. Takes some coins. Tiptoes back to the machines. Looks around... Puts in a coin. The noise of it dropping is like a freight train rolling through. Looks around again... No one is stirring. Drops in another coin...and another, until there's a soft *whack*, as a cup drops and then the sound of coffee squirting into it.

The smell fills the room.

Still no movement from the others. Maybe they're all dead from shock. Surely, they can't have slept through that old reprobate's performance.

There she sits on her blanket, leaning against the machine with her pillow behind her, sipping her coffee like the Queen of Sheba.

What's she doing now?

Rustle, rustle, rustle.

Enough noise to wake the dead – so Heddi guesses the others *aren't*, after all.

Oh! I don't believe this! A pipe?! The woman smokes a pipe?

Sure enough. The Brueghel's packing her pipe with... what? Marijuana? No. Smells like tobacco. Heddi's a Virginia girl. She'd know the smell of tobacco anywhere.

She's striking the match – that sharp smell of sulphur!

Sulphur, coffee, tobacco smoke. Cheap coffee. Cheap tobacco smoke, the lowest grade. But what smells! Elemental smells of Heddi's childhood. Those, and horse sweat, oiled leather, hay, kerosene from the stable lanterns. She can almost hear Tobias nickering for his morning apple and Amos, in that baritone that could soothe a skittish horse – or a frightened child – saying, "We-e-e-ll, good mornin' there, Miss Heddi. You up bright an' early dis mornin'."

And little Heddi, barely up to his kneecaps, smiling at his mock surprise, with one hand on her hip. "Amos, you know I come here this time every morning!"

And Amos, beaming in feigned confusion. "Is dat so, Miss Heddi? Now, how could I a forgot dat?"

Another elemental – her first flirtation. Those early morning exchanges with Amos filled her empty little heart and set high her expectations for all of male-female love – it would be tender, humorous and gallant. It would always cherish and honor her.

Yes, Amos, wherever you are, I am up bright an' early dis mornin'. And you would never, ever believe this world I've awakened to. Thank God you lived out your life among pitchforks and currycombs! You were made of too fine a stuff for the Age of AK-47s.

Pearl

Well, if this don' beat all! Pearl cain't believe she done fell inta such good luck! A good, safe nat's sleep, nice an warm, plenty a food, an good, black coffee! She's been roamin this earth fer a hunnert years an the Lord finally done smilt on her.

If her luck holds, they'll be in here fer a day or two more, an she cain rest up. Since Pop died, she confesses, she's been feelin poorly. Don' quite know what ta do with hersef. If she cain set a spell, she'll get hersef collected, she reckons.

José done her a good turn. She wonders what's happent ta his cousin, Maria? Hope she's alrat. Them tearists mean business. Another piece a good luck, she was in here when all Hell broke loose.

Alls she gots ta do is survive them women.

Sophie's a good egg. The nigger gal ain't gonna be no trouble. Betty, she strikes Pearl as a gal with a heart – but she looks ta be rat on the brink a hysteria, lak she'll bust out laughin or cryin or both, an fer no patic'lar reason.

Then, theys this Heady woman an the Onion. Pearl don' ratly know how ta consider them. Theys too high-toned fer the laks a her. Pearl watcht em at supper last nat, pickin through all the good food the Lord done provided lak they was lookin fer jewels in hog slop, little fingers prinked. *Too fine fer feathers*, her Granny use ter say.

Before everbody wakes up, Pearl's gonna get in that bathroom thar an freshen up. She'll rinse her out some undies an maybe soak her feet in the john. Loosen up some a them callouses.

The Lord done blest her today an she's gonna take full advantage of it.

Sophia

Sophia didn't sleep all night. She kept dozing and then instantly waking, the way you do in a combat zone, constantly checking on Erika. Sophia thinks she'll mend. Today will tell. If an infection's started, it'll show today.

Not a sound from the concourse all night. Where on Earth are the police? How could it take this long? They've got to have an army out there, by now – SWAT teams, ambulances, helicopters, FBI. Maybe even National Guard and tanks. A whole city of news trucks, at a safe distance. But not a peep, in here. It's eerie. What could be wrong?

Maybe they've taken hostages. That's probably it. They've got a whole bunch of people rounded up, somewhere in the terminal, and the police are afraid to come in. That must be it.

The terrorists must have a demand of some kind, she figures. They're negotiating. Otherwise, why do this? They could just send in a suicide bomber...get it over with, if they're just pissed and want to make a statement. No. They want something...passage to Libya, release of a fellow terrorist from prison...something like that.

That means no heroic rescue any time soon. Negotiations will take time.

Meanwhile, the police'll be planning a strategy. Spotting the lookouts. Setting up snipers. Reading the buildings with infrared to see where the concentrations of bodies are...living bodies.

She wonders if a decomposing body shows up on one of their scopes? Even a dead body emits heat. Then it cools. Then it starts to rot, which is a form of slow fire – so you get heat again. She'll have to ask someone when this is all over.

Betty

All Betty wants to do is cry. She's been lying here – how long? And she just can't stop. The tears just flow and flow. Thank goodness she keeps Kleenex in her purse.

Her nose is running, too. She's a big, blubbering mess – except she's not blubbering, not aloud anyway.

Betty's never cried like this before. When she cries, she always wails. But here she's trying to be quiet. But that doesn't stop the tears. They just well up and spill over, without her even thinking much about it. They have a mind of their own.

Heddi would want to know what she's crying about. Betty hasn't a clue. It's just scary and overwhelming. They're locked in here; dead people are heaped in front of their door; her family doesn't even know she's in trouble...or care, probably. This room is small and ugly. There's a gutted Coke machine looming over her.

Isn't that enough?

She just wants to do what it takes to get through this. Thank God Sophia and Heddi are with them! They seem to have some idea of what needs doing.

She just doesn't understand why she can't stop crying. Maybe it's because her backside is numb from lying on this floor.

Or maybe because she's hungry. What they had for dinner last night was nothing more than a snack. And breakfast this morning isn't going to be any better. Betty's like a vole – she needs to eat her own weight, every day, just to stay balanced. She's afraid she's waking the others up with the thunder rumbling in her stomach – another thing she can't control.

She can imagine that they'll be trapped in here for weeks, until they're reduced to drinking tap water. Maybe one of them will die, finally, and then they'll have to decide whether to eat her or not, just like that problem her high school philosophy teacher gave on a test: several men are on a boat, lost at sea. They're starving. They have no way to catch fish. Someone proposes that they select lots and the loser gets killed and eaten. Write an essay: did she think that was a good plan, or not?

Well, what kind of question is *that?* What L.A. high school student could relate to sitting in an open boat in the middle of the ocean, chewing on a raw hunk of human flesh? That's the kind of thing you only read about in the *National Enquirer*.

Betty wrote that she'd rather die than eat another person. Then, after she was dead from starvation, they could eat *her* if they wanted to – that way, her life would be lost for some purpose. She'd felt noble when she handed in her paper.

She doesn't feel so noble, now. She doesn't want to die – and she doesn't want anybody gnawing on her thighbone, either, thank you very much.

Ondine

All her adult life, Ondine has felt exhausted. She drove herself. Everyone thought she was Ms. Congeniality. She was always the one with the biggest picnic hamper at soccer matches. Always had the cleverest theme parties, like the time, for Richard's birthday, she transformed the backyard into a pirates' grotto. Or the Marie Antoinette wedding shower she gave for her friend, Joan, all pink and green.

Heddi says she's tired all the time because she's an introvert who's been living an extroverted existence. She says that kind of reversal of type can be extremely harmful, physiologically.

And in France, at Tante Collette's, Ondine finally started to understand what she means. One day, she felt so strange – she thought she might be coming down with something. Then, she realized – *I'm relaxed!* It had been so long, it felt pathological!

Well, this morning, after a miserable night of repositioning a roll of toilet paper at the back of her neck and awakening from near-hallucinogenic dreams, she's exhausted again.

She guesses escaping death at the hands of terrorists counts for extroversion.

Erika

Erika's glad to hear the others start to move around. She was beginning to think this night would never end.

Sophia's been shoving pills down her, but – *I'm sorry* – Advil really doesn't cut it when you've got a hole bored clear through you!

Sophia says she shouldn't eat anything. Who's hungry? And she wouldn't eat that junk, even if she were hungry – which she's not.

She feels hot and sweaty, and like something with big teeth is gnawing on her left shoulder while jabbing a red-hot wire right through the bullet hole.

Christ! She pays enough taxes. Wouldn't you think the LAPD could get it together to come and rescue them? Sometime soon? Like, before she dies.

X

Oh! She must have been sleeping!

Where is everybody? All the monitors are quiet.

Oh, there they are.

Still with that cluster of civilians who, for the most part, are still sleeping on the floor. A few are sitting up but with their knees drawn up and their arms around them like they need something to hang onto – or hide behind.

The Brothers are there, too, either standing and talking, or lying down, asleep. But where are the sentries? Maybe it's the changing of the guard, although she does not see anyone in the corridors right now. Are the Brothers becoming careless?

With those ski masks on, it's impossible to tell who is who. Could that be Jamal, over by the restroom door? She cannot tell.

Ah! Now they are moving. Six of them go off into the corridor and she starts to see them flitting from screen to screen. They split up into pairs and she monitors their individual trajectories through the terminal.

It is strange, seeing them moving past bodies that will never move again. One of them has stopped and is rooting through a pile of bodies with the barrel of his rifle. And...

Oh! He just shot someone who must have made a fake death. The body arcs up from the pile and then slams down. The Brothers move on, but more furtively, looking front and back. Probably they are worried the shot will have alerted the police. But they do not have to worry. She can see the police – or FBI or NSA or whoever they all are. They are on the monitor farthest to the left. They are still out by the main doors, massed like the starting lineup of one of their American football games – one that never begins.

She feels that she is playing an authentic role in this action, even though she is not out in the corridors killing people. With these monitors, she is the first to know what is happening outside – if only the Brothers were interested.

She turns on the news and there is the same blonde newswoman again.

In the camps in Palestine the women hold everything together, while the men sit around and roll cigarettes, smoke and talk politics. The women cook and tend the children and clean and sew and haul water and stand for hours in the aid lines.

Not one of those worthy creatures looks like this one, with her plastered-in-place, artificially-colored hair and her artificial frown and, when she forgets that it is a serious report she is giving, her artificial smile.

It makes X proud that she is a warrior; that she is not artificial. Her beliefs are part of her. So what if her hair is not golden? So what if she does not wear makeup? Jamal says she is beautiful. For whom else does she need to be beautiful? She does not need to flaunt herself over fifty states as this woman does.

She is beautiful because her heart is pure.

Heddi

It's hard to get enthusiastic about breakfast when the menu only consists of candy bars and chips. At least there's still coffee. That rallied everyone at bit. When that runs out...

This is going to be a really long day unless they can find a way to make it interesting. In the hallowed halls of her night's rest and the pillared temples of her deepest thoughts, Heddi made a plan. Now, she's feeling too chicken shit to propose it.

This is the biggest challenge of her professional career; the ultimate group therapy session.

Has she got the balls to try to pull this one off? Has she got the energy?

Poor Betty is dissolving – and they haven't even been here 24 hours yet. Ondine looks like she's just gone around the world in a hot air balloon. Sophia is strong but Heddi can tell she's exhausted from all her tending of Erika. And Erika looks like boiled Death under a vermouth demi-glaze.

The only person who seems to be thriving is that old lizard, Pearl. Heddi supposes you couldn't daunt *her* with a jack handle.

If she were going to do something, this would be the moment. Their royal repast is over; morning ablutions are finished. Everyone's kind of milling around or sitting there, dejected.

This is it...show time!

Heddi claps her hands. "Ladies, may I have your attention?"

And then she makes her pitch. "Since we seem to have nothing but time on our hands, how about getting to know one another better? What if we each told a story about ourselves? Anything. Happy. Sad. Long. Short. Just something to help pass the time and to help us get acquainted."

They're staring at her dully, like a pasture full of shocked cows. Finally, Betty asks, sniffing and wiping her nose on a paper napkin, "What do you mean?"

Heddi starts over. "Well, I just thought it might pass the time if..." Etc., etc., etc.

Ondine sighs and says wearily, "I can't think of a thing. If you start, Heddi, maybe the rest of us will get inspired."

Oops! She hadn't anticipated that.

There's a weak chorus of "Yeah" and "Good idea."

Tag! She's it!

She rummages around in her bleary mind for something that might catch their attention. The story she calls *The Holly and Heddi Show* might do it. It's not exactly the stuff of Jungian analysis, but it has a quality of low comic relief that might be...well...a relief.

"Okay," she says. "I'll tell you this crazy story about my step-daughter, Holly, and me. But you have to promise that if it's boring you stiff, you'll stop me."

"Ain't lak the Chip 'n Dale boys is about to make they appearance." This from the Breugel, seated in her domain near the candy machine. She's contentedly picking her teeth with the blade of a small pocketknife.

"Okay then. Here goes..."

Heddi tugs at the hem of her silk skirt, bringing it down over her kneecaps and squirms a bit, nestling her bottom deeper into the cushion of the orange Naugahyde chair. She clears her throat, glances to see if anyone is interested and finds, to her discomfort, every eye – even Erika's feverish one – fastened on her.

"Well, one day, Roscoe calls me, frantic," she begins...

"They're gone!" he screams. Heddi holds the receiver out a little from her ear.

"Who?" she asks.

"Both of them!" he screams again.

She's never heard him like this before, although Holly – Hal's daughter by his first wife, Sharon – has often told her, in afternoon saga-ettes while Roscoe is out in the orchards on the spray rig, contentedly dousing every living thing with toxins, that he frequently falls into these hysterical rages.

If you have to choose between Holly or the soaps, Heddi always tells her best friend, Linda, choose Holly. No commercial interruptions and the quality of immediacy is compelling. Only Holly and Roscoe don't dress as well as their TV counterparts, their at-home attire being selected from a wide range of sweat pants.

So, there is a short pause while Roscoe collects his wits. She hears his heavy breathing – which may represent volcanic emotions or just the pumping up of his energies before a belch.

"Both of *whom?*" she asks, with what she hopes sounds like patience.

"Holly," he gasps. "And the wolf."

"Together?!" Now, Heddi's screaming. Holly's not allowed to even touch the wolf. Why would Holly run off with the wolf? It makes so little sense that Heddi suddenly thinks, *Oh my God! The wolf ate Holly!*

While she's thinking this, Roscoe's talking and she's so addled that she doesn't understand a word of it. She has to ask him to start again.

"Holly ran away from home," he says, laboriously now, with exaggerated patience.

"With *Rosebud...?*" Heddi asks, incredulously.

"No! Dammit! No!"

The explicative shocks her. Not that she's a prude, but Roscoe is a devoted congregant of the Four-Square Revivalist Church of Born-Again Sinners and Ranting Righteous, down near the Crossroads. They don't swear, dance, sing, laugh, have parties or, more than likely, don colored underwear. Their major entertainments appear to be family picnics in front of abortion clinics and the on-going repression of the congregation's women and children.

"Then where is *Rosebud?*" Heddi's turn to speak slowly and patiently.

"If I knew, would I be telling you she's *lost?*" he fires back in exasperation.

"I mean," she says, gritting her teeth now, "*did* Holly, or *did she not* depart at the same time and in the same vehicle with the *wolf?*"

"No."

She's been hoping for years that Holly would divorce this idiot and now, one minute into this wacky conversation, she's convinced all over again of the justice of this intrusion of opinion into Holly's business.

They sit in less than companionable silence in their respective homes, gaining strength for the next go-round.

Heddi draws a careful breath. "So..." she says, "how did the wolf get loose?"

Roscoe suddenly sounds forlorn. "I don't know. I think maybe Holly opened the kennel before she left."

This, clearly, is the ultimate betrayal. Sleep with his best friend; withdraw his anally squirreled-away money from the bank and squander it on colored panties – you could work it out. But let the wolf loose, just when she was on the verge, through careful and constant pestering, of becoming the wildest, most savage watch animal in three counties: "*Et tu,* Holly?"

"Well, Roscoe," Heddi says with a sigh, "what can I do for you?" She knows Roscoe would never call her, except in the most abject desperation.

Like all "femi-Nazis," a cute term he picked up in his daily quasi-religious communion with Rush Limbaugh, Heddi falls well outside the pale of the prescribed associations of both Roscoe's church and his politics. Translated, this means she has a college education and a career – a situation highly subversive in Roscoe's view – and probably in Rush's, as well, although he and Heddi not being personally acquainted, that's only conjecture on her part.

Roscoe thinks Heddi is a bad influence on Holly. She is, she suspects, unwittingly the cornerstone upon which this latest crisis in his life is founded.

"I need you to come and stay at the house tonight," he says without hesitation. This is the rehearsed part; he's on terra firma, at last. "I can't go looking for Holly and stay home and wait for Rosebud to come back, too. You're the only other person Rosebud might come to. I need you to come here and watch for her. I've got some chicken defrosting in the fridge. If she comes around, lure her to you with a piece of chicken, then slip the leash around her neck. Think you could handle that?"

This last question oozes with such condescension that Heddi almost says a knee-jerk, "No!" But she really needs to see the scene of carnage that's been developing over at Holly's house over the last couple of days. Holly's described it in minute detail over the phone, but Heddi's still having trouble grasping it. She thinks about her weekend plans to finally plant the narcissus bulbs in the camellia garden and kisses them goodbye.

"Sure, Roscoe," she hears herself saying. "I'll pack an overnight bag. Give me about two hours and I'll be there."

"What's that, Ondine? Oh...Holly's mom? No, Roscoe couldn't call *her*. She's dead. After Hal, she married an exec from Mutual of Omaha. A few years later, there was an odd accident... There were always questions, but no one ever could prove anything...but that's another story. Anyway, no Sharon to call on, so..."

It's a pretty short drive from Malibu out to the hills of Ventura County. Hal bought Holly and Roscoe twenty acres of citrus trees for a wedding present. It's a nice spread and in their defense, they keep it pristine – even if it *is* through constant dousing with the wonders of modern chemistry.

When Heddi arrives, Roscoe meets her in the driveway. His face is normally red, but now it's almost a burgundy hue. He doesn't seem to realize that his hands are balled into fists, or that he's punctuating each word as if he were jabbing at a speed bag.

"Where are you going to start looking for Holly?" Heddi asks, keeping her distance. She has the sudden realization that Roscoe probably thinks she knows where Holly is and is hiding her from him. Actually, it surprises and worries Heddi a little that she doesn't. Holly always checked out every move with her before. She looks at Roscoe and wonders if she's in physical danger.

"I thought you might be able to tell me that," Roscoe snarls, squinting at her against the midday sun.

"Roscoe," Heddi says with all the sincerity she can muster, "I don't know. I really don't. Holly said on the phone yesterday that she was upset. That's the last I've heard of it." She looks him full in the eyes, earnestly. To her surprise, he believes her.

"I'm going to see the pastor, first," he says, mostly to himself. "Maybe he'll have some clue. Now, you remember what I told you about Rosebud?" He doesn't even stop to hear her response. "Don't forget to set the alarm system. I left the code tacked above the key pad by the back door."

Roscoe is twitching, already turning away, agitated and ready to bolt for his vehicle.

It seems like a perfect time to say something profound or soothing. *Good luck* won't do it because Heddi's not sure how she feels about him going after Holly. Most likely, Holly needs space, not rescue.

Heddi's tried very hard to like Roscoe over the years, love being clearly beyond her abilities in his regard. And to consider, under Dr. Copeland's tutelage, all the reasons why she should forgive him his outrageous misogyny, bigotry and stinginess. She does believe that we are, to a large extent, products of our upbringing, which in Roscoe's case may have been closer to downbringing. But she also believes that at some point in our lives, we have to take responsibility and rise above all that.

In all fairness, that may be exactly what he intended to do by joining the Wayside Chapel of Congregated Patriarchs and Askew Values. And how he came, just these last few days, to do what he did, which in turn has driven Holly, more forcefully than usual it would seem, away.

"Well, Roscoe," Heddi says, "good luck."

He nods distractedly, already halfway into the cab of his half-ton Chevy truck. He spits gravel as he goes off down the driveway without a backward glance, the back of his head bar-coded by the gun rack and his *Rush: Excellence in Broadcasting* bumper sticker proudly dead-center of the tailgate.

Holly's taste was never Heddi's. That she's been married to Roscoe for more than fifteen years is proof enough of that. And for added emphasis, there's her house. While Heddi's personal motto could be *Aesthetics Uberalis*, Holly's would be *Utility First*.

Every square foot of floor, for example, is done in beige linoleum – even the living room. The only rug in the entire house is a little pink cuticle of fluff around the base of the toilet. And every square inch of this linoleum could serve as dinnerware, so spotless, so highly polished, so basically antiseptic does it appear to any scrutiny except electron microscopy.

Holly even does her housekeeping while they're talking on the phone. Heddi will hear odd grunts and scratchings.

"What are you doing now?" she'll ask.

"I'm on my hands and knees in the bathroom, scrubbing the crack between the toilet and the linoleum with a toothbrush," Holly will say.

Heddi can see her there in her lime green sweat pants, her mop of frowsy red hair held out of her face by the headset that holds the phone so her hands are free to work, the antenna seeming to grow out of her left ear like a little antler.

Meanwhile, Heddi reclines on her seafoam green leather couch, propped up on the cushions she had made last year from mill ends of Scalamandré silk the color of a cold May ocean. The sun streams through French windows onto her antique Chinese rugs and the indigo glows in a kind of sexual incandescence from the stroking of the rays.

"That's great, Hol," Heddi will say.

So, now it's a shock to walk into her living room and see what has happened. The floor is still spotless, stretching out before her like a highly waxed desert. The two recliners in turquoise vinyl are still at perfect 30-degree angles to the big-screen TV. The *faux-bois* Formica coffee table still holds this month's issues of *Field and Stream* and *Sunset* at perfect right angles to the edges.

It's to the windows that Heddi's eyes leap in astonishment. There, just as Holly had told her through her tears yesterday, is the proof that her marriage has just taken a perfect 180-degree turn for the worse.

"You won't believe it," she gasps, snuffling. "He went to the pastor and the pastor agreed with him. They both think I'm possessed by an evil spirit...or maybe the Devil Himself. I'm not sure. So...so..." her voice fades into helpless weeping.

"So...*what*, Holly?" Heddi asks, trying to sound gentle and to urge her on at the same time.

Holly takes a deep breath. "So, the pastor blessed some oil for Roscoe. And then Roscoe came home and used the anointed oil to make crosses on every single window in the house!" Her voice rises to a pointy little squeak and then cascades into further weeping.

There is a considerable silence, while Heddi's mind adjusts to accommodate this new input.

"Just how *big* are these crosses, Hol?" she finally asks, trying to encompass the magnitude of this event.

"They cover the whole damn window!" Holly shrieks. "Top to bottom! Side to side! Every one of them. And I just washed them all yesterday!"

There's another long silence. "I see," Heddi says, finally. But it is clear to her now that she did *not* see.

"Well, Hol...maybe you can retaliate," she says, trying to make light of it. Sometimes, she can humor Holly into laughter, right through her tears. "What would freak Roscoe out, as much as he's freaked you out?"

Holly snuffles. "If I wrote *666* right over his damn crosses," she answers promptly. "In blood."

"In *menstrual* blood!" Heddi yelps, really getting into this fantasy.

"Yeah! In *menstrual* blood!" Holly chimes. And somehow, through the tears, she manages a giggle and before they hang up they're howling histrionically enough to raise the Devil, imagining all the things they could do to subvert the Little Temple of Living Misogyny and send its congregation, en masse, to its knees, praying for deliverance from liberated women.

So now, Heddi's looking at the windows and her knees are feeling weak. The midday sun is streaming through, baking a mooshed-up mess of blood and oil onto the glass. It looks like a chicken was butchered on there.

She tiptoes out of the room, goes down the hall to the bathroom. She looks in the wastebasket. Sure enough – Holly's on her period.

Heddi feels a little dizzy. She heads to the guest room, thinking she'll lie down.

Blaaghh!

There's blood and oil there, too, but not quite so dried out because it's the shady side of the house.

She pulls the blinds and lies down. Bit by bit, she fluffs out the wadded scraps of memory and tries to piece them together into a coherent whole.

"So what kicked all this off?" she asks Holly during a lull in their commotion.

"Oh..." Holly puffs. "It was that class I'm taking. Women's Spirituality. He picked up my textbook and read a few pages. It was the part where the Hebrew god Yahweh speaks through the prophets and tells them to destroy the goddess and cut down her pillars and groves.

"He made some remark, and I said that I thought we'd be better off if we still worshipped the goddess – and he just went ballistic! I mean, it was worse than when I said I thought Jesse Jackson would make a good president. He just went crazy. And then, he went to see the pastor."

Heddi gets up from the bed and goes in search of Holly's textbook. There it is, stowed fastidiously in the little bookcase by her desk in the corner of the master bedroom. She opens it at random. Neatly underlined in yellow highlighter, she reads:

> *Archeological evidence suggests that ancient goddess-worshipping societies were egalitarian and non-aggressive, the latter being inferred from an almost total absence of weapons at these sites. The monotheistic sky-god cultures that overran these earlier civilizations, however, were almost universally patriarchal, hierarchical, and dedicated to the arts of war. The subjugation of women, accomplished by rape, destruction of material goddess culture, and laws limiting women's rights, was justified by the fact that the male godhead was the model of superiority, in which first the king and the priesthood, and then all other males, partook.*

Heddi closes the book and returns it to its shelf, thinking about the day Holly called, bursting with the amazement of her discovery: *God used to be a woman!* Heddi always has the women in her Jungian study groups read Neumann and Gimbutas, so these things are old hat for her, but Holly was so excited!

That realization seems to have played an important part in unwinding the skein of Holly's very conventional, very married life and setting her on the apostate road of feminism. Holly couldn't wait to join a consciousness-raising group and to share in the empowerment that was going on there.

This semester, she was beginning to see her role from new eyes – so new that Roscoe thought they might be someone else's; someone Satanic.

Heddi thinks about Rosebud, lifts the shade and peeks out at the yard through the hideous smear of blood and oil; the goddess and the patriarchs, going *mano à mano* across the sliding aluminum windows.

"Holly, honey, the party's getting rough!" she mutters, dropping the shade.

That night, Heddi goes out under the night sky, all milky with moonlight and wispy clouds, and calls for Rosebud. Not that she actually expects her to respond, but she gave her word to try. The geese honk in response, down at the pond beyond the front lawn. In the dim light, she can see Snodgrass, the big white Chinese goose, rise up from the banks and spread phosphorescent wings as he throws his head back and *squonks* his answer. But no Rosebud.

Heddi goes back into the house, locks the door and sets the alarm for the night. In the guest room, she throws back the covers, changes into her PJ's and crawls into bed feeling a trifle undone by the day's revelations. The last thing she remembers is the quiet *shush* of the central air coming on and the gentle blast of cooling breeze from the vent above her.

Suddenly, she sits straight up in bed. She knows from the leadenness of her body that hours of deep slumber have transpired.

What's she hearing? What's going on?

Groggily, she listens and identifies the sound. The geese are in a tumult down at the pond! There is honking and shrieking enough to raise the dead!

Rosebud! The wolf, hungry after her release from the kennel and its regular feeding times, must be stalking the geese! Heddi leaps from bed and dashes down the dark hall into the living room. With blind fingers, she gropes for the lock on the front door, throws it open and rushes onto the lawn shouting, "Rosebud! Don't you *dare* touch those geese! *Ro-o-o-sebud!*"

The cold dew on the grass is showering her bare feet. The night has turned chilly and she wraps her arms around herself. Off toward the pond, she thinks she sees a vague, silvery tracer, leaping toward the orange grove. The geese squawk indignantly but the urgency of their alarm seems to have diminished.

She goes back into the house. *3:17*, she notes, on the digital readout glowing eerily beneath the invisible TV. She gropes her way into the hall, heading back to the guest room.

Suddenly, she's engulfed in sound! Sirens are going off somewhere in the ceiling over her head. An alarm making a whooping noise is blasting from somewhere in the living room.

The noise is deafening! She covers her ears and sinks to the floor, trying to shield herself. For a moment, she thinks that she has lost her mind; that she's finally having that acid flashback her friends warned her about back in 1969.

A brilliant, dead-white strobe light is illuminating the scene, surreally showing her Holly and Roscoe in their wedding photos, framed on the hall wall, now darkness, and then again, Holly and Roscoe, looking too young, and then darkness again.

A disembodied male voice, like God's over the black wastes of Chaos, cries out, "Identify yourself! Identify yourself!"

What can she say to this existential request?

"Female hominid, of Planet Earth?"

"Lone woman, unarmed?"

"Renegade Daughter of Eve?"

"What the fuck is going *on?*" she shrieks, instead.

The implacable voice demands again, "Identify yourself! Identify yourself!"

The strobe light is making her nauseous. She begins to crawl along the hall wall, making for the front door. As she passes the doorway to the bathroom, a bell somewhere within the recesses of the linen closet begins to clang, adding its uproar to the siren and the over-sized Whoopee Cushion.

She is screaming now. "Shut up, goddam you! Shut the fuck up!" and crying because of the violence of this assault on her slumberous nervous system.

She's almost to the front door when the whole thing suddenly stops. Silence descends utterly, and she experiences it with a kind of primordial awe – or maybe she's just been rendered permanently deaf. She can't be sure – until the telephone rings, a sound almost dulcet on her contused eardrums.

She gropes along the wall for the light switch but can't locate it. She crawls across the cold linoleum toward the sound of the phone. Instead of picking up the receiver, she knocks it to the floor in a blind swipe, and then has to hunt for it.

"Hello?" she whispers into what she hopes is the right end of the thing. She is impressed that her voice seems to have regressed at least five decades in so short a time.

"Hello?" she says again, hoping to sound more authoritative. It comes out as an unintelligible rasp.

"Who *is* this?" a stern male voice demands.

"Who is *this?*" she counters, suddenly fired up. "Don't you give me a hard time, you bastard! I've been through enough for one night without being harassed by some goddamn drill sergeant!"

"This is Delta Alarm Service. You have fifteen seconds to respond with the code word, or..."

"Or *what?*" she screams. "You'll shoot to kill? Launch Cruise missiles against me? You motherfucker..."

And she bursts into tears, her most maddening trait. She never can carry out a complete fit of pique, but must dissolve into these un-*macha* sobs.

"Oh *shit!*" she howls, and throws herself onto the floor in a heap, cradling the phone to her cheek like a security blanket.

"You sound upset," the voice says, not un-gently. "What happened?"

"The alarm happened," Heddi whimpers between snotty hiccups. "I tried to go outside to rescue the geese from the wolf and I forgot the goddamned alarm."

"Geese? A *wolf* was after the geese? Lady, there haven't been wolves in this valley for over seventy-five years!"

"Okay. Okay. I confess. I was trying to rob the place and in the process of lugging out this two hundred pound turquoise vinyl recliner, I set off the alarm. Now are you satisfied?"

"Tell me about the wolf. Oh...as long as you don't, by some chance, know the code word?"

"I do not."

"Who are you?"

"I am Holly's – the wife's – the owner's wife's – step-mother. Dr. Heddi Merriweather."

"What are you doing there?"

"Trying to catch the wolf."

"You really insist on this wolf?"

"I do. Such things are not unheard of – even in modern times," Heddi says stiffly, gathering her dignity about her. She's aware that somewhere in the last several sentences, they have changed their tone from confrontation to banter.

She's lying there on the cold linoleum of the living room floor in her pajamas in the 3:30 AM darkness, a failed wolf-catcher, needing to blow her nose and having a flirtation with the Delta Alarm Service switchboard guy.

What's next? she wonders. A flying saucer landing in the pasture? The imminent arrival of a marching band blasting John Philip Souza? The parking brake failing and her car slowly rolling backwards in the moonlight, down the driveway and into the pond? She has a brief epiphany concerning Life in Its Infinite Variety.

"My step-son-in-law has a wolf," she says wearily. The fight and the flirt have suddenly left her. "It got out of its kennel. I'm trying to lure it back in again. That's it. Nothing mysterious. Just a loose wolf and a forgotten alarm system. Period. End of report."

"I see," he says grudgingly.

Oh Mister, Heddi thinks, *you ain't seen nothin' like what I've seen, these last few hours! You don't SEE, at all!*

In the morning she makes the decision, while still lying in bed half asleep, to leave. She can't bear another day behind these grotesque windows. It's obvious that she is never going to catch the wolf. She needs the solace of the creature comforts with which her home is so richly appointed. She wants out of this madhouse.

She doesn't even take the time to make herself a cup of coffee because it's just instant coffee bags, anyway, and no cream, just one-percent milk. The image of herself perched on cold turquoise vinyl sipping this ghastly ersatz concoction is what propels her from bed and into a flurry of bed-making and jamming toiletries and PJs into her overnight bag.

"I'm not leaving," she mutters, "I'm fucking *fleeing!*"

Her car waits intact out in the driveway, not dripping with slimy green pond weed or showing signs that it has in any way been involved in the surreal business of the night. She opens the passenger-side door and throws in her purse and bag.

As she's going around to the driver's side she senses she's being watched. *Shit!* she thinks, her whole body jerking spastically. *It's the police! They've got guns trained on me!* She looks around fearfully.

There, by the pasture fence, sits Rosebud. Her silky silver and charcoal fur is blowing and glistening in the morning light. Her yellow eyes are trained on Heddi like scopes.

For all the trouble she's caused her, Heddi still loves this animal. From the first moment Heddi laid eyes on her, when Roscoe brought her home as a pup in the palm of his hand, she loved her beauty. And as the months went by, she learned to love Rosebud's wildness and her indomitability.

It was only through imprisonment and brute force that Roscoe had any influence at all on her. He wanted her mean. Heddi couldn't bear the spectacle of his abuses to this animal that never groveled and never broke, but only watched and waited and hated in some fierce recess of her ungiven heart.

"Good morning, Rosebud," Heddi says softly. She knows that in the kitchen there is a defrosted chicken waiting for just this circumstance. "You're looking very beautiful this morning," she croons. She doesn't make a move toward Rosebud, nor the wolf toward Heddi.

Heddi also knows that the alarm system is now fully armed. No one can enter the house without the code to disarm the alarm, which Heddi does not have. She's taken it from the wall, wadded it up and thrown it in the wastebasket. If she enters the house and tries to find the code, too much time will elapse and the alarm will sound again. Not only is she unwilling to endure this consequence a second time, but the sound will send Rosebud into the next county.

Roscoe, you clever paranoid, she thinks, with a sly smile, *you've outsmarted yourself.*

She looks Rosebud in the eye. They seem to be having a meeting of the minds. The wolf stands in a motion too quick and graceful to see.

"That's right, Rosebud," Heddi says softly. "This is your moment."

Rosebud shifts uneasily, still staring steadily at Heddi. The morning breeze sifts through her soft coat like fingers through fine sand.

Heddi raises her arms and shoos her. "Go!" she says, without much conviction.

Rosebud edges away a few steps. Heddi waves her arms, more agitated now. "Go, Rosebud! Go, girl! Go! Go! GO!"

Heddi is crying, now. She runs toward Rosebud, waving her arms and the wolf turns and begins a slow trot in the direction of the road. Beyond it, in the morning sun, the foothills rise, round and tawny with summer-dry grasses, a few minute's journey for a fleet-footed animal.

"Go, Rosebud! GO! GO! *GO!*"

Heddi's sobbing. She's running down the driveway and Rosebud's loping through the pasture, parallel to her and a little ahead.

Rosebud turns her long, yellow eyes and looks back, briefly. Heddi feels such a hit of wild love in her heart that she can scarcely breathe.

Rosebud's running full out now. She's streaking through the pasture grass like a silver wind.

And then, she's gone and Heddi is screaming, "Yes! Yes! *YES!*" and jumping in the air and shaking her fists like a madwoman.

"Yes! Yes! She's *loose!*" She kicks up a small whirlwind of dust, as she spins and leaps and shouts.

"She's loose! She's loose! She's FREE again!"
Heddi throws back her head and howls like a wild thing.

Ondine

They all just sit in amazement when Heddi finishes her story. She's told it with such verve and passion that Ondine is sure that she's not the only one with tears in her eyes.

Heddi has an odd look on her face, half-pleased, half-stunned, as if she's amazed *herself* with such a passionate telling.

It's Ondine who says, "And you want one of *us* to follow *that?*"

Everyone chuckles. They start to move and stretch and heft themselves up from their chairs and the floor. Sophia goes into the bathroom. Betty starts dishing out the flat Skip-and-Go-Naked Punch from the dishpan. Pearl cackles over by the candy machine and says, "Maybe we outta have a snack on some a them peanuts."

Ondine looks at the clock and realizes that two hours have sped by. It's close to 11:30. Heddi's plan to make time pass has worked perfectly.

Betty

Lunch is pretty dismal. They're all trying to conserve. They have chips again, Hershey's chocolate with almonds and some of Pearl's warm punch.

They vote that after the next person tells her story, they'll have a mid-afternoon snack. Betty's isn't the only stomach that's rumbling now.

So, they're all settling back in and Heddi's looking around for the next person who'll be brave enough to tell her story. No one makes a peep. They won't even meet her eye. So, to her own amazement, Betty raises her hand and says, "I'll go next, Heddi."

Betty really doesn't mind because she has this story that is really amazing about her neighbors, Bud and Angela. For years, Angela's been filling her in on the goings-on at their house and, in this case, Betty took part – to some extent.

"Well," Betty starts off, "this isn't a story about me at all, really. But I think it's interesting enough for you to tolerate. It's about my neighbors, Bud and Angela, and their son, Bernie. I'm like Heddi...if you're bored, just let me know.

"I'll start kind of in the middle, so you get the feel for how things are for them. It seems like there's always some kind of turmoil over there because of Bernie..."

"What's that sound?" Bud asks. He's just shambled out of the bedroom after sleeping off his job on the night shift at Anheuser Busch.

"It's Bernie," Angela says, not wanting to say much because she's right in the middle of Oprah and the transvestites.

"So what the hell's the matter with him? He got his dick caught in the silverware drawer again?" Bud is almost shouting now because the noise of Bernie, from the kitchen, is rising in volume.

"He's being a car alarm," Angela says, waving her hand to shush Bud. One of the transvestites, in a gold lamé floor-length dress slit to the thigh, is starting to tell his story and he's so beautiful, she just has to hear how it all came to happen this way for him.

"A car alarm? For Chrissake! BERNIE! HEY! *BERNIE!*"

Angela turns on Bud in a fury. "Don't you yell at him that way! You know he can't help it. How can you treat your own son like that?"

"Like what? He don't even know I'm talkin' to him. Make him stop, Angela. Just make him stop, for Chrissake. I work all night and then wake up in a loony bin. Men in skirts and a son who thinks he's an electronic device, for Chrissakes!

"I'm gonna do what Don Wilmer did and run off to Mexico. I swear. Make him STOP, will ya, Angela?" Bud throws himself down in his recliner, forgetting that Bernie broke it last week, and almost capsizes himself when it goes over too far backward.

Angela knows she has to do something before he gets to ragging about the chair, too. So she yells back, "And what do you think I should do? When he was two, I could put him outside in a playpen. At twenty-six, he's a little beyond that. What do you suggest I *do?*" Always best to go on the defensive with Bud before he blows sky high.

Bud now has the *L.A. Times Sunday Edition,* very fat, over his head and he is still lying angled slightly head downward in his chair and listing a little to starboard. He groans from under the paper, "Just do something, or I swear to God, I'm gonna get Don Wilmer's address from Gus and I'm gonna go to Mexico. Then he can be a car alarm, or a fire alarm, or a godamn fog horn, for all I care because I'll be hauling in blue fin in Baja."

Then he went quiet, very still, under the paper. And with Bud, this is always a very bad sign.

So Angela turns off Oprah, very reluctantly, because after the break, the men are going to tell their beauty secrets. But when Bud goes quiet, you sometimes have to make sacrifices.

Angela first learned this when Bernie was about five or six. Bud was reading her this article in the *Times* about how leaded gasoline was dumping twenty tons of lead on the L.A. freeway system every day. Angela said she didn't believe it. If that were true, their house, which is only five blocks from the San Diego Freeway, would have heaps of raw lead lying around on the lawn. It would be lying in layers all over everything – the car, the patio furniture, the concrete in the driveway. They'd have to bring City trucks and those machines with blades, like snow removal equipment, and be scraping the streets day and night, just to keep people from bogging down in lead. That's what she said.

But Bud said that was stupid; that it all went up in the air and they breathed it. And it did fall in layers and that was what that weird sticky black stuff was that collected on the backside of the Venetian blinds in the bedroom. He said it was like you took a five-pound box of laundry soap and you spread it all over the house. You wouldn't really know that there were five pounds of it because it would be laid out so thin. You'd just think it was a little here and a little there.

Well, in just a couple of minutes, Angela saw something out of the corner of her eye which turned out to be Bernie going down the hallway with a box of Tide, seeding it into the shag. That's the way Bernie shows his Dad how much he loves him – when he listens and then responds.

Well, that was the very first time that Bud went quiet. Only, since it *was* the first time, Angela didn't know what it was, so she thought he'd just gone to sleep in his chair.

"The green plaid chair, not the blue one he has now," Betty digresses for clarification. "Bernie destroyed the plaid one with lighter fluid – but that's another story."

By the time she'd wrestled the box of Tide from Bernie – who started screaming and rolling on the floor – and vacuumed the carpet, Bud was still in his chair and still quiet. But he had his eyes open, so then she had this moment of horror that he was dead. But, as it turned out, he was just in that place where he goes when there's really nothing left to say – or maybe he's ready to start screaming, himself.

So, Angela shuts Oprah off and goes into the kitchen and there is Bernie smearing peanut butter on Rye Crisps and stacking them up in long columns on a plate. He's making that sound, which is like no other sound, of a car in distress. He really is good at this. Really, if it were another circumstance than his father getting ready to run off to Mexico, you might even admire how well he does it. But obviously, now is not the time.

Now, with Bernie, he is impervious to the human voice when one of these things is upon him. He is so deeply involved with his discovery, whatever it may be, that he just doesn't hear. So, from the time he was a little baby, distraction was the name of the game.

So without a word, Angela walks into the kitchen, goes straight up to him at the counter and grabs the last peanut butter Rye Crisp from the top of the stack and shoves it into her mouth.

Bernie stops wailing like a vandalized car and shouts, "HEY!" very loud. He looks at her, outraged.

Angela smiles at him, chewing the dry, sticky mess as best she can, and mumbles, "Good!"

Suddenly, his round face, all puckered with concentration and anger, relaxes, and he gives her this smile that from the time he was a baby made all the rest worthwhile.

"I can vouch for that because I used to babysit for Angela, when she'd had enough and really needed a break," Betty explains parenthetically. "If it hadn't been for that smile, there might have been one more child homicide in Reseda. Not really, of course. But you just can't imagine how that child could push you to the limit!"

She looks around, is gratified to find that she has the undivided attention of the group, and continues.

"Yeah!" Bernie says. "Good!" And he holds out the plate to her, to take more.

Of course, he does it too fast and the columns of crackers, already pretty shaky, just topple over and smack to the floor, exploding peanut butter and cracker crumbs over every inch of her freshly waxed tile. But at least, while he's scrambling around on the floor picking up the biggest pieces and smearing in the rest with the knees of his jeans, he's quiet. He's forgotten he was formerly a car alarm and has become, for a few minutes, Angela's sweet boy again, worried because he's made a booboo.

So they are both cleaning up the mess for a few minutes before she notices a big silence, like a Black Hole, over near the refrigerator – and there stands Bud watching them with a look that, in all thirty-one years with him, Angela has never seen before. Then, he just turns, walks through the living room, grabs his Rams hat from the hook by the door and leaves.

Even Bernie is impressed. He doesn't ask, like he does twenty times each time it happens, "Where's Dad goin', Mom? Where's Dad goin'?" Even Bernie is afraid to ask and that can't be good.

So she goes straight in and calls Betty, who says, "Maybe you should call Madame Zola?"

Madame Zola has a place down on Reseda Boulevard with a big plywood palm and fingers, painted pink, the Life Line in black and *MADAME ZOLA – FORTUNES* in red underneath it. Her front windows always have the drapes closed and it seems like secret things are always going on in there behind those red curtains.

Betty first spotted the place years ago when she went to get a prescription for Bernie when he had allergies to grasses one spring, so bad that all he did was sneeze, one right after another, day and night, for three weeks straight. Poor Angela was so exhausted that she didn't want to drive.

Since then, Betty's been going to Madame Zola for years, even though Kathy Petersen's cousin, who was visiting from Tulsa, went to her and swore that she was actually a waitress who used to live in Oklahoma. She said that she was absolutely certain that Madame Zola used to work in a truck stop, nights, and was caught early one morning with the Methodist minister in the back of his car – "*in flagrant-ee*," as she said.

Kathy's cousin also claimed to know that the president of the bank said that when Madame Zola, whose name was Kim Something then, left town, she took a cashier's check for half of the minister's bank account with her. Kathy confirms all this – not because she ever knew Madame Zola before, but because she says Madame Zola had Oklahoma license plates on her car when she first arrived in L.A. Well, that may be, but even so, Betty thinks it's a pretty tall coincidence, and that Kathy and her cousin were just bored and it was a case of mistaken identity.

Even if she *was* once Kim, the truck stop waitress, Madame Zola gives good readings. Sometimes, she reads Betty's palm but more often, she pulls a long deck of Tarot cards out of a red silk brocade bag, thumps them importantly on the table and cuts them with the ease of a Las Vegas card sharp.

Her long red nails flick through the stack like little knives, cutting out the cards she knows psychically to be the ones for Betty. She always has some piece of advice or some warning about the future or some remark about somebody who's doing Betty wrong, that always turns out to be true.

Once, she saw a woman with red hair stabbing Betty in the back, like in a vision. Within two days, Betty found out that Dora Johnston, who dyes her hair the color of ripe tomatoes, had told her next door neighbor that Betty was on Prozac, which was a complete lie.

So you see, Madame Zola is a good person to turn to in a pinch – which Betty had been telling Angela for years. But Angela's a good Catholic and didn't want to risk it.

But on this occasion, Betty talks her into it and Angela calls and sure enough, Madame Zola has time that very evening to see her. Even though she doesn't usually work Tuesday nights, she says she's always available in an emergency.

So Angela takes the car and drives down to Reseda Boulevard to Madame Zola's place, near the Stop'n'Shop Center. It's a little house right on the edge, where the commercial district meets the residential district. Betty supposes it is a great location to catch people as they come and go, and put the idea of a little metaphysical intervention into their heads.

So, Madame Zola is waiting for Angela in the doorway, smoking a cigarette, holding it elegantly way out at the end of her fingertips, pinced in those long red nails. Madame Zola, who has never been familiar enough with Betty to reveal her first name, claims to come from Romanian gypsy stock. With her hooked nose, thin face, loose silky pants printed with roses and her long black hair in a gypsy shag, with layers of curls from her ears almost to her waist, she sure looks like it might be so.

And she drives a big 1960's Cadillac, white with a tuck and roll interior in red leather that must have been custom done across the border in Tijuana. Everybody knows that's the kind of car gypsies prefer.

So Madame Zola chooses her cards and slowly turns them face up but close to her, so Angela can't see them. She looks at each one for a long time and then lays it back down again. After she's looked at them all, she closes her eyes and is quiet for several minutes. Finally, she opens her eyes and says to Angela, "Bernie needs to get married."

It was winter, down around 68 degrees outside, and Madame Zola had the heater on, so maybe that was why Angela broke into a sudden sweat. Her whole body was hot and cold at the same time.

Angela sputters for a second and then shrieks, "*Married? Are you crazy?* Bernie, married? He's twenty-six years old and

he still can't tell the hot from the cold water in the shower –
and you think he should get *married?*"

Madame Zola just sits there looking at her like a big cat
tracking a panicked mouse. With the tip of one red finger-
nail, she slowly scratches her thigh through a big pink cabbage rose. She has that look of infinite wisdom and patience,
like an Egyptian queen or one of those silent film stars playing Mata Hari. It's a look that says, *Sooner or later, you'll see it
my way.*

When Angela calms down, Madame Zola says it again.
"Yes, Bernie needs to get married. And..." she looks at Angela very cold, very commanding, because she's starting in
with it again, "and I know the name of the girl... Myrna."

"Myrna who?" Angela asks weakly.

"Just Myrna. That's all I know." And then, Angela realizes that Madame Zola didn't know this Myrna personally
but she had had a vision or heard the name whispered by her
guides or however it works for her.

Myrna. It was a start.

"So how many Myrna's do you suppose there are in
L.A.?" Angela asks, not really being flip, just a little overwhelmed is all.

"It's not as bad as you think," Madame Zola says kindly. "Bernie will meet her at the youth group at St. Patrick's
church."

"Bernie hasn't been to church in 12 years," Angela says.
"Not since the visiting priest told him his brother in Ireland
had a German shepherd named Bernie, and Bernie barked
all through the service every time he was supposed to respond. He was an altar boy, you know...at least, up until that
day he was. When he sat up and begged for a communion
wafer, that was the end."

"What happened?" asks Madame Zola, lighting up a cigarette and leaning back in her pink armchair.

"The priest broke one in two and threw him a piece. Bernie caught it in his mouth. The whole parish was scandalized. That poor young priest was sent up to the Sacramento diocese in disgrace...which was too bad because he seemed like a nice young man and at least he smiled all the time, which is something old Father Foley never did. *He* always had a cloud of gloom and guilt riding on *his* shoulders."

"It's a typical story of patriarchal religion," Madame Zola says harshly, blowing out a streamer of smoke and surprising Angela with her tone of authority. "In my belief, the Divine Mother is central. She would never deny a poor boy just because he thought he was a dog. These priests and their Father God have got to go."

Well, to Angela, this was blasphemy – even though she hadn't set foot back in St. Patrick's since the day she led Bernie out, whining like a punished pup and trying to lick people's hands as she dragged him along. But Madame Zola was not going to be denied.

"I see Myrna in the St. Patrick's rec hall," she says, closing her eyes to slits and staring through a cloud of cigarette smoke at a scene only she can see. "She's dancing the polka. She has brown hair and she's quite petite. She has set her cup of punch on the edge of the table and the tremors from the dancing are about to jar it loose. Ohhh...there it goes!" Madame Zola shakes her head in sympathy.

"Just what I need," Angela mumbles. "A daughter-in-law who's a klutz. That should be good for the destruction of what's left of my house and marriage."

Madame Zola shakes her head to disperse the vision and looks at Angela sharply. "This is not about you," she says, kind of rough but not unkind. "This is about Bernie. The poor kid has raging hormones. Just because he's simple, doesn't mean he doesn't have natural desires. It doesn't mean he doesn't dream of being loved. Snap out of it, Angela. Bernie needs your help."

So they talk awhile about it and then, just as she's getting ready to go, Madame Zola begins tidying up the cards and Angela gets a glimpse of the last card as she's returning it to the deck. It's the *Ten of Swords*, all dripping with blood. Angela's heart freezes.

"What's that?" she shrieks. "What's that card? That's the Death card, isn't it? I know it is. What are you hiding, Madame Zola? What aren't you telling me?"

Madame Zola is so cool she's almost cold. She shoves the card deep into the deck with one thrust of her long red nail. "That card is none of your business," she says, so icy it almost shocks Angela. "A little knowledge is a dangerous thing, Angela. You just have to trust me in this," her voice a little gentler, now. "Bernie will be fine. If there's going to be a death, think of it as the death of an *old* way of life as Bernie takes on a *new* life all his own, that he shares with Myrna."

So that evening, instead of going straight home from Madame Zola's, Angela drives to Sears, which stays open until eleven on Tuesday nights, and buys Bernie a new pair of navy blue slacks, a blue and white striped long-sleeved shirt, a red cotton pullover sweater, navy socks and a new pair of penny loafers.

She takes them home, hoping Bernie will try them on. But he's already asleep, his arms wrapped around Burt, his big stuffed bear. Bud, of course, is at work – if he isn't already across the border, heading for Cabo San Lucas. So she piles the shopping bags under the kitchen table, goes into the living room, turns on the TV and falls asleep on the sofa, watching Jay Leno.

Sometime late, Bud comes in with beer on his breath, so she knows he's stopped in for a quick one at *The Spot* with his buddies on the way home from work. But at least he's home. He comes into the living room, and sitting gingerly on the edge of the couch, he gently rocks her by her shoulder. "Angie," he whispers. "Angie...are you awake?"

"Mmmmmm," she murmurs.

"Angie, honey, I'm sorry, okay? I'm sorry. I was a jerk. I know Bernie can't help it, okay? I know it's not your fault. I was a jerk, okay?"

Angela opens her eyes and looks up at him, so tired and sweet and helpless-looking, there in the blue light of the TV.

"Oh Buddy!" she whispers and bursts into tears.

Slowly, awkwardly, he just gathers her up and mounds her into a limp heap on his lap.

"Angie, honey. It's okay, Baby. I'm home now. Everything's gonna be okay." He pets her hair. He bounces her with his knees.

Silly big galoot!

Angela's just an itsy-bitsy thing and he carries her into the bedroom just like Scarlett O'Hara, and she remembers all over again why she married *him* instead of that dope, Craig Matthews, who both her mother and Betty's thought was the biggest catch of the century.

In the morning, after Bernie goes off to see if they've turned on the TV's yet in the window of the appliance store down on Reseda, Angela makes a pot of coffee. Pretty soon, the smell draws Bud out of the bedroom. He doesn't meet her eye, but he's smiling and that's always a good sign with Buddy.

So she starts right in. "I went to see Madame Zola, the psychic, last night," she says.

"Yeah? What about?" Bud is busy doctoring his coffee – two heaping teaspoons of sugar and two of Cremora. It always makes Angela shiver.

"About Bernie, of course." Angela pours out her own coffee, plain and black.

"And...?" Buddy is now alert because she's dragging it out and not just coming right out with it.

"And..." She takes a sip of coffee, not even a little bit sure how to say it, or having the remotest clue what Buddy will think, if she does.

Buddy begins to wave his hands like a traffic cop motioning her forward. "*And...?*" His voice is starting to rise.

"And so...Madame Zola thinks...well, she thinks...that Bernie ought to...well...ought to get married." She finishes in a rush, just to get it over with.

Buddy looks like he's just been popped right between the eyes with a pellet gun. He tries to speak, but only a sort of babble comes out. She can see he's on the verge of some kind of major tizzy.

"Madame Zola says we're being selfish. That Bernie has feelings and urges just like we do and that it's our place to help him, not to keep treating him like a baby. And besides..." She throws this in to gain time because she can see Buddy is slowly getting control of himself. "Madame Zola even knows the right girl. Her name is Myrna." She picks up her coffee mug and takes a big, triumphant swig. She can feel that something she's said has touched Buddy.

"Myrna," he says weakly.

"Yes. And she dances the polka at St. Patrick's Parish hall on Tuesday nights. Madame Zola saw her." Angela leaves out the part about the spilled punch, or it being in a vision. "So, in preparation, I went to Sears last night and bought these for Bernie." She pulls the bags from under the kitchen table and shows Buddy the clothes. "Won't he look nice?"

Buddy raises his eyebrows in that way he does when he's trying really really hard to be agreeable. He nods his head and he looks at the pants and shirt and sweater lying there on the red Formica. He says, "Nice. Yeah! He'll look real nice."

So, for Angela and Betty, it seems like it takes forever before next Tuesday rolls around. Betty calls the Parish and inquires about the Singles Club for Angela – not giving her name, of course. Just to make sure Madame Zola got it right, because sometimes she sees things but it turns out they're a year or two in the future. But as it turns out, there *is* a singles group on Tuesdays and anyone between 18 and 30 is welcome.

Then, Angela has to tell Bernie he's going, which is sometimes a problem. You never know with Bernie which way the wind will blow. Sometimes, he'll start to say no, even before you explain what you're doing. If you persist, he rolls on the floor, kicking his legs and yelling, "NO! NO! NO!" until you're afraid some neighbor will think you're over there beating him. Other times, he'll be docile as a lamb, give you a big smile and say, "Okay. Let's go," and that's that. You never know with Bernie.

As it turns out, there is no problem this time. He even seems quite interested when Angela tells him she is driving him to a place where he can meet girls and dance with them. "Okay," he says. "Let's go."

Then it takes her half an hour to explain to him that they aren't going right away. He starts to get cross, so to distract him she teaches him the rudiments of dancing; how you hold the girl and the steps of the polka.

Now, with Bernie, it's either a quick study or nothing. They've struggled for years to get him to turn lights off when he leaves a room, for example. But fortunately, it was a fast take with dancing. He always did have a great sense of rhythm.

So finally, it's Tuesday night and Bernie has had his new clothes on since 2:00, so he can show his dad before Bud goes off to work. And Angela drives him to the parish hall with so many butterflies in her stomach, she feels like the Monarchs are migrating right through her mid-section.

She drops him off because they were very specific when Betty called: no parents allowed. She watches him shamble up the walk toward the hall and says a prayer to the Virgin:

Mother, take care of my boy. Don't let them crucify him, like they did yours.

Well, to make a long story short, Bernie comes out of the place at 10:30 with a bounce in his step and grinning like she hasn't seen him do since he was twelve. He throws himself into the car, slams the door and turns to her with a face lighted-up as the full moon. "Met a girl, Mom. Myrna. She's gonna get me a job, Mom! A job, Mom! Good, huh, Mom?!"

Well, Angela is close to a complete wreck. She doesn't know whether to jump up and down for joy to see her boy so happy, or to burst into tears and sob.

Bernie, sounding like an accordion, hums polka music all the way home.

The upshot of it all is, Myrna really does get him a job at a local hamburger place, a drive-in where she's the assistant manager. Bernie is thrilled because now he's making money wiping down stainless steel and bagging Styrofoam for the garbage cans.

Five days a week, Angela drives him down there, but he won't let her come in and he won't let her meet Myrna. Eight hours later, she drives back and picks him up. He smells of rancid grease, he's grinning from ear to ear and all he can talk about is Myrna. What mother could ask for more?

Of course, Angela and Betty are both dying to meet this Myrna, but Bud says to mind their own business. "Bernie *is* my business," Angela tells him. But Bud can be very dictatorial at times and this is one of them.

"Give the kid some room to breathe, for Crissakes, Angela. He's been in your back pocket for twenty-six years. Aren't you ready for a break? Why don't you join a bowling league or somethin'?"

So Angela gets her feelings hurt and goes back in the bedroom and watches Oprah on the little black and white set and pouts, she's so mad at Bud. But in her heart, she knows he's right. It's just that...well, she's feeling left out, you know? Like for 26 years, she's been there every minute for this kid. And now, when the biggest thing in his life is happening, he shuts her out. So, really, she was mad at Bernie, not at Bud.

This goes on for weeks and then, one day, Betty is watching the noon news and the reporter says he's just been given a note that says there's a robbery in progress at Hazel and 12th, at a drive-in. It takes a second to sink in and then Betty screams, "Oh my *GOD!*" She runs to the kitchen and calls Angela. Then, she grabs the car keys from the peg by the chalkboard and runs out and jumps in the car without even her purse she's so panicked, because, *ohmygod,* that's the place where their Bernie works!

Betty stops and gets Angela and they can't even breathe they're so scared. When they get to the light at the corner, it's red and Betty's sitting there for 20 seconds before she realizes she's honking the horn over and over at the poor guy in the car in front of her – like he can read her mind and get out of her way, so they can go and save Bernie.

When the light changes, Betty guns it and almost smacks into his bumper. He must of thought she was nuts and, if she's really honest about it, she was. They've both been through a lot of things with Bernie, but never, ever did she ever think that she and Angela would get him all the way through his life-threatening childhood only to lose him at twenty-six to some cranked-up robber.

Betty takes the next few corners on two wheels and then there they are. The drive-in is dead ahead and there are cop cars all around. Traffic is backed up and people are in a group, gawking. Betty just leaves the car in the middle of the street and they both start running. Betty's sure they're going to find Bernie lying in the middle of that group, on the pavement in a pool of blood, and an ambulance nowhere in sight.

She lopes up to the people standing there in a little gaggle and, all out of breath, she gasps, "What's happening?"

Some woman with her hair shaved off and a hoop through her nose turns to her and says, "It's all over."

"*What's* all over?" Angela screams and Betty knows she's thinking its Bernie's life that the woman's talking about.

"The robbery. It's all over. The cops have the guy in their car over there." She points a finger that has an inch-long black nail and a ring like a snake at one of the cop cars. Sure enough, all the officers are gathered around it, talking to one another.

Betty turns to the woman. "What about Bernie?" she asks.

The woman snaps her gum and gives Betty this look out of the corner of her eye. "Bernie who?" she asks.

"Oh never mind," Betty says and she grabs Angela. They take off running again toward the drive-in. Now, she's sure that Bernie is dead – only instead of out in the street, he's lying inside on the floor. They make it almost to the front door when an officer steps out of the group around the patrol car and blocks their way with an out-stretched arm.

"Hey! Where're you two going? Stop right there!" he orders.

But all his authority is lost on Betty. "We're going in," she says, very firm.

"You can't be *that* hungry," he says, trying to make a joke.

Betty turns on him with some kind of fury, like she doesn't even know where it comes from, and she screams, "Our *Bernie's* in there! You get the fuck out of our way!" Even she is amazed by her use of the "f" word – probably more than the cop is because he's heard it all before.

"Bernie?" he asks. "Your son is *Bernie?*"

And then her heart sinks and she's thinking, *Oh God*, and her knees are starting to shake and get weak. She thinks she's going to have to sit down, and fast. She looks him full in the eyes and tries to read them like the headlines of the

L.A. Times. "Yes," she whispers. "I mean, no. Bernie is *her* son." She drags Angela close to her. "Is he dead?"

The cop reaches out and takes Betty's elbow and sort of slides her onto a wooden bench under one of the patio tables. Then he lowers Angela down, too. The shadow from the umbrella cuts out the sun all of a sudden, and Betty feels like she's sinking into some kind of hell filled with bleeding, rusted swords.

"Hang on, ladies," she hears the cop say from a big distance. He sort of molds her into position, so she's leaning on the table and doesn't fall off onto the concrete.

Then, he sits down across from them and puts his hand on Angela's arm. It's a good gesture, a kind thing, and Betty can feel his sympathy is right there with Angela.

"Lady," he starts, and Betty tenses up waiting for the worst. "Lady, your son Bernie is a hero."

So now, Betty's mind is really dizzy and she's trying to think – *did he throw himself in front of the gunman to save Myrna, or what?* Her mind is making up stories about how Bernie got shot and was a hero faster than you would even believe – she's always had this tendency to make up stories, you know. To fantasize. So, she sees him throwing himself across the counter and falling dead on the dining room floor; then she sees him out back, trying to club the fleeing bandit with a sack of used Styrofoam and getting shot. Betty doesn't know – the images are coming so fast that she can't really sort them out.

The cop pats Angela's arm and says, "You wait here." He slides off the bench and goes into the drive-in. Betty and Angela just sit there. They hardly see him go.

Angela whispers, "I feel like I did after I miscarried Bernie's baby sister...empty." Betty looks at her friend. In her face, there is just a huge emptiness filled with a grief that doesn't even have a form yet – just molecules of grief whirling around in emptiness. Angela puts her head down on her arms and begins to cry.

Then, there's the hand on her arm again. "Lady," Betty hears the cop say. "Lady, look."

And then Betty hears this familiar voice saying, "Mom! Hey Mom! What's wrong, Mom?" And she never heard a sweeter sound in all her life!

And there he is – their boy. He throws himself at Angela and gives her a hug that takes Jeff, her chiropractor, three visits to undo. And when Bernie's done with that, he starts dancing from foot to foot and that's how they know he has a big story to tell.

"I stopped 'em, Mom!" he warbles. "I stopped 'em good." He's dancing with delight.

Angela looks up, dazed, at the officer, who's still standing there. "That's right, M'am," he says. "Your son's a hero."

They both look at Bernie in disbelief. Not only is Angela's son not dead, but he's a hero, too. Betty's having some trouble taking it all in.

Just then, another officer comes up and the first one introduces him as Captain Somethingorother and says that Angela is Bernie's mother. The Captain reaches out to shake her hand and Angela reaches back, but Betty can see that her hand is as limp as a fish. She's not quite in her body, even.

"Congratulations!" he says, beaming at her. "Your son Bernie saved the day today. He probably saved someone from getting killed."

And then he tells them how Bernie is back in the back, pouring oil in the fryer, when he hears the robber come in and yell at everyone to get down on the floor.

Of course, the robber is talking to the people in the dining room and he doesn't even see Bernie, back by the fryer. So Bernie, being very quick-witted, steps out the back door and comes around the outside of the building to where he's sure the robber can hear him. And then he starts making a noise like a police siren. He starts out like the sound is way off in the distance and then makes it louder and louder, like its bearing directly down on the drive-in.

Of course, the robber panics and runs out the door, jumps in his car and drives away. Only he's going so fast that he skids as he swings out of the driveway and his rear end hits a cop car that's just turning in to the drive-in for lunch. And when the robber jumps out and tries to run away from the scene of the crime, the officer apprehends him.

That's it. That's the whole story. It was over before Betty ever even heard it on the news. And there is Angela's boy, just dancing with delight because he's saved the day. Betty feels like she's going to faint again, but this time from pride.

Angela's beaming at her boy, when all of a sudden this strange person comes up and throws her arms around him. Angela and Betty are staring now because Bernie throws his arms around her, too, and they're hugging very intimately. Only, this young woman comes about to his waist. Betty knows instantly – this is Myrna.

Why Bernie never mentioned he was in love with a dwarf Betty can't say. She doesn't think he was afraid to tell them. More likely, she thinks it never occurred to him that there was anything different about Myrna. That's their Bernie; he just takes people as he finds them and loves them, one and all.

So Angela was really worried about the wedding. Because as soon as this thing happened, they were so aware of how either one of them could have died without ever getting to be married, that they decided to do it right away. So Angela was worried about finding a dress. How many floor-length wedding dresses are there, after all, that are only three feet long, shoulder to hem?

But it turns out that Myrna has been making her own clothes since she was a teenager and is an excellent seamstress. She made herself a beautiful wedding dress all in taffeta and lace and little pearl buttons. And Bernie looked so handsome up there at the altar in a tuxedo! Bud and Angela just sat there amazed by their beautiful kids standing up there, taking their lives into their own hands. At the end, Bernie did a perfect imitation of an organ playing the recessional.

So two years pass and the kids are doing fine. Then one day, Bernie and Myrna come over to Bud and Angela's so full of themselves, so proud, to tell them the news: they're pregnant! Bernie is practicing Lamaze breathing, while Myrna tells about the tests at the hospital and how she's already started a college fund for the baby.

After the kids leave to go back to their apartment, Angela can't find Bud. She goes into the back of the house to the spare bedroom that used to be Bernie's room. And there is Bud lying on the bed, crying. Not crying, really – sobbing.

"Bud!" she says in alarm. She rushes over to him and kneels beside him. She's thinking he's had a heart attack or something. "Buddy! Sweetie! What's wrong? What is it?"

And he turns these big, swimming, blue eyes up at her and tears are running down all the creases in his face that he has from so many years working outside on a forklift.

"Angela..." he starts, and then can't finish and sobs some more.

"Angela..." He wipes his nose on the corner of the chenille spread. "For twenty-eight years, I've loved that kid. Twenty-eight years!" He hiccups. "I thought he would break my heart. All I ever wanted was a son I could go fishing with, you know? Someone to go to the ballpark with. Maybe even the drag races, once in a while. And what I got was Bernie."

Buddy kind of slithers around, so he's sitting on the floor leaning back against the side of the bed, and Angela's still kneeling next to him holding his arm like she's going to keep him from shattering into a million pieces.

"How many times I'd hear guys at work saying, *My son this* and *My son that*. And I'd get a knot in the pit of my stomach and I'd cry out to God, *Why did He give this kind of kid to me?* when all I ever wanted was a normal son who wanted to tear down lawn mower engines in the garage? Angie, I've been an enraged man for twenty-eight years, that's the God's truth."

He grabs the corner of the spread and scrubs his nose and then his cheeks, which must have been itching with salt by then.

"And now...now..." he begins to sob again, so Angela can barely make out his words. "Now, I swear to *Christ*, if He gives those two kids...those beautiful kids who love each other so much...a weird kid...I'll...I'll...I'll never speak to God *again!*"

So now, Angela is crying, too, and her and Buddy sit on the bedroom floor, holding each other and crying and rocking and crying some more. Because, let's be honest, they love Bernie with all their hearts but, as Angela told Betty, "I wouldn't wish another Bernie on anyone, especially my own son and daughter-in-law. It's too hard. I can't begin to tell you. It is just too hard a thing to ask of anyone."

Buddy and Angela were really shaken to the core, so the next day Angela takes herself down to Saint Patrick's and marches right up to the head Virgin, up there on her pedestal, and lights a candle and says, "Mother, you're a woman. You understand these things. Your son was crucified, and so I expect you were, too, in your heart. How could you help it? So please hear me when I say that Buddy and me are just not up to this. Twenty-eight years was enough. We can't start over with another little Bernie. So please, for our sakes and especially for the sake of Bernie and Myrna, and most especially for the sake of the baby, who has to come into this wicked world and suffer what people do in their ignorance and cruelty, please, Mother, please...make this a normal, healthy baby. That's all I ask. Oh...and that Buddy not lose his faith in God, too. That's it. Thank you, Mother. Thank you for hearing my prayer." That's what she said to Her. And then she lit a second candle, just for good measure.

Also for good measure, she stopped by Madame Zola's. As luck would have it, Madame Zola had time to give her an appointment. She was right in the middle of giving herself a dye job and her hair was wadded up under a plastic cap with little rivulets of black dye running down her forehead that she kept wiping away with a wad of Kleenex. She set a timer, so she wouldn't keep the dye on too long and then she pulled out her Tarot deck and rummaged through the cards, pulling a few.

She looked at them for a long time and then she said, very gently for Madame Zola: "Go home, Angela. Stop worrying. Say your prayers for this baby that's coming. Everything's going to be fine."

In retrospect, they don't know why they worried so much. Bernie and Myrna are like two halves of one whole. Myrna's smart as a whip and is even thinking of going back to college to get her MBA. Bernie's so strong that anything little Myrna can't do, he can. And they're so tender with one another, it would make anyone just cry to see it. Together, they make a great team.

So it must have been the same with their genes – Bernie threw his good, strong, handsome ones into the pot and Myrna put her big brain ones in – and *Presto!* Out came little Mikie, cute as a bug, healthy as a horse and already lifting his head and smiling at them all like it's Christmas.

So now, the kids come over for Sunday dinner every week with the new baby. It's a wonder anyone has time to eat because they're all just fighting over who gets to hold Mikie next.

So, Buddy and Angela stand on the porch after dinner and watch them go down the walk. Myrna is carrying Mikie and Bernie is carrying the diaper bag and the car seat and crooning some lullaby of his own composition to the baby, who is crooning back.

Bernie helps Myrna arrange the baby in the back seat. Then, he opens the door and helps her into the driver's seat and gets her all buckled in behind the special controls she uses because her feet don't touch the floor, and then he comes around and gets himself buckled in. They both turn and wave, just as they start off down the street at a snail's pace.

Buddy turns to Angela and he has a little smile, which is always a good sign with Buddy. "Angie," he says proudly, "I think I see some fishing trips in my future."

"With Bernie, too?"

"With Bernie, too."

And he whacks her on the bottom and gooses her and she starts to giggle and he grabs her and waltzes her across the kitchen toward the bedroom, with her squealing, "No! No!" But meaning yes. *Yes*.

"I have to stop now. I'm kind of choked up."

The others are so quiet, Betty looks around for the first time wondering if they're all asleep. But they're just staring at her.

"I'm sorry," Betty says, mopping her eyes. "Everything's making me cry right now."

"What, exactly, is making you cry?" It's Heddi's voice, full of her clinical authority.

Betty's caught off guard. "Well...I don't know...I..."

"But you *do* know. You know perfectly *well* what's making you cry right now."

Betty looks around, kind of embarrassed. What must the others think? She looks at Heddi, beseeching her, but she's adamant. She just stares at Betty like she does during their sessions. No one else makes a peep.

"Well, I guess I'm crying because I'm happy for Angela and Bud. And for Bernie and Myrna. And Mikie, too, of course."

"Really."

And that one word cuts right through to this place where Betty's emotions are like feet standing on slippery, slimy rocks full of crawdads. It's a stranded place that she just wants to get to shore from, but first she has to wade there – and try to keep her balance at the same time.

"I...I..." she stammers.

And then up it comes, like bad food. "I guess what I'm feeling is...I wish that it had ended for Larry and me the way it did for Angela and Bud. I wish Larry, just once, would of said how pretty my flower arrangements are...and danced *me* around the kitchen.

"I guess I'm really scared and it feels just raw and terrible that my family doesn't even know where I am or what's happening to me...or even care, as far as I can tell."

And then Betty can't talk anymore because all she can do is sob.

Erika

Wow! This Heddi plays hardball. She just reduced that fat chick to tears. If Erika could learn to hit people that hard right in the gut, she could rule the world!

Between bouts of pain and with Sophia's help, Erika's been trying to get her cell phone to work – but nothing. She needs to call her office and let them know she's alive. Talking to somebody official like the police wouldn't be bad, either. Gently nudge them to come and fucking *rescue* her!

Sophia got her laptop set up for her, but WIFI isn't working, either.

That fucking deal in Berlin's gonna go down without her! Man, that's a burn! She worked her ass off on it and now Lathrop's gonna get all the credit.

These women and their stories are about to make her puke. Who gives a rat's ass? Now everybody's clustering around, giving Betty hugs.

Yuck!

There's one good thing about being shot – everybody leaves her alone. They let Sophia deal with her and that's fine with Erika. Sophia doesn't get all touchy-feely.

All she wants is to get out of this fucking hellhole and get on with her life. Every hour she spends in here is costing her money.

Ondine

Everyone's taken a break and now they're settling in again. Heddi whispers, "How do you think things are going?" Ondine tells her she thinks her idea is brilliant.

"You go next, then," Heddi whispers.

"*Me?* What will I say?"

"I don't know. Whatever you want. Tell them about your aunt's house in France."

"What about it?"

"Anything. I doubt anyone else in this room has an 18th-century house on the ocean. *Anything* you tell them about it will be interesting."

So Ondine agrees and Heddi gets everyone settled in again.

What on earth should she say?

"Heddi says I should tell you about my aunt's house in France. I inherited it when Tante Collette died two years ago.

"I just came from there. Just now...when...all this... Well, anyway...

"I've been staying there for a month, trying to decide if I want to live there permanently or not. I've had it for those two years, but until now I've never really thought that I might want to live there.

"I love the house. I love the area it's in – on the Atlantic seaboard, you know. And I love France. So I'm not sure why I can't make up my mind. Anyway, let me tell you about the place..."

It's an old house, from the early eighteenth century, and it breathes at night – random creaks and pops and groans, and there's a kind of *shush*, like a velvet coat being dragged across the floor behind someone invisible.

In the night wind, it sighs as if it's remembering.

Ondine likes to think that its history, deep in its bones – in those dry, hand-hewn timbers and sleeping stones – is dreaming. And she's the current dream; this woman recently arrived with her leather mason's satchel of mallets and chisels, a folding French easel and jars of raw pigments.

The house likes her, she thinks. It's waking up, popping its eyes open in curiosity, asking, *What century is this?* Is that a mistress to King Louis? Old Marie with her chamber pots and brooms? Does she wear bustles or an apron or beaded flapper gowns? When she cooks, is it cabbage that fills the air or roast meat? What manner of occupant is it, this time? What's her station in life and what's her rhythm?

The floorboards already know her. She walks briskly but lightly, sometimes tripping when her foot catches the edge of the parquet. She doesn't mince, or drag along, old and weak and tottering – and neither did Tante Collette, by the way. Her stride was always slow and stately.

The windows tremble in the night wind like muted tapping on a drum. A tree branch scrapes against the slate roof with the sound of an old woman sweeping, feeble and irregular.

There's marble dust in the studio – a faint, crystalline powder sparking in the moonlight, lying in the grooves of the planking like pale ribbons of vapor. On the easel, the black lines leap forward in the silver light and colors recede, leaving an inky, tangled calligraphy where image was. Shadows run like ink along the baseboards and pool in the corners.

The stairs click and sag, remembering a dozen generations of feet; small and bare; large, heavy and booted; satin slippered; slow and labored in wooden clogs. The old walnut wood remembers, by emitting a faint scent, the hands with veins like grapevines, patient and firm, that rubbed in beeswax and lavender oil.

In the master bedroom, the bed is a carved and tangled garden under an antique silk canopy. Old Turkistan carpets gleam like an enchantment when stroked by the moon. And two matched *Louis Quinze bombé* dressers with pink marble tops lift their smooth knees in a courtly nocturnal dance.

When she awakens, the morning sun is enflaming the rose-colored plaster of the walls. There's a sweet odor of apples rotting in the orchard and the squabble of sparrows. She is, momentarily, both dreamer and dream.

She has to lie still and remember: this is Tante Collette's bedroom, not the cathedral-ceilinged one with the view of the southern California beach. She's alone in bed, not lying tense, wondering if *he* is awake, too. A day stretches its morning stretch, all hers. It won't be chopped into appointments, arguments or shopping mall feeding frenzies.

Alone! She's gloriously alone!

Ondine can't tell them the relief!

When she gets up, the house unwinds before her as she moves toward the kitchen. There's a long hall with a Persian runner, family portraits, yellow ochre plaster; then the dining room, pulsing with morning sun. She's put apple branches there in a huge apothecary jar to force them into bloom, on a table carved with the initials *C.B.* – by Charles Baudelaire.

Finally, there's the swinging door, nine feel tall and paneled. The kitchen will still be sleeping in shadow. It's cold and smells of mustard and asparagus. There's a blue-enameled cast iron cook stove hunkering against a wall of cobalt tile. A massive butcher's block at center stage, with its heavy turned legs, reminds her of a squat old woman with her hands on her hips, defiant, like some ancient kitchen deity.

She's still vague about the layout. It's all dreamy, as if the rooms move around in the night. Twice, looking for the bathroom, she's blundered into the linen closet.

Little Ondine – the barefooted version of herself, ten years old with wildly curly auburn hair down her back – remembers it still differently. *I think the library's in there*, she'll say, directing Ondine, instead, into the music room, where Paderewski's edition of Chopin's mazurkas still lies open on the music rack of the Bösendorfer. Deep indigo toile drapes are gathered back. Behind them, Alençon lace sheers mute the brilliance of the day outside, where bare branches hold shards of sky in their black fingers. The stillness in this room is deep, as if the walls were still straining to hear Tante Collette's long, magical fingers trilling.

The house is a dreamscape partly because of Tante Collette's long association with the *Nabis*, the French Symbolist movement of which she was a part – colors in odd juxtapositions, a certain sense of enchantment, nature honored and invited in, books everywhere, paintings, and upholstered chairs in little coveys, seeming to gossip.

"A sensual atmosphere of mild *tristesse* and pure lucidity," as Tante Collette once described it.

"This house is the Keeper of Hours," she told Ondine that summer long ago. "Dawn, rising sun, day, dusk, and night, with its moon and stars – *Matins, Lauds, Tierce, Sext,*

Nones, Vespers, and *Compline* – every room is canonical. You will see."

Why does a person retain such a comment for three decades? It was full of mystery then and mystifies her still. But she sees the sun already moving through the dining room, as she enters with steaming *café au lait* in hand – moving from left to right, pushing the room's blue shadows westward like sands in an hourglass flowing horizontally.

And last night's moon was one long beam angling through the bedroom French doors, an hypotenuse of light. Tante Collette would have plucked the string of that geometry of wildness, producing a pure note that vibrated with the feral perceptions of the *Nabis.*

"Strength is not in the arms," she said to soothe Ondine, the day she fell out of an apple tree because she couldn't chin herself on a limb like the neighbor boy. "Strength has other muscles that articulate in the soul. It means being able to endure what we know as women. To be ligamentous. It means being able to stand and live."

Her blouse, Ondine remembers, was aqua silk cut velvet patterned in leaves, soft and sensual as a cat, with a large pink cameo at the throat. Little Ondine looked up the length of her aunt's long, kelp-colored skirt, as if it were a tower and listened, uncomprehending.

Even so, she remembers. This time, when she returned to *Quatre Vents* – that's the name of the property, *Four Winds* – she thinks she may have gotten a small inkling of what Tante Collette perceived: how her whole life was washed in the flat white light off the Atlantic and moved by it, the way music moves to a metronome.

"You must keep the sea always in your heart," she told Ondine on the summer of her fifteenth year, when she was struggling to birth her nascent feelings into poetry. "Once you've mastered the cadences of the sea, the spark of salt crystal, the coilings of the fog and the dirge of the wind, then poetry will live in you – and you in it."

Not much has changed, really, since that long-ago summer. The house scarcely shows the passage of time. Its edges were rounded then, its stairs scooped into parabolas by generations of feet, its windows a hand-rolled waver of lustrous glass *semé* with sparks. And so they remain.

Only the garden seems to mourn Tante Collette's passing. A ramshackle pergola of roses needs pruning; fruit trees haven't seen a long-handled saw in several seasons; the walkways of hewn limestone are furred with long grass fanned across them by last winter's heavy rains.

The fountain in the shape of Pan – Tante Collette called it her *fauntain* – splashes into a pool clogged with last autumn's black, viscous leaves. Roses and *Vigne Vierge* lattice the music room windows.

The entire place – house, garden, orchard – holds a stillness that's both serene and highly energized, as if a gong had been struck and even though its note has disintegrated past hearing, it still vibrates in the air. It's like a sleeping princess awaiting a reviving kiss.

At ten, Ondine's daydream was to live there, chaste and pure, to write and paint and sculpt. She imagined her sculpture stand out under the willow tree in summer and in the studio – the converted dairy – in winter. She envisioned laying out her chisels, files and mallets on the crude workbench and the stone, half roughed-out, sitting solidly in its ruff of dust and chips.

The place itself inspired such visions in Little Ondine, with its framed photos, grainy and dreamlike, of Tante Collette's friends, the *Nabis*, painting in her garden, or in smocks and berets, wielding hammer and chisel in the studio. These artists of the French Symbolist movement became Ondine's friends, too, in the imaginary land of her childhood.

It seems impossible that Tante Collette's life bridged theirs and Ondine's. The artists of the *Nabi* are like the knights of some distant quest to Ondine – lost in time. It was Tante Collette's father, really, who was of that generation and who made his reputation painting as a Symbolist, while young Collette appeared in many of the artists' paintings as a lithe and lively model, and served as their resident *femme inspiratrice*.

She was Ondine's great aunt, actually, which is hard for Ondine to believe because Tante Collette seemed, even in great age, so young. Ageless. Preserved in some inner *aqua vitae* of joy...

"I...I really *miss* her!" Ondine stops to dab at her eyes with a hanky dug hastily from her bag.

The women sit quietly, their attention unblinking.

"Can you really be interested in all this stuff?" She gazes around her, with tear-glossed eyes.

Heads bob. She sighs, and then continues.

Tante Collette lived in a manner that was part affectation, part fiscal necessity and in large part the manifestation of her inner aesthetic and creative force. Her sensibilities were too refined for the rough-and-tumble of public life. She belonged, Ondine always felt, within the magical confines of her high garden walls, behind her thick portal doors. Like some exotic animal, she needed them as bulwarks against extinction...

"I see you giving me that look, Heddi. I can hear you thinking, *Projection, projection,* and *projection!* Well, maybe you're right. I do feel safe there. Safer than... well...anyway..."

The gatehouse – a majestic structure with massive double street doors on one side, the garden gate on the other,

and stone benches in deep shade along each inner wall –
sports a classical pediment in gray stone over each portal,
netted in climbing roses. There Tante Collette kept an ancient, balloon-tired bicycle for mundane travel.

"I love this elderly conveyance, with its willow basket,"
her aunt once told her with great dignity, when Little Ondine teased her about it. "The bicycle is a noble invention
– it requires balance, rigorous effort all of one's own and the
willingness to brave the natural world – not unlike art. Or
life."

Her forays into the world were highly selective. Even at
the end of her life, she'd sally forth for shopping in the village, peddling at a leisurely pace, her posture as upright and
proud as if she straddled a Lipizzaner stallion. Off she'd go
down the dirt road, always following the right hand rut, rais-
ing little puffs of dust in the summer heat.

And always in a skirt. Ondine never saw her in pants, except in her garden or studio, where she wore tailored men's
trousers, cinched by a large leather belt.

"She and Coco Chanel were contemporaries and modest
friends – but sisters in elegance."

"She *knew* Coco Chanel?" Heddi, doyenne of fashion,
gasps incredulously.

"Yes. In fact, someone told me once that it was Tante
Collette who first started wearing men's wear – and Chanel
stole her style and then took all the credit for it."

"My God!"

"Who's Coco Cha-what's-her-name?" This, from Pearl
who has been leaning against the candy machine, quietly
paring her nails with her pocketknife.

"She's a fashion designer, Pearl," Ondine says patiently.

"Well, I been wearin men's clothes all mah life, an ain't
no one never cared one way or t'other."

Heddi and Ondine share a long look.

"Well, it was probably just a rumor, anyway."

"This is interesting, Ondine," Betty pipes in, "don't stop now. Tell us more."

An ancient housekeeper, Marie, whose life was apparently dedicated to cleaning and polishing as a religious calling, underpinned Tante Collette's elemental yet aristocratic life. Marie's gnarled old fingers wielded broom, dust cloth and polishing rag like holy relics, and she fed the carved legs of tables and chairs with good local beeswax and lavender oil as if she were genuflecting to administer the sacrament.

Tante Collette's banker was another of her ancient retainers, who handled all her accounts and managed the small fortune that her husband, Ruban, had left her when he died young. It wasn't a happy match, she always implied, and she apparently loved him more for abandoning her in comfort than for any more romantic reason.

Once a month, she'd stop at the bank and her old friend, although long-retired, would meet her in a private room to discuss the state of her resources which, given her modest needs and conservative spending, was ever-normal.

But Ondine doesn't want them to get the impression that Tante Collette was stodgy or boring. Quite the contrary.

"When I was little, I always used to confuse her telephone, in my mind's eye, with the hand-held porcelain shower head attached to her bathtub. They seemed equally complicated and exotic, and both were all white and gold, with big horns on the end, perforated with little holes. I pointed the similarity out to her one day, when I was sitting in her huge bathtub, surrounded by a foamy mattress of bubble bath.

" 'The French do not invent things,' she told me with a twinkle in her eye, 'they *fantasize* them.' Then she picked up the hand-held shower and, instead of rinsing my hair, she put the thing to her ear and shouted, 'Allo? Allo?' in her heavily accented English.

"Pretty soon, she had me giggling, as she carried on an imaginary conversation with a *desmoiselle*, one of the local fairies."

Ondine shakes her head in amusement.

Occasionally, Tante Collette would embark on more worldly travels. Maybe there would be an invitation to an art opening in Paris. As one of the last of the *Nabi*, she was always lionized. Or maybe she simply needed to replenish her underwear and nightgowns at *Galeries Lafayette*. And there'd always be a stop at *Chanel* for something deliciously simple to augment her wardrobe.

And in the depths of winter, almost until she died, she escaped the cold Atlantic winds by embarking from Marseilles for Morocco, where she kept a tiny house with a walled courtyard, close to the *kasbah*.

"I own that now, too – and what I'll do with it is anybody's guess. I'm afraid to go to North Africa, with all the terrorism...

"Are you laughing at me, Heddi?

"Oh! I get it! Afraid to go to my aunt's house in Morocco, but then, here in L.A...! Very funny...

"It *is* pretty ironic, isn't it?

"So, are you bored to death, yet? No?

"Okay. Let's see... What more can I tell you?"

Tante Collette always sailed in the keeping of a young seaman who clearly adored her, a Captain Fouquet. There are photos of her bundled up on a deck chair like a film star, with him hovering over her like a handsome leading man.

She never talked much to Ondine about these migrations to a warmer climate, but there would be huge amber beads against her couture blouses, or heavy silver earrings worn with cashmere sweaters that attested to her secret movements through the labyrinths of the exotic.

It suddenly occurred to Ondine, during this last trip, that all this is hers now. But in a house so saturated with Tante Collette's essence, could anything ever really belong to Ondine? If she chooses, she can go to the jewelry chest and, with a little rummaging, find those Berber earrings and wear them.

Imagining that gives her a guilty sense of pleasure. At a time when her own identity is at its nadir – when she feels formless and chaotic – she can don Tante Collette like a mask and hide behind her panache.

"Always create with compassion," she wrote Ondine in her last letter. "With compassion, courage and originality." Always, she insisted on addressing the artist in her, despite Ondine's protestations that she hasn't created anything in the way of real art in almost two decades.

Would her aunt think her cowardly, if she crawled into her skin just for an afternoon and drew the last warmth from it? Put on her *aubergine* cashmere sweater, her amber beads as big as quail eggs and pretended, if she cannot feel it, that her soul vibrates to the same pure note that Tante Collette's did?

Would she say Ondine is creating herself compassionately? Or simply that she lacks originality?

Eventually, Ondine had to try it. She dressed in her aunt's clothes; a pale aqua silk sweater, an ankle-length wool skirt of deep sea green, Tibetan turquoise beads with a repoussé silver locket, topped by a full-length down coat of teal silk. For what, she had no idea. There was nowhere to go. No one to see. She simply needed her aunt around her, like protective coloration.

Thus attired, she went out. The wind was silvery and cold like the handle of a coin silver spoon, thin and sharp.

Silver seems, in fact, to have enchanted the land as if everything lay enmeshed in it. The sky, snared in a scrim of black branches, is that fragile blue that comes in winter with the cold. It is late afternoon and clouds are heavy in the west, deep blue-violet streaked with raspberry.

The sun pulses above the western horizon, fiery apricot, hurling lances of lemon yellow. The far hills are deep, soft lavender blue, misted over with pale silver. Leaves that have survived the wind gleam like green-black glass in last light and the pale vanilla hemisphere of the moon is already mid-journey in the sky.

Such beauty! It's as if Ondine were seeing it through her aunt's eyes, and for the first time.

The front wall of her heart aches and burns as if the flesh were seared. And behind the pain, there's a tremulous beating, so weak it seems to be announcing its ambivalence about living.

She's as insubstantial as her own shadow, wafting through bushes, stretching over the frosted grass, so vulnerable and unsure. The absolute integrity of what grows from winter soil rebukes her, as if speaking for Tante Collette.

She feels like the Unluckiest Woman in the World, resisting even thinking about the things she cherishes, for fear the hellish curse of her lucklessness will waft towards them like a blighting frost.

Yet, here she stands in the ruined garden with its shining black leaves, its red berries rimmed in a foil of frost, the thick grasses like a tangled pelt. Her passing leaves them undiminished, apparently.

Maybe – just maybe – here at Tante Collette's stronghold, where her magic still reigns, Ondine's luck will change at last.

And then, suddenly, the beauty invades her and she is resistless. She seems to fall back into the child she was, wild and free and so sensitive to the natural world.

What has happened to that fairy child of the past, with her wild fantasies and sprightly ways, the hubris and the innocence...?

"You are Ondine," Tante Collette told her that summer she was ten, gazing at her thoughtfully – worriedly, even. "The water sprite."

Ondine felt special and preened a bit. No other child she knew came with a myth attached.

"When she married a man and bore his children, she lost her soul." Tante Collette paused, watching this dire news spread across her niece's complacent face. "I begged your mother not to name you after her."

"What does it mean?" Ondine asked, alarmed. "What can I do?"

Tante Collette shook her head slowly, as if already grieving Ondine's future misfortunes. "Nothing. Unless you choose not to marry. Not to bear children."

She broke a pink rose that proffered itself from the long hand of a vine reaching through the music room window, and clipped it under Ondine's barrette over her right temple.

"How lovely roses look in that auburn hair!" Tante Collette stepped back to admire her.

"Or..." she continued with a sigh, "once your soul is lost, you shall have to set about finding it again."

"Your only duty in life is to remain true to yourself," she wrote in response to Ondine's ten-page howl of pain, when she discovered her husband Richard's betrayal. She was the only person who could say something so trite and get away with it; she, who'd followed her own dictates for more than nine decades.

So then, how could she know how it is with Ondine, who has no idea what being true to herself might entail, who is as soulless as an old shoe?

"Imagine that your own genius is at hand," Tante Collette fired back, this time by telephone. Ondine could picture her at her desk, holding the ivory celluloid and gilded brass receiver of her 1920's phone. "Nothing comes into being without imagination. *Imagine* yourself with a soul! What would a woman of your age, with your talents – with a *soul – want?*"

"A bullet to the brain?"

"Oh, Child!" A rare burst of exasperation. "Don't you know that pain and chaos always herald *Eros?* You have birth pangs, for heaven's sake!"

"People die in childbirth," Ondine intoned mournfully.

"Now, you listen to me!" Tante Collette's voice was suddenly cold. "If it takes you through the very holds of *Hell,* you honor it. You honor this passage. Or you are a woman *without* honor – a thing which is an abomination to me." And with more vigor than one would have guessed a nonagenarian arm could possess, she slammed down the receiver.

Now, the orchard lifts its un-pruned suckers like a wiry mauve haze in the westering light; wind soughs, indistinguishable from surf. Cindery trunks rise up all around her, brandishing black branches that scrawl a calligraphic account of her sorrows on the evening sky. She has come here to this wild Atlantic coast – to Tante Collette's, to *Quatre Vents* – to begin the search.

Ondine seems fated to live her life at the edge of continents, as is only proper for a water sprite.

In southern California, where the ground shakes and waves periodically invade beachfront homes, while other houses simply slide down the cliffs with the first real rain, it all seemed evidence of the instability and marginality of her own life. It was proof that her psyche was neither here nor there – neither fully conscious, nor sufficiently immersed in the unconscious to be creatively endowed.

At Tante Collette's, however, she considers a new possibility: that she, Ondine the water sprite, might find her soul here, close to the waters of the Atlantic. This is not the plasticized beach of L.A. with its carnival atmosphere and a heat she always found suffocating. While others lay out in it slathered in oil, worshipping it, it wilted Ondine.

The air of the Atlantic, though, is bracing, the wind like a god. That morning, walking along the bluffs, she looked down into a coffer of jewels – aquamarine, sapphire, emerald, citrine, and diamond – all caught up in lacy nets of foam that tear and are rewoven again and again. Such unbounded renewal must surely have the same effect on her.

Mustn't it?

She finds as they become reacquainted that the house, too, is a treasure chest. One morning, looking for a coffee spoon, she pulls open a kitchen drawer and there is Tante Collette's good silver where she had expected to find the everyday flatware – which is lovely enough, with its thin nickel silver spoons engraved with sweeping initials and its ivory-handled knives.

But this collection sends her instantly into a kind of reverie. Lying on deep green velvet are implements of wondrous proportion and weight, the tines of forks half again as long as usual, the spoons with deep, lustrous bowls, vaguely webbed in scars of use and age. The knife blades are broad and curved like palette knives, inviting the spreading of rich butter and slow-cooked jam. The silver handles are thick and bumpy with ornament – flowers, birds, leaves and ribbons – not engraved, but sculpted in low relief. Oxidation lies in the crevices like black shadows under the plantings of a magic garden.

Ondine is aware of the ticking of the old wooden clock on the wall, of the smell of coffee, and a thick atmosphere of silence and satisfaction. A damask linen tea towel draped across the Moroccan tile of the counter catches the morning light with a kind of promise – but of what? Blank canvas? The slow elegance of a life fully lived? The richness of everydayness?

All this, as she gazes into a kitchen drawer.

And every inch of the house contains these vignettes.
At all hours of the day, sun sweeps through room after room
igniting the soul of old wood, of silk draped into shimmering
clouds, of softly knapped leather books with sparking gold
edges and embossings. And especially, it incandesces the
fabulous, bright images of the *Nabi*, glorifying the garden of
Quatre Vents.

Ondine stops to sip from a can of Squirt and glances
around apologetically.

"All this about the house must be awfully boring..."

She encounters Heddi's ferocious stare. Its message is
unequivocal. Ondine sighs.

"...and besides...I guess I need to tell you what's happened to me here in L.A., instead of hiding inside Tante Collette's life. Heddi knows. It's really hard to talk about..."

She looks tentatively at Heddi, who nods silently in
response.

Ondine sighs again, heavily.

"It's just that, one day when I was still married to Richard, I was returning to our house in Malibu, just above Point
Dume. I'd just been to my aerobics class and I'd picked up
my daughter Jackie's cheerleader uniform at the dry cleaner's. I was thinking about what to fix for dinner..."

On that terrible afternoon, Ondine runs up the front
steps with Jackie's uniform over her arm in a dry cleaner bag,
throws open the door and prances in, still in her hot purple
Spandex workout leotard, to find her son Kyle on the entry
hall floor in a heap, screaming and flooded with tears.

She knows instantly that it's disaster – but what?

She opens her mouth to ask, but her tongue is paralyzed
like the warped leather of an old boot.

Kneeling, she scoops Kyle into her arms. This child who,
since the age of five, has been Southern California cool is

now a drooling, hysterical rag of a huge teenager. And she holds him and rocks him and croons to him, while her mind turns to razor blades in a blender.

"Baby! Baby! Kylie, Baby!" she says over and over, rocking and rocking.

Before she can calm him enough to tell her, though, there is Richard, looming over them with the most horrible expression on his face. He looks down on their pitiful *Pietà* like an Old Testament Jehovah, colder than an ice storm, his face clouded with incipient judgment.

"*What?!!!*" Ondine screams. Even Kyle, lost in his inner hurricane, jumps at the shrillness.

"You *cunt!*" Richard hisses, no trace of his handsomeness left, all viperous tongue and curled lips.

Ondine recoils but screams, again, "*What?!!!*"

"Jackie, you cunt. It's Jackie." His foot lashes out and he kicks her in the thigh. Then he kicks her again.

She's holding Kyle. She's screaming. She's in a darkness shattered by jagged lightning bolts.

"*What?!!! What about Jackie?*"

"She's *dead*, you cunt! You *bitch!*" He's kicking her metronomically now – hard, up and down her – from head to foot.

She doesn't remember it for a while. It's a blur of horror. There's pain, denial, terror, and sickness in the pit of her being that comes raging up like a rabid animal in ragged screams.

What she remembers next, very clearly, is Kyle clinging to his father's leg, yelling, "*Stop! Stop!* Please, Dad! Please, Dad! *Stop!*" His face is red and gooey with tears and mucus.

Her family has metamorphosed in those instants into something unrecognizable to her, including Jackie, whom she knows to be, without any question – almost without surprise – dead.

She feels as outcast, as if Richard had kicked her, narco-
tized and without a parachute, out of an airplane over the
open ocean.

Their nice, calm, prosperous life is blown up. In an instant, everything is changed forever. What is the *meaning* of
that?

That's what Ondine is grappling with now. Can it be that
some hidden benefit is tucked into her being, something
positive and strong that's boring its way out from the middle
of this catastrophic heap of rubble that she is?

And where does one begin looking for a lost soul? In
what direction does one point oneself? What rituals does
one perform; what obeisances make? What are the necessary sacrifices – as if more could possibly be required – and
what is the desired restitution?

It's no different, really, than if she had died and not Jackie. The first half of her life is dead. She went there, to Tante
Collette's, to discover if there is anything or anyone left to
be reborn. Is there a Phoenix in these ashes? If so, she has
no clue where the energy or direction or rigor might come
from to resurrect it.

She's caught in a *tsunami* of black ink; tumbling, not
knowing which way is up, down, or sideways, in a rip tide
that's bearing her away from all known shores. Is this madness, or the very bones of realness, stripped of every shred
of padding flesh?

They've all gone off to their separate camps to recover –
if recovery's possible.

Kyle's in his first-semester dorm room at U.S.C.

Richard's gone to his lover's apartment, or at least that's
the gossip her friends tell her.

And Jackie's gone to ash in an urn in a wall in a mauso-
leum in Forest Lawn...

What hour of any day hasn't been haunted by her image?
Those short, chubby legs, so cute under her cheerleader's

pleated skirt. That fragile blonde hair, striped white by beach sun. So her father's daughter and so like his mother that she seemed to Ondine, sometimes, not her own.

With her tiny snub nose, her wide blue eyes that always seemed too empty of expression – not trusting, really, but just too little imagination to sense anything other than 365 days of sunlight, unlimited credit card usage and well-fed ease. There was not the smallest shred of angst in the child. No passion for the unknown.

How, then, could she be Ondine's child? Where was *she* in her? Surely, some part of Jackie reflected her mother? Wasn't it that little particle of Ondine in her that enraged Richard?

The bruises on her side were ripening from plum to sickly yellow but he felt no shame. He shouted at her for days, making Jackie's death all her fault.

"You started her going there," he snarled, jerking at the knot of his tie. The day of the funeral; his good black Armani suit; the tie of rich cerulean silk patterned in gold *fleurs-de-lis*, Tante Collette's final Christmas gift; southern California sun beat back by the low, cool throb of air conditioning; the bedroom carpet innocent and pristine as a newly-born, pale-apricot lamb.

"What business did that kid have at a coffee house? All that poetry? Open mic, or whatever?"

She opens her mouth to protest: *Why not?* But she knows in the base of her empty being, it is pointless. Instead, she concentrates on centering the seam of her pantyhose in the exact middle of her crotch. Try as she will, there is always an S-curve right below her belly button.

"You knew. You knew it was bad for her thighs – but you did it anyway."

"Her *thighs?*"

He's describing the strange land he's walking in, she knows. This is the road map of his thoughts, if she can follow.

The coffee house is a landmark. Her taking Jackie there in the first place is a landmark. Jackie's thighs are a landmark. How the dots connect is not marked. She's in open country here, looking for a sign.

"All those *lattés*. All that cheesecake. You know what my mother's legs are like! And cholesterol. And you let her do it anyway. How was she ever going to get a husband?"

All this addressed to his svelte and distinguished form in the full-length mirror. How long has it been since they met one another's eyes?

A pale flame of protest licks upward in the bright sunlight bouncing off the Pacific, then falls feebly back. "But, you could have said something yourself, surely, if it..."

"You were her *mother*, goddamn it! It was *your* job! You know I'm busy. You know a doctor's life is a goddamn living hell of work. Couldn't you pull yourself away from the goddamn aerobics classes long enough to keep your daughter from *dying?*"

He has his back to her now, his foot up on her vanity bench, jabbing at a spot of dust on his mirror-finish black shoes. "Can't you be trusted with *anything?*"

She's drifting away now, aware that some inner part of her is being beaten, stabbed and strangled – but she's leaving her behind, the silly wench. Why does she stay and take such abuse?

She had known the day she picked him up from the plastic surgeon's, with his eyes stitched up, his face sanded raw, the paralytic rigidity of Botox injected into him, that they were through; that he'd donned an impenetrable mask behind which she was no longer welcome.

His voice is like distant thunder. Her head is round and empty and blue inside, like a pale spring sky on one of those tremulous mornings when anything is possible. She floats away into it, his angry voice like the diminishing drum of black rain.

What got her through that terrible time was thinking of *Quatre Vents*. Right after the funeral, she flew to France and spent three weeks there, just trying to put herself back together; trying to decide what to do next.

Part of the magic of Tante Collette's house is its backdrop of constant sound from the sea. Her property extends over a little hill with an orchard, down through some low bushes and bunch grass rooted in sand, all the way to the beach where the Atlantic churns against the rocks.

Even when the garden is saturated in the smell of roses, as Ondine remembers it from her childhood, there is always the tangy under-note of brine. It gives the place a certain air of sturdiness – some suggestion of men in wooden boats putting out to sea with nets – and also of mystery, as if the fathomless deeps of nature have found a portal there, with the high garden walls as their *temenos* and the house, their temple.

On that brief visit, in her devastated, barely-embodied state, the growl of the sea was tonic. It reminded her that eternal verities underpin this transient life. People have come and gone – in this house, this town, this continent, this world – for who knows how many generations?

Her aunt lived richly, deliciously, at *Quatre Vents*. Now she's gone. Her daughter, with her silly little social existence as cheerleader, perennial dieter and heartless cell-phone gossip, is gone. Her hollowed-out marriage, like a puff pastry *sans* filling, is gone.

And half of Ondine's life is gone.

On the first night at *Quatre Vents*, she dreamed that she has ten minutes to dress because she's expected to be the head of a parade in a wonderful costume. She can't find her shoes – other women had borrowed them...

"My other selves, Heddi? That southern California social fixture? That soccer mom? That loveless, dutiful wife?"

Heddi just stares at her with fathomless, sibylline eyes that say she's listening with her entire being.

...and when she opens the bottom drawer of her dresser where she keeps her fancy things – embroidered Spanish shawls, antique *huipils*, hand-woven *rebozos* – it's empty.

The shock is profound. In a panic, she opens the next drawer. It's empty, too!

Quickly, she opens the third drawer, the next to the top, and – Oh! Sweet relief! – it's stuffed full of the most marvelous fabrics. Not one but three *rebozos*, each more fabulous than the last, in bright cadmium yellow with intricately woven designs in rich colors. And at the bottom of the drawer is an ankle-length skirt of sky blue *ikat*, woven with hazy white clouds.

She shakes the skirt out, expecting it to be too wrinkled to wear, but it ripples down invitingly, without a flaw. She feels a strong desire to slip it on.

But still, she dithers, making excuses. The parade has probably started by now. But in her mind's eye, she can see people still milling about, sorting themselves into parade formation. There will be no parking in town – even though she'd planned to walk. And she has no right to head the parade – this, in spite of her vision of herself, carrying a towering silk banner embroidered with strange symbols, that billows in the wind, with skirts flying and shawls swirling about her.

Most alarming is the radiance of her face. Her absolute presence in the moment. Her joy...

What right has she – the killer mom – to such prominence, immanence and abandon?

She awakened delirious with indecision: to rush out and head the parade or to shrink back, cop out and become anonymous? The decision isn't so easy as the waking, rational mind might think.

But those two empty drawers! The first half of her life gone, emptied out!

And that third drawer so full of riches – all those beautiful adornments so ready to leap into the fray, to whip like bright flags in the winds of life.

If they'd been common clothing, the decision would have been simpler. But these were vestments; the sacred garb of the Feminine, created by the most skilled hands – woven by Isis or Athena Herself, maybe.

Surely, she couldn't face the shame of keeping such treasures hidden, could she?

Tante Collette was right: she's lost her soul and now it is her burden – she can scarcely imagine it might also be her delight – to retrieve it.

The morning after the dream, the weather turns frigid. It's February and a heavy gray sky lours over the bare orchard. Ondine digs Tante Collette's ankle-length black mink out of the fur vault in the basement, along with its matching Tatar hat. She twines a long scarf of slubbed Thai silk, sea green iridescing to peacock blue, around her throat, buttons the coat from top to bottom and goes out.

The western garden door groans on its hinges and exudes a smell of mold, as she follows the path toward the shore. She reminds herself to oil both wood and metal when warm weather comes. The grass of the orchard is bent under heavy dew, wetting her boots as if it were wiping its tears there, protesting its neglect.

Over the crest of the hill the low bushes begin, with their pale, leathery leaves and twisted black branches. She stumbles downhill toward the sea over coarse bunches of bleached grass. Wind whips up the slope, magnifying the roar of the agitated surf below. Dry seedpods, like blackened string beans, rattle ominously on the bushes. The entire scene is dramatic, Shakespearean, filled with the shamanic intensity of Macbeth's witches.

She imagines the southern California beach today, with people in shorts and tee shirts, the sun shining, and the smells of hotdogs grilling and cocoa butter sunscreen overpowering the ocean's salt. While here she is, skittering down toward the icy Atlantic, wearing fur. She feels the rightness of that in her cold bones.

When she reaches the beach, the roar of the sea obliterates all other sound. The ocean is whipped by wind into ice green tunnels fringed in foam. Wind lifts the foam, rolling it in airy balls across the beach until it snags in the grass.

A balloon of it skates along the gale and smacks into her face. Immediately, it begins to disintegrate, its tiny bubbles popping deliciously against her skin. When she licks her lips, she tastes salt and minerals that feed an utterly primal hunger she didn't even know she possessed.

Heddi would say that the beach is liminal space: "In dreams, the beach holds contents emerging from or disappearing into the unconscious." This, one day as Ondine sat in Heddi's office, gazing blankly at wavelets of light that lapped across the ceiling and east wall, refractions off the afternoon ocean.

So here in France, it's an appropriate place for a stroll, given Ondine's soulless, semi-vaporous state. Maybe a rogue wave will come and simply sweep her into the obliteration of the unconscious; or a serpentine leviathan of the deep arise, bearing as a gift the Pearl of Wisdom in its hoary jaws.

As she struggles up the beach against the wind, a gull is hanging in air, breasting the gale. Positioned directly over the tide line, he strokes his wings, seeming to advance, only to be pushed back by powerful currents of air. He bobs forward and backward by inches.

Ondine stands watching him for some minutes. At any moment, she expects, he will disappear into those vast spaces only birds can inhabit.

Instead, he hangs suspended.

She is overcome with the desire for him to do something; to exert some kernelled energy and soar off over the ocean, or to tilt and fold his wings and wheel inland booted by the wind. But this endless exertion accomplishing nothing annoys her. What the hell is he doing? What does he hope to accomplish?

She picks up a round sea cobble and hurls it at him. Of course, it misses.

She shouts at him, "You stupid bird! Move, for God's sake!" And she lobs another stone.

He's sublimely indifferent to her existence. He stares unblinkingly out to sea. He flaps and is blown back. He bobs above the waves, going nowhere.

"God damn you!" Ondine screams, scooping up a fistful of wet sand and hurling it with all her force. It blows back into her eyes and she hops around in supreme irritation, rubbing her eyes and brushing her face with damp gloves, shrieking.

"God damn you, you stupid, stupid bird! You useless, indecisive piece of shit! You weak, helpless goddamned piece of garbage. God damn you! *God damn you!*" She wipes away strands of spittle with her suede glove. Tears hot as lava gush down her icy cheeks. "God damn you to Hell!"

And she turns and runs for the house. She doesn't even need Heddi's decree, "Projection!" She knows it well enough on her own.

She's halfway up the slope to the orchard when she remembers Heddi also saying, "The bird's a symbol of the spirit. Like, when the dove of the Holy Spirit comes and hovers over Jesus at His baptism."

When she gets back to the west garden door, she can't get it open. The latch is rusted and simply refuses to lift. She struggles ineptly and vainly for a while, like some well-attired Lear locked out of his own castle.

She exerts all her strength in one last attempt to rattle the door loose. It doesn't budge. The *temenos* is doing its job, expelling the unclean and unready.

In complete humiliation, she has to march down the road in ankle-length black mink to find a locksmith. She's sure they're *still* talking about *that* epiphany in the village.

"The memory of country people is long," Tante Collette used to say – in which case, they must also still remember the fairytale wedding Tante Collette gave her at *Quatre Vents*.

It's been over twenty years since that afternoon saturated with such joy and sureness, when Ondine wed Richard under the trees of that garden. Then, they were in full leaf and heavy with fruit; apples, pears, apricots, cherries and peaches, each in its separate state of ripening. Their mingled fragrance was luscious in the warm air of early summer. Birds dipped and chattered. Roses and honeysuckle twined their scents with the marvelous foods being presented at the long, linen-clad tables beneath the trees.

She had thought herself so adult that day, so gracious, so the Lady deigning to stoop to guests – little knowing that her own state of ripening was close to rock-hard green.

Maybe the de-souling happened that very day, when she went away, proud and sure, with the handsome man she scarcely knew. Out of the Garden, so to speak. De-Edenized.

Or maybe it was more gradual. She remembers putting up a fight at various junctures along the way. Demanding a sitter for Kyle and Jackie four days a week, so she could finish her MFA. Refusing to iron Richard's shirts as a nod to feminism. Squeezing in time while the kids were at school for dance and exercise classes that kept her figure trim, maintaining the illusion of her sylph-self.

What she could not have known, what is barely coming to awareness this moment, is that it was, from the instant the vows were spoken, a losing battle.

Whether in the frenzy of a Christmas-time shopping mall buying blitz, or during quiet nights in a lonely bed wondering where Richard was and what was keeping him so long, or in the ball-cap-on-backwards, hamper-lugging, interminable weekends of the children's grade and high school soccer matches, her soul was quietly, step by stealthy step, stealing away.

Unlike the people of the village, she *cannot* remember. She feels lobotomized. When did her bright hopes for an intimate relationship with Richard first have a head-on crash with reality? When did she first realize that the mature companionship of equals she had envisioned was really just a charade of male dominance and female passivity?

At first, she tried cajoling: *I love you – can't we work this out?* Then, she fought it, calling it by name, railing against it – only to win herself a reputation as a ragging bitch. Then came withdrawal, at the point when she could no longer speak her disappointment. And finally, the glossy, well-portrayed, scooped-out facsimile of a happy, pampered wife.

She lay down inside like a suicide inviting inundation on a beach. She let the green waves of his icy neglect bury her, batter her against the rocks, stop her breath and drown her soul.

And she did it all effortlessly, in Italian sandals, silk gauze skirts and Dior tee shirts. It was no small feat, when she stops to think about it. Maybe she's missed her calling in film or on the stage.

"Heddi talks about my marriage to Richard as a regression. She says I was letting Richard act like an emotionally abusive father, while I played the docile little girl.

"I couldn't disagree – what docile little girl would? It was just easier, that way...less stressful."

Ondine's eyes sweep the group, looking for the antsyness of boredom or the blank stare of withdrawal. All eyes are still on her, though, and it gives her the courage to continue.

Heddi isn't impressed by that logic, at all: "You think living this way is *easy?*" They're sitting in her office, with its tranquil ocean light off the afternoon Pacific.

"What else can I *do?*" Ondine flips her hands upwards and then drops them listlessly in her lap, a gesture of futility.

"There's a kind of heroism," Heddi says, "that comes through meeting the banal demands of everyday life – including standing up to a husband whose will to power seems overwhelming. If not for yourself, then for the children. What kind of role model are you for them? Do you want your son to abuse his future wife and children? Do you expect your daughter to endure an anti-erotic marriage of emotional compliance and cowardice?"

In truth, Ondine never really bought that argument. Kyle was always so out-going and friendly, she could never imagine him holding his future family as emotional hostages. She'd known, right from the first moment he stumped off on his solid little toddler's legs bent on investigations pertaining to himself alone, that his life would go just fine.

And Jackie was always so...well, it's hard for her to say it and not sound monstrously cold. She is – was – her daughter, after all, her own flesh and blood. But the child, right from the womb, was unnaturally passive. Sweet-natured, no trouble at all. But somehow limp. There was no fight in her at all.

Ondine came to think of her as the new genetic dispensation, bred especially for southern California, where fight-or-flight is more concerned with whether or not to skip school to go surfing than with battling saber-toothed tigers. She was born with her hand shaped to a cell phone. She was the easeful life, embodied. A domineering husband would scarcely have been a problem for her. She'd probably have welcomed never being called upon to make a decision regarding her own existence.

In the weeks after Jackie's death, people complimented Ondine on her grace under pressure, her heroic stoicism. They sent emails saying things like, "Thank you for being a courageous example to us all."

Only Heddi wasn't fooled. "Where are you stuffing the grief?" she wanted to know.

And when Ondine replied, without a glimmer of self-awareness, "What grief?" Heddi just stared at her without a word.

Ondine wasn't fooled, either. She knew with terrifying certainty that something major was wrong with her. She went through her paces like the good trick pony she was. The sun shone; waves rolled languidly up the beach. She ate at excellent restaurants with loving friends. She even shopped for clothes.

All the while, it was as if novacaine had been injected directly into her brain. She was a walking, talking, robotic model of a human being.

And there was no place to recover from the shock, either, because her home went from being a smoothly operating mechanism of family life to a war-torn, bombed-out battleground, over night.

Richard, who had almost always deigned to keep his cruelty cleverly hidden behind smooth words and general physical absence, was suddenly and terribly present. He attached himself to her like a demonic possession.

Whoever said that marriage is about doubling joys and halving sorrows never imagined *their* hellish household. Richard continued to place the blame for Jackie's death squarely on Ondine, and his mother, Rose, a pretty creature resembling a plump, faded film star, began to show up daily in her opalescent *crème*-colored Coupe de Ville to aid him in this.

Rose's chirping voice and adolescent giggle warble from a body plumped by too much daytime TV and too many dates with her girlfriends at the ice cream parlor. Her thighs – the very ones, according to Richard, that Jackie had inherited – stand out a good six inches on either side of any other point on her body, and it's no improvement that she chooses to wear Spandex stirrup pants and a platinum blonde bubble. She's round and white and tender as *gnocchi* – but she's got a core of elemental iron.

Her only real interest in life being position and power, she rides Richard like a winning racehorse, with whip and spurs. And her hatred – Ondine's friends say jealousy – of Ondine has always been complete.

So Rose developed the habit of dropping by unannounced to "support you during your time of mourning." With both her and Richard in the house, Ondine was caught between hammer and anvil.

At first, she played a good game of duck and dodge. If they were in the living room, she went out to prune the garden. If they discovered her there, she pled the need for a shower and retreated to the bathroom, locking the door behind her.

But there's only so long you can stay in the bathroom, especially with water rationing.

If she tried to cook, Rose horned in, meat cleaver in hand, and Ondine was never sure if it was the veal or her fingers that Rose was aiming for.

Rose's conversations went from thinly veiled to overtly acidic. Ondine's clothes, cooking, housekeeping, interior décor, friends, lifestyle and artistic creations were all fair game. Especially her mothering, which had never met with Rose's approval, anyway, but now was forever categorized as slipshod at best, but more accurately, lethal.

At issue, of course, was the fact that Jackie died at a coffeehouse. At first, Ondine tried to defend herself. Girls her age went there. It was not in a dangerous part of town; it was *Glendale*, for heaven's sake! Close to the college. There was an occasional legitimate poet who passed through and always an open mic. Some amusing and intelligent material. She liked going there, herself, sitting back in the shadows with an espresso, sipping in the rap and the self-indulgent angst.

So she took Jackie there. She thought it might give her an alternate vision of herself – something a little to the left of the mall. Maybe political consciousness would seep in by osmosis.

And Jackie did seem interested. Ondine only took her that once and she warned Jackie never to go there without her.

So how was Ondine to know that Jackie's friend, Amanda, turned sixteen the next week? Or that her parents gave her a brand new Porsche convertible for her birthday? Or that Jackie would propose a jaunt into Glendale as one of their first outings?

Would Ondine have said "No," if Jackie had asked permission?

Yes! She thinks *surely* she would have because she would have doubted Amanda's driving ability – especially on the tangle of freeway interchanges around Glendale that's always clogged with high-speed traffic.

But she never got that opportunity.

Jackie and Amanda were full-blown in the stage where parents are terminally stupid. They communicated with rolled eyes and pained sighs.

When they were still dependent on Ondine for rides, they were more or less loosely under her control. But with a car – especially one she didn't even know existed...!

Ondine had no idea that they had been loosed on the world, adolescent whim in full cry.

Even the police defended her: a drive-by shooting in *Glendale?* In *that* part of town, close to the college? It was unheard-of. It was a weird fluke. No one could have predicted it.

Even the shooter, when he was caught, admitted that his friend who was driving had taken the wrong off-ramp. They wanted to go to L.A.'s South Central. But then they thought, what the hell? "Hunting," they called it. May as well hunt Whitey. It was a novel approach. They kind of liked it. It was kinky. And two hotties in a Porsche convertible? *Shee-it!*

None of that mattered to Richard and Rose. For them, it would never be anything but Ondine's fault, completely and utterly.

And it didn't help when Amanda, in her tearful funeral remembrances, trying for a little humor with the teenagers who were there, gasped out that Jackie had wanted them to go to the coffeehouse to prove, once and for all, how terminally lame her mother's taste really was.

"The poor kid," Richard muttered, driving home, "she was so embarrassed by you!"

So why can't Ondine grieve? Why is there only stone where her living heart should be?

The only thing she can think is that it's not possible to grieve for anyone else until you've truly grieved for yourself.

"Heddi says Richard is an extroverted thinking type. Can you explain that again, Heddi? I'm still not too clear on it."

Heddi smoothes her skirt before responding, trying to formulate an answer that will be comprehensible to the others. "Well, basically that means that he formulates a vision of reality based on objective facts and communal values. In other words, from things outside himself. He has no expectation of finding anything of value in his own inner life."

Ondine nods enthusiastically. "And that, of course, puts him at complete odds with me, the artist, whose inner life is everything," she says, launching back into her story.

Watching her as she tells her long and convoluted tale, with her beautiful, pale, worried face framed in clouds of auburn hair, Heddi envisions Ondine as a mermaid newly arisen from the depths, her white skin coated in salt crystal that sparks and glows around her like an aura in the blazing sun of consciousness.

She has a sudden, hospitable realization. *How painful the Sun's glare must be for her*, she thinks.

As a doctor, Richard is completely oriented toward objective data. It is a short step, according to Heddi, for him to elevate his intellectually oriented formula into the ruling principle of his life. *Shoulds* and *oughts* stud his speech like cloves in a ham. In the world he inhabits professionally, this makes him a powerful ethical voice for quality treatment of patients and for reform of lax procedures in the hospital.

Ondine can't begin to list the committees, the panels and the honorary degrees that Richard has accumulated. She could paper his study walls with certificates and diplomas, not to mention the glossy photos of him shaking hands with important people at important events, always tall, elegant and commanding, immaculate in his Armani suits, the very archetype of the Hero Doctor.

At the dinner where he was to accept the position of hospital Chief of Staff, one of his nurses leaned toward Ondine during happy hour and whispered, "What's it like living with a god?"

Apparently, his nurse was confused about the difference between divinity and autocracy, because at home, at the real center of his power, Richard was tyrannical. Maybe that nurse was right in a way, though: he *was* like the Old

Testament Jehovah, who withers the life of everything that doesn't conform to His dictates.

Heddi opines that that's because the unconscious attitude of such a rational man, the flip side, is an egocentric hysteric. Ondine shudders at the thought of anyone trying to tell *Richard* such a thing!

But Heddi's right about Richard's hysterical tendencies: the need to make himself interesting; the impression management; his effusiveness that morphs so often into either a lie of self-aggrandizement or imaginings of wrong-doing on the part of anyone close to him. The children suffered often from his morbid fantasies of their divergence from his dictates but, of course, Ondine was the perennial favorite focus of the dragon's scorching breath.

One afternoon as Ondine is heading into Heddi's tranquil office, built onto the back of her big house in Malibu, she has an insight. The house, what she can glimpse of it coming down the side walkway, is all done up in Oriental rugs, French furniture and old porcelain blue-and-white jars. Bronze rain chains hang from the eaves into the moss carpets of a Zen garden studded with lichen-covered boulders and antique stone lanterns.

It's perfect, all of it. Everything is here, except the warmth, she thinks.

She doesn't mean it to be catty. It's just that after years under the rule of Richard's perfectionism, she's more than a little leery of Heddi's. She wonders what kind of shadow lurks beneath those polished surfaces. It's hard for her to hold such an apostate thought – and she's quite sure she hasn't the courage to share it with Heddi.

On this particular afternoon, Heddi is laying out for the first time the full picture of the man Ondine has married. It astonishes Ondine that anyone could know him so accurately and intimately without ever having met him. It's two years into her analysis and she still hasn't fully accepted that depth psychology can actually reveal anything important to her – or maybe she's just wary of being caught in another perfectionistic trap.

Heddi says, "Richard is an icon for our culture," in that conversational way that always puts Ondine at ease. "He completely embodies one of our cultural ideals that says that a truly enterprising person has to concentrate everything on a single goal."

"What does that mean?"

"That means that his professional focus has been absolute. Almost all his libido is consumed there. But the unconscious always compensates for the conscious attitude. So the unconscious attitude of such an extraverted person is subjective, but in an undeveloped, infantile way. Which would make him, unconsciously, terribly egocentric."

Ondine feels as if Heddi is gazing into a crystal ball, seeing with mystical clarity something that has, for years, troubled her home like a phantom.

"Jung says that the extrovert's unconscious attitude goes far beyond mere childish selfishness; that it verges on the ruthless and brutal."

As if Heddi had triggered a secret spring mechanism, something that has lain ever more tightly coiled in Ondine is suddenly released in a wordless shriek, both agonized and ecstatic. Both of them are startled by the violence of the sound.

"I'll take that as an affirmation," Heddi says, honing the sardonic edge of dry humor.

Ondine nods, speechless, her mouth agape.

"It must have been terribly hard for you, all these years," Heddi says gently. "The whole world idolizes your husband. And I'm sure you tried hard to do the same..."

She leans across the space between their two chairs to hand a tissue to Ondine who, without knowing it, has begun to leak sparse, reluctant tears. One by one, they gather like drops of acid in the corners of her eyes and then trickle down her cheeks, furtive and stinging.

"How is Richard's health?"

The question catches Ondine off guard. "F...fine," she stammers. "He's...he's indestructible."

"I wouldn't count on that." Heddi's voice is dry, soft and sure.

"What do you mean?"

"When the conscious attitude becomes so absurdly ex-aggerated, there is a resulting deepening of repression of the unconscious. All the trapped energy in the unconscious can only come to light in symptomatic form. Often, that takes the form of a catastrophe."

"What...*kind* of catastrophe?" Ondine can't tell, in that instant, if she's terrified or hopeful.

"It can take various forms. A professional collapse through some kind of misstep. A nervous breakdown, where the unconscious simply paralyzes all conscious action. A life-threatening disease. Or even suicide."

They sit in silence awhile, as this information slowly seeps through Ondine's defensive crust. She can hear the faint grind of traffic out on the Pacific Coast Highway. Heddi's wristwatch gives the tiny beep that signals only five minutes left of the session. Ondine dabs a few more fugitive tears, wondering if her mascara has run.

"But Richard's *indestructible*," she repeats inanely.

Heddi just stares at her without a word, as if Ondine's head were a crystal ball in which the future is fulminating darkly.

"I guess I've gone on and on. I'm sorry. This isn't really a story like Heddi and Betty told. It's just a ramble.

"I won't keep you any longer, except to say that Heddi was right. The reason I've come back to L.A. is that Richard's sick. In fact, he's apparently dying.

"You see, it turns out that Richard was in the closet all those years and, after we divorced, he went to live with his lover. But now, he's got AIDS and his lover's abandoned him. I'm here to tend to him, while he dies."

"Why doesn't his wonderful mother do that?" Betty asks.

"Oh! I forgot to tell you. Rose had a stroke about seven or eight months ago. She's in an extended care facility in Burbank. She can't even speak much less tend Richard. Kyle thinks it happened when Richard finally had to tell her he's gay and has AIDS."

"Talk about the return of the repressed!" Heddi mutters to no one in particular.

"And you don't have...?" Betty asks, tentatively.

"No, I've been tested. I got lucky. I'm fine."

"But won't it be awkward to see him?" Betty persists.

"Probably. But I guess he's too weak to make it too awful. The first thing I'm going to do is paint his bedroom. Kyle says it's all white...so stark you'd think he was already in the morgue.

"So I think I'll paint it rose, in honor of his mother."

Heddi

Well, that's Ondine for you; everything in her life viewed in terms of color – even her bruises.

In her mind, it all turns into paint on canvas or sculpted forms. Even death becomes a *Pietà*. Maybe there's only one thing a person like Ondine *can* do – just do the obvious and turn life into art. Maybe that's all that's asked of her in this life.

Pearl

Well, Pearl cain't ratly make heads or tails a the Onion. From what she cain tell, she's god-awful sorry fer hersef cuz she's so darn rich.

An as fer yer man beatin on you – that's a story old as stones an don't hardly bear mentionin.

Now, Pearl cain relate ta losin yer kid. She's lost a passel of em. Ain't nothin, never, gonna make that rat.

Now everone's had a break an used the john, an that Heady gal, she's turnin her eyes on Pearl, who espects she's got ta do it, if only ta keep all them women from gabblin lak a gaggle a geese.

Well, Pearl laked her corner. Even on the coldest days it gots shelter from the wind an the afternoon sun keeps it warm, rat up til it goes down in the ocean. It's betwixt a surf shop an a greasy spoon called *Pop's*. Jes the way they built the places, both with angled front winders, makes a little *V* Pearl jes fits in, her an her pack an cart.

She spreads out her cardboard – the best is a water heater box, good an thick – an gets out her pillers an lap robe. Digs out her pipe an lats up. Sets out her can.

Don't take long. Some bleached blond young feller from the surf shop, or some old fart comin belchin outta Pop's'll drop some change in, an the day's off ta a good start.

Long's she gots enough ta buy her some tobaccy, she's fine. Pop makes sure she's fed. He'll fry up a burger after the noon rush. She uses his john. She don't need much. Never did eat much.

Yer the skinniest child in the Choctaw Nation, her Granny use ter say, sizin her up. *Must be that nigger blood a yer pappy's – you got bones half the size a anybody fer ten miles in any direction.*

She warn't being mean. It was jes her way ta say a thin as it come ta her. She was kinda short on eti-cut, but you always knew whar you stood with Granny.

One thin you can say fer California, the weather's fine. Back in Oklahoma this time a year, a gal woulda froze ta death, settin out lak Pearl does. The Roads Department'd have ta haul her off lak one solid block a human ice. But out here, thar's but a few days she cain't set out in the fresh air an smoke her pipe an watch the world go by.

When it gets blustery – an it do, sometimes, bout three, four times a year – she goes ta the homeless lounge an cools her heels. But she don't lak it cuz they won't let her smoke. An them white bread an cheese samitches they hands out at lunchtime is a scandal. Pop wouldn't a let such a puny thin cross *his* counter, she'll tell you that!

She sure does miss Pop, since he up an died!

People worry bout her at the shelter, too. They fuss over her an that jes irritates the hell outta her. Theys afraid – afraid a this an afraid a that. Asceerd she'll be attacked. Asceerd she'll catch pneumonia. Asceerd she'll be raped.

Hell! If life is so damned sceery, how come she's lived to be a hunert an twelve?

She's exaggeratin, a course. She ratly forgot how old she is – lost count a few years back at 91.

Not that she don't get a little stiff, settin on the cee-ment, all day. But she gots her cushions. It's the gettin up an down that's the hard part. The transitions, you mat say. Once she's up, once she's down, she's fine. It's the limbo in between whar she's dubious.

Speaking a Limbo, she's been settin here thinkin bout her husband, Abel Johns. Now that man was a scandal, an if he's dead he ain't in no Limbo, if you catch her drift.

If thar's a afterlife, that man jes passed rat through Limbo in a dead drop straight ta Hell.

In fact, ta kill him, God prawly had ta shove him inta a big ol cosmic mineshaft, plungin rat down ta the Fiery Furnace.

Lord! That man was a tribulation. She don't know why he's on her mind so much these days. Maybe it's cuz Alma Mae, down at the shelter, was come an brung home by her kin. They jes up an arrived one day an took her away. Built a room over the gee-rage fer her, with its own bathroom an everthin.

Got Pearl thinkin about Abel Johns an all the lil Johns they done made together. Ever one of em in they grave. Poor thins. Never stood a chance with that heathen fer a father. What drink didn't plug inta they little bodies in ways a weakness, meanness done took what was left.

Pearl declares, she don't know why a soul would even *come* ta this earth, knowin *that* was in store fer it. God must blindfold us before He kicks us outta Heaven. Ain't no way, otherwise, no soul in its rat mind'd come an take up residence in any body related ta the Johns family. She was wishin, after Alma Mae done rode off with her kids – and them no young'uns theirseves by the look a thins – that she still had *one* child ta come an take *her* away. Put her in some nice new room smellin a fresh paint, with a flush toilet close by. Maybe a TV.

It was a moment a bitterness, she gots ta confess. She's ashamed ta turn her face up ta the Lord fer such ingratitude. An here she gots her health, too, an poor ol Alma Mae so stove in with arthritis she cain't hardly walk.

Pearl thinks bout her Granny, round this same age. Tough as boot leather. Couldn't a kilt her with a shovel. Woes jes done shed off a her lak water off a goose's rump.

When the Lord invented her Granny, He musta said, *Ye'll get no quarter from me, Woman. I'll give you nothin but misery an you give Me nothin but praise an we'll get along jes fine.* The kinda contract some Stillwater lawyer'd make.

And Granny jes answered back, proud an proper as beets, *You bet, Lord. If that's the way You want it, that's the way You'll get it.* An she never deviated from their contractual arrangement in all the years she lived – except one time, which Pearl remembers cuz a it being the exception that proved the rule.

That one slip-up a Granny's was when she got religion. But it warn't the Christian one. It was Choctaw; a Choctaw revival.

It started with the men. Pearl heerd it happen one nat when a bunch of em was out round a bonfire, drinkin applejack an howlin at the moon. Some old geezer started warblin one a them old songs. Somebody found a 5-gallon can an started a beat. Some others – prawly stumblin over theirseves, lak she'd seen em so many times – started dancin.

They raised a ruckus all nat – a reg'lar war party.

"I'll never fergit it," Pearl says, taking in her audience in one squint-eyed glance. "Wakin up in mah bed, asceerd, an Granny comin in an sayin, *Hush, Child. Ain't nothing ta be asceerd of.*

"*What is it?* I axed, all fearful. *Wuves?* I'd never seen a wuff, but ever child knows that wuves cain be the cause a what frights em.

"*No,* Granny says, *somethin far more dangerous then wuves. It's a bunch a Choctaw men raisin Hell. No danger ta us, though. Jes ta theirseves. You go ta sleep now.*"

But a course she couldn't go ta sleep. She laid thar inta the dawn listenin ta them wild yelps, the wailin an the chantin an the big bass beat a the drum. An she confesses, she warn't scairt by mornin. Her whole sef was *alive* lak fresh, fallin water – all frothy inside. Somethin in her jes perked rat up.

She reckons it was the same fer Granny cuz soon after that, her an some a her friends started ta join the men's circle that was a regular thin now, ever night.

They took Pearl out thar cuz they warn't nothin else ta do with kids.

It was pure magic – that bonfire shakin flamey lat across they faces, an makin the bunch grass look lak it got up with its own shadow an danced, too.

The best was the beat a them drums, cuz now they'd found more thins ta beat on – old kettles, a 55-gallon oil drum. A couple a them old farts had they grandpappy's *real* drums, skin ones, an Pearl could always hear the voice a them drums risin above all the others lak a clear voice singin, certain an true.

An the men was chantin *AY-AH-YA-YA AY-AH-YA-YA*, an givin little yips lak a whole den a cay-otes. An the women was movin out in the shadders at the edge a the lat, shoulder ta shoulder in a ring, sidestepping, they feet raisin little dust storms as they stomped.

You'd think them kids woulda been runnin round lak crazy people, screamin an chantin an wagglin they arms. But no. They was quiet as mice. They set back thar in the shadders under the black prairie sky in a little cluster an stared with eyes as big as the moon.

Oh, it was strange an unsettlin. Sometimes, she din't know who she was, or whar, or when. It felt lak she'd fell down a well in time an them Choctaws was a livin river a memory an voice an rhythm that come outta ferever an went off inta ferever.

Some a the little kids'd doze off, all wrapped in blankets, but not Pearl. If somebody axed her, she could hop up off this floor an dance them dances yet, this very day, yellin, *AY-AH-YA-YA AY-AH-YA-YA*, lak she'd been thar yesterday; lak she jes seen it happen.

She reckons in some deep part a her it jes *did* happen – or maybe it *always* is happenin. Maybe them dance circles never rest, but keep on spinnin lak them galaxies they talk about – only somewhar in the deep space inside a *her*; somewhar that all the white man's bullshit never shat on.

That deep.

She thinks it could be so. She knows thar be springs that rise up outta the earth even in the driest years. Pearl thinks it mat be lak that with her. All parched an wrinkled on the outside, but somewhar deep inside, risin up, still dancin.

X
=

"On this second night of the terrorist stand-off at Los Angeles International Airport, in the floodlit night, the assembled army of agencies, with their warriors and experts and their multiple technologies, waits. No one seems quite sure what they are waiting for."

X watches with heavy eyes as the eleven o'clock news begins. The incident's Public Information Officer steps up now, speaking various platitudes before the cameras for the benefit of the television audience. These only manage to annoy, not inform, her.

"Terrorism is violence perpetrated by a sub-state entity upon innocent citizens," he says, in response to a reporter's question. X considers this, repeating it to herself until the meaning of the words is clear to her. It is, she grudgingly admits, an accurate, if skeletal, definition. But it does not say the things she so deeply knows; the level of disenfranchisement one must reach before terrorism becomes on option.

According to the blonde reporter – with whom X now feels a certain scant sisterly regard, also grudging, as they both endure the grinding hours – various technologies are gradually assembling a picture of the problem. Infrared sensors have detected the locations of living bodies entombed within the luckless building. Listening devices are picking up snatches of conversation, some of it in foreign languages that then need translation. Drones and robotic scouts have been sent into the corridors, only to be foiled by heaped bodies, closed doors or deliberate blockades. One negotiator has been sent in who has failed to return, and that option is thus considered to be officially closed.

"SWAT teams and the FBI Hostage Rescue Team lean into the restraints their orders impose on them like tethered warhorses that, smelling blood, are eager for the fight. In full battle gear, they lie on the floor of makeshift shelters trying to rest, or pace their confines, coffee in hand, muttering to one another about the irritating delays. Among them the feeling is universal that immediate action would prove more fruitful than careful deliberation. The smell of adrenaline-generated sweat hangs about their quarters."

Despite this poetic description, X can see that the woman's enthusiasm is feigned. She is tired, just as X is tired. Along with the rest of the world, X asks herself wearily, *What are the Brothers waiting for? What do they want?*

The camera pans as the newswoman, in a hoarse voice, speaks her closing words for the night. "The second day of the terrorist stand-off closes with the accumulated glare of red emergency lights, halogens, media spots and helicopter beams throbbing like a fulminating sore on the civic body of The City of the Mother of the Angels."

Day Three

Heddi

After the night's sleep Heddi just had, it almost seems preferable to have been killed by the terrorists.

There's just no way to get comfortable, sleeping on the floor. If one side of her relaxes, the other goes numb. If she's got her head cradled on her arm, her elbow aches. And the bruises are more painful today, not less. It's impossible.

And when she did sleep, she had terrible dreams – chaotic, violent and bloody. It doesn't take a Jungian analyst to figure out how badly their psyches are traumatized.

Last night, Heddi could scarcely believe her ears when the Bruegel – Pearl, she's got to start calling her Pearl; she deserves that much, at least – when Pearl told her story. Under mangled syntax and an accent that must be part Choctaw, part Oklahoman with a tinge of Middle English, and part street slang, there's a surprising intelligence at work, even a poetic sensibility. Heddi was amazed.

Dr. Copeland always says she's a snob; that she judges people harshly because she's projecting her own insecurities onto them. Jung said the object of a projection has a psychological "hook" that makes a perfect place to hang the entire projection. Pearl has so many hooks she's positively barbed.

Heddi just can't bear the wizened old con artist. She doesn't like to sit next to her because she expects her to stink – which she doesn't. She looks filthy, like dirt has been ground into her pores that no amount of scrubbing will get out – even though she's not.

Her whole body is like some old rag of a dress you'd find at a thrift shop – wrinkled, faded, snagged, both shrunk-up and stretched out, and turned in by its last owner grimy and spotted with past meals.

Heddi just can't get beyond her revulsion for her. Dr. Copeland would say she's obsessed. He'd want to know what she's projecting onto Pearl.

And Heddi would give him the obvious answer – fear of old age; fear she'll get as lumpy and basically repugnant as Pearl is, some day.

But that's not really it. After so many years of analysis, it's impossible for Heddi not to wonder what's *really* going on here. The other women seem to like Pearl well enough, and she and Sophia have actually become thick as thieves. So what's Heddi's problem with her?

The answer snuck up on her in the night and she felt it eating in the pit of her stomach. But before she could go there and see the little mousie of emotion with her own eyes, she did this quick little thing in her brain and switched over to hating Pearl, just visualizing her and imagining she smells like pee – she doesn't – and remembering the same little annoyances, over and over and over. And the little mousie just ate its fill and departed, with Heddi none the wiser.

Dr. Copeland would want to know: "Why the avoidance?" Then Heddi would get snippy with him. Maybe get up and walk out ten minutes early. Then she'd obsess all day, thinking of that scene and blaming her analyst.

God!

Maybe she's just obsessing over Pearl to avoid thinking about the reality of their situation.

Heddi's been optimistic until last night. On every side, she heard groans, muffled swearing and tears in the darkness. Everyone is starting to come undone – except Pearl, of course, whose peaceful snores would be enviable if they weren't so dreadful.

And there's another concern. Sophia's prediction is apparently coming to pass. There's a distinct odor now, more than just their unwashed bodies and clothing; a kind of sickly sweet smell.

At first, Heddi thought it might be Erika's wound, because Sophia confided in her that infection has set in and Erika needs antibiotics soon. But now, she's thinking the smell is exactly what Sophia predicted – decomposing bodies on the other side of the door.

Where the Hell are the police? She thought they'd be out of this room a day ago. They can go to the Moon, but they can't disarm a few terrorists? She's not sure who "they" are – but she's mad at them, just the same.

She feels as if the entire world has stopped. Died. That they're the only ones left – and they just don't know it yet.

Sophia

One good thing about exhaustion – it numbs the fear. These gals are going to be too tired to *move* today, let alone quake.

But someone's going to have to muster the energy to help Sophia do the unthinkable. Today's the day. There's no putting it off now. They have to unblock that door and move those bodies. She'd know that smell anywhere – and, like a toothache, it never gets better, only worse.

Still, she hesitates, thinking...maybe...maybe they could hold off one more day. It's not too bad yet. No sense in going out there, if they're about to be rescued.

She hasn't heard any movement in the hall at all. It doesn't make sense. If the terrorists are still in control, you'd think she'd hear them patrolling. If they're not in control, then where the hell are the police? The only thing she can think is, the terrorists have control of both ends of the concourse, so they don't need to patrol it.

That means if they're lucky, they can open the door, dash out and drag the bodies – where? Somewhere far enough away, so that the stink isn't overwhelming – and then get back in and block the door again, without their spotting them.

And if they do spot them? *Oh Goddess!* She doesn't even want to think about it.

Talk about being between the Devil and the deep blue sea!

Betty

Heddi told Betty once that there's a kind of behavioral therapy where they make you go and face your fears. Like, if you're afraid of flying, you fly and fly until you lose your fear. Or something like that. She said she didn't recommend it.

Anyway, being locked in this room, threatened with death, half-starved, sleeping on the floor, may be God's form of that therapy. Betty can't imagine ever being bored or depressed again! If she ever gets out of this mess, she'll fall down and kiss her wall-to-wall carpet. She'll say Grace before every meal, every snack, every breath mint.

She'll make time to assist in Sam's homeroom. She'll help Serena start a hamster farm. She'll write Larry a letter of apology – she'd do it now, if she had paper and a pen.

What was that little song they learned in French class in high school? *Au Clair de la Lune?* Betty begins to hum under her breath:

> *Au clair de la lune, mon ami Pierrot,*
> *Prêtez-moi ta plume, pour écire un mot;*
> *Ma chandelle est morte. Je n'ai plus de feu.*
> *Ouvres-moi ta porte, pour l'amour de Dieu.*

Some poor guy begging a pen, wanting his friend's door opened so he can have light and warmth to write by.

This experience sure gives *that* new meaning! Betty wants the door opened, too. And she wants a friend, not a foe, to do it. And she wants a pen and paper, so she can write her family – just in case it doesn't happen that way.

What would she say to them? How can she even begin to express what she's feeling?

She feels like she's made the most colossal mess of her life! How could she just let her family walk out like that? How could she just let Larry go? The love of her life? And Sam? And Serena? Has she been completely crazy?

This *is* reality therapy and, if she survives it, she'll never be the same again – which is a *good* thing.

Ondine

By some miracle, Ondine slept an hour or two last night. Sheer exhaustion, probably. And with sleep, came dreams...

She's on the beach below Tante Collette's house. The sea is unusually pacific and gulls are soaring in a cerulean sky. Down the beach, she spots Tante Collette coming toward her, moving with that stately grace so uniquely hers. She is all wrapped in some kind of aqua and celadon silks that breathe and flutter in the wind.

Ondine's heart just leaps with joy! She starts running towards her.

Tante Collette stops, holds out her arms. Ondine runs into them and reaches up to receive her aunt's kisses – only to see a Death's Head grinning back at her!

Of course, it woke her straight up. But she was so tired, she'd doze again, and again find herself on the beach. She must have dreamed the same dream at least five times, with variations on the theme.

Until those dreams, she didn't really understand the seriousness of her situation. Somehow, it's seemed like *this* is the dream – this little room, these women, being trapped here. She's been in denial, thinking this would suddenly all just go away magically, like a terrible nightmare that evaporates with the dawn.

But now she feels that Tante Collette has appeared to warn her of real danger – to say that Death is a reality.

Tante Collette always was her Early Warning System, using age as a promontory from which she looked down on everything that seemed like a jumble to Ondine. From her eminence, chaos must have showed as patterns, like Ondine seeing the mandala in the heart of Paris from the plane.

So the pattern Ondine's weaving now – or being woven into is more the case – is Death. And she guesses it's not so much the dying that scares her. It's all the unlived Life.

Erika

Erika thinks she's going to die. She can't get any relief from the pain. She feels sweaty and hot – then icy cold.

They're just going to fucking let her lie here and die!

Pearl

Whooo-eee! Pearl ain't had a good sleep lak that in a coon's age. She done fergot what it was ta sleep indoors an not have ta worry bout some feller a-sneakin up on her; some junkie lookin fer dope or money, or some prevert lookin ta take his pleasure on her ol body – now ain't *that* the very vision a desperation!

She wonders what's fer breakfast an hopes the coffee ain't run out yet. She sure do enjoy a cup in the mornin!

She's gettin spoilt.

Ain't it amazin how quick a gal gets use ter the high life?

X

X cannot believe herself. Here she is, watching television and eating Oreos out of Fat Guy's lunch box like some American housewife!

It is the body again; it does not want to die, especially by starvation. Her stomach is rumbling so loudly she thinks it will give away her position!

If the police ever bother to come, that is.

When X first came to America two years ago, she was so excited! She wanted to become an American – to think like one, dress like one and eat like one. She discarded all her mother's notions about food and dress. Instead, she consumed Big Macs and fries and wore jeans. She thought she was so chic, hanging out at MacDonald's with her friends!

She cannot believe now that she was so naïve.

No one from the organization of Christian churches gave her any instruction. She was just brought here straight from her hiding place in Jerusalem because her English was good and her parents were dead, and because she had excelled in her classes.

She knows certain people risked their lives for her, and that she was favored by luck or she would not be here now. She would have missed this opportunity completely.

Still, they just threw her in the water and no one really cared if she would sink or swim.

The first year was devoted only to study. She was determined to excel in all her courses because she was afraid to lose her scholarship. It was not until the Imam and Father Christopher brought them together that she began to see the error in her ways. When the Kultur Klub was formed, everything changed.

First of all, she met Jamal. In the beginning, it was so frightening. What would her parents say, if they were alive?

An Egyptian Copt and a Palestinian Muslim? She thinks she would be stoned to death.

But the entire point, according to the Imam and Father Christopher, was to break down the old prejudices that have left them all orphaned. Ibrahim and Hassan are from the Palestinian camps, like her; Abbas lost his parents to the intelligence agency VEVAK's assassins in Iran; and Bros is an orphaned Croat. Slobodan's entire family was murdered in Bosnia. Yuri's parents died in a Russian bombing of Chechnya. Abdullah has permanent genetic damage from Saddam Hussein's gassing of the Kurds that killed the rest of his family – eighteen of them! And Hansi has one hand missing from the massacre in Rwanda that took his family of ten. There's even a Jew, Abraham, from a frontier village in Israel that was bombed by the Palestinians. She thinks he may still have a sister left alive somewhere.

It was only a fluke that X was included in the Klub. The Imam and Father Christopher located every foreign orphan they could find on campus and all the rest just happened to be male – or women too frightened to join.

But she doesn't really want other women included. She's proud to be the only one. She wants to be the token female and show how strong her gender can be. In Women's Studies, they studied women like Ida Tarbell, Harriet Tubman and Madame Curie; women who did not let gender prejudice defeat them, who broke through the barriers and opened the doors.

X wants to be one of those women. She wants girls in Lebanon and Egypt and Palestine and yes, even America, to read her name in books and say, *I want to be like her!*

Even though, meeting after meeting, she had to go to the restroom and be sick, she made her spirit stronger than her body. She did it by overcoming the body's natural prejudice for life.

She had to make herself willing to die.

Sophia

Thank the Goddess the food's holding out. Breakfast was a little sparse, but potato chips taste pretty good with coffee when you're ravenous.

Something's going on with Betty. She's roaming around in major meltdown, so distraught that she doesn't even realize the green plastic chair is pinched on her enormous bottom like a squashed animal, its stiff legs protruding backwards in a kind of supplication.

A new take on having a reserved seat! Sophia wants to smile, but thinks she might burst into tears, instead.

Heddi and Ondine are hovering.

Sophia's got to catch Heddi's eye and get her to calm her down. Hysterics that loud could be heard outside.

Heddi

Complete hysteria! She's got to get this creature quieted down before she draws the terrorists to them like wolves to a wounded deer.

Betty

"Okay. Okay.

"Let me catch my breath.

"Okay.

"Okay.

"I'm sorry. I'm so sorry.

"It's just...just that...

"It's my family. They all hate me.

"They don't even know I'm here...or care, if they do know.

"Heddi says I should tell you *my* story – not the neighbor's – and I don't really know where to begin.

"I guess it should be with the flowers.

"Heddi says that flowers are a symbol and that flowers are my fetish.

"I don't really understand that. I always thought the flowers just created a nice, homey atmosphere. Celebrated the seasons and holidays. That's what I thought they symbolized...a nice, loving home.

"For whatever reason, though, what started out innocently has become a big problem. I don't really know how it happened, it was so gradual...

One Halloween, as she was arranging a plastic pumpkin full of corn stalks, Betty conceived a noble project. She would assemble a huge bouquet of flowers for every holiday and every month of the year.

For years after that, her secret vice was to drive by various shops – K-Mart, if she was poor, and the local gift shop, if she was flush – and buy a stem or two of plastic roses or holly or yellow daffodils, whatever the season or holiday dictated.

Her collection kept growing. It filled up the basement and so she started hanging things from the garage rafters wrapped in old sheets, with manila labels dangling on white string: *Christmas; Valentine's Day; Memorial Day; Feast of the Assumption.*

It was her nod to spirituality. She was as industriously ceremonial as any pagan. On February 15th, the red roses and flocked red hearts on stems came out of their Styrofoam block, were dusted under running water, left to dry on the drainboard, then bundled back into an old florist's box and returned to their crypt in the basement, as vivid and everliving as Dracula.

Then out to the garage for the Styrofoam Presidents Lincoln and Washington in their polyester winding cloth, swinging from the spanners like primitive tree burials. Along with them came embalmed foliage – whatever she could as-semble that was red, white and blue.

She had the routine down pat: take the step ladder from its hooks by the window; mount three steps; untwist the wire holding the bundle to the two-by-four; twitch her nose against the dust; lower the package and herself carefully down three steps; rest the bundle on the hood of the car; put the ladder back on its rack. Then scoop up the prize and scuttle away with it to her living room bay window like a spider with a fresh fly – all very neat and tidy.

Of course, with so many different themes, she needed lots of containers. At first, she just crowded them on top of the refrigerator, but then one fell off and broke and that led to the complete emptying-out and repainting of the old butler's pantry to keep them safe and display them better. Then, slowly and insidiously, they began consuming the can-ning shelves in the basement.

Larry called it *The Invasion of the House-eating Vase Crea-tures*. He said all those open mouths gave him the creeps.

They came from garage sales, the Salvation Army, Wal-Mart, her friends' gift rejects, and mail order catalogues. They were tall, squat, elegant, cozy, shiny, matte, plain white, brightly colored, patterned, wide-mouthed, narrow-mouthed, metal, porcelain, pottery, wood, plastic and bas-ketry. Each one was tawdry and uneventful in its own right, but as a collection they assumed gravity and power. In com-bination with the flowers and the enormity of the holidays they took on the grandeur of sacred relics.

So it was only right, a matter of religious virtue, when Betty refused to let her husband's departure from her life dissuade her from her mission.

One day, Larry just couldn't take it anymore. He was up-set because he couldn't reach his fishing pole without mov-ing a bale of hot pink spider mums she'd found at a discount store for pennies. And that was that. He threw his shorts and socks in a brown paper grocery bag, slung his shirts over his elbow and left.

But Betty wasn't alarmed. She knew it was the Universe telling her that he wasn't the right one. Flowers trump fishing poles, cosmically. Everyone knows that. Besides, Betty was sure – at first – that he would come back, even though Madame Zola was dubious.

It wasn't long before her 10-year old, Sam, speaking from the banana seat of his half-sized bike, said in his soft, squeaky voice, "I think I'm gonna go live with Dad."

This occasioned another departure, somewhat more majestic than Larry's, of trucks and balls, bedding, chest of drawers, even the rug – although Betty knew he'd soon be rejecting it with its motif of Teddy bears frolicking – all carried out by Larry, a couple of his drinking buddies, and a bevy of neighborhood youngsters as sober and fastidious as a sultan's slaves.

This hurt, there was no denying it. To keep herself from flying to pieces, she turned Sam's room into her studio, a kind of Holy of Holies, and started making flower arrangements for every room of the house.

Not long after that, her 16-year old, Serena, opened the door to her bedroom, shrieking, "If you ever put another of these fucking things in here, I'll kill myself!" and lofted a basket of plastic forget-me-nots into the hall.

She slammed her door. The bouquet smashed against the far wall, but nothing was broken. There was no water to mop up, no dirt spilled, no broken stems. Betty just scooped it up from the carpet, flounced it all back together again and took it into the master bedroom and wedged it onto the nightstand between the alarm clock and the box of Kleenex.

A few weeks after that, she smelled a weird smell in the hall. She sniffed around and it seemed to be coming from Serena's room. Getting down on hands and knees, she put her nose under Serena's door. For sure, the source of that smell was behind it somewhere. Betty didn't want to intrude on Serena's precious privacy, but that smell...

She knelt in front of the door like a penitent, trying the knob. It was locked.

She went to the kitchen and found an ice pick; got her reading glasses; knelt again, this time as focused as a safe-cracker; leaned close, took aim, inserted the ice pick in the lock and jiggled it around. The pin sprang back with a little thump and she was in.

Betty opened the door and shuffled forward, still on her knees. How long had it been since she'd seen Serena? Was that basket of pink peonies on her toilet too much? Had it pushed her over the edge, even though they weren't, technically, in her bedroom?

She floundered into the room, sniffing as she went, anxious for sight of her, thinking, *Did I make her breakfast this morning? Or was that yesterday?*

All she could remember was Serena snarling at her, "This place sucks."

Was that today? Wednesday?

There was her bed, unmade of course. Betty struggled toward it through drifts of dirty clothes like a snow shoer in deep powder. She groped around in the sheets and cast-off clothing.

No. There didn't seem to be any bodies buried underneath.

But the smell! The smell...

Her eyes darted around: a huge pile of movie magazines on a chair; the desk, stratified like an archeological dig with papers, books, print-outs, notebooks, clothes, rat-tailed combs, used dental floss, what might be a dirty pillowcase...

And then she spied it; the metal cage on the dresser under a pile of flung clothing! And little furry bodies, plump and slow, clinging to the bars, running frantically on a metal wheel or asleep in piles.

What in God's name were they? Whatever kind of creature they were, they – they! – were the source of the smell
in Betty's house!

And lots of them! Lots and lots and *lots* of them!

"Just an aside – I don't often say a thing like that, 'in
God's name.' I think it's blasphemous. I was raised by God-
fearing parents who never uttered an oath in their lives –
well, almost.

"I do remember my father watching TV when Nixon
resigned and him saying, 'The damned Communists have
finally won!'

"I didn't really know what he meant at the time. I just
remember being shocked that he would swear right there in
the front room in front of Momma and me.

"I remember Momma swatting him on the thigh and
hissing, 'Judd! Hush!' and throwing a look in my direction.

"But Daddy just said it again. 'I mean it! The damned
Communists have finally won!' And then he got up, took his
coat off the hook by the front door and went out.

"I heard the car starting in the driveway and saw the
look on Momma's face; a burning red blush and the shame
in her eyes.

"That was the only time I ever heard swearing in my
home, growing up. It seems to me that young people are ir-
reverent nowadays. It's *f___* this, and *screw* that, and Jesus'
name attached to everything but what it should be."

Betty used to like going to church on Sundays as a child.
There was a nice, quiet atmosphere, somber and special, and
always a fresh bouquet on the altar. It wasn't until she was
about seven or eight that she realized that she'd seen some
of those bouquets before, and maybe that's when her passion for fake flowers was born.

They get confused in her mind with organ music and old hymns and that smell church had – maybe some kind of cleaning agents, wood polish, the old paper and soft leather of the hymnals, and probably the mixture of different colognes worn by the congregation.

At Christmas, they had green candles on the pulpit, short, fat ones, and the place smelled of cedar and cinnamon. Betty always associates those smells with the Holy Ghost, like His epiphany is heralded by smells of the holidays.

She buys those same candles now for Christmas, and along with the lights on the tree – which of course doesn't smell because it's plastic – they make her house fill up with some of that holy energy she used to experience in church.

Nowadays, she doesn't know if there is a God, but she she hopes there is and wishes He were as easy to contact as those candles are to buy. She could use Him right about now, with this thing with Serena.

She doesn't know what to do, really, and she wishes He could at least send an angel or something to clue her in. Wouldn't you think that with all the churches there are in Los Angeles and all the candles burned – look at the Catholics, alone – and all the pretty flower arrangements, that the Holy Ghost maybe would come every few months, at least, on some kind of regular round, like a circuit rider?

She just wants the others to understand that she had a solid religious upbringing, even though Heddi says she's transferred her religious function onto flowers and forgotten about God:

Heddi leans back in her office chair, the soft light off the ocean playing across her elegant face, and says, "The gods choose their moments to intervene. You're in an ages-old situation, Betty, the very nature of which is meant to stir you to the depths until you remember the gods."

"Well, for one thing, is it God or gods?" Betty asks in pique. "Sometimes, I think it's you, Heddi, who's confused! And what have the gods got to do with Serena, anyway?"

So Heddi has her go over the incident that was the turning point with Serena one more time.

That afternoon, at the hour for Serena to return from summer school, Betty sits on the couch in the living room, composing herself.

The arrangement in the bay window, a huge burst of silk sunflowers, honors Summer. One of her splurges, silk. Not quite as durable as plastic but more lifelike.

The afternoon sun slants in and the sunflowers blaze, proclaiming Summer, and Betty sits, wondering how she's going to keep her last remaining family member from running screaming from the house, when she announces that really, definitely, the Creatures have to go.

What in heaven's name are they? she practices saying. *Rats? Gerbils? Hamsters? How did they get here? Take them back. Take them back where they came from. We can't have them in this house.*

She can see Serena's face, so plump and pink, with her brown hair lying tight against her skull like a helmet. *Pull your hair back,* Betty's always telling her. *You've got such a pretty face. Don't hide it. Wear some eye makeup. Wear some barrettes.*

And Serena always giving her that poisonous look, the one that says she wishes Betty was dead.

Whether it's hair or hamsters, Serena's not going to capitulate. Betty can feel it in her bones.

How can this child of a neat, clean home that celebrates Beauty be so involved in dirt and disorder? Is that what Heddi means when she talks about family members having to live out parts of Betty's unlived Shadow? She notices her hands in her lap; her fingers are laced and balled together like hibernating worms. The tips are white from tension. She looks at the clock. My God! It's 5:30! She's missed Oprah! She's that upset!

And still no Serena.

She can hear the grandfather clock ticking in the family room. It's a nice room, with turned maple furniture she inherited from her grandmother and beaded board wainscoting with wallpaper above, a tiny floral, and a matching border at ceiling level. The TV's in there, with an arrangement of coral roses on top. It's a nice room. It's just that there's no family there to enjoy it.

It's 9:30 before Serena finally unlocks the front door. Betty is standing there, ready to say – what? She's almost speechless by this time.

Serena throws her one of those looks that says, *Don't even...!* as she brushes past. And Betty stands there and can't say a word.

There's a space of about 15 seconds with nothing. Then the scream – a sound like some animal that's both badly wounded and truly enraged.

Then instantly, she's there in Betty's face, in a fury.

"My room! You've been in my *room? You've fucking been in my room?!*"

Betty's hands fly out on their own, as if possessed, and make vague dancing gestures in the air between them. They're trying to explain, to ward off her rage, to placate and cajole.

"It was the smell..." she begins, feebly.

"What smell?" Serena screams.

"Of those...of those... They smell. I smelled them. From out in the hall."

"No way! I clean the cage every day. No way, Mom. You had no right!"

"Well, you never asked. I mean, I didn't know. Where... how...did you get them? Where did they *come* from?"

Betty is leaning against the hall wall now, her backside lodged against a little gold bracket holding a vase of pansies.

She feels defeated, like a cornered rat with a terrier snarling at it.

"It's none of your business," Serena scowls.

"Now listen, young lady!" Betty bristles. "I think it *is* my business. This is *my* house too, you know, and I am your *mother!*"

"Yeah, right."

"What's *that* supposed to mean?"

"Like, when? On alternate Tuesdays?" she asks in that *duh* voice that the girls have all cultivated; the *You're So Dumb* inflection.

"I pay the *bills* here, young lady. I put the *food* on the table for you to eat."

"Well, *yeah! Duh!* Because Dad sends a support check every month. Because you kept the bank account and he took *nothing!* Big fuckin' deal, Mom! Great White Hunter, Mom! Bringin' home the bacon!"

Betty didn't ever intend to hit her. Her entire intention had been to have an adult confrontation. And it wasn't really a hard slap. It sounded like a rubber band snapping, is all. A *big* rubber band, she admits, but no more than that.

Betty has never seen Serena move so fast. She spins as if the slap has put her into gyration. Two steps and she disappears down the hall. Her door slams. The weeping commences, loud and long. Then the rising and falling cadence of a telephone conversation that goes on and on.

Betty sits outside of Serena's door, her ear pressed to it, and can't understand a word, just the aggrieved tone.

She isn't about to apologize. Where had that child learned such insolence? She used to be such a sweet little thing when she was younger.

So, Betty barely saw her, after Serena discovered that she'd discovered the creatures – hamsters, as it turned out. She left the house early and came back late. When she came at all.

Betty would have to call around to find out where she was. Usually, she was staying at her best friend Julie's house. Sometimes at her father's. Some nights, she never could locate her and just had to trust that Serena was still alive; that she didn't need to call the cops and put out an Amber Alert or an APB.

Things weren't going well. Betty was feeling nervous and unfocused. To keep her sanity, she called in a landscaping company to tear out the front lawn and replace it with Astroturf. Then she had them cut holes in it, along the sidewalk, and put in juniper bushes – they don't shed – with tanbark around the trunks. She bought herself a yard vac and vacuumed her new lawn every day.

In late August, just when she was thinking it was time for the Back-to-School arrangement in the ceramic book-vase, the final blow came. Serena flounced in the door one afternoon and Betty nearly fainted.

She'd dyed her pretty brown hair blue. Her nose was pierced with a gold stud. Her earlobes were hung with tiny crosses, safety pins and little metal symbols that looked Satanic. Her eyes were rimmed in thick black pencil and her mouth was white. The knee that protruded through the hole in her left pant leg was tattooed with a bat, hanging upside down.

Betty felt like she was going to have a heart attack. She couldn't breathe.

"I'm leaving," Serena said flatly.

Cold as ice, she reaches into a big shoulder bag of Indian mirror cloth and pulls out a manila envelope. "This is for you."

"What is it?" Betty wheezes.

"It's my Emancipated Minor paperwork. It was final today. I'm moving out."

"But...you can't!" Betty is staring at her in horror. She can't think.

"Why not?"

"Because...I..."

She can't say, *Because it will leave me all alone.* There must be some reason it's good for Serena, too. She just can't think of what it might be, right now.

"Sweetie, let me fix you some soup. Have you had lunch?"

Serena just stands there staring at her, like she's the Mother from Hell.

"I'm taking my things," she says. "Julie's out front with her car."

"But where will you live? How will you get money?"

"It's all there," Serena shoves her chin at the manila envelope. "The court won't let you emancipate unless you have a job."

"You're *working?*"

"Yes, Mother. I *can* work, you know. I'm not a complete imbecile...or a parasite like *you.* God!"

"Couldn't we just talk this over?"

"No."

"Why not?"

"Because you're a loser, Mom. Because your values suck. Because I'm finished trying to talk to you."

"But, we never really got started..."

"Yeah! *Duh!* No shit!"

"Are you...are you going to take those...things with you?"

"Yes, Mother. I'm taking the hamsters with me. God knows I wouldn't want to leave them here – where nothing *living* is welcome!"

She turns away toward her room. Betty turns toward the kitchen. She leans over the sink and begins to cry. She can hear Serena throwing things into the hall and her friend Julie saying, "You want this?" "You gonna take that?" "I think the cage will fit in the trunk." Things like that. These terrible little decisions; so paltry, so final.

When it's over, Betty feels like her entire being has been lashed with burning electrical cords. Everything stings and aches and throbs and feels empty, all at the same time. She can't sit without needing to jump up, can't read, watch TV or eat. All the usual stopgaps don't touch the scraped-raw place she's feeling.

Finally, in desperation, she decides she needs drugs.

She calls her friend Emily, the most neurotic, drug-fortified person she knows. "Bring tranquilizers. I'm dying."

"The ones I have won't kick in for two weeks," Em says. "You need something that's gonna work right now."

"What?" Betty rasps. "A gun?"

"I'll be right over. I'm taking you to Heddi."

And that's how Betty came to be the patient of a shrink. She doesn't know if it's working. She still thinks drugs would have been faster. In fact, she's sure of it.

But talking to Heddi twice a week is an improvement on sitting alone in an empty house listening to the clock tick, waiting for Oprah. And even Oprah doesn't interest her much right now. She's that wrung out.

And she hasn't made a flower arrangement in weeks.

"I'm sorry...I'm sorry. I just can't stop crying.

"I'm sorry.

"Please forgive me...I'm so sorry!"

Erika

"Honky bitches! Every one of you's got things so good you don't know what else to do with yourselves except fuck things up.

"Try growing up in a fucking garage, you cunts! A garage in Oakland with seven brothers and sisters, one toilet, a junkie prostitute for a mother and an alcoholic child molester for a father.

"Jesus Christ! Give me a fucking break!"

Ondine

Poor Betty! She's just a puddle.

And what's with Erika? She's moaning and groaning this morning, like she's trying to talk, but nothing comes out that's intelligible. Is she getting worse? But then, how could she *not* be? Two and a half days without medical care...it's a wonder she's still alive.

Even so, Ondine doesn't like to go over there near her. Even half dead, she's got a fierce energy. Thank God Sophia's here!

She spent the waking hours of the night wondering if Richard realizes she's in here, in this mess? Does it tickle him, thinking of her as a hostage? Or dead? He probably thinks it's justice being meted out; an eye for an eye.

Her life to appease Jackie's.

Pearl

These here women is a trip! Reminds Pearl a one a them Baptist prayer meetins. Everone rollin round, moanin an groanin an carryin on. Wearin shirts a agony an britches a sorrow.

Pearl don't ratly give a hoot. Maybe she's jes been wrung out, lak boilt laundry. Only so many tears God gives a body in this lifetime an Pearl used up her share, long ago.

Sophia

Time to shift the energy in here before everyone loses control completely. The only one who seems solid is Heddi. Maybe Sophia can get her to tell her tale.

Of course, there's Pearl. She's steady as a rock. But she's off in some space, sucking on her pipe. Sophia never knows if the old woman's in this world or some other. Pearl's a true crone. It wouldn't surprise Sophia if she already knows the outcome of all this.

Or if she simply doesn't care, one way or the other.

Heddi

"Well, my life doesn't seem all that interesting. So I don't really know what to tell you. I mean, I've never had any really great adventures...until now, that is!

"I just went straight through my life like an arrow. I set my sights and off I went. And nothing really stopped me until this thing with Hal.

"When Ann Landers first got her divorce, all my gal pals and I howled! We thought it was hilarious! Here was the doyenne of advice, missing all the clues in her *own* life. The irony was too delicious.

"Personally, I was never one to miss a beat. Straight out of high school, I did my pre-med, then entered medical school, then a specialty in psychiatry and then off to Switzerland to become a Jungian analyst..."

Now, after decades of practice and hundreds of her patients' life stories, Ann's humiliation doesn't seem so funny to Heddi. It seems damned pathetic and all too common.

She's seen it all – or at least enough not to want to see the rest: drug addicts driving Mercedes, with season's tickets to the opera; frumpy little nothings working two jobs to hold the family together, while the old man drinks himself into oblivion, beating the kids on the way there; spoiled brats, hating their parents, while sponging off their money; victims of childhood abuse so scarred by rage and shame that no balm will heal them. And it goes on and on, as if her analytic practice were the confluence and summation of human psychological disaster.

The hardest for her to deal with are the simple neurotics who chafe against every aspect of their lives, blaming everyone and everything, while failing to lift a finger to save themselves. They're full of angst and ennui without the slightest clue that they're their own worst enemies. The smallest hint that they're responsible for their own pain sends them into a rage. The barest whisper of self-realization can send them skulking out of analysis altogether.

They wring their hands, weep, and flounder in a lack of focus remarkable for its tenacity. Theirs is not so much an inability to imagine a productive life as a refusal to do so.

Because isn't it imagination, after all, that gets people out of bed in the morning? Or that motivates them to spend years, even decades, working to accomplish some personal goal?

It might be simply to rear a healthy family, or to become a brain surgeon, or discover a new star, or to reevaluate, pare down, and simplify, revealing the essence of character the way fire brings up the grain on charred wood. Heddi has several patients who are working in that direction, by sitting in Zen meditation or working in Catholic soup kitchens or writing poetry or returning to school.

Which makes the neurotics even harder to take: all they can imagine is ingesting Prozac for the rest of their lives.

So imagine Heddi's astonishment at finding herself in Ann Lander's place! In her meditative moments, she supposes that it was inevitable: *that which I have despised has come upon me.*

It's a scenario too limp and worn even to credit it with life, but it's alive, all right. It's sunk its parasitic tendrils deep into the tree of her being and sucked her life force without her even being aware of it, just like mistletoe – and not the kind you hang up over doorways to get kisses, either!

It's almost predictable now that she thinks about it: 40 years of marriage, and Hal's got a babe.

And to garnish trite humiliation with further trite humiliation, she's only 26. And he ferries her about in a brand new, shiny red BMW convertible.

Can throat lifts and hair transplants be far behind? Maybe a new Harley and a road trip to Phoenix? The wilds of the aging male mind are as yet unmapped. Anything is possible. Jung never prepared her for this.

Ann could have her last laugh if she were around, but she's departed this wicked dimension for another and Heddi wishes her Godspeed and hopes she finds conditions improved there – wherever.

So now Heddi has a little more understanding for her neurotic patients. They used to drive her crazy – even though that's a cliché scarcely fit for an analyst.

Sometimes, they seem to have everything: brilliant husbands, beautiful homes, healthy children, all the time and money in the world to lavish on themselves; often, they're smart, rich and socially prominent – and slender. God! For that alone, most women would kill!

And still, they come to her office in their designer jeans or silk dresses, pampered as any women on the planet, with dead eyes, with sighs and woeful countenance.

(At this point, Heddi is careful to avert her eyes, so no one will realize Ondine is one of these problem patients.

What do you want? Heddi sometimes asks her in exasperation. And Ondine just sighs and shakes her head, completely innocent of an answer to one of life's most fundamental questions.)

So Heddi's frustrated, dealing with her neurotics. Sure, maybe their relationships lack intimacy. People always complain about marriage as if they didn't know beforehand what they were getting themselves into. And they could have a closer relationship with their children, but what mother couldn't say the same?

The real problem is a lack of imagination about what to do with themselves, plain and simple.

They aren't without assets. They have fine educations, good minds and economic support. They could do or be anything. Instead, they come with vague complaints, both physical and emotional, wanting prescriptions for this and that, especially Prozac, which Heddi steadfastly refuses to prescribe.

Even when their lives take a terrible turn, when there's death or divorce or illness, there's a vacancy where true grief should be. Their tears are mechanical. Obligatory. They're as empty of genuine emotion as wind-up dolls.

With some – Ondine especially, if she could say it – Heddi ends each session more frustrated than the patient. She's begun to have a sense of dread on certain appointment days. Anyone with half a grip on depth psychology could have told her that the counter-transference was at work, showing her her own dark emotional underbelly. But Heddi has lived so ideal an existence for so many years that that simple and unpleasant possibility just didn't occur to her.

And her own analyst was either asleep at the wheel or far too subtle when he should have been poking her in the rump with a cattle prod. They both missed it. By the time the obscure became the obvious, things had gone way too far to repair them.

What had her own lack of imagination wrought? Well, an errant husband, for starters. But that was just the first trump to buckle in the house of cards she'd built for herself.

She went into a profound slump in self-esteem. When had her jaw line become so slack and crepe-like? When had she developed kimono-arms? How good an analyst could she be, if she'd let this thing burgeon right under her nose? How would she survive the social humiliation of having her husband escorting his girlfriend into the homes of their friends?

Who would love and protect her? Would she die old and abandoned?

The questions descended deeper and deeper into the depths where gas rumbles and gurgles in the intestinal pipes – right down to the second *chakra* which, as every true Californian knows, is the level at which survival issues are housed.

It was as if an elevator cable had broken and a freefall into the emotional basement were in full plummet. You would have thought Heddi was about to become a street person, eating out of Dumpsters and sleeping on window ledges...

"Oh...Sorry, Pearl – no offense meant."

Why is she speaking of this in the past tense? Is she under some delusion that she's passed the danger point? Hardly!

For entire weeks, all she's been able to do is cry. No...cry is scarcely the word. Weep. Wail. Carry on. Wring hands, saturate tissues, dissolve through tears into helplessness and hopelessness.

Sometimes, she even acts out. She throws things. She screams. All she's wanted – longed for, searched for, demanded – is escape from the pain.

Heddi is aware that Ondine and Betty are both staring at her in disbelief. She ignores them. There's a certain perverse satisfaction in coming out of the closet of her analytical cloak, with producing astonishment.

When she can think of anyone else at all, she thinks about her neurotic analysands and a whole new appreciation for their plight begins to simmer in the cold cauldron of her heart. When the rug has been pulled out from under you emotionally, no matter how solid your financial and social picture may be, a floating anxiety buoys you through life like a rubber duck riding heavy surf. It's the very inner emptiness that keeps you afloat.

They taught her all about this during her psychiatry residency and in Zurich at the Institute. It was couched in abstracted clinical terms: *lack of appropriate affect, dissociation, repression.* She passed tests requiring this information. For years, her clinical notes have been filled with terminology appropriately describing just this passage in a patient's life, always with that edge of superiority that the well feel when dealing with the sick.

So now it's Heddi at *her* analyst's office, snuffling, pleading for Prozac. And it's he observing her with that vaguely superior glance, that slightly amused twinkle, refusing.

It's Heddi screaming at him that he let her down and he saying calmly that that is an interesting projection. And it's she leaving the fifty-minute hour as empty and unsatisfied as when she went in.

She wonders if Dr. Copeland is beginning to dread her appointments the way she dreads Ondine's? Or if the smug Dr. Copeland's marriage is as vertiginously imperiled as hers was? Is his lack of empathy imagined, or is he the next to gain experiential understanding that pride, indeed, goeth before a fall?

It's doesn't matter. Heddi doesn't give a rat's ass about Dr. Copeland or his equally smug wife. Everyone seems smug to her these days. Everyone looks as if they are sassy and well fed and in the know, as if they are seeing right into her shattered interior, pitying her. Coolly, gently, heartlessly ostracizing her for committing that most cardinal social sin: experiencing her genuine, raw, emotions – and showing it.

But there's the real rub. She's *not* experiencing her genuine emotions. Even in this wasted state, she's astute enough to know this about herself: she's not being authentic, at all.

Oh, she's creating plenty of Sturm und Drang, but it's all play-acting. The real truth is, it's all just the howl of the wounded ego. Her humbled pride. Her hubris...

In her *inner* acting out, though, she's throwing herself against a glass wall, hammering and yammering and pounding to get out of this vitrine she's inhabited. And what's outside of it, should she be so lucky – or so unfortunate – as to break through? Is it Truth or Madness or Authenticity that she dimly views through the darkened glass?

She's not got a clue. And therein lies the terror.

"Oh my! Look! It's already lunchtime!"

Pearl

Well, alls Pearl cain say is, that Heady is ratly named. Pearl's Granny use ter ax, *What's in a name?* an Pearl never did know quite what she was drivin at. But she thinks this here bout clears it up.

Now, Heady's axed Pearl ta tell more bout herself, but Pearl points out that that Sophia gal ain't told her story yet. She been hidin behind that thar colored gal lak she was a duck blind.

Fair's fair. An besides, Pearl's jes enjoyin coolin her heels today. Ain't gotta go out an hustle. Got plenty a food. All the coffee she cain drink.

She don't ratly feel lak bein bothered today. Let one a them other gals go a-huntin fer possum. Pearl's gonna set rat here an smoke her pipe.

Sophia

"Well, I'm not sure what to tell you, but I do know I've been thinking a lot these past two days and maybe you'd be interested in that."

It says in the Bible that in the end times, young women will begin to dream dreams. That's kind of vague – women, young *and* old, have *always* dreamed dreams. Sophia's sure that from the super-conservative pulpits of this land, preachers have found ways to turn that against women – probably by considering dreams as fantasies or diversions from the truth or instruments of Satan – because in many ways, the Inquisition never stopped; the hatred of the feminine seems eternal, and the flames of the Burning Times still cast their lurid light and black shadows across the earth.

When you've lived long enough interiorly like Sophia has, though – and she's surely no young woman – you come to know that dreams are anything but fantasies. Dreams are the bucket that pulls up the living waters of our own deep knowing.

Before the Loma Prieta earthquake in 1987 – the one that flattened the freeway overpasses in Oakland and dropped the roadway out of the center span of the Bay Bridge – Sophia had a dream, maybe three weeks before. She saw the collapsed sections of concrete stacked like pancakes. There were emergency vehicles and medical personnel tending to people on the ground.

When the earthquake happened and everyone was in shock, Sophia wasn't. She was sad because of the loss of life but she wasn't surprised. Because of things like that – and it started when she was a really young child – she's learned to pay attention to her dreams.

But when she awakens most mornings, feeling shaken by what she's seen in the night, she often hasn't a clue what her nighttime visions might mean. That's the funny part about these powers that visit her. Sometimes, they give information before the fact that is only relevant after the fact. What's the use of that?

No use, as far as she can see. So she's had to start considering herself an imperfect vehicle. The information's there, but she can't carry it all into the light of day. Things fall off and get left in the weedy margins of wakefulness.

The only thing she can really rely on is her Little Voice. It knows everything and with complete assurance, but its visitations are sporadic and she can't summon it up at will.

Pearl's nodding her head as she squints at Sophia through a cloud of pipe smoke. The others, however, are looking confused.

"How do you know the difference between your little voice and just imagining something?" It's Heddi, direct and clinical.

"I don't *know* how I know, Heddi. It's...a kind of quickening, I guess. Sort of like jumping into cold water on a hot day. My entire system — body, mind, and spirit — just comes alive in a burst."

"It's more a powerful sensation, then?"

"Yes... I feel it very strongly..."

Ondine interjects in a voice too soft to hear.

"I'm sorry, Ondine...what's that?"

Ondine gives a little cough and almost whispers, "You've always heard this voice, then?"

"Yes, I've always had this ability for as long as I can remember."

"Why do you think you have this, while others don't?" Heddi, again, her tone dubious, obviously thinking this sounds a lot like inflation.

"I attribute it directly to having spent my entire life on a mountaintop, away from the barrage of civilization."

"What do you mean?" It's Betty, this time, who's never been on a mountaintop in her entire life.

"I mean, things like electronic bombardment from telephones and television..."

"You had no *television*, growing up?"

"No. Not even electric lights until I was five."

Pearl's chuckling softly to herself, as Betty exclaims in astonishment, "Where did you live...*Siberia?*"

"It may as well have been, I guess."

"So no electronic assault. What else?" Heddi asks, sounding unconvinced.

"No socializing influences, like church, or even Girl Scouts. Not even other kids close by to play with. I was just left to my own devices and I guess it's a kind of instinctive ability that grew out of being in nature all the time."

"What about your parents? Didn't they try to influence you?"

"I don't know what to tell you, Heddi... I just sort of grew like Topsy, as my mother used to say. My parents were busy with the business of survival. I was just left on my own most of the time – which was fine with me – and that allowed my inner being free rein."

Ondine, from the depths of her coddled years, is trying to understand. "I *think* I get it. Something similar happens to me when I'm painting or sculpting. It's like another intelligence steps in. But, Sophia, it must have been so difficult for you, as a child. What was it like to be so neglected?"

"What was it like? Well..."

As a child, she loped around the mountain like the spawn of the Wild Mother; one of those mythical beasts half imaginative child, half instinctual creature or bird. She was always rooting in the underbrush like a fox kit nosing for the teat, plunging fearlessly into gullies that smelled of moisture, leaf mold and minerals leaching from the red clay banks. Snakes, spiders, lizards and bats were part curiosity, part kin. She could read the adventures of the night in the baby's handprint of the raccoon, the black spiraling scat of the skunk and the owl's lost feathers, like some children read comics.

In ravines where water rises in furtive springs that trickle through mossy stones, she met the elfin strain, the familial bloodline that dangled like roots back into the invisibles, the magical half-wild ones, carriers of culture too ancient and rich to fathom...

"You mean *fairies?*" Heddi interrupts, barely maintaining a courteous neutrality. It's all she can do to keep a mocking smile battened down.

Sophia doesn't answer. Her lips clamp down and it appears that she'll be stubborn about opening them again. An awkward silence ensues.

"Tante Collette used to say there were nature beings that inhabited *Quatre Vents*," Ondine finally says, timidly. "She called them *incantadas* or *demoiselles*. She said they're particularly fond of *Quatre Vents* because it's associated with wind and water. I guess the *demoiselles* can summon up the wind at will, and calm it just as quickly. And the *incantadas* live near water."

"Really," Heddi counters, deadpan.

"Yes. She told me when I was little that *une petite demoiselle* guarded the spring that feeds the fauntain, and lived inside a little carved door at its base. She said the *demoiselle* wore a little white dress with a blue sash, and flowers grew at her feet wherever she walked. I used to pick flowers and leave them on the little doorstep."

"Children are much more sensitive to these things than grownups," says Sophia, coming out of her stubborn silence. "And they just naturally know how to honor the Others by performing rituals for them."

"Yes," Ondine agrees. "And apparently, it goes both ways – the *demoiselles* are very protective of children and of the country people, and can be quite fierce when they think an injustice has been done to them."

"That's the craziest thing I've ever heard!" Betty chimes in.

There is a short but pregnant silence broken by Pearl's rough cackle. "Ever Choctaw child knows theys creatures out thar in the woods an prairies. Theys smart – they don't stick round whar people is, but theys thar, an they gots ta hold the entire web a thins together. That's they job. *Without them little people, wouldn't nothin grow nor water flow*, mah Granny used ter say."

Another awkward silence follows, finally broken by Heddi.

"Jung wrote extensively on the archetypes," she intones professorially. "And indigenous peoples the world over believe in a realm of diminutive nature spirits. I guess we don't need to settle that issue today.

"Why don't you continue, Sophia? Tell us more about growing up on the mountain."

Well, the point Sophia's trying to make is that she grew up like a feral child, really. Barefooted, scratch-legged, curly-headed with leaves in the coils, skinny, malnourished and bold, she could track a deer for miles along trails roofed in bear clover, the cloven, heart-shaped impressions like Hansel and Gretel's white stones in reverse, leading her deeper and deeper into unknown territory, into mystery.

She was always more lost than found, more in danger than safe, but she knew herself to be watched over. There were eyes everywhere, all benign. The trees, wind, rocks and the Others were her knights, her personal bodyguard, hers mothers.

She was no bigger than a snack for any prowling mountain lion, mostly naked except for some sawed off jeans and a holey tee shirt, streaking down deer trails, bounding barefooted over fallen branches, past coiled rattlesnakes, moving like the deer that were her teachers.

It was too erotic to explain. Each smell was distinct. The Mountain Misery was tarry, leaf mold musky, manzanita flowers delicate and sweet as fairy honey. These smells, compounded by wind and sun, were a perfume of volatilized scents so sensuous that it dizzied and elated her and got her high.

Later, in the '60s when everyone was getting stoned, she tried it and found it pitiable. *That* was what they thought was *high?* The smell of buck brush blooming, rising up-canyon on a full moon night, capped acid by some measurement known only to physics – light years or megawatts or angstroms.

And that was just the smells. There were all the other senses left to indulge – like sound! There on the mountain, the wind always speaks in a low moan through the pine boughs, day and night. And in a storm? The voice of the gods! Wotan bemoaning his scooped-out eye! Isis anguishing for lost Osiris!

And the conversation of birds and animals is the subtext; trilling and hooting, coughing and chattering, howling and snuffling – a poetry too mellifluous, a symphony too polyphonic to convey. We rational beings, so stunted, asensual and sad, lack the vocabulary or the instrumentation. We grownups.

She's carried those childhood experiences with her into adulthood and that, she supposes, is why her dreams are so vivid and premonitory now. In sleep, that well-honed instinctual self is still roaming the woods of the unconscious, picking up cues.

So, many mornings she's gone through her routine in a daze, still pondering the inner images and whisperings, and just waking to the gossip of the natural world. First thing every morning, she puts the kettle on for tea before going out into the cold morning wind to split kindling and lug in firewood, so the wood stove can take the chill off the house.

This time of year, the east wind is a gale as she steps out into the dawn light. It cuts right through the wood-hauling jacket she always throws on, that's snagged from hugging oak logs close to her chest and sticky in spots from pine pitch.

Splitting sticks of kindling off the straight grain of a cedar round, she uses the strokes as a metronome to orchestrate the images of the last night's dream – like the one she had just before she flew down here to L.A...

She's in a city intersection, surrounded by buildings. Power poles support scalloped black cables that cross the intersection diagonally, marking a big X in the yellow sky. She's under the X in the center of the intersection with traffic rocketing all around her, not paying her the slightest heed. She looks over her shoulder and sees a white delivery van bearing down on her. There's no way to escape. A step in any direction and she'll be mowed down by traffic. She stands there helplessly as the bumper of the truck comes at her like the lowered horns of a bull.

And then, of course, she wakes up, with her heart pounding.

So while she's still lost in those images, she's pulling back a black plastic tarp and beginning to stack wood in the crook of her left elbow; a few small pieces of limb wood to feed the first flames from the kindling, some medium-sized logs to add next, and just at the edge of her arm's strength, one big split of oak to top things off.

She lays the fire the same way every time, with crumpled newspaper first, then crossed sticks of kindling, a couple of thin pieces of limb wood balanced on top of that. That just about fills the firebox. She closes the damper so the updraft won't blow out the match and lays the flame against the bottom wad, where it hesitates before grabbing hold of the paper and then eats greedily.

When the fire's fully engaged, she opens the damper and the heat rushes up the stovepipe with a roar like the afterburner on a jet. Once she hears that sound, she can relax. When a stove draws like that, a fire isn't going to smolder down to nothing; it's going to burn like a barn in August.

Winter on the mountain can be trying. Storms race in from the Pacific and dump rain or snow, then keep blowing eastward until they thump up against the Sierra crest where they moil and toil around a day or two, dropping snow and scouring the peaks with wind. Then the clouds wheel around and come charging down from the heights laden with cold they've picked up over the eternal snowfields and glaciers.

When they reach the high foothills where she lives, they're moving with the power and speed of a runaway freight train and, because the house sits right on a ridge, the east winds slam into it like the Furies. The whole house concusses, as if it were being beaten by a giant sledgehammer.

When the east wind blows, there's really no way to keep the house warm. Frigid air seeps into every crack. Sophia stuffs the stove full and it eats and eats logs, all day long. By evening, it's warm enough to sit by the fire in comfort. An hour after she's gone to bed, the place is frigid again. In the morning, she starts the process all over again.

She likes living that way. It keeps her honest. There's no ignoring the cycle of the seasons or denying the intensity of cold or heat. There's nothing artificial about the way she lives; she and Earth commune.

In November now, she limits her time outdoors and treasures her indoor hours. When spring comes, she'll throw the doors open and let the fresh wind cleanse away winter's smoke, while she washes windows and scrubs floors.

Her day is made up of these small, elemental rituals. She keeps her life simple and deliberate. She digs and weeds and plants in her garden; she goes for walks with her dogs; she washes and irons her clothes. She writes in her journal. She sews or reads or cooks...

"But Sophia," Ondine blurts out, "how do you make a *living?*"

Sophia shrugs. "Money's usually the last thing on my agenda. I'm not a person who cares to have it. It's simple necessity, nothing more."

Heddi scowls. Ondine looks at her in confusion.

"But...I mean...you have to *live!* You've got bills, surely. You've got a car. You need to eat."

Sophia shrugs again. "I grow most of my own food. But you're right. I do have a few bills; property taxes, if nothing else. And I have an old '57 Chevy truck that I maintain myself...but it does need gas once in a while."

"So...?"

So she does astrological readings for a living, by phone or by mail. Every once in a while, she gets a client who insists on meeting with her personally. That's always a bit of a jangle to her nerves because she's so reclusive, but it's interesting to see the face of the person she already knows so well through their chart.

Seeing their reaction to her and her situation is pretty interesting, too. They always arrive a little shaken. There's a narrow, twisting, five-mile grade up the mountain, with a 500-foot drop into the canyon. People have to really *want* what Sophia's got. And fortunately, she has a good reputation, so they keep coming even if the journey's death-defying.

Once they pull in, they sit in the car for a minute or two, sort of collecting themselves. When they finally do open the garden gate, it's with the trepidation of Vasilisa sneaking into Baba Yaga's hut to steal fire.

Sophia admits her place is a bit odd – an accretion of her personal aesthetic and the materials that fall to hand.

There's a high wall around house and garden – that's to keep the deer out, or they'd eat not just the roses but her kitchen garden, too. Also, it's a psychological boundary between her little enclave of civilization and the surrounding woods. Otherwise, her place would feel like a raft in the middle of an endless ocean.

The wall's a daub and wattle affair she pieced together out of oak branches, suckers pruned from the fruit trees and woven into screens, boulders and local clay. It's a toss-up whether it supports the rose and grape vines, or they support it. It gives the place a distinctly medieval ambience, as if serfs in coarse tunics bearing scythes might come stooping by any minute.

Inside the garden gate – an old cast iron bedstead that she's outfitted with leather hinges – the courtyard is filled with herbs and native plants that she uses for her concoctions. Wind chimes clank in the branches of the fruit trees and fetishes of feathers, twigs, and colored twine, binding little sacks of this and that, twirl in the wind.

The compost pile is lying ripe and black in full view. The woodpile and her chopping block are to the left of that, with the kitchen garden beyond. Chickens scratch under the rosemary and lavender bushes and peafowl strut among the cabbages.

A huge iron hog-scalding cauldron dominates the center of the courtyard – not to scald hogs, Heaven forbid! – but as her primary aesthetic statement: the Vessel of the Divine Feminine. It's six feet across and four feet high and must weigh two tons, if it's an ounce. Too large to ignore or to take lightly, it looks like something from a cartoon about cannibals cooking missionaries for lunch. It always gives people a start when they first see it, a momentary intuition of their mortality, she supposes, looking into the maw of the Life-and-Death Mother.

When she comes down to greet them, that gives them a jolt, too, because she always puts on her ceremonial garb. What's the use of arcane practices without ritual trappings? Would you go to a wedding in a bikini? The opera in your nightshirt? So why do a reading about the designs of the Cosmos in bib overalls?

She's been working on her robes for years, starting in her early twenties with a coat that she found at a thrift store, stitched from a two-point Hudson Bay blanket. From the early days of the fur trade, she explains, point blankets were made into hooded coats called *capotes* by both natives and French Canadian voyageurs. Whoever designed this one was off to a good start – wide straight sleeves and a pointed hood with a long streamer cut from the border hanging down the back. It's bright rosy red with two black stripes running around the hemline and the two 6-inch points along the front edge. She figures it was well over a hundred years old when she found it.

When she bought it, it was full of moth holes, so she spent the next ten years embroidering moths over every hole, using her insect field guide for accuracy. The smallest is a tiny gray thing barely half an inch long and the biggest is a full-sized Luna moth in an exquisite pale green that looks very exotic against the fuzzy red wool.

The coat is never really finished. Every summer, when she stores it away, the moths eat new holes. When winter comes, she begins stitching all over again – which is okay because there are still so many moths to choose from in the book.

If butterflies are the symbol of the soul, she thinks of moths as night steeds that carry the soul into the deep realms, other dimensions or alternate realities – places into which she's never been afraid to venture. They're bringers of the energy she needs for the readings.

But red was never really her color. She's a Pisces and drawn to cool, watery shades. So she's made herself a skirt of aquamarine silk cut from a single old drapery she found at the flea market. The places where it folded outward and caught the sun are faded and the interior folds are dark, so it has the tonal variation of water that she loves.

Being so big – not fat, of course, but just so tall and broad-shouldered – she's lucky to have all that curtain yardage for her outfit. She's like one of those jokes men tell about women who have their clothes made by Omar the Tentmaker.

And she's also working on a cape that's to look like sea foam when it's done. The base is a curtain of handmade lace, one of a pair that a friend gave her when she cleaned out her grandmother's house. It's wide and long and trails behind her a bit because she doesn't dare cut it.

Then she started gathering bits of lace, old linen napkins, a tattered antique Chinese shawl in white silk pongee, embroidered in white with flowers and birds. That, she stitched down whole over the shoulders, using the ends to tie the cape on. The other scraps she just sews side by side, making an incredible patchwork of white fabrics and textures: old crocheted doilies, lengths of tatted trim, bobbin and Battenburg lace – anything white and feminine, and only those treasures actually made by women's hands.

She started at the hemline and after about seven years, she's reached the waist. Other than the shawl it's just lace from there up, but she wears it anyway, just like the moth coat. Probably neither one will ever be finished.

Someday, they'll bury her in her unfinished finery.

So with her gray hair hanging to her waist, her aqua skirt, red coat and white cape, she supposes she's quite a spectacle coming down the stairs to greet her clients.

She doesn't do this to alarm or impress them. She does it to honor the old gods and goddesses who honor her with their inspiration. She knows the God of modern religion doesn't care if you're in polyester or Spandex, as long as you're decent. But she believes that her goddesses *do* care – they'd rather she came naked than in synthetic fabrics. Natural fibers are gifts they give us, and using them in ritual is part of the sacred cycle.

She always starts her astrological readings with a Tarot reading. She never touches the cards without washing her hands first. Then she prays over them that only the truth will manifest there, that the best and highest good will come through them.

Sophia stops and glances around to see the women looking at her oddly.

"You must think I'm incredibly weird. Sometimes, I think so, myself. But really, I was just born in the wrong century or the wrong culture. Women like me have been carrying forward the rituals of humankind since we lived in caves. I'm just a latter-day shaman, is all."

Sophia sings the sun up in the morning and down again at evening, in Sanskrit – the *Agni Hotra*. She blesses the yogurt to set while it's still liquid and thanks her vegetables and flowers before picking them. It takes so little effort and energy to honor the sacredness of the world.

Lately, she's taken to blessing road kill, those poor little creatures and rags of bloody fur that people whiz past so thoughtlessly. They break her heart, so she prays for their souls. She's sure they have them, just like people do. So as she's rolling along in her pickup, she says her prayers. Her eyes aren't what they used to be and if she blesses a grease rag or a shoe lost beside the road, so what?

The other day, she mistook some fast food trash for a dead skunk and was well into her prayer before she realized she was praying for a bag of Taco Bell Styrofoam. Well, who's to say Styrofoam doesn't need our prayers?

Sophia looks around at her audience again. Pearl is lost in some reverie of her own. Erika is tossing in a sweat-glazed doze on the couch. Ondine looks listlessly at the floor, while Heddi and Betty stare – Heddi with fathomless eyes, and Betty as if Sophia might suddenly straddle the broom and dematerialize through the wall.

"I think I must be boring you to death. Let's take a break, shall we?"

Heddi

The archetype of Diana the Huntress, as she lives and breathes! The purest example Heddi's ever witnessed in all her years as an analyst. It's easy to imagine Sophia on a full moon night, with her pack of dogs, cloaked in fierce independence, striding out into the inky shadows of the oak woods, intent on performing her secret rituals, or dancing naked to the rhythms of the night wind. Amazing that so pure a type could still exist in 21st-century America!

Betty

Well, that's the weirdest story yet! Even the bag lady isn't as strange as this gal. What is she – a witch? A pagan? Betty's father would have said she's Satanic. All that talk of fairies and goddesses and Tarot cards! If it weren't for Madame Zola, Betty wouldn't even have a clue what she's talking about.

And all these little details of her life! Should Betty care how she builds a fire in the morning? Or what the weather patterns are at her house? They've got weather in L.A., too, but Betty never bothers with it and she'd never bother anybody else with it, either. She guesses when it rains and the freeways flood, it's a big deal, but really...!

Betty just can't get on her wavelength, at all.

And all this talk of dreams... Heddi does it, too. Every session: "Did you dream?" Well, yes, of course Betty dreams – but it's all just nonsense.

But she *does* daydream. Some, she's been working on for years, kind of perfecting the plot. Then there's a new one that she's started, just since they got trapped in here. It helps her cope. She just sort of slips away into it like mental knitting; how you always want to do just one more row before you quit. Her story's like that. She wants to imagine just one more detail before she has to come out of it and deal with what's here and now.

Heddi wants her to start imagining living things instead of dead flowers, so it's kind of strange that in this latest story Larry is dying of prostate cancer, but that's what her imagination is dishing out.

On his deathbed, Larry calls for her – and forgives her...

"I made a promise, 'til death do us part. I'm glad we didn't finalize the divorce. I'm glad I can keep that promise to you... Don't cry, Betty. I need you to hear this.

"I've got a life insurance policy you never knew about. It won't make you rich, but it'll get the kids through college and help you get started in whatever you plan to do next."

Betty sits by his hospital bed, silently weeping. She is filled with shame and gratitude.

"Now you listen to me, Betty! If I so much as hear a peep on the Other Side about you spending one cent of it on fake flowers, I'm going to come back and haunt you. Do you hear me?"

He stops for a weak, hacking cough that produces nothing but exhaustion. When he continues, it's in a rasping whisper. "That money is for moving on. Do you understand? For the kids to have the education that'll help them move on. And for you to start a new life.

Something real this time, okay? Something not artificial. Something living."

He slides his hand limply across the blanket in her direction. She sits there, frozen – but only for a moment. She grabs his hand quickly and holds it with a fierceness she didn't know was in her.

"I love you, Betty. Always did, kid. Whatever happened between us, it wasn't because I didn't love you. You hear me?"

She can only nod dumbly.

"Come here." He pulls her to him with a little jerk of his head, like he always used to.

She creeps onto the bed and lowers her big body down gently, so she won't jar him and ignite the pain that's smoldering in his bones.

Gingerly, she rests her head on the shoulder he offers her. His arm comes around her protectively, lying across her shoulder with a pale warmth.

"Always did, kid. You know that, don't you?"

She nods, working the top of her head underneath his chin. And slowly – oh, so slowly, as if it were a frozen hand reaching up from frigid water through ice – she watches her hand rise up, then float gently down and settle over his heart.

She hears Heddi and Ondine talking and it distracts her. Heddi's saying, "I know it seems like the terrorists are winning, but in the end I think they will fail. The healthy psyche – and even the unhealthy one – has to withdraw periodically, so that the inner voice can be heard. The Self demands it. That's why fanatical political action is incompatible with individuation."

And then Ondine's soft, tentative voice: "But the problem is, so many of these terrorists seem to be young men. They're too young to have felt the urge for individuation. Their strength comes from the collective... from being a hero in the eyes of the group."

And then Heddi: "It's true that the collective opinion distrusts and rejects the bringing to life of psychic images and revelations. There's a fundamental collective resistance to the unconscious because its messages rock the boat. But depth psychology shows us that when unconscious forces are repressed, they gain strength in the darkness and then erupt in terrible, pathological ways."

"But isn't that exactly what terrorism is?"

"Yes, this is what Jung warned about at the end of his life – destructive collective energies. But I think it's also that the ego is unable to free itself from extroverted rational prejudices. The ego doesn't want to relinquish control and admit that true liberation in our time can only come from psychological transformation. What does it matter if one dies for one's cause, if the cause recognizes no meaningful goal in life – no goal for which it's worthwhile to be free?"

"So, only if a person can create something meaningful is it worthwhile to be free?"

"Exactly. Isn't that what freedom *is* – to be at liberty to live and create authentically? And that's why the individual voice – the one that's developed during the process of listening to the deep psyche – even if it's a whisper, is so much more powerful than the communal shout."

Their voices go on and on, attempting to put an intellectual corral around the crazy, chaotic energies that are encircling them like Attila's hordes. Betty hopes it gives them comfort, the same way her story does for her.

So where was she?

She's lying beside him and she slides her hand over his heart...

They bury him on a cold day in early spring.

In the days between his death and his interment, Betty fights her addiction. She plans wreathes of spring flowers, of rosemary for remembrance, of evergreen. She even goes so far as to start pulling bundles of them down from the garage rafters, getting herself all dusty and wheezy in the process.

But in the end, she forces herself to drive by a florist's shop. She goes around the block three times before she has the courage to park and go in.

When she pushes open the heavy plate glass door with its little tinkling bell, it's like Sisyphus pushing his rock. Just like Heddi says, anyone who hasn't experienced it can't believe the actual weight of psychological resistance.

She steps into a room that is really just a narrow passageway between banks of ferns and tubs of flowers. The heavy, penetrating perfume almost makes her faint.

It's the smell more than anything that makes her want to bolt. It's so alive — like the voices of children calling out for love; so desirous to be regarded and cared for.

It's too much. Everything in her is gathering strength to turn and flee.

But she's there for him. For Larry. And he wanted something living. So she starts poking around in the tubs, pulling out some daffodils here, some hyacinth there. Kind of clustering them in her hand and pushing them into one another until the colors begin to harmonize and hum together.

The owner has the good sense just to leave her alone and let her create. Betty can see him hovering back behind the counter but she ignores him. She's going to get this thing over with and get out, ASAP.

But as she works, a funny thing begins to happen. As she handles the flowers — the cool waxiness of the bulbs, the dry feathers of asparagus fern, the lush, satiny roses — it's as if something is moving inside her like a tightly furled bud breaking open.

At first, it's painful and alarming. She has a fleeting thought that she might be having a stroke. But it gets easier and more fluid. It slides beneath her skin like a cool wave, lifting and plumping as it comes. She wants to be afraid, but it's too pleasurable.

This must be what Heddi was saying about a lightning bolt from the gods. It's so simple, really, that it's hard to believe how amazing, how profound, it is. How much of a miracle.

It's Larry's last gift to her, and his parting shot of vindication, too.

Because she's falling suddenly, madly, in love with living flowers. Some passion that had gotten all balled up in acquisition, in ownership of heaps of dead things, suddenly threw the entire weight of its being into love of the ephemeral. Every blossom a hymn to the fleeting moment. Each a treasure house of color, scent, form and giving Grace...

A vile smell draws her out of her reverie. Pearl's pipe! What a rancid, nasty smell! A rose it's not, by any name.

Ondine and Heddi are still talking. Heddi is saying, "To take the unconscious seriously is really an act of personal integrity and courage."

And Ondine replies, "I can see how the loss of the power of religious symbols is compensated by a kind of scientific excitement, as we delve into the unconscious on a strange new kind of ethical adventure..."

Betty should be listening to all this. She could learn something that might help her make sense of this analysis she's taken on – or even this situation she's in. But the narrative keeps drawing her back in with an irresistible attraction.

She handles living flowers now, with love, every day. She works at the florist's shop.

She handles Herb – he's the owner, well, half-owner, Betty's the other half – that way, too: with love. He's a good man and they're happy together, mating their flowers to one another; mating themselves to one another.

They live in a kind of bliss of fragrance and color. It's like opening a door in a dream and walking through and finally finding yourself in your own life. What a surprise!

And then comes the part that she's just working on. It's hard and she can't get it to flow. It's about Serena.

Things are so broken between them. She can't imagine anything – even the actual death of her father – that would bring them back together again.

In fact, her father's death and Betty's remarriage would most likely send Serena screaming out of Betty's life forever. She'd blame Betty for her father's death. She'd accuse her of wicked things. Betty knows all that. But she at least wants to be able to *imagine* that things could be better between them.

The last time she saw Serena was terrible beyond description. She came to the house looking like a street whore. She'd dyed her hair carrot orange. She had so many piercings Betty was afraid of infection. And tattoos! All her clothing was sawn off or shrunk up or ripped open to show them off.

She came to announce she was moving into a new apartment – with her lover!

Betty'd scarcely grasped the meaning of *that* proclamation when in came this new mate: a woman of about 35! She had on motorcycle boots and a black leather jacket and she took possession of her daughter's body in a familiar way that made Betty nauseous.

Betty thought she'd faint.

But the worst part was that Serena didn't come for Betty's blessings or simply to inform her. She came to torment her.

And she succeeded.

X is digging in Fat Guy's lunchbox, listening to the news with her back to the television when she hears it – that *voice!*

She spins around and there is a man in an FBI jacket talking to the blonde newswoman. He is saying things but she cannot really understand them because her heart is beating so hard.

It is *he!* It is the man who came to talk to the Brothers at the Kultur Klub meeting! She knows it! It is a very distinctive voice – deep, with a small way of slurring his words that makes her believe he may be from one of the southern states.

She did not hear the announcer say his name. Who is he? What is he doing here? She tries very hard to focus her attention.

"We believe the terrorists are holed up in the food court," he is saying.

"And why haven't you gone in for them yet?" The blonde is shoving the microphone at his mouth in a way that is almost sexual.

"Because they're holding hostages. We're sure of that, now. We're waiting for them to make a demand."

X cannot concentrate on his words. The blood is pounding in her ears like a drum.

She feels dizzy and sick, the way she felt spying from the next room, that night.

This is the man who provoked the Brothers to this action! What is he doing here?

She feels sick in her stomach.

"Commander, can you give us a way to think about terrorism?" the newswoman asks. "I'm sure many of us are grappling with that, right now." The reporter thrusts her microphone toward him and, with the other hand, pushes her blonde hair, blown by the wind, back from her cheek.

The man clears his throat and shifts his stance. His eyes are on the ground. Around him a herd of television cameras waits on his opinion with the black, inscrutable eyes of animals. "Well, basically, terrorism is comprised of violent acts by sub-State actors against noncombatants," he intones, unaware that the PIO has already stolen his line.

The reporter nods her head enthusiastically, as if in full comprehension – while wondering if her mascara has smeared by this late hour, X guesses. "Can you be a little more specific?"

"No, actually, I can't. And that's because terrorism is taking so many forms these days. Some terrorists are moved by political concerns, some by religious conviction, and others by tribal loyalties. Sometimes, all three. Or by other things, like economic oppression, environmental erosion, simple hunger and thirst. It's impossible to generalize further. Each event calls for a different understanding of motivation."

He shifts his feet again, clearly desiring to leave this obligatory interview and return to his command post.

"What are the factors in *this* case?" the reporter persists.

"We're just beginning to put together profiles of the individual terrorists. I'll let my Public Information Officer fill you in on what we know." He shifts his weight away from her and, taking the cue, the reporter lets him go.

"Alright, thank you, Commander."

Before she can continue, his back is already disappearing through the media throng, the emblazoned *FBI* glowing eerily in the artificial light with a cold phosphorescent fire, long after his human form is dissolved in darkness.

"We'll take a commercial break and then we'll be hearing from the FBI's Public Information Officer with some very interesting information on the background of the terrorists."

She lowers the mic and snarls into the glare of the lights. "Where the hell is Stacy? I need my makeup checked, like, *yesterday*," unaware that she is still on camera.

So now X understands: it is not that her body is cowardly and weak. It is that it *knows!* It knows danger and it knows when to eliminate or refuel – and, it knows the voice of betrayal!

Her entire being is quivering like a frightened animal. She cannot think clearly. How did this man come to be in their lives? How is it that his promises of glory spurred them on, so that she is here now in Fat Guy's room eating his tuna sandwiches and shaking with shock? None of it makes sense.

After the meeting when the man came and she was dismissed, she asked Jamal what had happened, even though she already knew.

His answer was strange. "I think the President needs an incident – and we are it."

When she tried to get him to explain, he said he was sorry he had said anything and would respond no further.

Later, she heard him arguing with Ibrahim, asking, "Are we pawns in the game of rich men, then? Is that what you think we should be?"

And Ibrahim answering coldly, "What difference does it make how we do it, as long as we make our point?"

The argument went on and on and, at the time, all she wanted was to get away from their harsh voices. Now she realizes that she should have listened and learned.

Can it be possible that they are here to be exploited for the present administration's political gain? Is it possible that the President is so evil as to wish death on his own citizens, so that he may then be a hero, soothing them? Or even that he might use their attack as a pretext for war?

Allah! What have we done?!

She glances at the television, just as the Public Information Officer steps before the cameras. He's a slender man in his thirties, handsome in a weak way, with perfectly razor cut and moussed hair, and a well-tailored suit. He holds a sheaf of papers in his hand, obviously aware of the expectant hush that falls around him.

"Our agents have been working tirelessly," he begins, "to identify the terrorists. Tonight, I will reveal the identity of some of them and give a brief synopsis of their lives." He shuffles the papers importantly and then begins his delivery.

His information, the PIO claims, comes straight from investigators who have been poring over notes in Father

Christopher's files, discovered in his university office two days ago.

X suffers a second shock because Jamal comes immediately to her mind and his closeness is almost palpable. She is remembering him coming to her apartment, acting oddly, only a few days ago.

"Why are you acting so strangely, Jamal?" she had asked him, her brow furrowing.

"I have something to show you," Jamal answered, looking about him as if there might be others in the room.

X laughed out loud. "You are acting silly, Jamal. You are not in some American film. We are alone, obviously!"

He shrugged nervously and gave an embarrassed smile that faded too quickly. Reaching inside his jacket, he pulled out a large but not very thick black book and held it indecisively, still glancing about nervously.

"What is that?" X asked, approaching him curiously and reaching for the volume.

Jamal jerked it up, out of her reach, his nostrils flaring and his eyes wild. X became suddenly frightened.

"What *is* that?" she asked again, almost in a whisper. "What have you got there and where did you get it?"

"Sit on the couch," Jamal said, jerking his head in its direction. X wanted to bristle, to assert her rights as a woman, but something warned her to be compliant. She went dutifully to the couch and sat. Jamal came to sit beside her.

"This is Father Christopher's journal," he said flatly.

X frowned deeply. "How do you come to have this thing, Jamal?" she asked warily.

He looked her in the eyes for the first time that evening, with a mixture of fierce pride and apology. "I stole it."

Her eyes grew large with alarm. "Jamal! Then you must take it back!"

"Yes," he said. "Yes, I have to take it back, and I will – but not before you see what he has written here." And he opened the book to a place that was marked with a piece of torn paper.

Her head was shaking by its own volition and she looked at Jamal with confusion, pleading, "Please, Jamal! You know this is not right!"

But Jamal had been firm, almost cold, when he responded. "Just sit still and hear what I will read you." And so, she had.

"'The Dean has asked me to compile some notes on the members of the Kultur Klub,'" Jamal began reading, in the accented English and soft baritone that X loved so much. "'I assume his interest is personal, although I can see that the success of the Klub could be a political feather in his cap, as well. I will begin by assembling what little I know about the various members.'"

"Do you see. Father Christopher has been spying on us," Jamal said, his eyes flicking fiercely in her direction.

"Oh, I don't think..." X began. Then she shrugged her shoulders and said softly, "Go on."

"'Hansi Nyirabazungu'"

"'Hansi first came to my attention in 1994, when Sister Elizabeth went to work in Rwanda, immediately after the massacre at Gikondo. From the assassination of Juvénal Habyarimana on 6 April through mid-July, at least 500,000 people were killed. Sister Elizabeth left her mission in Uganda immediately upon hearing of the commencement of hostilities and narrowly escaped death herself, as violence between the Tutsis and the Hutus swept the country.'"

X took advantage of Jamal's presence, an increasing rarity as the training had intensified, and snuggled closer to him on the pretext of reading along with him.

"'Sister Elizabeth's reports were almost not to be believed, so vast and horrible did the cataclysm of death seem to be. She talked of heaps of bodies lying bloated in the hot sun; of men, women and children maimed horribly, most often by machete. The disruption of communities was disastrous, as well. People fled, often without even the basic necessities of food and water or clothing and bedding, creating a huge humanitarian crisis.

"'She was working, one day, in a Tutsi refugee camp, trying to organize things – to get latrine pits dug, cooking fires going, shelters rigged. Suddenly, a band of Hutu militia charged into the camp, machetes swinging. People ran screaming in all directions. Sister herself was saved when someone reached a hand down from the branches of a tree and pulled her up to be hidden in the leaves. From that vantage point, she watched, terrified, as the soldiers sliced and hacked for more than two hours.

"'Finally, exhausted with their labors, they began to hobble their victims by slicing their Achilles tendons so that they could not run. Then, the soldiers took their leisure for an hour or more, rummaging the camp for food, resting in the rude shelters and rinsing blood from their bodies in the river. When they were sufficiently rested, they followed the blood trails of their crawling victims and finished them off.

"'At last, when it seemed the militia had no one left to kill and was about to depart, a little boy of about three or four came to hide behind the tree where Sister Elizabeth was perched with her benefactor. A soldier spied him, came running and, with one swoop of his machete, cut off the boy's hand. Screaming, the boy collapsed against the trunk of the tree, holding his wrist from which blood squirted. And he cowered there, awaiting the killing blow.

"'Just as the soldier was about to strike again, however, he was himself struck from behind. A tree branch landed solidly on his head and he went down. It was the boy's mother, apparently, who then threw down her weapon and ran with arms out to rescue her son.

"'But it was not to be. Two more soldiers, witnessing the scene, ran over. Meanwhile, the first soldier had recovered his senses and was pushing himself up from the ground. In concert, the three of them reached for the mother just as she was about to snatch up her child. They threw her violently to the ground and one was about to decapitate her with his machete when another of the three had an idea – they should rape her instead.

"'Sister Elizabeth watched in horror. All she could see from her vantage point were the woman's lower legs and feet, which first beat the ground in frantic struggle but, as first one man, then the next, and finally the third brutally mounted her, subsided and then went limp – whether in a faint or in death Sister could not tell.

"'All the while, she had a clear look at the boy who still leaned against the tree trunk, holding his severed wrist tightly, his face blank with shock. He witnessed the violence meted out to his mother without uttering a sound.

"'When it was over at last and the militia had departed, Sister Elizabeth came down from the tree. She saw instantly why the mother lay so still. Her throat had been cut. And still, the little boy leaned against the tree trunk, as if turned to stone.

"'Sister Elizabeth herself was in profound shock. Her only thought, just like the Tutsi refugees, was to flee – and this she did, but not without reaching out for the little boy. Tying a crude tourniquet around his wrist and sweeping him up in her arms, she fled. After two days of walking, she was able to hitch a ride to the capitol and from there, a plane back to Uganda.

"'There, she got medical attention for the boy and then placement in an orphanage run by Dominican sisters. Then, she requested refuge in a Dominican motherhouse in Belgium, was accepted and departed Africa, still in deep psychological shock. In Bruges, she took vows of silence and is, as far as I know, still living a silent, contemplative life. I sincerely hope that she finds it healing.

"'The boy, who when he was finally able to speak, called himself Hansi, took a long time to heal psychologically, even while his severed wrist quickly mended. His teacher at the orphanage, whose last name was given to him – for he could not remember his own, if ever he had known it – reported that he was very bright but too quiet in class, only responding when spoken to and then as briefly as possible.

"'Nevertheless, he passed the next years excelling in academics. So when it was time for his college education, his teacher helped him get a scholarship to this American university and it was here that I met him, at last, and encouraged him to become a participant in the Kultur Klub.

"'According to his professors, he is doing well in his classes. However, I have discovered that he lacks completely a religious life or even an obvious personal philosophy, and also cares nothing for politics; nor is he the least bit interested in sports, societal issues, or even girls. He seems to dwell in an inner space that is devoid of anchors, therefore, as if his roots, having been severed so early, never again were able to penetrate into the soil of human culture.'"

Jamal glanced briefly at X and, satisfied that she was fully engrossed in his reading, continued.

"'Jamal Faleh'"

At the reading of Jamal's name, X drew her breath in sharply. "Oh, Jamal! It is *you!*" Then she gasped again because it suddenly occurred to her that, if Jamal were in this journal, her story might be in it, as well.

Jamal gave her a knowing look and continued:

"'I first met Jamal a year and a half ago, at the very first gathering of the Kultur Klub. I was struck instantly by his appearance, for he is tall for an Egyptian, yet has those wide, dark, dreaming eyes and delicate features that characterize some of his people, like a male Nefertiti. The Imam whispered to me that he is a Christian and with a smile, hissed, 'He's in your camp, my friend, yours to attend to.'

"'So I introduced myself to Jamal and began to elicit his story, for one thing was sure: he would have one. All the members of the Kultur Klub do, as the Imam and I have chosen them precisely for this reason. Each is an orphan and the survivor of some horrific human cataclysm, and some are heirs to conflicts in which they are the born and sworn enemy of other members of the Klub. The Imam and I feel that if we can get these disparate people to know one another and to hear one another's stories, it will break through the walls of hatred and prejudice and there will be a possibility for healing to occur, both individually and culturally.

"'Jamal's family has lived from time out of mind in the southeastern area of Egypt, far from the capital in Cairo and thus, far from access to power. In recent years, the government has been relocating people into their area, causing land disputes with the Faleh family and with the Bedouins, now no longer nomadic, who are their neighbors. Even though the Falehs are Coptic Christians, they get along well with the Bedouins. And so, both groups were outraged in one another's behalf when the government usurped their lands for outsiders.

"'Jamal explained to me that the Copts are the oldest and largest Christian community in the Middle East. They call themselves the Church of St. Mark and claim descent from that apostle, who brought the church to Alexandria during the reign of the emperor Claudius. For centuries, Copts were the majority in Egypt until, in 641 during the advent of Islam, most were forcibly converted or became Muslims to avoid the heavy taxes imposed upon them.

"'Presently, he said, the Copts are discriminated against because of the rise of Muslim fundamentalism. There is, for example, an official ban on the building of new Coptic churches and even on the repair of old ones, without express presidential permission.

"'Also, evangelical churches from America have been using the Copts to proselytize among the Muslim majority and this is causing widespread and explosive anger, both because of the unpopularity of America in general and because changing religions is considered to be a grave disrespect to Mohammed. There are numerous instances of Muslims who converted being killed. Random violence against Copts is increasing, as well.

"'Also, Jamal explained to me that in some villages, young Coptic girls are kidnapped and forcibly married to Muslims, and appeals to the authorities to find the missing girls are rarely followed up, nor are strong penalties for abduction enforced.

"'These are the tensions that grew to surround the Faleh family who had lived a peaceful pastoral existence on their lands for generations. In 2001, their fields were seized by the government and parceled out to relocated Muslims from the Cairo area. Numerous complaints to the government failed to bring restitution.

"'Then, in 2002, two events brought disaster to Jamal's family: his grandfather, the patriarch of the family, was caught grazing his sheep on his ancestral lands and was summarily beaten almost to death. Shortly thereafter, Jamal's sister, Yasmin, was kidnapped and forcibly married to one of the Muslim intruders – an action that the family, quite justifiably, considered as rape.

"'The Faleh family assembled and marched, en masse, to retrieve the girl, armed with pitchforks, shepherd's crooks and shovels. They were met by unequal force, however. The new settlers had guns and, in the melee that ensued, the entire Faleh family, including the kidnapped girl, was massacred. Jamal, who was home on vacation from his first year at university in Alexandria, was the sole survivor.

"'Although badly injured, he had the presence of mind to play dead and then, in the night, to crawl away and take refuge with the Bedouins, who nursed him back to health. Through the intervention of one of the evangelical churches active in the area, he was able to come to the U.S. on an academic visa, and that is how he came to be one of founding members of the Kultur Klub.

"'He has survived a terrible physical and psychological calamity. And yet, Jamal is emotionally open and sensitive to the stories of the other members. Often, it is Jamal who leaps into the fray to calm arguments and to insist on the efficacy of peaceful communication.

"'Although he was slow to share this part of himself, it gradually became known that Jamal is a poet. Only once was I able to convince him to recite for the Klub and it did not go well. Ibrahim was a disruptive influence, whispering and nudging the fellow members to either side of him throughout Jamal's presentation. After that, Jamal refused to try again.

"'Nevertheless, Najat has told me shyly that Jamal favors her with his newly minted poems. Also, he is apparently a scholar of the 13th-century poet Rumi and Najat reports that he can recite Rumi's verses in Farsi by the hour.'"

Jamal stops reading and turns accusing eyes on X. "You have talked about me to Father Christopher, Najat?" She is shaken by the anger in his voice, but also that he has, after so many weeks, used her true name again.

"Jamal, be careful! You know Ibrahim has forbidden it."

"So...is Ibrahim here tonight?" Again, Jamal looks around the apartment, suspiciously.

She sighs. "You know that he is not."

"Then I will speak to the woman I love in the way that *I* choose!" His jaw is rigid with anger. "And you discuss me with Father Christopher, Najat?"

She hangs her head. "Yes," she whispers, "I have talked with Father Chris about you...but only because I am so proud of you and so happy that we are together."

He does not respond, but resumes reading, his dark eyes liquid with turmoil.

"'Jamal's professors are impressed by his brilliance, by the quality of his attentive listening and by his respect for all whom he encounters. Several have expressed the opinion that he should become a diplomat due to his charismatic charm and his obvious skill at compromise and negotiation. Of all the Klub members, I would judge him the closest to that model of diversity and peaceful coexistence that the Imam and I have envisioned for this group.'"

Jamal stops reading, so she is able to insert her mollifying thought. "See how respectful Father Christopher is of you! See how he honors you with first place in the Klub!"

But Jamal's eyes are dark with mistrust. "He is collecting this information for a reason, Najat. Something is not right. Do you imagine the Dean asks for information about the members of the ski club, or the debating team?" Without waiting for an answer, he continues reading.

"'Ibrahim Yassin'"

"'By far the most controversial member of the Klub is Ibrahim. The Imam and I actually argued over his inclusion, a thing we have never done before or since. That is because Ibrahim is older than the rest by nearly a decade and, therefore, has more mature leadership abilities. This would not be a bad thing under most circumstances, but Ibrahim has another striking quality: his outspoken Muslim fundamentalism and his overt rage against the Israelis.

"'The Imam and I expected that each Klub member would present certain religious and cultural attributes that are deep-dyed and rigid. Indeed, it has been our hope that the very tragedies that bring these young people to America might also be the catalyst to break through certain cultural barriers and insensitivities that are the essence of international conflict. With Ibrahim, however, the prejudices are excessive and I confided in the Imam, and ultimately argued with him, that Ibrahim is too fully cast in iron ever to have his heart melted – even by the tragedies of the other members. Allowing his bid for leadership, then, appears to me to risk leading the Klub astray.

"'Nevertheless, the Imam carried the day, arguing that Ibrahim is the very model of the student we seek: orphaned, traumatized, confused and, therefore, vulnerable to persuasion. Certainly, on hearing his story, one would have to admit that he is in need of the solace we hope the Klub will provide.

"'Ibrahim is Palestinian, born on the southernmost border of the Gaza Strip in Rafah Camp. It is a refugee center of 95,000 souls that, under the Camp David agreement, was split down the middle between Egypt and Israel. At the time of that division, families were arbitrarily torn apart. In this way, Ibrahim was separated from his extended family when he and his parents were forced into the Egyptian side, while the remainder of his relatives stayed on the Israeli side of the divide.

"'Although only a hundred yards or so separate the watchtowers of the Egyptian and Israeli sides, the refugees have neither the money nor the papers to cross over, even for a short visit. So each day of his childhood, trudging through sand and heat, Ibrahim was brought by his mother to the border of the Egyptian camp. They would come to the barbed wire and lean against it, squinting into the desert glare across two paved patrol roads, one Egyptian, one

Israeli, to the opposite fence line where the women and children of their family would also be gathered, waving at them.

"'In the moments when the desert wind fell and there was a hush, the women shouted news to one another across the divide, holding up new babies to be blessed or wailing the sad tidings of death. And they shouted out the reassurances that keep the bonds of family alive: "I miss you!" "I love you!" "Give my love to Mother; to Aunty; to my sister."

"'Ibrahim told of a day when he was about ten and he and his mother were at the wire. He was playing war in the sand using rocks for tanks when his mother suddenly reeled back from the fence, collapsed to her knees and buried her face in the sand, a posture that did nothing to muffle her agonized screams. Terrified, Ibrahim ran to her, thinking she had been shot.

"'Her head veil came loose and slid onto the sand and her long hair came undone and spread around her head like a black cloud, as she pounded her forehead against the ground, shrieking and flooded with tears. Her agony so alarmed him that he claims he was infected by it from that moment onward.

"'"I will never forget it, as long as I live," he told me, vehemently, "and I will never forgive it, either." His tone held such cold menace that I could not help but believe him. And I confess, he frightened me a little with the power of his venom.

"'As suddenly as she had flung herself onto the sand, Ibrahim's mother leapt up and threw herself against the barbed wire again, screaming to her relatives across the way. Her cheeks were gritty with tear-annealed sand and she scrubbed it away with the cuff of her dress.

"'She was hoarse from shouting before Ibrahim understood what was happening. Someone on the Israeli side had attacked a guard and, in retaliation, the Israelis had launched a rocket attack. As her parents sat innocently over their midday meal inside their makeshift house, a rocket tore into the house next door and a huge explosion and fire erupted. Ibrahim's grandfather, two of his aunts and five of his cousins were killed outright. His grandmother, burned almost to a cinder, was still alive and, most terrible for his mother, was calling plaintively for her daughter, over and over.

"'Ibrahim's mother was frantic to get to her mother before she died. She ran down the fence line to the first guard she encountered, grabbed him by his shirtfront and screamed at him that she needed to get across the divide with no delay. A guard in the nearest watchtower, thinking she was attacking his fellow soldier, simply raised his rifle and shot her, without hesitation.

"'Ibrahim's mother did not die immediately. Instead, she lay in agony for five days, weeping both from pain and for her mother, until the simple flesh wound in her thigh festered, became necrotic and finally killed her.

"''In any decent place, in any civilized situation, my mother would not have died. The doctor would have stitched her up, given her antibiotics and she would be alive today. But no...'' Ibrahim told me, his eyes reddening with the internal flames of rage. "No. She was condemned to die because no one cared. No one came to help her. There was no doctor. No medicine. Not even clean water for my poor father to clean the wound. My mother died in agony because of the cruel stupidity of the international community that does not recognize the existence of individuals. My people are a 'humanitarian dilemma.' We are 'refugees.' In the eyes of the world, the Yassin family does not even exist! And to the Israelis, we are no more than targets!"

"After his mother's death, Ibrahim's father, formerly a political moderate, became more and more radical until he finally joined the Palestinian Liberation Organization under Yasar Arafat. He trained with the PLO militia and carried out several daring adventures outside the wire before he was shot and killed, somewhere in the no man's land between the Egyptian and Israeli sides of the camp.

"By this time, Ibrahim was eighteen, old enough to join the PLO himself. He spent several years training with their militia before his application to university in America was accepted and, under a student visa, he came to this country.

"In his introductory talk to the Kultur Klub Ibrahim said, "Do you know, there is a saying among the United Nations soldiers in our camp: *If you think you understand the Middle East, you have not been properly briefed.* They think this is hilarious.

""But I will tell you something else. My people, the Palestinians, are intelligent, well-educated people. Liberated and united as one people, we could control the Middle East. All the big players know this – the Russians, the Arabs, and especially Israel and the United States. Oh, they very well understand the situation in the Middle East!

""Now do you understand why the Palestinians cannot be allowed to be reunited in our homeland? We are a political threat to the big powers, that's why. And because it serves their interests, they hold us in slavery and destitution!" He slammed his fist into the dais.

"The others listened respectfully, without a murmur of dissent. What could they say, after all? They, who understand all too well the gravity of the captive state?

"In talking to Ibrahim's professors, I find them divided in their comments, just as the Imam and I are divided. Some find him intelligent, articulate and engaged. Others find his obnoxious, dominating the class with his rhetoric, anti-Semitic to an alarming degree and outspoken in his hatred of this country, although it shelters him. All agree, however, that he is a good student. Not a brilliant student like Jamal or Najat, but thorough, well prepared, and with a deeper than average understanding of the subject matter.

"'Personally, I still reserve judgment. While I respect the progress he has made in overcoming a life of tragedy by coming to this country and challenging himself to attain a university degree, I cannot feel comfortable with the intensity of his emotional fixation on his perceived enemies, nor with the distortions of Islam that attend his fundamentalist stance. In particular, I object to his treatment of Najat, a fellow Klub member and Muslim, whom he treats despicably simply because she is female.

"'Only because the Imam is so firmly set on his inclusion in the Kultur Klub do I tolerate Ibrahim Yassin. And even the Imam has expressed his doubts.

"'"You know," he said to me when we were alone together after Ibrahim's first interview, "I am among those born before the camps existed. I remember how my people were. The Land of Milk and Honey was never a paradise, my friend, but it was a pleasant place. There were olive groves and fields with crops and herds of sheep. People lived simply but they had enough – and they were free.

"'"Then, in 1948, when the land was taken and my people were herded like their own sheep into the camps, that generation – my parents' generation, the first in the camps – expended all their energy just surviving. My generation had the benefit of their hard work and some of us were able to get educations or to establish small businesses. The children of my generation, though – that's a different matter. They were born in captivity and they are angry. They have no outlet for their energy and intelligence. Their rage and frustration grow by the day.... Even we are afraid of them."

"'If it were my decision alone, I never would have invited Ibrahim to join, nor would I tolerate his continued membership now. There is something about this young man that makes my hackles rise, may God forgive me for my intolerance!'"

X draws her breath in sharply again because, gazing over Jamal's arm, she sees that the next journal heading is her own name. Jamal glances at her, his jaw set, as if her unwitting appearance in Father Christopher's journal were a deliberate impropriety on her part.

"'Najat Barbary'"

When he reads her name, Jamal's voice is rough with anger.

"'The sole female member of the Kultur Klub is Najat, a delightful, petite young woman who is clearly extremely bright. She speaks, by my last count, seven languages, including two dialects of Arabic, English, French, Spanish, German, and a smattering of Farsi. And I believe her boyfriend, Jamal Faleh, is teaching her the Egyptian language, as well – a special Coptic Christian southern Egyptian dialect laced with Bedouin, the name of which I do not know. I believe she is majoring in pre-Revolutionary Spanish literature, of all things!

"'Najat is self-possessed and sophisticated. Of all the Klub members, she has made the largest strides in fitting into American late-adolescent university culture. She has a cell phone. She wears jeans, has her ears pierced multiple times, and once said the f__ word in front of me, then turned beet red and burst into giggles – a display of modesty that charmed me! With her shoulder-length black hair, her delicate features and huge dark eyes, she is a real beauty – an observation that may seem out of place for a Catholic priest but that is too obvious to ignore.'"

Jamal stops reading, to glance at Najat, who keeps her eyes lowered modestly. She does not need to see his face. She can imagine the mixture of pride and outraged protectiveness that is playing across it now. The hesitation is short and then Jamal begins to read again.

"'Her story, like that of the others, is a bottomless mess of injustice and tragedy. She was born nineteen years ago to well-educated parents in Rafah Camp, the same camp where Ibrahim was born. Her father had been a school administrator and her mother, not surprisingly, a university linguistics professor.

"'*UNRWA* – the *United Nations Relief and Works Agency for Palestinian Refugees in the Near East* – acknowledges that Rafah, out of a total of sixty-one camps, is the worst of the worst. Refugees are unspeakably crowded and the living conditions are atrocious.

"'Najat's family's home was typical of dwellings there: a concrete shack measuring 9-by-13 feet – and housing *seventeen* members of her family! Sewage stands in open channels throughout the lanes (there are no streets) running among the hovels. Flies, filth and stench compete with the uproar of so many compacted lives to create an atmosphere of incredible stress.

"'"The lives of the women are intolerable," Najat said softly during our first interview. She shook her head worriedly, looking down at the floor. "They try to keep things clean, but the floors are dirt and there is no water. Every drop has to be carried from the communal faucet and in my family's case that faucet was more than a hundred yards away. My mother, my aunts, my sisters and I – we all made trips many times a day to the faucet where we had to wait in line. Sometimes, the Israeli soldiers urinated in the water to punish us for some unrest, but worse was when the water just stopped and we would go without it for days.

"'"Can you imagine – women give *birth* in those conditions! They try to raise their children, keep them fed and clean! It is an endless labor and completely without thanks. Their men abuse them, too, sometimes. And there is no one to protect them."

""The only job that Najat's mother could find was a very low paying one in a sweatshop making T-shirts from cloth imported by the Occupying Authority. The finished garments are then transported back into Israel for sale, as the Palestinians cannot afford them. Najat's father, along with the other men in the camp, was mostly idle, spending his days in conversation with other men or sipping coffee in the makeshift coffeehouse.

""'You must understand our dilemma," Najat said during that first interview. "The Gaza Strip is only 7 miles wide and 25 miles long. In that space, until 2005, lived 2,400 Israelis in nineteen very fertile settlements subsidized by Israel. Those settlements used one third of the land and 96 percent of the water. The remainder of the land and water was for us, the Palestinian refugees – one and a half *million* of us! Can you *imagine?* The Gaza is the most densely populated and poorest place on Earth!

""'It is so hard for the women, especially. The mullahs and the Rabbinical Courts of the Israeli Occupying Authority forbid contraception or abortion. Can you see what happens? Women cannot control their own bodies. They are pregnant again and again. Many have ten, twelve, even fifteen children!

""'I know one woman, Deen'a, who has *twenty-five* children! Can you imagine such a thing? Her husband will not let her stop because the boys are getting killed fighting as guerillas. She must keep having babies to support the PLO, as if her body is a machine for making weapons! She has gone to the clinic, trying to get the doctor to say she has cancer so she can have her uterus removed. But the doctor is a fundamentalist and he told her husband, and she was beaten.

""'The bodies of the women are exhausted and yet they still must care for their children. And how do they feed them? There is no work. Their men are depressed and they cannot or will not work – even if there were jobs, which there are not."

"'Najat's hands, lying in her lap, were twisting about one another. She could not meet my eyes because hers were filled with tears. Nevertheless, she kept on in a determined whisper.

"''The lucky ones qualify for Special Hardship Case. That means they get food rations twice a month – some flour and sugar and four small cans of meat. They can get used clothing and blankets when they are available. And they receive two dollars for each family member, per year. Can you imagine? And what of those who do not qualify? On what do you imagine *they* survive? No, Father Christopher, the situation is impossible!"

"''But Najat,' I protested, 'you're a woman, and you got an education. Your application says that you were in university, even before you came to the United States.'

"'She lifted her head, then, with a glare that shot right through me. 'University!' she spat. 'Do you want to know about that university? That university was founded by the Saudi Arabian government – and it is fundamentalist Muslim. Hamas and its *Izz ad-Din al-Qassam* Brigades hide their weapons there!

"''Al Hazar University in Cairo – the greatest seat of Muslim learning in the world, as I am sure you know – refuses to accredit our university in Gaza. To go there, I must wear the full *hijab* – a head veil, a complete body veil, my face covered, even *gloves* on my hands! If I would wear *this*...' She swept her hand from her shoulder to her knees, taking in her jeans and sweater in a gesture of dismissal, 'they would stone me. So yes, I was in university – but did I learn anything but the suppression of women? No, I did not!'

"'I was astonished by the vehemence of her manner. I had not expected it from so small and delicate a woman. Her anger seemed larger than her physical body, extending out beyond it like an aura of flame.

"'Apparently, the women of Najat's family are exceptional in that they are instrumental in a women's movement aimed at educating the young women of the Palestinian camps.

"'"There is an underground movement – very secret, very dangerous. Women teaching women. If they are caught, they are beaten. There are no leaders. There is no meeting place. It is all very – what is the word? – *fluid*. The women whisper it among themselves at the water faucet, or waiting at the clinic.

"'"My mother and her sisters – my aunties – were very involved in this. They felt that because they are literate, they must share their knowledge with others who have less fortune.

"'"My Aunty Zahira can sew and embroider, so she taught the other women, and now they have started a cooperative to market their work. Aunty Rada knows how to read and so she goes to the women's homes while their husbands are at the coffeehouse, and teaches them. She gives them books for practice that they must hide so their husbands do not find them. If they find them, they beat the women and also, they watch them so they cannot meet again.

"'"When I was very young, I learned to read from my mother and then I, too, began teaching. One day, when I was at a woman's house – her name was Isam – her husband came home early. He saw us with the book. He became so angry! It was very terrifying. He threw the book into the cooking fire and then he hit Isam so hard that her tooth flew out of her mouth. He kept hitting her and hitting her. What could I do? I was only twelve and very small for my age. I ran away. I am so ashamed to tell you that. I ran home and I never went back to see Isam again."

"'That concluded my first interview with Najat because she burst into tears and ran from the room.

"'I expected that she would not return. Perhaps it was too daunting, I thought, to ask a woman to be part of such an overwhelmingly masculine organization. The Imam and I have searched for other foreign women who are orphaned through traumatic political circumstances, but they are hard to find. The few whom we did locate refused to consider joining the Kultur Klub. They were frightened and clearly felt that the Klub exposed them in ways that would only increase their vulnerability.

"'So it was quite a surprise to me when, the following day, Najat suddenly appeared at my office door.

""'I am so sorry!" she began, her eyes averted from my outstretched hand. I was at fault – the reflex reaction to shake her hand offended her cultural restriction against women being touched by men not of their family.

""'Yesterday, I was such a coward. Please forgive me."

"'I protested; I soothed; I got her seated with a cup of hot tea. I said that she was very courageous, indeed, to re-turn to face me. Somehow, we made it through the opening difficulties and returned to the previous day's explorations.

""'It makes me very sad to talk about these things," she began, by way of explanation. "The situation is so – *crazy!* The women want to learn. They want to work. They want to limit their family so that the children have enough to eat and so that they can be educated.

""'But our religion does not honor women... Let me say that differently. Islam *does* honor women, but the fundamentalists interpret the *Qu'ran* so that women have no power at all – even if it will help the family to have more money; even if the father *knows* his daughter is very intelligent and deserves an education. Still, the men see this as a loss of power, if their women have such advancement. And so, the intelligence and the ambition of the women are wasted. It is a very terrible situation. That is why the women of my

family were part of the underground movement – not like
Leila Kahled, of course..."

""'I'm sorry...who?"

""'But surely you have heard of her – Leila Kahled? She
is famous for hijacking airplanes to protest the treatment of
Palestinians. She says that occupation of our native lands by
Israel and the United Nations is the true terrorism, and that
the PLO is a legitimate organization of resistance."

""'Ah yes! Now I remember." But in truth, I didn't. Later,
I did some research and discovered that this amazing woman, beautiful and passionate, repeatedly stated that the aim
of the hijackings was to gain international recognition of
the plight of Palestinians. They are not a refugee problem
to be resolved through charity, she claimed, but an issue of
national dislocation and of the desire for self-determination
and the rightful return of sovereign Palestinian land.

""'She's someone you admire?" I asked, fishing for information that might jog my memory.

""'Oh! But yes! She is...is...an *icon!* The women in my
family adore her!"

""'You come from some very strong women, it seems."

""'Yes. But just listen to what happened to them! My
Aunty Zahira was arrested by the Occupying Authority
and taken away to prison in Israel. Do you want to know
why? Because the authorities came to destroy the house of
a woman who was learning to embroider. Her son, who was
only ten, threw a stone at a soldier, and that is what the
Israelis do in return: they come with a bulldozer and knock
down the house. But this poor woman had eleven children
and her husband was killed in the PLO. If they destroyed
her house, where would she go? What would happen to her
children?

""'My Aunty Zahira was so angry! She stood in the way
of the bulldozer and she shouted at the soldiers, so they arrested her and we have not seen her again. We have heard

that people are tortured in the prisons in Israel and so we are very sad."

""Najat paused and I searched for something I could say that would be appropriately compassionate. But in truth, I was too horrified to speak. I had no idea that such things went on! What could I, a sheltered and privileged American male, say to this woman?

"""But what happened to my Aunty Rada is far worse," she went on in a small but determined voice. "She was in a home, one day, teaching a woman and her two oldest daughters to read. They did not know, but the oldest son was outside the door, listening. Suddenly, he came into the room and just as it was with me, he started to beat the woman. He beat his sisters, too. Then, he turned on my Aunty Rada, who was trapped back in the corner, and he beat her, too.

"""She came home covered in blood, but we thought she would be okay. But he hit her too hard. Something happened in her brain. She got a terrible headache – and then she went into convulsions and died."

""Najat took a deep, ragged breath. "My mother was so depressed, then, without her two sisters. She cried and cried and then she stopped crying, and that was even worse. She sat in the corner and did not work. She did not speak. Her eyes were open, but they looked at nothing.

"""It will not surprise you, I think, what happened next. She got sick. There is always sickness in the camps. It waits like a devil for the people who become weak. And so, two months after my Aunty Rada was killed, my mother died, too."

""We sat for a long while in silence. Finally, I ventured, very gently, 'And your father, Najat? What happened to him?'

"""Ayyy, my Papa! He was a good man, you know? Not like the others, so crazy against women. He was educated.

He had lived in the world and he understood – that is why he allowed my mother and my aunties to do what they did.

""This is what happened to my Papa. He found out that one of my brothers, Abdul, was using drugs. Yes! I see you are surprised. Drugs in the camps! Can you imagine? How do people get the drugs? How do they have the money? You are wondering the same questions that my father thought.

""He began to ask questions. He discovered that drugs are brought into the camp from the sea, smuggled in through tunnels under the wire. And there is more. The Occupying Authority knows this! Oh yes! They turn their eyes away and pretend they do not see. Why? Because a young man stupefied by drugs is less dangerous than one training to shoot guns, that is why.

""And do you know what? The mullah knows it, too. My father went to him and asked him to do something; to use his authority to stop the drug trafficking. But the mullah said that my father was wrong...that there are no drugs. Two nights later, a gang of men found my father and beat him to death. The women told me that Papa was foolish. He should not have gone to the mullah because the mullah makes money from the drugs. He gains power by being the connection. Can you imagine such an evil thing?"

""So, what happened to *you*, then? It must have been very dangerous for you."

""Dangerous? Father Christopher," she said very slowly and deliberately, as if she were addressing a simpleton, "Every. Single. Day. Of my *life*. In Rafah Camp. Was *dangerous!* Do you somehow imagine that there is a *safe* place there?" She looked at me, stymied, as if I hadn't heard a single word she'd been telling me.

""Well, no, of course, I understand..." I stammered. I couldn't continue. She was holding me in a gaze that completely flustered me.

""""Yes, of course. You understand." She stated it so flatly that my own words condemned me.

""""Najat, forgive me. I'm a man. And what's more, I've had male power and privilege my entire life. I have no right to tell you that I understand what you've experienced."

""""Thank you," she said with icy dignity.

"'Then, after a pause, "So, you want to know what happened to me. Okay. This is what happened. I was going to the clinic. I had some symptoms like my mother. I met a doctor there – a woman. She knew about me. She was a friend of my mother and aunties. She told me that I had to leave the camp. She had a way to do it. She is part of an underground movement of women on *both* sides of the wire.

""""Can you believe that there are Israeli women who are willing to help us? Yes! It is true! These women are working for peace, while our governments wage war on each other!

""""The doctor gave me admission forms for this university. She told me to fill them out. I laughed at her. 'How am I going to go to America when I cannot even go to *Jerusalem?* But she told me there is a way. When I had completed the forms, she put them in a mail pouch with medical forms from the clinic. The pouch went to a clinic on the Israeli side, where her friend waited for my forms.

""""This woman – may Allah always protect her! – had false papers made for me and sent them back in the pouch. With those papers, I was able to cross over into Israel. That woman – I cannot say her name because I promised – kept me in her home. She made the arrangements for me to come to America, with the help of a Christian church group. Can you imagine? And I cannot even write to thank her. It is forbidden. But I pray for her, every single day of my life."

"'I am humbled by my interviews with Najat. She is correct. I don't have the smallest idea of the abuses she has suffered in her young life. After that second talk, I was forced to consider that the Imam and I have started the Kultur

Klub because God willed that *we* should be educated and opened to the suffering of the world! It frightens me, the thought that these young people are martyrs to *our* ignorance and arrogance.

"'I have spoken with all of Najat's professors. They are unanimous in their praise of her. They cannot say enough about her intelligence, her sparkling personality and her beauty. Clearly, I am not the only one who has been captivated by her!

"'If I have any reservations about Najat's membership in the Klub, they revolve around the male members. I have heard Ibrahim being verbally dismissive and abusive to her. And some of the young men sniff around her like hyenas around a piece of meat. Only Jamal seems to have genuine respect for her.

"'I am resolved to keep a very close watch over her, so that the Klub does not become yet another anguish in a life already so lashed by them.'"

Jamal stops reading and they sit for a long while in silence, each lost in their separate thoughts and griefs. Finally, Jamal reaches out and squeezes her hand, briefly and hard. "I must take this back before Father Christopher is finished teaching."

She nods numbly. "Yes," she whispers. She does not even rise to see him out.

X stares emptily at the television screen, lost in remembrance. After a commercial break, the television station will return to its special news programming, the announcer says. Soon, X imagines, the media people in the field must begin to pack up their equipment, weary from a long day. She is weary, too. Without awareness that it is happening, her head droops and she sleeps, still sitting at her post.

Almost immediately, she begins to dream:

In the tent of the Incident Commander, a short conversation takes place, as he enters a portable sound proof booth and speaks into an encrypted line in the voice she knows so well. "Sir? It's done. The bird has flown. Tomorrow, this will all be finished... Yes, Sir... All major networks, yes, Sir... Yes, Sir. Good night, Sir."

In her small room, X awakens, having forgotten some important part of the dream. There is something white – is it a piece of paper? A sheet? And there is a figure – a man, she thinks. What is he doing? Something with the white thing. She tries to remember, but is interrupted by the voice of the FBI's Public Information Officer, who is beginning to read his information sheets, identifying the terrorists, twelve in all, with a brief synopsis of their personal histories.

As he reads, X is frozen in horror: her name and that of the eleven Brothers are being reported on television!

They know who we are! Allah!

What truly stuns her, however, is the version of their lives she is hearing: Hansi, a Hutu militiaman responsible for murdering hundreds of Tutsis! Jamal, a member of a co-vert Egyptian death squad! And she – *Allah! What have we done?* – a murderous operative of the PLO, a latter-day Leila Khaled!

Day Four

Sophia

She's in the corridor. The lights are still on and, to her astonishment, Muzak is still inanely serenading the bodies sprawled down its length. It is deep in the earliest hours of the morning – she can tell by the fatigue that refuses to relinquish her muscles. Her brain, however, is perfectly awake. She knows what she must do.

She grabs the ankles of the first bloated, reeking corpse and, straining backward, begins to drag it off the heap in front of their shattered door.

Her ears are alert, over the soft shushing sound of the dragging body, for any other sound. She comes to a corner and turns to the left, but too sharply. The upper body of her burden wraps itself around the corner and refuses to budge. She strains and snarls under her breath, "Come on, you bastard! Come *on!*" She gives a last pull and the body breaks loose and lurches toward her. Its heels, shod in expensive Italian leather slip-ons, shoot forward and smack into her breasts. She pushes back from them in disgust, then keeps on pulling.

Suddenly, her rump collides with something and, dropping his ankles, she spins in alarm. There, her face white with terror, is a small woman all in black who is in the act of dropping the ankles of a huge, bloated man whose legs she has been holding at her waist like the traces of a cart. She and Sophia stare at one another in astonishment.

"Who...who *are* you?" Sophia manages to breathe.

The woman stares back at her, too terrified to speak.

Sophia's eyes descend, taking in the handgun thrust into the woman's waistband. "Are you...one of *them?* A *terrorist?*"

Slowly, numbly, the woman nods her head, a movement so slight Sophia barely sees it.

Without hesitation, Sophia lunges for her, her left hand reaching for the gun, her right striking a blow under the woman's chin that jerks her head backwards. It should have been a killing blow, but Sophia is out of training. The woman sits down hard, her eyes wide in surprise, her fall cushioned by the huge corpse. She lands squarely on its belly, sinks in and is almost enfolded.

And then the corpse emits a huge, foul-smelling, very noisy fart.

Sophia's eyes meet those of the small woman. Something simmers between them, something ageless and pure. Something female.

They both begin to giggle.

With the gun trained on the woman, Sophia backs away and makes her exit, still laughing.

The smell is what wakes her, a smile still crimped on her lips. It's getting overpowering; she can barely breathe. Something has to be done.

Betty was in the bathroom retching, early this morning. And for a group that's been without a square meal for three days, no one seems to mind that breakfast is a Saltine and a slice of cheese with black coffee, eaten in silence.

She just can't figure out how to move the bodies without exposing them to maximum danger. It isn't just moving the drink machine from the door – even if she can. It's so heavy, and now the linoleum is wrinkled underneath.

She doubts she can do it alone, and who could possibly help her? Ondine? She's so slight, it's not likely. Heddi? No way. She's the type who strains to lift her own suitcase. Betty's too hysterical. The smell would probably make her sick,

right when Sophia needed her most. Erika's out, obviously.
That leaves Pearl. Goddess knows, she'd give it a try – and it
would snap her old bones like dry sticks.

Even if she can move the thing, then the real problem
comes. They'd be completely exposed and vulnerable. Once
she goes out into the corridor, she's a sitting duck. And if
she's spotted – or if they kill her – it would lead the terrorists
straight to the rest.

And where is she going to drag the bodies *to*? The terrorists, if they're patrolling the ends of the concourse, doubt-
lessly look down it and know where every body is lying by
now.

It's just one of those Devil and the deep blue sea situations – which doesn't mean they can just ignore it.

"Ladies, listen up! We've got a problem and we've got
to deal with it. I'm sure you know what I'm talking about."

They look at her with haggard, deadened eyes. No one
says a word.

Pearl begins rooting around in her pack, her head half-
submerged in it, industrious as a dog unburying a bone. No
one even looks her way. The rest look like they're on heavy
drugs.

"I know it's hard, but we have to..."

Pearl emerges from the mouth of her pack and victoriously thrusts something into the air on the end of one gray
claw.

"I gots it! I knew I had one in thar somewhar. An here
tis!"

"What? What is it?" They're all squinting at the thing
Pearl's waving around, like an excited child.

"A mirrah. A dentist mirrah. I dug it outta his trash a
hunert years ago an I been carryin it round ever since. I
knowed I'd need it one day fer somethin!"

They're all staring at her, mystified. What can she possibly be thinking?

"Explain your plan to us, Pearl. Please."

"Doncha see? Sophia thar, she leans the machine for-wart, an someone small, me or the Onion, we squeezes back behind thar an sticks this here mirrah through one a them bullet holes in the door. An then we cain see what's out thar without havin ta move that damn machine!"

Sophia has to admit, it's a start. It doesn't get the bodies moved or even the machine, for that matter, but it at least gives them some notion of what they're up against before they un-barricade the door.

You might know it would be Pearl who would come up with a solution. She's as pleased as punch with herself, too.

"That's a brilliant idea, Pearl! Let's do it!"

Sophia pushes herself up off the floor and it seems to take almost more energy than she's got. Even the war never brutalized her like this has – but then, she was a lot younger in those days.

Pearl clings to the front of the candy machine and pulls herself up, too. The rest look at them with dawning but completely passive interest, as if she and Pearl were on television.

Sophia pats Pearl on the shoulder, as she scuttles past. "You gonna be the one to do this?"

"Well, I been a-waitin fer the Lone Ranger ta come along, but looks lak he's been delayed."

"Okay, then. Let's get 'er done."

Sophia braces her right shoulder against the corner of the machine and reaches toward the back, engulfing it in a big embrace. Her fingers find the back edge and she grips it like the jaws of a trap.

"Okay, Pearl. I'm going to pull it forward onto me. You tell me when you can slip back behind it."

"Ready!" is all Pearl says. She's braced like a runner about to start a relay race, one foot forward, the dentist's mirror in her fist like a baton. Just for an instant, Sophia thinks she sees something else; something eternal – one of the Furies shrouded in gray mist, or Hecate in her swirling cloak of night – and she feels a bolt of love for this old woman go through her, so fierce that it's like a pain.

Then, she summons every ounce of her strength and pulls the machine onto her chest, like a lover.

Heddi

If that machine topples, it'll smash Sophia flat, but the three of them just sit here like toadstools. Maybe it's the stench that's gotten to them. Heddi feels as if she'd been administered ether.

As soon as a crack opens at the back of the machine, Pearl wedges herself into it like a scabrous old rat darting into a hole. There's the crackle of glass grinding underfoot and then a long pause.

Heddi glances at Sophia. She's bent backward at the waist, hugging the machine and Heddi can't see her face but she hears her breathing coming in the kind of deep, measured breaths that weightlifters use.

Finally, Sophia grunts, "What'd you see, Pearl?"

There's another long pause and Heddi's beginning to wonder if Pearl went back there and died. She had a rat do that behind her refrigerator once.

Then there's the scrape of glass again and Pearl sticks her head out to make her pronouncement. "Nothin," she intones gravely.

Suddenly, Ondine is up off the floor and dashes over to her. "Pearl," she whispers urgently, "what do you mean? Sophia can't hold this thing much longer."

Pearl shakes her head like a truculent child and steps out from behind the machine. "Ain't nothin out thar, I tell ya."

Ondine snatches the dentist's mirror from Pearl without a word and wedges herself behind the machine.

Sophia gasps out one word: "*Hurry!*"

As if in a trance, Heddi sees Betty struggle out of one of the plastic chairs which clings, momentarily, to her rump. She pushes it off with annoyance. Then, with surprising speed, she moves to Sophia and braces herself against the upper corners of the machine.

Pearl is doing a kind of shuffling dance, like a molting and deranged chicken, craning her head sideways, trying to see into the crack where Ondine has disappeared.

Heddi alone is disengaged. This is a complete descent of libido. She can't lift a finger.

Ondine's slender backside comes wiggling out of the crack. She's holding the mirror in her fist by its thin handle, like a disheveled fairy queen with her wand.

"Pearl's right!" Her creamy forehead wrinkles in puzzlement. "There's nothing out there!"

Pearl gives a victorious cackle, as Sophia and Betty heave the machine back against the door. It slams back with a leaden thump and a grinding crunch of shattered glass.

Betty puts an arm around Sophia, who is breathing like a freight train and white with fatigue. She brings the plastic chair for her to sit in. Heddi knows she should offer her the armchair, but she seems to be unable to move.

"Tell us," Sophia wheezes.

Ondine steps into the center of their ragged circle, still holding the mirror as if ready to bless them or grant a wish. "Pearl's right. There are no bodies out there."

They look from one to another, blankly.

"I think the bodies have been dragged away in the night. There's a trail of blackened blood smeared down the corridor toward the right. I think the smell will get better now. There's a pool of coagulated blood right outside the door. That must be what we're still smelling."

As if that announcement has exhausted her, Ondine sinks to the floor in one graceful, yogic motion.

"How could that happen without us hearing it?" Betty asks, puzzled.

"Maybe we're all so exhausted, we're sleeping better than we think," Ondine says, with a shrug.

A long silence ensues.

"Well," Sophia says finally, "either the Good Guys are making some inroads at last, or the terrorists are preparing to storm our battlements. And there's no way to tell which it might be."

Sophia

It must be the heat. The bodies produce heat, just like she thought. They have to get rid of the bodies in order to scan the building and find where the living bodies are massed. All that decomposition is throwing their readings off. That must be it.

And that means they're preparing to do something – finally.

But how will they know who's a terrorist and who's a civilian?

Things are about to get dicey.

Heddi

It's as if a plug has been pulled and their little group of automatons has ceased to function. Heddi's got to rally herself before the silence encases them like wet cement. She clears her throat, as if revving up the requisite energy.

"I guess I'll invite myself to start this morning.

"I've been lying awake all night, pondering my life. What it'll be like, if...*when*...we finally get out of here.

"This event that we're experiencing is like a huge axe that's come chopping down, just cutting all the former years of my life off from all the years that will follow. Everything from now on will be *BTA* or *ATA* – *Before the Terrorist Attack* or *After the Terrorist Attack*.

"We talk in depth psychology about transformational events in the psyche – but I never *dreamed*, either literally or metaphorically, that something of this magnitude would happen to me."

Before this, she's been trying to keep everything as normal as possible. Hal may be gone – and it's looking like he's really gone for good – but she doesn't have to have every part of her life disrupted. Her lawyer says Hal'll have to give her alimony once this thing goes to court. In the meantime, there's plenty in the bank – savings and checking both – to sustain her. And she has the income from her practice. And there's the trust fund that her father set up years ago, and the investments to divvy up. Financially, she's fine.

Keeping things going as usual means keeping Antonio to do the yard, and his wife Alma for the housework. It's too much for Heddi to do herself and she's not inclined to do those things anyway. It means keeping the house, while Hal moves out. It means keeping the furniture and the art because most of it originally belonged to her parents. In other words, it means keeping everything just as it was, with only Hal missing.

But last night, she got this wild hair. She thought, *What if I changed everything?*

What if she sold the house and moved to that retirement community up on the north coast? She's betting there are lots of women there at loose ends who'd love to start analysis. Maybe do something physical for the first time since she was a girl – abalone diving or sea kayaking.

Or maybe she could go back to Zurich to the Institute and teach.

Or retire, and take up watercolors.

Or write that book she's been imagining, compiling everything she's learned in all these years as an analyst.

Sometime in the night, the ideas just started wriggling inside her, like minnows waking to a spring thaw.

Lying here on this cold linoleum with a roll of toilet paper under her neck has done what fifteen years of analysis with Dr. Copeland couldn't. It's been a portal into a new life.

And all she has to do is live long enough to get there!

Or...*almost* all she has to do.

And it's that other thing she has to do that she wants to talk about this morning. She hasn't been fully honest with them. She's presented herself as a successful doctor whose main fault is a kind of professional blindness that allowed her life slip through her hands.

That's all true. But it's not all.

They've all been so forthcoming. They've exposed vulnerable parts of themselves in a way that would take years in analysis. That, Heddi supposes, is the gift of this horrible experience, if gift there be.

Last night, as she lay here and reviewed each of their stories, she was just amazed by the integrity they've each brought to their lives – the willingness to examine them and endure them and transform them.

And she'll be honest – it made her ashamed.

"Oh, Heddi!" Ondine protests. "You're being so harsh with yourself!"

"Yes, ashamed, Ondine. I know you want to leap in and soothe me. Fix it, so that I can see myself in the same kind light you do.

"And maybe in good time, I will. But first, I have to do some disclosing of my own. And that's what I intend to do this morning, if you've all got the time for it."

Pearl chortles, her back to the candy machine. "Some-one call mah stockbroker fer me – tell him I cain't come rat now fer that meetin."

"Yes, and cancel my hair appointment, while you're at it!" Betty chimes in.

"And here I was just going out for pizza," Ondine adds.

"Alright, all of you! I'll get you! This'll be the longest, most boring story yet!"

Heddi comes from a very wealthy family, as she supposes they may have guessed. There was a big house, fancy parties, a stable of horses of Derby caliber, tennis courts, an Olympic-sized pool with a faux-Grecian-temple pool house – the works.

She attended the best girls' school on the east coast and could speak French before she was twelve and do Latin declensions like a Roman. She learned how to sit like a lady, greet people with aplomb, and set a table with everything from fish knives and sorbet spoons to five different wine and water glasses. She also learned that women of her class never buy clothing that is too tight or made from synthetic materials, to jump a horse, dance the waltz and foxtrot, and boss the servants. Her school groomed her to be cool, classic and superior.

All this, of course, was not to fit the girls out for authentic lives, but to make them marriageable to men of their own – or better still, an even higher – social stratum. The thought that they might have ideas of their own about how to proceed with their lives never penetrated the silk-lined confines of Miss Pryor's School for Girls. Such notions, in fact, were discouraged when they erupted, *sui generis*, from their heads, like Athena from the head of Zeus. They were considered as freak emissions of working-class mentality; young ladies were not meant for lives of labor but of courtly ease and elegance.

Heddi's mother was such a product of such an upbringing. Oh, she was beautiful! Elegant! Always so coolly remote in her beige cashmere crewnecks and pearls, her designer slacks and skirts and jackets. She always looked like she'd just stepped out of a beautician's chair, a designer's boutique, or a glass box where she was kept against any disturbing influences upon her perfect blonde pageboy or her spotless white linen.

And Heddi's father was her perfect match, taller than she by a good foot, two years older, wealthy, tanned, handsome and charming. His ebullience was the perfect compliment to her composure. They were the social catch, the couple to have at any party, wedding or funeral, and Heddi was their sole, perfect child. They were considered to be the first family, nonpareil, of their town.

That was the operative myth that Heddi grew up with: they were perfect, beyond reproach. And more than that, they were ultimately desirable, enviable and the subject of endless inept emulations.

"Imitation is the sincerest form of flattery," her mother used to say when Heddi complained that some town girl had run out and bought a pair of red shoes or a pink belt or a green sweater just like hers. It went without saying that such behavior was gauche and pathetic.

She guesses she was about six when she first became aware of the night terrors, although it's more than likely that they had begun long before that. In dreams, bad men menaced her. She would flee in terror through dark ruined hallways with tattered wallpaper hanging in shredded curtains, and black, gaping doorways giving onto empty, echoing rooms. Alone and in terror, she would run and run while the bad men pursued her, gaining on her, reaching for her... and then she would wake up, screaming.

Night after night, her nanny – a huge-bosomed black woman named Matilda – would come hustling in her terry cloth robe and fuzzy pink slippers, and hold her to her giant breast, rocking and crooning, until Heddi could sleep again.

Once, her mother took her to a psychiatrist, who rec-ommended tranquilizers. Her mother hustled them out in an elegant huff. The women of their family did not *need* tranquilizers, even if – or especially if – they were not yet women.

After that, the onus fell on Heddi. She was being naugh-ty. She was failing her elite upbringing – to be out of control emotionally was simply *déclassé*.

Heddi has a filmy recollection of those early years. In the evening, she would have her supper in the nursery, be bathed, dressed in her nightie and put to bed. Then, magi-cally, the door would fly open and Mother, looking like a fairytale princess, would swoop in. Maybe she would be in a slim black dinner dress, or a pink lace sheath by Balmain. Best was when she was on her way to a fancy ball and she would appear in floor-length silk taffeta or chiffon, with glit-tering jeweled necklaces and her beautiful hair swept up to show off her long, white neck.

God! She was a vision!

Like a dog who knows by the shoes you put on whether he's going to get a walk or not, Heddi came to know by her clothing what her mother was scheduled to do: dinner in, dinner out, cocktail party, civic event, afternoon or evening wedding, or charity ball. And Heddi, as devoted, hopeful and forlorn as any dog, took her mother's meager offerings from her jeweled fingers as if they were tidbits of sirloin.

Her mother would bend and kiss her and call her her Little Angel and then, with a silken rustle like the sudden start of birds' wings, she would depart as quickly as she had come, leaving the room vibrating with her beauty and sigh-ing with her French perfume.

Matilda would stick her head in and say, "Now, you lucky Little Angel, you go to sleep now, you hear?" And she would turn out the light. Heddi would snuggle down in the dark-ness feeling like the luckiest, most loved little girl in the world.

And a few hours later, she would erupt from sleep, screaming in terror.

Sometimes, after her evening bath, instead of a nightie she would be dressed in a pretty dress and Maryjanes and Matilda would use a curling iron to make sausage curls in her fine blonde hair. Then, she would be hustled downstairs to make an appearance.

In the salon, there would be a crowd of elegant people, sipping from martini glasses and making a subdued murmur. When Heddi arrived, pushed from behind by Matilda's firm hand, the murmur would suddenly stop. All eyes would turn toward her. Either Mother or Father, whoever was closest, would take her by the elbow and say, "Say 'good evening' to the nice people, Heddi," and Heddi would curtsey to no one in particular and everyone in general and say, "Good evening."

Then, she would be led to certain strategic figures in the crowd by whom she was duly greeted and whom she greeted in return, always with a curtsey. Men would hold her hand just a bit too long and make vague sexual innuendos about what would happen to her when she was "of age," and wom-en would coo over her, saying, "My! Aren't you the prettiest thing!"

Then, she was allowed to take a canapé or a bonbon from one of the trays and was ushered to the door where she was expected to curtsey once again and say, "Good night." Her mother or father would kiss her once on the cheek and she was handed back through the portal into Matilda's wait-ing hands.

This was the regular order of business until, one night when she was eleven, her mother killed herself.

Or at least, that is what Heddi later came to understand. The official cause of death was listed as an automobile accident, but Little Miss Big Ears, frantic to know what was going on, loitered outside the kitchen just beyond the all-seeing eyes of the servants and there she heard words like *hooch, dead drunk* and *suicide*.

In tones barely audible even at close range, she heard a whispered tale of tremendous speed and her mind provided the details: her mother, clutching the steering wheel of her silver Mercedes convertible in strangler's hands – but clad in suede driving gloves, nonetheless – her eyes staring the glazed stare of the possessed, as she tore down the road at blurring speed.

On a straight stretch where no one, not even a dead drunk, would lose control, she inexplicably cranked the wheel and rolled herself over and over into a creek bed where she came to rest, upside down. Her lovely head hung from the shattered side window, her neck broken, her long blonde hair floating in the shallows of the creek.

Blood alcohol level was whispered and a number given, and *tsk tsking* issued from various lips. The Sheriff's name, the time of night, the existence of a note, and the condition of the car – these were gobbets of information Heddi's young brain could not presently register but stored away to be remembered years later in an analytic office in Zurich.

After her mother's death, she was sent off to Miss Pryor's School for Girls as a boarder rather than a day student. She rarely saw her father, except on major holidays and then only as he slipped off to other events. She grew up and went to college, taking the strange notion that she wanted to be a doctor, and studied pre-med. Her father was too otherwise occupied to object.

Heddi was about to graduate when she met – or re-met – Marcus Wilbur. The Wilburs were a good family and had been close friends with hers before her mother's death.

Heddi and Marcus had never been friends – who *had* friends, really, under such circumstances? – but they had had a mildly conspiratorial acquaintance that allowed for forbidden adventures like tree climbing or creek wading and tadpole catching.

When they met again at a luncheon at the country club, they were both twenty and on the verge of graduating. They must have recognized immediately that they, born into the same class and educated in the same ways, were destined for one another. Things transpired quickly, and soon Marcus came to the house to ask her father for her hand in marriage.

Into the library they both went, with Heddi anxiously waiting in the salon. A faint wave of cigar smoke wafted through, as Heddi arranged the pleats of her linen skirt with nervous fingers. A long silence followed.

Then, suddenly, the door of the library burst open. Marcus charged through as if he'd been shot from a cannon. Heddi thought he was headed straight toward her, to sweep her up, kiss her and claim her for his own. Instead, he raced blindly past her and, not waiting for the butler, threw open the front door and was gone.

Heddi stood thunderstruck in the entry hall, her mouth hanging open just like the front door, as if to call him back with words that would not come.

Slowly, she turned to see her father standing in the doorway of the library, glaring at her. "You are forbidden to see that boy again," he said coldly. Then, he turned his back and closed the library door.

Heddi was too numb to cry. The shock simply stunned her.

Everything was so right. Marcus had studied diplomacy and had his first posting already promised in South Africa. His father had bought him a house in Durban with a sweeping view of the coast and large formal gardens. She and Marcus had fantasized big game hunting on the veldt and explorations into the mysterious Congo. They even had the name of their first child picked out: Francesca Duchesse, if it were a girl, Marcus Aurelius, Junior, if it were a boy.

How could this be happening?

One time only she dared to ask her father for an explanation, and he became so enraged that she retreated in terror, while the servants scurried around her, eyes downcast, as if she were a leper. She tried to call Marcus's home several times, only to be told by the butler that Mr. Wilbur was not presently available.

Finally, in desperation, she got into her car one day and drove into the south part of town below the railroad tracks. This was the black section and she, a well-heeled blonde girl in a powder blue Mercedes convertible, aroused more than passing interest.

At a stop sign, a man lounging against the side of a building shouted, "Girl, you better git yousef home rat now. You don' have no *idea* what you doin."

Instead of heeding his advice, Heddi shouted back, "I'm looking for Matilda Johnson's house. Do you know where it is?"

He ambled out from the shade and leaned on the passenger door of her car. A bolt of fear went though her and she thought he was about to climb in and abduct her. Instead, he pointed languidly down the street.

"You go down ta the second cross street an take a lef. Den you go down two streets ta Vine Street an take a rat. The third house on the rat is Matilda's."

"Thank you, sir," she said primly and gunned the car.

"You be careful, you hear?" he shouted after her.

Matilda hadn't changed much in the intervening years. Her hair was a little whiter than gray, her girth somewhat increased, her breasts heavier and lower. She walked a little stiffly, as if something had frozen up in her hips. Other than that, she was as gruff and kindly as ever.

Heddi explained her mission.

"I think I even wept. I *know* I did because I remember her clasping me to her huge bosom just like when I was five, and rocking me. I can remember her smell to this day – a combination of bacon, onions, something spicy like cinnamon and an exotic, musky aroma that must have exuded straight from her own pores. It was a scent from my childhood and it calmed me down.

"What I didn't expect was Matilda's reticence..."

"Marcus Wilbur? That's who you been seein?"

"Yes, Matilda. And I love him so much! I want to marry him!"

Matilda was silent in a way that made Heddi uncomfortable. She seemed to be rummaging deep within herself. Finally, she said, "And you Daddy don' want you ta marry him?"

"No, Matilda. Like I told you. He ran Marcus off. And now Marcus won't even answer my phone calls."

Again there was a deep, ruminating silence. Finally, Matilda sighed and said, "Well, Baby, I think you better listen ta you Daddy. He's got you best interest in his heart."

"Oh Matilda, no! Not you, too!" Heddi moaned.

"Baby," she sighed, "they is some things is best lef alone. You know what I mean?"

"No, Matilda. I do not."

Matilda hoisted herself up from her armchair and, turning her back on Heddi, began plucking yellowed leaves from the African violets on her windowsill. She seemed to be lost in thought and Heddi knew this mood in her and didn't dare interrupt it. If she did, Matilda would automatically take the opposite view from hers. If she let her come to her own conclusions, however, she invariably softened, relented, and supported Heddi however she could.

Heddi glanced around the shabby room. An antique Regulator clock in a chapped brown case ticked lazily. The couch and mismatched chair, both in faded floral upholstery, sagged contentedly. The walls were painted a soft shade of rose, dappled with the slowly fanning shadows of trees. The air was warm, humid and soft, as if they were sunk in a forest glade somewhere in the farthest reaches of Africa – one of those glades she'd hoped to explore with Marcus.

She thought, *So this is the best she can afford, after all those years of taking care of a little rich girl?* And she was ashamed.

Finally, Matilda sat herself down in her armchair and asked, "How old is you now? Seventeen?"

"Matilda! I'm twenty!"

"*Twenty?* My! How time flies."

"I'm going to graduate from college in two more semesters."

"My! Imagine!"

Again, the silence lengthened, wrapping itself around the tranquil room.

"Baby," she began at last, "I don' know I outta be the one who tells you this. Or if *anyone* outta be the one ta tell you. But you done asked an I done thought about it an I think you's old enough ta know."

"Know *what?*"

"Why, exactly what you asked...why you ain't bein' allowed ta marry Mr. Marcus."

"Well...*why?*" Heddi's heart began to race. She knew she was on the verge of a life-altering revelation.

"Well, Baby, because...because..." Matilda sighed deeply, as if releasing the last of her inhibitions, "because Marcus Wilbur is you half-brother."

"My...my...*what?*"

"I know. I know. It ain't easy ta understand. But it's true. Mr. Marcus is you half-brother."

"*How?*"

"Because you Daddy had an affair with Miz Wilbur, that's how."

"How do you know this?"

For the first time, Matilda laughed, a hearty contralto that cleared Heddi's mind to hear it.

"Oh, Honey Child! What *don'* the help in white folks' houses know? They ain't a thing goes on that somebody don' hear or see an report ta everone else. That's what kitchen's is *for*, don' you know? I bet you thought they was for *cookin!* But they is *mills*, Honey Child. Gossip mills, pure an simple. Cookin is always second ta gossip in the white folks' kitchens. That's the Law."

"*Well...!*"

Marcus was her half-brother. Matilda had said it and that meant it was the truth.

Heddi went back to college, to her sorority house, and spent two miserable semesters finishing up.

She confided in her best friend, a sorority sister, about what had happened. "I made *love* with him, Jenny! My God!"

Jenny just laughed. "I practiced sex with my older bother from the time I was twelve. It's a safe way to learn about it," she said with a toss of her head. "Incest is best, Heddi!" she crowed. "Don't sweat it."

Her father came for graduation, bringing a diamond bracelet as a present. He kissed her on the cheek, said he was proud of her, took her dutifully to dinner and departed. He left a three thousand dollar check on the dresser, "for expenses."

Let me know when you need more, his note read. *I expect you'll be wanting your own apartment now.*

And that was that. Heddi entered medical school and did well. She was in her psychiatric residency when she got the call that her father had had a heart attack and died.

Going home to that house was one of the hardest things she'd ever done. It was so huge and silent there at the end of the drive. The servants had been laid off by her father's lawyer and for the first time in her life, she unlocked the big front door with the key he'd given her. It hadn't even occurred to her that she now owned the place. She felt like a trespasser and realized that she had *never* felt welcome there – and nothing about that had changed.

Her father had died in his bedroom and, for some macabre reason, Heddi needed to go up there. Maybe she hoped to see him still lying there, so she could believe he was really gone.

But the room was in perfect order. Tillie, the upstairs maid, would have seen to that before she departed.

Heddi opened his closet. There were his suits hanging neatly spaced, his starched shirts, his sport coats and topcoats. There were neat stacks of cashmere golf sweaters in gorgeous, muted colors and clear plastic boxes holding various hats.

In the drawers of his dresser were neat rows of folded socks, ironed handkerchiefs, rolled belts. There were underwear, tee shirts, pajamas, and silk long johns for skiing. In the narrow top drawer were his watches, tie tacks, cuff links and pins from fraternal organizations. And at the very back, a small black book.

Heddi pulled it out and flipped it open at random. It had blank pages that her father had ruled by hand into separate entries.

Alice G. was the first entry she read, in her father's tiny, neat hand. *Carleton Hotel, Savannah. April 2nd, 2:00 PM.*

The next entry read, *Miriam. 4:30 Wednesday. Prada Towers, Rm. 345.*

The next, *Wilma Herrington. 3:30, Tues., April 10. She will call with arrangements.*

And so it went. In the back was an address book, containing the names, addresses and telephone numbers of over three hundred women, some of whom Heddi knew. Some were the wives of her father's friends, some the mothers of *her* friends and some were her mother's friends. Some were his secretaries, or waitresses and shop girls in town. Some were complete strangers.

They were all rated with stars, from one to five. The dates went back to before Heddi was born.

One of his most consistent trysts during the years Heddi was growing up was Anna Molina, a day student two classes ahead of her at Miss Pryor's School for Girls. Next to Anna's entries were neat calculations: *$500, $250, $350*. All the students knew Anna was from a poor family and they'd always wondered how she managed to pay tuition and wear such pretty clothes. Anna had a five-star rating.

At the beginning of the book were his earliest conquests. For a couple of years around the time of Heddi's birth, Marcus's mother, Millie Wilbur, was a frequent entry. She rated three stars.

In Zurich, Heddi's analyst made her burn the little black book, saying it was therapeutic to do so.

Heddi thought she'd dealt with the collapse of her family myth. She started her analytic practice; decades passed.

By then, she'd married Hal Merriweather. He was a roofing contractor, which was a choice that would have shocked and disgusted her parents. A *big time* roofing contractor – like roofing the opera house or the university library, that kind of thing. High rise buildings, entire housing developments. He was a wealthy man and a happy, lively soul, but still, from working class origins.

She'd had her practice for several years and was successful in her own right, in spite of her inheritance. She married Hal because he made her laugh.

And then the Jon Bennet Ramsey case hit the news.

When the Ramsey thing first broke, she was instantly galvanized. Her fascination was complete. At first, even Dr. Copeland was mystified by her near-obsession.

"Does this child remind you of yourself at her age? The careful presentation? The repression of natural spontaneity?" Dr. Copeland stared at her through his thick horn-rimmed glasses, a frown creasing his forehead.

And Heddi would shrug and do a quick glance out the window, like an animal judging its ability to escape.

"I would study the photos of that poor, doomed child – she was so perfectly turned out, so poised. So *posed*. She was a little sexpot in miniature, a tiny Marilyn Monroe – and just as tragic.

"And I knew – I *knew* from the first time I saw her picture – that she was being sexually molested. I could *feel* it exuding from her, even on paper.

"I started cutting out her photos and putting them on the fridge in the kitchen. When that became too crowded, I started pinning them to the wall."

"What's your thing with this Ramsey kid?" Hal would ask her from time to time.

Heddi would scan her wall of clippings and mutter, "I don't know. I just don't know."

Finally, one night, the dream from her childhood returned. The bad guys were chasing her again and she was running down the hallway. But this time, it wasn't in a ruin, but in her family home. She ran and ran and the bad guys got closer.

But instead of waking up at the crucial moment, the dream continued. This time, she was caught. Rough hands dragged her down. She was frozen with fear. Her clothes were ripped off. There was hot breath on her cold skin.

There was ramming and pain and she felt like she couldn't breathe.

Then, she woke up.

"And I mean that in the fullest sense. The full realization of my situation."

She knew the sweet aromatic scent of tobacco smoke, the exotic tinctures of expensive aftershave. The rough abrasion of Harris Tweed she knew intimately, as it rubbed and abraded her flesh. She opened her eyes as a five-year old child and looked into those of her father as he breathed his hot, alcoholic breath into her face...

"The Compleat Cocksman," her analyst muttered when she told him. Even dear, bland, impassive Dr. Copeland couldn't subdue his disgust.

"The Compleat Narcissistic Asshole."

"That, too."

"I'm still dealing with it...that betrayal. That use of me. That utter disregard for the sanctity of my being. It's left a ragged hole inside of me. Hal's leaving hasn't helped, either. And now...this.

"Am I going to spend my entire *life* in the hands of terrorists?

"I...I...think...

"That's all...I can do...for now."

Sophia

As brave as she believes Heddi to be, Sophia can't help thinking that her story is ill-timed and self-indulgent; ill-timed because these women are frayed, by now, almost past enduring; and self-indulgent because, like it or not, Heddi is a leader.

She organized the storytelling and the women tell their stories to her, as if she were their therapist – or even their mother. In bad times, the leader has to stay invulnerable for the sake of the others.

Sophia's afraid her show of emotion will be interpreted as weakness. Whether they realize it or not, these women will be demoralized by her revelations, not strengthened.

And besides, which one of them hasn't been terrorized in their lives, long before being trapped in this little room?

Ondine

Ooolala! Heddi's a mess!

Never, never, never would Ondine have guessed what she was going to reveal!

Heddi is so cool, so consummately in charge. She's every bit of that classic, reserved woman she described her mother as being.

Ondine wonders if this will change their therapeutic relationship? Will she be able to trust her once she cloaks herself again? Or will Ondine always see this – this mess, weeping and disheveled, in an orange Naugahyde armchair?

Is that really selfish of her to even think that? About *her* needs?

Or does she even believe, anymore, that they'll be rescued? Maybe it's best that Heddi had her say like the rest of them – a sort of final confession.

An unburdening of the soul, so it can fly.

Betty

Betty wants to say to Heddi, *Now, Honey, don't cry. Everything's gonna be all right*. But, she doesn't think she would appreciate it. It feels like, if she put out her hand to comfort her, she might bite it.

All of a sudden, Betty feels like she can't stand this anymore – like she's got to go to that door and push that machine aside and go out, even if it means getting shot.

What is it that Heddi says she should do at times like this? Put her head down. Close her eyes. Breathe deeply. Count.

She's counting. She's counting.

But her body is screaming, *I WANT OUT!*

Her heart rate must be over a hundred. She feels like she can't breathe. She can smell her own sweat, that rank smell that comes with fear.

Just keep counting.

Pearl

Well, if that don't beat all! That Heady gal gots a heart after all.

Ain't nothin better'n a good cry, her Granny use ter say. Not them tears that's self-pityin, mind ya. But the ones that comes from down deep, whar they's thins thats been fergot. Thems the ones Granny says makes the apples bloom on yer cheeks. Them tears is the waters a health.

Speakin a health, Pearl's startin ta get restless. These ol legs has been doggin it fer four days now. She needs ta get out an push her buggy an feel the wind on her face.

An she's almost outta tabaccy. That thar is serious.

Ain't it a wonder. She done survived so many thins – Abel Johns whorin her around, all her children dyin or gettin lost, livin from hand ta mouth most a the years a her life. An now, do you suppose the Good Lord gots up His sleeve that she's gonna die rat here in this little mouse hole that's all shot-up an closed-in, without ever havin another breath a fresh air or seein the sun?

It makes her ratly ashamed a herself. The Good Lord done give her them thins ever single day a her life an did she give thanks?

Well, yes. In truth, she always did give thanks fer ever little thin come along – fer the burgers Pop flipped fer her an the good solid clink a coins goin inta her can.

But that warn't enough. It warn't the same as what she's thinkin now. It ain't the same as feelin the simple gift a life down deep in yer marrow bones. It ain't the same as this pinin fer the open air an the winds a God sweepin round everwhar, pushin the clouds about an fillin her ol lungs with life.

Pearl done looked the Angel a Death in the face many a time an oft in this long life an thought dyin would be a gift, pure an simple. But the plain fact a the matter is, she don' want ta die here in this here place. Call her a ingrate fer questionin the ways a the Lord, but she gots ta feel the free air on her face one more time fore she passes.

This here is why she always hated zoos. Cain't ratly keep a wild thin in a cage. That wild critter gots ta be free. An so does she.

Starting sometime late in the night, the monitors began to show activity: people sneaking through the front doors of the terminal, all in black with guns held at their shoulders, very stealthy.

X is sleepy, so at first she does not comprehend what is happening.

Then, suddenly, she is very wide-awake!

They are coming! Finally, they are coming for them!

But that is not the case. Instead, they begin removing the bodies lying in the concourse. Several men with guns cover the ones who simply take the bodies by the ankles and drag them away, as fast as possible. This goes on for several hours. There are hundreds of bodies and they remove many of them. Then they leave, scooting backwards, their guns still ready to shoot.

X does not know what it means, but she thinks things will change now. And she is very frightened.

Thank Allah they did not come this far. But that means they did not take Fat Guy, who is beginning to stink very badly.

Now someone is moving again on the monitors. He is one of the Brothers and he is moving in places where they have not patrolled for many hours. Why is he alone? Their rule is to patrol in pairs.

She thinks she must have fallen asleep. It seems to her it was just morning. She cannot remember the last time she looked, but now it is almost five o'clock. She would not know if it were 5:00 AM, except she can tell by the television programming that it is afternoon.

Now, she is hungry again and her bladder is full. She hates being trapped here with her own bodily needs. It is the opposite of heroic action.

If heroic action is what this is. Since last night's news report, her clarity of purpose has been devastated. Fat Guy's small, cramped room seems to close in around her now, like the jaws of a trap.

On the television, there is no news, only commercials. The people are all well dressed and all they care for, apparently, is shopping and curing bad breath. She wonders if they even know that Palestine exists?

The man on the monitor is moving this way! He is moving carefully. X can see by his movements that he expects to find police behind every door and around every corner. From where she sits, of course, she knows that this caution is unnecessary. It is troubling, actually, how little police intrusion there has been.

When she digs in Fat Guy's lunch box, she finds a bag of Fritos and a peach. The whole box is starting to exude a fruity smell of decomposition because it is full of wrappers and apple cores and banana peels. There is also a plastic box with something homemade in it – maybe lasagna? She has been saving it, but soon will have to eat it or it will spoil and be wasted. Besides, she is too hungry – which is affecting her eyes and her judgment.

She can see on the monitors that the Brothers are eating well from the food court and even sharing some with the hostages. They all have access to toilets, too. She has watched now, many times, a hostage raise a hand to be marched off to the bathroom at gunpoint.

Meanwhile, X has put her latrine can out in the hall because the smell is overpowering. She knows this is dangerous but she cannot help it. She only drags it in when she needs to use it.

The man on the monitor is getting close! Could it be Jamal, finally coming for her? It is impossible to tell because he is in full battle dress, with his balaclava over his face. His weapon is held up in front of him, ready to drop and fire in an instant.

On television, they are advertising a medicine for stomach problems, and California cheese. She likes the happy cows. They make her laugh.

The man is very close now. She can't wait any longer. She believes, without any proof, that this man is Jamal. Maybe it is the way he moves, or his height. Or maybe she just needs so badly for it to be him.

When the monitor shows him a little closer, she is going to open the door.

Heddi

Heddi is so damned mad at herself she can't stand it! She thought she could tell the whole thing and then she broke down and didn't finish.

"Please excuse me, all of you. I don't mean to make a scene."

"Maybe making a scene is the best way to heal your wounds. After all, isn't it exactly what your parents – your whole *class* – would have despised? Isn't it a true strike against them and their abuses of you to act as you truly *are* and not as you *should* be?" Ondine is so earnest that it touches Heddi's battered heart.

"Yeah," Betty agrees. "Didn't you tell me that becoming authentic is the work of mid-life? Getting rid of all those *shoulds* and *oughts* and discovering who you really are underneath? What's so bad about tears? People have been crying them forever. Why should you be left out?"

Heddi drops her head and nods tearfully. But she's not mollified. She wanted to say it all. The late-night tippling, the coldness she brings to the marriage bed, the unexpected panic attacks...

"Hamm boff tubaba. Bada bam...Gaba...Ahhhh... Uhnnnn...Haba nuf...nuf...Muhhhhh...Ahhhhh..." Erika suddenly erupts, thrashing. Sophia dashes to keep her from rolling herself off the couch.

"Pearl! How many pills do we have left there?"

"Only five."

"Oh, Goddess!"

Heddi's such a damn mess, she's ashamed for herself. She's got to do something to get these women focused again. It's all her fault. She can feel them unraveling, even through her snivels.

"Sophia...Sophia. Help me out. No, I mean help us all out. While I'm collecting myself, why don't you tell us how you came to be so proficient at medicine?

"I understand that you don't want to talk about it, but just consider what each of the rest of us has been revealing..."

Sophia looks at Heddi hard, and then nods almost imperceptibly.

"You will? Oh, thank you. If you'll excuse me then, I'm going to slip into the powder room. Don't stop on my ac-count. I'll just tiptoe back, in a minute."

Sophia

"Okay. Well..." She sighs, and shrugs her massive plaid shoulders, as if trying to throw off a burden.

"I grew up around guns and shooting and blood. My fa-ther used to hunt deer with a pack of dogs every fall. I can still hear them, baying down in the canyons, driving the deer uphill. We didn't have much money when I was growing up and hunting was just a part of our lives, a way to fill the larder."

Their neighbor, Pat Clark, the ditch-tender, would sit on the road in front of the house, right at the crest of the ridge, with his rifle across his knees, drinking coffee laced with whiskey and waiting for the first deer to break from the brush. Two or three other men were there, too, spaced out every couple of hundred yards, each with his khaki-and-red plaid Thermos of coffee, his red plaid hunting shirt and his thick, lace-up work boots.

They'd pick off two or three deer that way in one day, field dress and hang the carcasses, and then later they'd get together and butcher and share out the meat after it'd hung for a day or two.

Sophia, the tomboy, was always buzzing around the hunters and their kill like a gnat. Her father taught her to shoot when she was just five and the rifle was taller than she was. She was never one of those kids, though, who went around shooting birds and squirrels. Her father taught her to respect life, to take it only out of necessity. But she could knock a can off a fence post at a hundred yards with her little .22.

Sophia was interested in Indians as a girl and she used to take the deer hides and tan them, using an old oak stump that was half rotted-out for her soaker. Tannic acid in the oak wood, maybe they know, is what cures the hide.

Probably she never would have left the mountain. She liked the way things were going, but her folks worried about her.

"You gotta get an education, Sophie," her father used to say. But of course, there was no money for a college education and in those days, school loans weren't so common.

So finally she decided to join the Peace Corps – but to her surprise, they wanted nothing of her, because all her skills were the same ones that people in Third World countries already had. What the Peace Corps wanted was someone who could teach English or engineer a water system.

So she licked her wounds for a while and then went down to see the local Army recruiter. She'd heard the Army would give you an education, if you signed up.

"Oh yes," they said. Anything she wanted to study, as long as it was a field they needed.

Well, all those years of butchering had given her a fair understanding of anatomy – of deer, at least – and so she thought she'd do well as a medic. The recruiters weren't too keen on agreeing to that. Maybe they weren't as clear on the connection between butchering and being a medic as Sophia was, but she refused to sign up unless they gave her a contract. So in the end, she went off to boot camp and after that to train as a medic.

She guesses they can imagine what happened next. The Vietnam War was heating up and before she quite knew what was happening, she was serving in a field hospital outside of Saigon.

Sophia would never forget that first step onto the tarmac as they deplaned, in-country. The asphalt was actually sticky under her boot soles. The temperature must have been over a hundred with humidity to match.

And the smell! She's always had an acute sense of smell, almost like an animal. It's impossible to describe the compounded stench of that place: diesel, rotting vegetation, ripening fruit, hot asphalt, the sulfurous smell of munitions and of course, blood, sweat and the acrid scent of fear.

That, and above all, the burning shit cans. Every night, they'd light off dozens of 55-gallon drums of shit from the latrines and they'd burn all night long. It's a sickening reek. Anyone who's never smelled it can't imagine it.

She remembers, when she finally made it back home to the mountain, the first time she unzipped her Army duffle. The evil smell that rose from it was so rank that it revolted her. It's the smell of Death; the smell of Hell.

She was in a hooch with a bunch of Army nurses. In those days, they didn't let women go into battle. The women had to stay behind and tend to the wounded. There were plenty of those and Sophia got her fill of stitching up wounds.

And a couple of times, when a doctor was too drunk to function, she even performed surgeries, with one of the nurses reading instructions out of a surgical text. Sophia was never afraid. She knew her way around a body, especially under the skin.

She just sort of hunkered down inside and tried to wait out her year so she could go home all in one piece. That's what she wanted most – just to survive, intact. Every night, there were rocket attacks or warnings broadcast by loud-speaker that there was a sniper inside the wire.

"You never really sleep in a place like that. There's sand in your sheets and they're never really dry because of the humidity. And the blood and the suffering gets to you, pretty quickly.

"About six or seven months into it, I was starting to doubt that I'd make it – and that got more intense when one of my nurse friends was shot in broad daylight as she was walking to surgery.

"Just when I thought things couldn't get worse, though, they did. The Army was pushing northward and there were big battles going on up by the DMZ. And one day, the captain came to our hooch and told us to pack up. We were being shipped up north. That's when things got *really* spooky."

Even though they'd been dealing with the broken bodies of soldiers every day, and there'd been constant attacks on them, none of the nurses had ever been in a full-out shooting war yet. They were scared.

They were all standing out on the tarmac close to the edge of the compound, waiting for the plane to come and take them up to the DMZ. On the other side of the chain link fence, there was a stand of some kind of fruit trees, very large, very old.

She watched a group of women gathering there, graceful as dancers in their traditional *Áo dài*, with mandarin collars and long, side-slit tunics over loose pants. They always watched the Vietnamese carefully – you never knew when a washerwoman might fold a grenade in with your socks.

But these women weren't the least bit interested in them. One woman took her baby from the sling across her breast and laid it on the ground on a piece of fabric. Sophia thought they were just going to have a rest in the shade, but then another woman proceeded to wrap the baby up like a mummy and finally – she can still hardly believe she saw this – they tied the little bundle up in the branches of the tree. And then they all began to wail.

Only then did Sophia realize that the baby was dead. And as she stood there amazed, she saw that the big, spreading limbs of those trees were festooned in bundles!

"I'd thought they were bearing huge fruits and instead..."

Sophia's face crumples with a depth of sorrow that is unfathomable and she does not continue for a very long space. The others wait, silently.

"...and I remembered that old blues song that Billie Holiday used to sing, 'Strange Fruit'..."

That was a moment in her life! A dawn of realization. What were they doing there, anyway? Why were they there, killing these gentle people and their babies? She was sickened. Disgusted. She hated the Army, her country, and herself in ascending order.

All she wanted to do was to go home.

But of course, she couldn't.

So they ended up a few miles from the DMZ and things were really crazy up there. Patrols would go out, day and night, and sometimes people would return and sometimes whole patrols never did. The wounds she and her friends tended there were fresh from the battlefield and they were too terrible to describe. Feet and legs blown off, bullet holes through chests, head injuries – it became an endless assembly line of bloody, shattered parts.

Sophia thought she might lose her mind but she was too exhausted to do it. The drama would have taken too much energy.

And then, right in the middle of that terrible time, a miracle happened. One of the nurses invited her to the NCO Club for a blind date.

"A *date?* You want me to go on a *date?*" Sophia hooted at her. "Sherry, I'm six feet, two inches tall, in case you haven't noticed. Who would want to date *me?*"

"Someone who's six foot six?" Sherry said, with a kind of sly smile.

"You know this guy?"

"Yeah. Well, a little. Actually, he approached me in the mess. He asked me about you."

Sophia was stunned. She'd never had a single tumble from a man in her entire life.

"What'd he want to know? My shoe size?"

"Hey, Sophie, cut it out! You're a beautiful woman. He wants to meet you. Come on! Get a shower. You got anything that's not covered in blood, wear it."

So they went and she met John. It wasn't just that he actually towered over her or that he was handsome or even that he seemed to be a really decent guy, in spite of that crazy war. What really turned Sophia on about John, at the start, was that he was so clearly, and deeply, interested in *her!*

She really didn't believe in love at first sight, but pretty quickly she came to think that when two people are meant for one another, they know it, right from the get-go.

For Sophia, it was like she'd been out in a black rain on a cold night, and a stranger opened his warm overcoat and took her inside it. She couldn't maintain her shell with John. He just covered her, shattered as she was, with solid, loving energy.

Meeting John changed her whole experience of the war. She'd been sinking into a morass of depression. Suddenly, she couldn't wait for a new day to dawn.

They found a hundred ways to run into one another. It's amazing, the magnetism of love. It just drew them to one another, without even any thought.

She'd be covered in blood and he'd be smeared in mud from head to toe from having just gotten off patrol. It didn't matter. They were beautiful in each other's eyes. It didn't matter that they were defying Army regulations. It didn't matter that they were in the middle of a war zone. All that mattered was seeing one another one more time. And then another. And another.

They were both short. Sophia had two more months and John had two and a half. They knew what they'd do when they got home. They'd get married. They talked about how many kids they wanted and what kind of house and where. And in their imaginations, they lived forward into the future and the rich and happy life they'd make together.

She never would have believed it but when her time came to leave Vietnam, she was reluctant. Who could believe such a switch? She even tried to extend for two weeks so they could leave at the same time but her request was denied.

So home she went, and she waited. It was only two weeks but it seemed like an eternity. Finally, two weeks passed but there was no call from John. Sophia was worried but she thought there must be some excuse. Another week crawled by. And then three more days.

And then! Miracle! A letter arrived bearing the Army postal stamp and clearly having been through the brutalities of a tropical posting. She was so excited she couldn't breathe. She ripped the letter open and her eyes leapt to the page...but the letter wasn't from John. It was from his buddy, Rick.

In it, he related how they'd gone out on patrol, just two days before they were scheduled to come home, and gotten pinned down in a firefight. Everything was chaos, he said.

For a while, he could hear John shouting, trying to rally everyone. But then Rick lost track of him. They were pinned down for hours before gunships could come to their rescue. And when they did, no one could find John. He'd just disappeared. They went back a day later and scoured the area.

But he was gone – just gone...

"That was almost forty years ago and it still...
"...was he...
"Did he get blown to smithereens?
"Did he fall in the river and just float away?
"Or was he taken prisoner? That's my worst nightmare. My John, a POW. Even now, it's more than my heart...
"I have dreams, still. I go out looking for him. The jungle's dark even though the trees are on fire. Danger's lurking everywhere, but I charge through the undergrowth, calling for him. Bombs go off and the ground heaves and everything lights up a lurid red. But I keep looking and looking and looking...until I get so desperate, I wake up..."

After that, she stayed on the mountain. When her folks passed on, she inherited the home place. She turned her back on everything that had to do with the war and became a vegetarian so she'd never have to deal with another hunk of bloody meat again. She rejected God and Country and became a Goddess worshipper. She hated everything patriarchal and honored everything feminine.

As the decades passed, she came to see how the way she was living wasn't just a reaction against something, but it was really a reflection of who she is; living close to the earth, and honoring all creatures, the higher powers, the stars. It was a return to all she'd already known, as a child.

She looks to her happiness after she passes from this world, now. Nothing here can claim her, if John can't.

"So...that's how I got so proficient at stitchery, Heddi. I hope that answers your question."

Pearl

They ain't nothin gonna break this gloom lessen Pearl does. Sophia's story near sunk the barrel, fer sure. Theys tears in ever eye an the fat one, Betty thar, looks lak she's gonna wail lak a ambulance any minute.

Even that Heady gal ain't got a word ta say. She looks lak a drown rat, all kinda slicked down with water and red-eyed since she come outta the john.

What is she gonna tell em ta keep em from fallin apart?

Well, Pearl knows what Sophia means, bout doctorin. It ain't never easy, an she gots a tale from when she was jes a little slip of a thin ta prove it.

Sometimes, settin here, her mind slips an she falls back inta the past. She's five or six again, wanderin amongst the log decks at the mill. Her daddy worked thar buckin logs with his partner, usin a 5-foot double buckin saw with teeth two inches long an a handle at each end. Back and forth, back and forth – all day long.

Pearl's job was ta fetch him his lunch at noon. She'd carry the pail high in her rat hand, lak a lady holdin up her skirts. In winter, she'd sink in mud over her ankles that'd suck at her red rubber boots, pullin em rat off her heels, skinnin off her little thin cotton socks, rat with em. Many's the day she'd limp home with her boots full a muck an her feet freezin.

The mud is whipped up from all the wheels churnin through, what with the wagons an mule teams goin back an forth. It's lak quicksand, black, gooey, watery, stirred with wood splinters, hunks a bark and snarls a wire.

The whole conglomeration sinks an don't surface again til the hot weather, when the mud turns ta dust. In summer,

Pearl's barefoot, pickin her way cuz spikes a wood is angled lak spears trapped in the dry mud an buried outta sat in dust. Once, she hit her foot on a spike. She thought it warn't nothin but a flesh wound, but she couldn't dig it out with her lil pocketknife. She din't worry none cuz in a couple a days it should fester an the pus'd jes raft the splinter rat out.

In a couple a days, though, it's hurtin purdy good. She squeezes an squeezes. Pus comes out – but the splinter don't.

Pearl don't want ta tell her Mama cuz that means her Daddy'll come at her with his big ol pocketknife an whittle the damn thing out. But her Mama catches her limpin along an she's busted.

When he comes home from work, smellin a smoke an pine pitch, her Daddy holds her foot in his big ol paw, skin lak sandpaper, the roughest grit, with a grip lak Death Hissef. No amount a wrigglin a her upper body cain budge what's trapped down lower.

He makes some beginnin pokes that even her gritted teeth cain't keep the scream in. But her Daddy don't get mad lak she espects he will. He looks kinda puzzled lak an holds her foot up closer ta his eyes – not seemin ta realize it bout twists Pearl's leg outta the socket ta do it.

Then he says ta her Mama, who is kinda hoverin round lookin white, "Git me some plars."

Now, Pearl ain't sure if the pain or the terror gots her more. She gots the feelin a trapped animal must get, the ones that gnaws they own feet off ta get free.

Her Daddy takes them plars an he grabs the end a that splinter an he gives a maty jerk that yanks Pearl's foot rat off his knee an two foot in the air. An thar's her foot, hangin up thar by his face, still danglin by that dang splinter which is still in the side a her foot lak it was another bone she done sprung.

Well, the look on his face is almost worth the pain! He couldn'ta been more surprised if Mama'd said they'd won the lott'ry. He jes stares kinda slack-jawed at her foot hangin thar from them plars, til Pearl's howlin wakes him outta his trance.

Theys a kitty her folks kept in a ol coffee tin on the top shelf in the kitchen. Down it comes, an her Daddy says, "Take her ta Doc Lamb." An that's that. Out they go, her hand clamped in her Mama's.

Her Mama marches her down the street with Pearl hoppin along on one foot an touchin t'other down, as if it was plantin itsef on a hot griddle with ever step.

In they go, ta the waitin room a Doc Lamb's office that smells a bleach an antiseptic an starch from Wilma's uniform.

Wilma's Doc's nurse an, bein no fool, she cain see rat now this is somethin that ain't gonna wait. She don't even have ta say nothin ta the folks settin round in chairs waitin. Wilma jes opens the door ta the exam room at the back an jerks her head fer Pearl's Mama ta come rat on through.

Old Doc Lamb comes shufflin in after a piece in his starched white coat. He gots his heavy jowls an bent back on, same as always. He gots the look a someone who ain't never bothered ta straighten up betwixt exams.

"What've we got here?" He looks at Pearl. He's talkin ta her! At home, don't nobody talk ta her. Her job is ta shut up.

Pearl stares at him. He jes keeps on starin back, waitin fer a answer.

Finally, Pearl whispers, "Mah foot got hurt."

She's lookin down at the floor with its beigy, worn carpet an her big, bare, dirty, swollen foot planted rat on it – not at him, with those big eyes that don't blink.

"Ah!" says he. "Did you bring it with you?"

Pearl looks at him, then. What in the world is that suppose ta mean? Did she bring it with her? Her foot? The splinter? The hurt?

A regular eternity passes.

Then she realizes he's makin a joke. She smiles, a thin lil lick of a smile, unsure an wan. She nods an whispers, "Yes," in a lil breath, lookin down again. Doc beams. She cain hear his satisfaction in his voice. "Let's have a look."

Then she's hoisted onta the exam table in a big high arc. Out comes the lil drawer in front ta support her leg. Doc bends his bent shoulders some more an breathes on her skin, ticklin her.

"Hmmmmm..." he says. "I don't know which is bigger, yer foot or this piece a wood you got lodged in it! Let's get this thin out an you cain take it home ta use fer kindlin."

He turns ta Wilma who is standin by, with Pearl's Mama hoverin behind. "Get me a syringe a pain killer," he says. He actually says the name a some drug, very specific, but this is a hunert years ago an Pearl cain't remember what it was.

But she sure as hell remembers that syringe! Good Lord have mercy! That thing was a block long an thick as a knittin needle! Doc come at her with that thin an she thinks she's about ta puke. But fear ain't *nothin* compared ta when he rams that sucker rat inta that poor red, swollen flesh.

Lord God Almighty! She done fainted dead away.

When she come to, thar's a big ol white bandage on her foot, layers an layers a white gauze, an the smell a adhesive tape still in the air. Her Mama is standin next ta the table holdin the upper half a Pearl, which jes done leapt rat off the side, by her best reckonin.

Then she realizes a few thins all at once. Her foot don't hurt cuz a the shot. Doc an Wilma is kinda standin off, dryin they hands, lookin satisfied. An Pearl's Mama is holdin her.

Holdin her!

An fer that instant, Pearl feels as happy as she ever felt – safe, warm an cared fer. It was a revelation! It was all of a piece: the white walls, so clean an cheerful, the clock tickin, the smell an rustle a starch, an especially the scent a her

Mama, the soft, greasy feel a her apron bib under Pearl's cheek, an her strong arms under her.

When Pearl dies an goes ta heaven, it don't have ta be nothin more'n that ta satisfy *her!*

Well, they house was in the mill yard rat thar betwixt the road an the backside a the log decks. Them big pyramids a logs stacked up, bleedin pitch from the ends, jes kinda hunkered round that house lak big animals.

Finally, Pearl's Mama made the mill stack em endwise ta the house.

"What if they started ta roll?" she axed, holdin Pearl's hand, leanin in toward the mill boss. "They'd flatten that house lak a rollin pin on pie dough!"

So they was a flurry a work – men with cant hooks, the house fillin up with grunts an shouts, an the thunder a logs rollin. Three a the log decks was skidded out, then dragged back with the butt ends a the trees facin the house.

It was a lot a work an her Daddy was mad. He got the flak fer it an they docked his wages ta pay fer the time it took four men an two mules ta do the job.

Even then, her Mama warn't satisfied. "You be careful out thar in the mill yard," she'd say ever time Pearl set out with her Daddy's lunch bucket. "Them decks cain shift. You keep a eye an a ear out, you hear?"

Pearl's Mama was kinda psychic. She knew thins. She saw thins fore they happened. The mill yard was dangerous. She saw that. She knew.

Pearl had a friend – her first friend – an Bonnie Lee was her name. Two names she gots, not one lak Pearl. Bonnie Lee was a year older then Pearl. Her house was across the road, a shack no better'n Pearl's, built low an slopin, without benefit a no T-square nor chalk line.

Bonnie Lee had fine blonde hair with a bit a curl ta it, so it was always tied in little knots an snarled, an stuck out from her head in a little halo a neglect. She gots a bath once a week in a big ol galvanized tub in the middle a the kitchen floor jes lak Pearl. In between baths, she was smeared an grimed with food an mill dirt – also jes lak Pearl.

Bonnie Lee was fine-boned an delicate, though, even in her raggedy dress – *not* lak Pearl. Pearl thought she was beautiful.

They use ter come across one another out thar in the mill yard, totin lunch buckets back an forth. "Hi," Pearl'd say.

Bonnie Lee'd smile this barely-thar smile. "Hi."

Sometimes, they'd go down ta the crick an grub around fer frogs, or wade when it was hot, or play with Lucky, they poor ol black dog with long matted hair an skin an bones from worms. They'd throw a stick an Lucky'd run an fetch it, then chew it up. That was the game. Sometimes, if they had the strength, they'd play tag.

Pearl reckons she was five when it happened. Somebody come ta the door an she cain remember her Mama thar bent out the doorframe, whisperin. She cain still see her backside, with that limp apron bow, a cotton print skirt hangin down her skinny brown legs, an baggy socks an scuffed tie-up shoes.

Pearl strains ta hear but it's jes *Buzzbuzz* from the neighbor lady an then *Buzzbuzz* from her Mama. But thar was a energy ta it that told Pearl it warn't good.

And she cain remember ta this day how her Mama looked when she turnt back inta that room. Her face was dazed, kinda, an long-lookin, an hard, lak what lil plumpness they ever was thar was sucked off, sudden-lak. Her eyes din't blink an she looked ta be starin a-far off, even though it was jes at the planks on the floor.

An jes lak that, Pearl knew. She knew it was Death. She din't know whose, but she knew fer sure that a black shadder done stooped over them that day an wiped somebody clean away, lak a eraser on a chalkboard.

"That's the Injun in mah Mama an me. Us Choctaws, we gots the Sight.

"An that was the end a mah friend, Bonnie Lee, cuz it was her that got took. Thar she was in the mill yard, an the deck shifted. The top log rolled off, pickin up steam as it come, an Bonnie Lee, her daddy's lunch bucket an all, was jes flattened lak dough under a rollin pin."

That thar was Pearl's first funeral. Her Daddy was good with his hands an he built Bonnie Lee a little coffin usin wood from the mill, still bleedin pitch. Her Mama an another lady, Alice, done stitched her up a new organdy dress.

First one she gots, ever, an she was dead an couldn't enjoy it. Ain't that the way life goes, though?

Thar was a lid on the coffin. Pearl wanted ta see her friend ta say goodbye but they wouldn't let her. She heerd some a the ladies gossipin an they said Bonnie Lee's skull was cracked lak a egg, with brains oozin out lak yolk. Hell, a strong backhand'd a done that, she was so fragile – let alone three tons a rollin log!

Pearl heard her Mama an her Daddy talkin in the nat bout how it coulda been Pearl, an how her Mama was jes about ta send her off with the lunch bucket when the word come.

Her Mama wanted ta leave that place. She never did lak it much an after that she jes lost all heart. Thar was cracks betwixt the kitchen floorboards a inch wide an she'd jes stand thar with her broom, anglin dirt down them cracks a hour at a shot, lost in a dream. Maybe she was stretchin out her mind, searchin out the next place whar they'd be movin. She was lak that. She saw thins in advance.

Seems lak it warn't but a week or two after Bonnie Lee died, ol Lucky up an died, too. Pearl was the one who found him, layin by the crick with his snout in the water lak he got took rat in the middle of a drink.

Pearl wanted em ta bury him next ta Bonnie Lee, but everbody jes laughed at her. The men come an fetched him an threw his body on the big heap a sawdust under the main saw, down under the mill.

Pearl slipped round thar, when nobody was lookin. His body was already half-buried. With ever board that was cut, more sawdust jes drifted down. In a hour's time, he'd plumb disappeared.

Don't seem rat that a body can jes be wiped away clean lak that, with no ceremony an no one grievin. Even a dog.

So Pearl made up this story bout how Bonnie Lee was thar waitin fer him. An how they went off inta a beautiful meadow full a flowers, an how God give em a big basket a food ever day, settin it on a big rock out in the middle a the grass. An bout how happy they was an how purdy Bonnie Lee looked in her yaller organdy dress.

If some preacher axed Pearl what heaven was lak, she'd tell em that story. She espects theys playin thar yet, Bonnie Lee an Lucky. An when *she* crosses over, the three of em'll go down ta the crick an chase pollywogs again.

Cuz this much she knows: once childhood's over, they ain't *nothin* a heaven in this life after that.

Well, that story took a morbid turn, after Pearl done left Doc Lamb's office. She din't mean ta make thins worse, but from the looks on ever face that's what she's gone an done.

But then that Heady gal, she says, "Pearl, I think you're telling us what we need to hear. It's a somber day. Why don't you just keep on going?"

So Pearl sets a spell loadin her pipe an she thinks about all the thins that've befallen her in this long life – an she discovers that *she's* in a funk, too. An so she thinks, *What the Hell? I may as well tell it all.*

Well, Pearl's husband, Abel Johns, he never gots much of a bringin-up. Nobody never taught him not ta spit inta the wind, so ta speak. So he jes ended up gooberin hissef an everbody that done got close ta him. He was lak a big baby, goin through life wavin his fists an gettin mad at whatever done crossed his path, over nothin. Fightin his fate you mat say, when he was the one creatin most a it, hissef.

An he was a drunk. An not the happy kind that laughs an stumbles round lak a fool. No, he was a *mean* drunk an when he was in his cups, thar warn't nobody – neither man nor beast – that could face him.

Ever livin thin jes annoyed the heck outta him on sat when he was drinkin. Jes livin an breathin was enough ta outrage him an make him want ta kill. Many's the nat Pearl hustled the kids outta the house an hid with em somewhar – the woods, a barn, under the house. Jes anywhar outta his sat an mind.

With his temper, thar was always trouble. So Pearl had ta be prepared ta move at a moment's notice. She'd jes throw everthin they owned inta gunnysacks in about five minutes flat an off they'd go. Sometimes, they gots a ol dilapidated car. Sometimes, they gots ta hitchhike. An most times, they'd have ta sneak outta town through the woods or fields cuz somebody was lookin fer Abel Johns ta beat him up, or with a shotgun ta finish him off.

Lord hep her, but they was times she prayed they'd succeed.

An then they was the times that she warn't fast enough. Abel Johns'd come through that door already fired up an her an the kids'd be cornert. Jes the very sat a them'd send him inta a rage an he'd pick up anythin that come ta hand – a fryin pan, the broom, the poker – an jes start wailin on the first one he come ta.

That's how Pearl come by this here crease in her head. Feels lak you could roll quarters inta the slot he done made with a poker one nat, when she come betwixt him an her third son, Abner.

Abner warn't but seven or eight an it was his cowerin that set Abel Johns off. "Ain't no son a mine gonna shrink lak a girl! You come out here an take it lak a man!" And he picked up the poker an went fer him.

Pearl leapt across that room lak a buck in rut, but she warn't in time ta save that poor child a whack that broke his arm. The last thin she remembers was Abner's hand hangin backwards, an then nothin.

When she come to, Abel Johns was gone an so was Abner. Thar was blood from Hell ta breakfast – a big pool near the stove an splatters everwhar.

She went ta find her other little ones an they was huddled under the bed, as far back as they could get against the wall. Pearl axed, "Is Abner in thar with you?" And some one a them poor tykes answered back in a squeaky whisper, "No, Mama."

Well, she gots blood runnin down in her eyes an she's half crazy with pain an worry. She goes chargin out inta the darkness, a-callin Abner's name. Next thin she knows, theys hands around her throat an a stink a whiskey that'd gag a skunk. An this voice lak a sick panther roars at her, "You shut yer mouth woman, or yer the next one I put in the ground."

Well, she was so insane with what he done hinted at that she kicked backward an got him a good one in the balls – an the fat was on.

She scratched an clawed an he punched an she bit an he clobbered. An in the end, he drug her inta the house by her hair an throwed her down on the bed whar her poor babes was hidin, an would a had his way with her but he couldn't get it up. An while he was tryin, he just plumb passed out.

It was a pure act a mercy on the part a the Lord. Pearl gathered her chicks an they fled out inta the nat lak the hounds of Hell was upon em. They ran an ran til they saw the lats a town. She had no notion whar she should go, but she wanted folks round em, that much she knew.

The first place they come ta was a church an, as luck would have it, the doors was open an a heavenly singin was rollin out inta the nat. Pearl jes herded her flock in thar an they hunkered down on the first pew they come ta, way in the back.

They musta been a sat ta behold! Pearl lookin lak the wreck a the *Hesperus*, an her five children – who shoulda been six – settin thar lak they done seen a whole *herd* a ghosts. Good Lord! If ever they was folks that craved sanctuary, they was them.

Afore long, up an comes a gal, skinny as a bedpost an dressed all in black. "Good Lord have mercy!" says she. "What have we here?" She stands a-hoverin above em lak some avengin angel, scowlin down lak she was witnessin the final atrocity at Gomorrah.

Try as she mat, Pearl cain't get a word outta her mouth. If Abel Johns'd cut out her tongue, he couldn't a silenced her no better. So thar she set, her an her chicks. Pearl crusted in blood with a crease in her skull lak a trough a gore, an them all covered in dirt an patches an they eyes red from weepin. The Good Lord don't look down on nothin more pathatic then they was.

Pearl don't ratly know how long they set thar with that thar somber gal, a-lookin down on em lak they was a tableau a the Last Judgment. She seen a hunert thins go through that gal's mind, quick as minnows. She din't ratly know whether ta call the cops or weep fer pity. Finally, she jes says, "You all come with me," an nods her head towards the door.

Pearl's thinkin the gal's about ta send em packin an she gathers up her lil ones as best she cain. Theys lookin lak they legs ain't gonna carry em much further – she's packin the youngest, Sadie, in her arms. It's a moment a purest despair: them poor babes so tared an Pearl with no place ta rest they heads, let alone food ta put in they mouths. If she coulda jes laid down an died, she'd a thanked God fer the mercy.

But this gal has somethin else in mind. She marches em down the church stairs an then points down along the side, instead a out ta the street. An Pearl an her kids jes foller along, meek as lambs ta the slaughter. She could be leadin em straight inta the mouth a Hell, fer all Pearl knows. She's too tared an dispirited ta care.

They straggle down the path past the church an come ta a lil house no bigger then a matchbox, but with the lats on an lookin warm an cozy. The gal stops outside an turns ta Pearl an says, "This is the parsonage. You cain take refuge here."

Well, even the poker din't whollop Pearl lak that. She jes sunk down ta the ground an wept. An all her lil ones done clung ta her lak baby possums ta they dead mama.

Then she feels hands under her arms an she's bein lifted an half dragged inta the house. An she heerd a man's voice, sayin, "May God have mercy on the man who done this ta this woman," an it sounded lak he was bout ta cry.

An then, she don't ratly member much. They was hot water an someone scrubbin at her head, an later another man's voice that musta been a doctor cuz in the mornin she gots stitches in her head, an a headache the size a Pittsburg.

She opens her eyes, but it's lak they won't budge. Finally, she forces em open in slits with her fingers – and what do them poor swollen eyes see but her cherubs, all in a row on the floor, scrubbed clean an sleepin sweetly, all nestled in quilts.

She had a moment a pure delirium, the joy jes took her. But then, all anxious, she counts em an theys but five. Her Abner ain't among em an that knocked her clean flat on her back again. She jes laid thar with a heart heavy as a gravestone.

Well, ta make a long story short, them good people kept Pearl an her babes fer a week. The entire congregation sent food ta em an the Sheriff come an took Pearl's statement.

That thar was the hardest part cuz she din't ratly know what had happened ta her boy, Abner. She could guess at it, but it was a dark vision, an she told the Sheriff she din't ratly believe it was possible.

The Sheriff went out ta the house an a course Abel Johns warn't thar. He'd turned tail, leavin all they thins behind. The Sheriff had a look around in the woods an afore long, he come upon a pile a fresh dirt an it din't take much diggin ta uncover what was under thar.

They din't want Pearl ta see him, but she was lak a mad thin. She'd a kilt anybody that stood in her way.

That poor child was broke lak a jar. Warn't one bone in his poor lil body left whole. Thar he was, lookin lak a lump a mincemeat. Even his poor lil face was so battered an bruised, Pearl couldn't a recognized him from Adam.

"Thar ain't...no words...fer what I done felt...
"Thar jes ain't no words...
"Well..."

By week's end Pearl was sure even them good church folks was ready fer em ta move on, an the only place she had ta go was back home, so back they went. Nobody'd seen hide nor hair a Abel Johns an she figgered it was safe – that he'd be ten counties away by then.

But she figgered wrong.

One nat, bout a week after they'd come home, she heerd a sound an afore she could do anythin, thars that stink she knows so well an them hands, grippin her lak Death Hissef.

"You filthy bitch!" he spits in a whisper that makes her hair stand on end. "I outta kill you fer sicin that Sheriff on me!"

He's got his hands so firm round her windpipe, she knows her eyes is buggin out an she cain't say a word, let alone scream ta warn her babes.

"You git outta that bed, you whore, an you git this house packed up. An you do it rat smart, or I'll whollop ever one a them brats jes ta punish you."

So Pearl jes flies round that shack, throwin thins inta them sacks lak she was harvestin potatoes a gold. And Hissef jes settin thar, weavin back an forth lak the Devil's own rattlesnake that jes crawlt up from the holds a Hell.

The last spoon warn't in the sack when he snatches the bags an lugs em out, sayin, "Get them brats out ta this car in two minutes or I'll kill em all."

The poor creatures was awake, a course. Who could sleep with the Devil Hissef on a rampage? But still Pearl was shakin lak a leaf in a gale fer fear he'd come in an start beatin on the poor thins.

She gots em all in the car an off they go. An whar, pray tell, had Abel Johns got that car from? Pearl din't know – but she had a purdy good idea. They was flyin along the county road in a car that properly belonged in some sleepin somebody's front yard.

Heddi

"I cain see by yer faces that yer're shocked. Well, I don't blame you one bit. It was shockin fer me, too, as you cain imagine," Pearl says.

"That time was what mah Granny'd call a Blood Year. It's what you all is havin, rat now...a Blood Year."

Heddi has to ask, "What's a blood year?" and she sees Ondine give her a startled glance.

She didn't mean to put such an edge on it. It sounded so hostile, like she's saying, *You know damn well we don't know what you're talking about, and I'm going to bust your little game wide open.*

It's just an opening gambit, conversationally, for Christ's sake, she tells herself, *not a fucking complex you've got to hunt down with a flashlight in one hand and a 9 millimeter Glock in the other.*

But Pearl isn't offended in the slightest. She smiles as if recalling something sweet, takes a contented drag off her pipe and rests it on her knee. The way she leans back into the angle of the vending machines is a matter for envy. She seems to be experiencing solid comfort, her scrawny body soaking up the cushioning of her pillow of plastic bags like it was made of goose down.

Heddi notices that the others have stopped squirming around and that an unusually deep, listening silence has fallen on the room.

Something in her feels bitchy as Hell.

"Mah Granny use ter say they was different kinds a years. She had names fer 'em: Moon Year, Leech Year, Flood Year, but the hardest, most hateful year a all was the Blood Year. Granny said that a Blood Year was terrifyin cuz yer in the grip a somethin that you *know* ain't gonna let you loose.

"*A Blood Year bites inta you lak the teeth of a wild dog,* Granny use ter say. It breaks through yer skin. It starts you bleedin. It pierces yer muscles. It don't stop til it hits bone. Sometimes, it crushes that open, too, an sets rat down in the river a yer marrow an drinks.

"I declare, I don't know why Granny din't call it a Marrow Year," Pearl pronounces, and closes her eyes the way a cat sitting on a sunny windowsill does, a kind of creaturely basking.

"Maybe that wild dog hits a artery an yer scairt yer gonna bleed ta *death.* A Blood Year shakes you an draws on yer strength til yer lookin Death straight in the eye."

"Is there a point to this?" Heddi is almost hissing. Honestly, if Pearl doesn't take offense at that tone, she's missing a good chance.

Pearl opens her eyes slowly, the tiny pleated wrinkles around them furrowing like a tilled field. She looks straight at Heddi; meets and holds her eye, unflinchingly.

"I espect they is." Pearl closes her eyes and the tissue of thin, fine wrinkles relaxes again. Just for a moment, a spasm crosses her face, like a sudden pain. Heddi thinks she's about to cry. Instead, she keeps on talking, with her eyes closed as if she were drawing up what she has to say out of some deep well of memory.

"Granny said that Blood Years was the luckiest a all..."

There's an explosive guffaw. "*Lucky?*" Heddi is hooting, the contempt in her voice not even barely concealed. "Well, that's the biggest pile of rubbish I've ever heard! If your Granny had ever actually *had* a Blood Year, she'd never have said such a thing."

Heddi is astonished by what's coming out of her own mouth. So this is the Shadow, then, released from repression's cage by exhaustion and ready to devour whom it may! And what form does it take? Heddi, the adored Only Child, can scarcely believe it – sibling rivalry!

Pearl opens her eyes just a squint and stares at her the way a lizard looks at a fly.

Ondine, over on the other side of the room, squirms in her lotus posture and silently mouths *Ooohlala!* to no one in particular. The silence deepens uncomfortably.

"What's that you say thar, Heady? Granny musta never had a Blood Year ta say such a thin?

"Huh! My Granny done *fergot* more bout Blood Years than *ye'll* ever know," Pearl says softly. The edge of contempt in her voice is subtle. You have to listen for it, but it's there.

That's the thing about Pearl. She has nothing. She's the Queen of Cardboard – but a queen, nevertheless. She bows to nobody. And *that's* what's pissing Heddi off.

Pearl goes silent, sucking on her pipe, her eyes closed, as if she has withdrawn into her royal boudoir. Heddi can hear the wall clock above the door ticking and the low pant of the machines keeping their last few drinks cool.

Finally, Ondine breaks the silence. "Pearl," she says in a voice like a rivulet of honey, "won't you tell us the rest, please? I think we all need to know."

Pearl's entire torso begins to bob slightly, like a wild grass stem in a breeze. She holds her pipe just beyond her lips in her right hand, her elbow supported in the cup of her left. Her crepey eyelids veil the moment she deigns to leave her boudoir and enter again into the halls of memory.

"Anyways...Granny said a Blood Year was the luckiest a all," she continues, as if there had never been an interruption. None of them moves a muscle or even breathes – Heddi included. "She said it was a gift from God."

Self, Heddi thinks, staring down at the floor, *if you snort, or so much as crack a snide little grin, I'm going to smack you.* But she doesn't. She feels locked in some inner room of her own; some place where capital punishment can be exacted, where an axe can fall and the hated parasite of memory can be severed forever.

"The thin with a Blood Year, you see, is it cracks you open. Whatever closed system a thins you done set up, it's busted. Whatever you think is the way thins is, you find they ain't. Whatever you thought yer limits was, they wasn't. Maybe you thought you couldn't stand no more pain – an then, you find you cain. Or so much of it – an you discover you gots more room in thar fer it then you thought.

"*You gots ta crack the nut ta get at the meat,* Granny use ter say. *Gots ta break the shell ta get the chick out.* An the years that's hardest, the Blood Years, they cracks yer bones ta get the marrow a yer own meanin out.

"That lil river a the soul that lies deep in thar feedin yer poor, dried-up sef ain't a place you cain always get to. Blood Years, you goes down ta the river an drinks.

"Or falls in an drowns.

"Ain't no other way ta get at it.

"Cept maybe through joy. But that's a different thin – an it don't usually last a year. Ain't no Joy Year in Granny's calendar."

You gots ta crack the nut ta get at the meat, Heddi hears Pearl say, at a great distance. *You gots ta break the shell ta get the chick out.*

Is *that* what all this hammering has been, then... salvation?

Pearl's pipe has gone out but she sucks on it anyway, her eyes still closed. Her face glows like the Pythoness's over the abyss; their own Delphic oracle.

The resentment Heddi feels towards her is eating her like battery acid.

Why is she *like* this?

She knows from depth psychology that there *are* Blood Years. They just call them initiation, or the archetype of descent, or the *nekyia*, or the Night Sea Journey, or the Dark Night of the Soul, or a creative illness. So why is she resisting this woman so?

For some reason, Heddi wants to weep, just to double over and howl. She knows – *feels* – the exact place in her body where the wild dogs are gnawing.

And she doesn't know whether she's terrified, or if some secret part of her is rejoicing.

X has decided she will throw open the door when she sees by the monitor that the Brother is only a few steps from it. She is able to judge this by her latrine can that is clearly visible, sitting right next to Fat Guy in the hall.

She stands with one hand on the doorknob and her eyes glued to the screen. She is thinking that it will be best if he comes to her. She imagines him knocking at the door, calling her name urgently in a whisper. But she will hesitate, causing him to wonder if she is still alive. She will make him wait – only an instant – but in that time, he will feel the same longing that she has felt.

And *then* she will have the dignity of opening to him.

But when the instant arrives, she is so overcome that she does not wait. She throws open the door and...he is not there!

He has already moved past and now, with his back to her, is continuing down the hallway. Now it is she who must whisper urgently, "Jamal!" and when he continues on, a louder call, "*Jamal!*"

Like a cat, he spins in place and X is looking down the barrel of his gun. She cannot see his eyes within the balaclava and suddenly she is unsure. Is this Jamal or another Brother – or even some stranger?

She screams involuntarily, "No!" and ducks back into her room. She is trying to slam the door when he pushes through, knocking her aside.

He seems to fill up the room. His energy is huge and fierce. X stands with her back to the corner, staring at him in terror as he spins, looking for someone to shoot.

At last, he stops and focuses on X. "What are you doing here?" he demands roughly.

When she hears his voice, she knows at last that it is Jamal.

"Jamal! Please! Take off your mask. You are frightening me."

He does not respond. He seems to hang suspended between answering her request and something else that occupies him more completely. At last, slowly, he reaches up with his free hand and slips the mask up, revealing his handsome face.

X moves toward him, her hand raised, wanting to touch his cheek, but he steps back, tossing his head to the side like a wild animal.

"No!" he shouts.

X stares at him in horror. "Jamal! What is wrong? What is *wrong* with you?"

She is thinking that all the killing has damaged him, made him a little crazy. Again, she moves toward him, wanting to touch him, to soothe him.

But he is too fast. In an instant, he has lowered his gun and is pushing her away from him with the barrel.

"Jamal!" X is crying now, not from fear but because she feels her heart will break. "Oh, Allah-God, Jamal! Why are you *like* this with me?" Her tears are not an embarrassment now. They are simply the only language she has.

Jamal is staring at her; his large brown eyes are almost black. She cannot see into them. His face looks as if it is made of iron. It is set, rigid, hard. This cannot be the same man who touches her so gently and murmurs Rumi to her in Farsi.

They are frozen; he to the stock of his rifle and she at the end of its barrel, staring into one another's eyes. It seems to last forever.

"They told me you were dead," he whispers, finally, his voice hoarse with shock.

Then, slowly, very slowly, he lowers the barrel of the gun and whispers, "Don't move."

He turns his back and lays the gun on the desk. X hears the high metallic sound of a zipper. Then slowly, he turns back toward her.

In one instant, she understands. She begins to scream, "No! No! No! *Naaaahhhhh!*"

Her knees buckle and she crashes to the floor, circling her head with her arms. She cannot stop the wild shrieks that erupt from her mouth. She has never heard such sounds, except in the camps when someone is killed and the women grieve. She did not know she was capable of making such cries.

"Stop it!" she screams. *"Stop it, right now!"*

"I can't," she hears him say hoarsely, "or I would. You know that even better than I. There is not much time."

She cannot stop screaming. Above her own loud noise, she hears his; how he turns away with a gritty scrape, the metal of his zipper closing, the soft thud of his gun lifting from the desk.

"Say something to me!" she screams. "Say *something!"*

She does not have to look to know that he is by the door now, looking back at her where she is crumpled on the floor, completely undisciplined, in utter disarray. But X does not care. She is a warrior of another kind now.

"Say something, Jamal! Please! *Please!"*

And he does. "I love you. I always will," he says in a voice like boots on gravel.

"Then, don't go..." she begins, pushing herself up from the floor. But he is gone already, with a soft whoosh of air and a faint click of the door closing.

And X is left with an image engraved on her heart: Jamal standing before her, his hard eyes gone pleading, asking for understanding; his hands holding open his vest – and his chest covered in explosives.

Ondine

"Pearl," Ondine says, but glaring directly at Heddi, "there's such wisdom in what your grandmother said. Won't you continue your story, please?"

"Yeah," Betty agrees. "I like communing with your grandma."

"We all *need* to commune with her," Sophia adds. "She's become an important part of our commune of women." She sweeps an inclusive hand around their ragged circle, as if Pearl's Granny were seated among them.

Pearl strikes a match, lights her pipe and takes a long drag before she begins again. "I reckon she'd feel rat ta home here. If they was a disaster wrought by the hand a man, Granny'd somehow get sucked inta it, lak a turtle in quicksand. She'd be settin rat here, sayin, *Ain't nothin ta be asceerd of. Everthin's gonna be alrat.*"

Pearl takes another long, contemplative drag on her pipe, as if concentrating the smokes of memory deep inside her.

Pearl

"Well, ta get back ta Abel Johns...that was the beginnin of a season in Hell. We was all in the hands of a madman, no two ways bout it. We done traveled the back roads from county ta county an state ta state. An when we needed money, that unholy bastard'd stop at some seedy roadhouse an go in... "

The first time it happened, she was completely caught off guard. After a spell, the door a that bar opened an lat spilled out ta whar her an the kids set waitin in the dirt lot, an three men come out.

Abel Johns comes an yanks open her door an says, "Come here, bitch," an grabs her by the arm.

He pulls her round ta the back a the car an slams her face down against the trunk an holds her by the neck. An in a dream a terror Pearl hears him ax, "Who's goin first?"

She feels strange hands grippin her an her skirt pullt up an her panties ripped off. An then the most God-awful pain a some bastard's big dick rammin her. Ta this day, it don't seem possible ta her that she endured such a thin. But she knows it's true. They ain't no use denyin it.

It went on an on. The drunken bastard couldn't come, ferever. An jes when she knows it's finally over, she hears Abel Johns say, "It's yer turn, partner. Whar's yer five bucks?" An the whole natmare begins again.

That filthy devil, Abel Johns – may he rot in Hell! – kept her an her kids prisoner fer most a year. Spring turnt ta summer an finally the days cooled down an it was autumn. An still, they was travelin, never stayin more then a nat in any one place.

An ever place they stopped, he found customers willin ta rape a woman fer a price. In fact, the more she'd protest an fat, the better they laked it. She learnt soon enough ta play possum. It din't hurt as much an they din't get as excited.

She found out what he was tellin em that made em so eager. He was sayin, "I got this here wife that I found out is a whore. She done lied ta me an her punishment is ta do it out in front a God an everbody til her cunt falls off." Ain't hardly a man on the planet wouldn't get a hard-on ta punish a wayward woman.

Somewhar in Arkansas that summer, her oldest, Harold, done run off with a truckload a laborers, goin bout harvestin crops. She never did blame him. She was glad fer him. But her heart still aches cuz she never seen him again. He warn't but twelve.

Then, she had her but four young'uns. She did her very best fer em, which warn't much, she cain tell you. The life they was leadin was pure madness.

They was but one time that the Lord turnt His baleful eye upon that heathen husband a hers. They was somewhar in Alabama, she reckons, an Abel Johns was drummin up business at a roadhouse. But what he din't know was, the folks he was runnin his number to was all Baptists, sneakin a beer after choir practice.

They all come out in a herd, bout a dozen of em, an looked at Pearl an the kids waitin out thar in that old jalopy, lookin purdy tired an wan, she reckons.

"This woman the mother a these children?" one feller axed.

An Abel Johns nods an says, "Yes, sir, she is."

And then that feller does somethin completely unespected. He looks Pearl's daughter, Annabelle, rat in the eye an he axed, "You love yer mama?"

An poor Annabelle, scared spitless, stares at him with eyes lak a trapped rabbit an jes nods.

But the feller ain't done with her yet. "Is she a good mama ta you? Is she kind ta you?"

An Annabelle manages ta whisper, "Oh, yes sir. She is."

Now, Pearl's thinkin this guy's bout ta demand Annabelle in place a her, an she's plottin really fast how she's gonna kill em, if he lays so much as his lil finger on that poor child. She's searchin round the ground with her eyes fer a rock – anythin.

But then, the miracle happens. "Boys," says the feller ta his friends, "I think we need ta confer with Mr. Johns out by the outhouse. What'd ya say?"

And thar's a murmur among em an they kinda move round Abel Johns an take him by the elbows an shuffle him off round the back a the roadhouse.

Pearl's thinkin, *Good Lord! Theys bargainin fer a group rate!*

She gets outta that car – a thin she is forbidden ta do – an she creeps inta the shadders, follerin along behind.

Sure enough, when they get ta the outhouse, they stop an she cain hear em talkin. An she hears Abel Johns' voice startin ta rise above the others. And purdy soon, she hears him screamin an she's thinkin, *What the thunder...?*

One a them fellers comes flyin past her so fast he din't even see her hunkerin down thar in the shadders. He jumps inta his car an revs it up an comes tearin round the side a the buildin an stops with his headlats full on the scene. An then he jumps out, leavin the lats on, an joins the crowd again.

Now, Pearl cain see theys got Abel Johns rat in front a the loo, with the door open. Theys pushin him in an he gots both arms an legs on the doorframe, resistin with all his mat. But thar's no way one man cain fat off a dozen, an fore Pearl quite knows what's happenin, theys pushed him in an slammed the door shut.

Pearl cain't quite make out what these fellers is up to, but soon it becomes clear as well water. One of em's got a hammer an nails an he nails the door shut. Some others, they gots a can a gas from the back of they truck an they douse that lil house down with it real good.

And then, lak a kinda ceremony, everone gets real quiet an the first feller steps up an takes a book a matches outta his pocket. Very slow an deliberate, he folds back the cover. An pulls off a match. An closes the cover.

By the lat a them headlats, Pearl cain see a glitter down in the deeps a the crescent moon cut in the outhouse door, an she reckons it's Abel Johns's eye, watchin and gettin as big as full-on terror cain make it.

A great caterwauling commences. He's poundin on the door an screamin lak a panther with his toes in a trap. The whole buildin's rockin lak it's about ta explode cuz he's slammin hisself inta the walls tryin ta break through or ta capsize the whole she-bang altogether.

Then that first feller strikes the match an holds it up so's everone cain see the flame an thar's a murmur amongst the men. And then, lak he's the Archangel Michael stokin the fires a Hell, he bends down an puts that match ta the side a the loo.

Well, a building lak that, it's dry as tinder anyways. Hell, a cigarette'd ignite it, if the wind was rat. But soaked in gasoline...?

It goes up lak a torch an Pearl cain hear Abel Johns screamin an beggin an poundin inside.

Now, any decent person'd try ta stop such a thin. They'd rush rat in thar an demand the release a the prisoner. So, it's a commentary on how depraved she had become, livin with that devil, that she did nothin. In fact, she stood thar amazed, hopin against hope that that monster was breathin his last.

But them fellers knowed this trick. They'd done it afore an they knowed the outcome long afore Pearl figgered it out.

Afore long, thar ain't no more screamin an Pearl's thinkin that them fellers has made a widder outta her. But she sees theys shovin one another in the ribs with they elbows an sayin thins low that makes em all laugh.

An she thinks, *Everthin I ever heerd about these here Baptists is true, an then some! Good Lord! These here is even worse heathens then Abel Johns.*

At least he gots the good grace ta feel guilty over what he done ta poor Abner – even if his way a havin it is ta punish Pearl. But these fellers here, theys laughin an hootin an carryin on lak killin is nothin but good sport.

Finally, the buildin burns rat down ta the ground. Theys nothin but smokin timbers an the stench a burning poop. An them fellers is crowdin rat in thar, anyhow, as if this was the best part. An theys laughin an howlin an pointin.

And *finally*, Pearl gets it: Abel Johns is still *alive!* An he's took the only escape route available – which is *down*. Down through the wooden potty hole inta a pit a shit!

Well, then Pearl starts ta hear him screamin again, beggin ta be pullt up from the depths. But theys not a one a them fellers who's about ta lend a hand ta a hand covered in shit.

Theys had they good time an theys tared of it. One by one, they turns an shuffles back ta the parkin lot, gets in they cars an drives away. Theys purdy quiet then, lak dogs that done kilt the chickens an know theys done wrong – but is lickin they lips jes the same.

The first feller is the last ta leave an Pearl hears him talkin down inta the pit. "Yer a fornicator an a pimp," he says. "An yer turnin yer good wife inta a whore. Get a taste a Hell, my friend, cuz that's whar you're goin. Don't ask *me* fer a hand out. Ask *God*. High time you started prayin, instead a pimpin." And with that, he turns an leaves, with Abel Johns still down in the hole.

As he comes by, he sees Pearl cowerin thar in the shadders. He reaches inta his pocket an pulls out some bills an hands em ta her. "Take this an get outta town," he says, an then he hops inta his car an tears off inta the nat.

Well, Pearl's more'n ready ta take his advice but – here is her downfall – she's jes *gotta* see that man a hers swimmin in sewage. God hep her, but that was a sat too rich ta miss. A gal could wait a lifetime an never get such a chance again.

So she tiptoes up ta the lip. Theys still boards layin on the ground, smokin an winkin with lil red coals. The smell'd gag a maggot. Jes revoltin. An down in the blackness whar she cain barely see em, thars this figger sloshin round, most up ta his neck in muck. He's swearin an flailin an sobbin, all at once.

Pearl heerd once that they was this thin called the Divine Comedy. She reckons this was a scene straight outta that. If'n that din't make God laugh, He's too straitlaced an that's the plain fact a it. It was enough ta make the angels pee they pants. She knows she did hers. She ain't laughed lak that afore or since.

"Heeeee! Heeeee!

"Lordie! Listen ta me whinny! It makes me laugh still!

"Heeee, heeeee, heeee!
"Whar's mah hankie? Lord! I'm plum outta breath!
"Heeeeee, heeeee!
"Who-eeee!

Well! When she'd had her fill a that, she turns an makes fer the car. She ain't never drove one but she figgers this is the time ta learn. A gal cain be a quick study when a shit-covered demon's on her tail.

Cuz one thin she knowed fer sure: Abel Johns'd find a way outta that pit. Fer all she knowed, a devil straight from Hell'd come an *lift* him out, jes so's his deviltry'd keep on a-goin.

So, she's out thar in the parkin lot, tryin ta get under way. But she cain't co-ordinate the gas an the clutch. Her an her chicks is lurchin round that lot, the gas is roarin, an the car is jerkin lak its got a fit, an Pearl's still half crazy with laughin, so's the kids got it by contak, lak a bad cold. Theys all in that ol jalopy jerkin along, howlin lak a cage a crazed monkeys, when...

Good God! Some kinda monster throwed itsef onta the hood!

It's black an glistenin an stinks lak the holds a Hell. It plasters itsef against the windshield, a-hangin onta the whapers lak they was reins. Pearl cain't see the face – but two big red eyes is starin rat at her through the glass – an she ain't laughin no more.

Pearl tries ta step on the gas an throw the thin off but she stalls the car instead. And thar they are.

"Lock the doors!" she screams. But it's too late. The thin is rippin the door open an pullin her out onta the ground.

Well, thar ain't much more a that ta tell. The beatin she took near kilt her. An the kids din't fare much better. The only thin that stopped him from killin em all was he was so exhausted.

Pearl reckons his own smell did him in. He jes collapsed right thar in the parkin lot an slept til dawn, with the hair on his head still smokin, an covered in slime lak some creature vomited up out a the gorge a Hell.

Then, after sun-up, he had Pearl hose him down an off they went, silent an stinkin an beaten lak a carload a the damned.

Well, that incident set Abel Johns inta a foul mood that lasted fer weeks an it spurred his ambitions concernin Pearl. He'd drag any ol drunk out ta screw her, even if the feller din't have any money. He'd let him do it jes fer the spite a it.

Pearl's spirit was bout broke. She was thinkin she'd cut her wrists an be done with it. She couldn't even think ta defend her lil ones no more.

But then one day, she come inta the motor court whar they was stayin, luggin a basket a wet laundry from the crick. An she stops dead in her tracks cuz thar's Abel Johns an he's got his mouth on her daughter, Annabelle, who is only six, in a place whar no man outta have it.

Somethin happened ta Pearl then. Her blood run cold as ice. Her mind settled down from the chaos that was its daily habit ta a focus hard an sharp as a whetted axe.

Maybe some shred a decency was left in that monster, after all. When he saw Pearl come in, he stopped his unholy act an even had the good grace ta look ashamed.

A course, that only made him worse that nat. He took Pearl from tavern ta roadhouse ta bar til she was so sore she screamed when they touched her down thar, an her knees was so weak them bastards had ta hold her up against the car trunk or she'd a just crumpled down in a heap.

But all the while, she's keen as a hawk's beak. Her mind never rests on the pain but skips over it ta what's ta come — cuz she knows that bastard, Abel Johns, is gettin drunker an drunker. An sooner or later, he'll be fallin inta a stupor that a air horn cain't rouse him from.

Back at the motor court, jes as she figgered, he stumbles onta the bed an is snorin fore his feet leaves the floor. Quick as a lizard, she hurries the kids inta the car an tells em not ta come out unless God Hissef comes fer em.

"What's God look lak?" Buford, her second boy, axed. He wuz bout ten then, she reckons.

"He's a great, huge man with a long white beard an his eyes glows lak the full moon. Lessen you see *Him*, don't you dare move a muscle til I get back."

Now, out back, she'd seed a woodshed with a choppin block an a axe. An now she went out thar, bold as brass, an took that axe an marched inta that room an stood over the sleepin body a Abel Johns an searched her heart fer one tiny *bit* a compassion.

An then, findin none, she raised that axe high up above her head an brung it down with all her *mat,* an she chopped that bastard's head clean *off!*

Whar she found the strength, tared an battered as she was, she'll never know. But she's guessin it was a divine dispensation, pure an simple.

She found her a shovel in that same shed an she went out back in a weedy field an dug an dug an dug lak a woman possessed. Then she went back in an she drug that bastard an his head in the bedclothes, out the door, round the back an inta that field. An she din't roll him inta that grave. She *kicked* him in.

An then she took a notion. With that shovel, she dug another hole an put his head in that one, separate, so the two a em – body an head – cain never unite again even if they *was* some kinda reintarnation.

An afore she buried it, she done *spat* inta that gapin mouth an says inta them eyes that done sprung open, "This here is fer *you,* Abel Johns," an she pullt up her skirt an squatted down an *peed,* rat in his face.

An then she buried the body an covered the dirt with weeds an put back the shovel an the axe, an then she went in an turnt the mattress an scrubbed down that room all nat til the dawn come.

An then she showered off all the gore an sweat, an then went an brung her babies in an says, 'You been up all nat. You sleep tat now fer a few hours an I'll be rat back.'

An then she marches hersef down ta the police station an reports Abel Johns missin – run off on her an her kids. An she makes sure they know that he's wanted fer murder a his own child back in Oklahoma. An then she marched back an axed the manager a that motel fer a job cleanin rooms an he give it ta her on the spot. An she worked that day, straight through. An in the evenin, she gots her pay an fed her chicks the food she done bought with it. An then, she crawlt inta bed an slept fer three days straight.

Sophia

Sophia can't wait any longer. She has to tell them what's been growing in her for the last hour.

"Excuse me, Pearl, but..."

She glances at Pearl, wondering if she's affronted by being interrupted just at the climax of her story. But Pearl's gone into that space of reverie she slips into periodically, looking serene as the Virgin.

"Ladies, I have a feeling. My Little Voice is telling me that our ordeal will soon be over."

"When? Right now?" Betty perks up considerably.

"No, Betty, I can't give you an exact time. All I can tell you is that the energy's shifting. Something's happening. The oppressive weight is lifting...but the energy's getting more...more...I don't know...more *urgent*."

Sophia stops to listen but the only sounds are their breathing, the ticking of the wall clock and the faint purr of the drink machines.

"How do you know?" Heddi asks acerbically.

Sophia questions that herself: how can she be so sure of what she's feeling – no, *knowing* – right now? After all these years, she still has to remind herself: all her life, she's moved among mysteries and she knows when the Mysteries are moving in her!

The smell of water in an arid landscape; of snow before it falls, of ozone just before lightning strikes. Her nervous system dances with these and sings with them in ancient harmonies.

And always, out in the woods at the periphery of sight and sound and touch and smell, there is the flicker of something deeper, wilder, older still. Beings armored in exoskeletons of old ivory, winged like butterflies, singing like the stars, powerful, uncanny and evasive, with the black, lustrous eyes of goats, sensual, amoral, humorous, vengeful and wise.

They could morph from the gnarled roots of trees, from rocks scaled in lichens, from shadows glimmering through the deep trees. Their songs drifted through the air of the woods like fishing lures sinking through the shallows. They sank their hooks deep in her flesh and reeled her in. She was theirs. They took her and changed her and taught her their ways and then threw her out again to wander home in twilight or dawn light – dazed, blissful and only nominally human.

Heddi is staring at her with a look half hopeful and half profoundly dubious.

"If you think I'm crazy, Heddi, then so be it," Sophia snaps.

Heddi just shakes her head but keeps on staring, as if Sophia might suddenly grow horns, or vanish with a *poof.*

"Maybe I *am* crazy." Sophia shrugs. "Sometimes, I have doubts, myself...but then, madness must be an absolute form of truth because sometimes I just *know* things."

Pump her full of Thorazine; light her up with electroshock like a Christmas tree; paste her with labels from the *DSM IV* like an old steamer trunk – she will never recant!

She's lived in alternate dimensions. Only a part of her soul belongs to what this world calls reality. The bigger part has colored wings and kites through the canyons, baying like a wolf!

"If you want to know how I know..." Sophia shrugs brusquely. "I've seen things."

Ondine

That's the first time any of them has heard Sophia being snappish. She's been a rock of patience, but Heddi's so bitchy it would drive anyone over the edge.

It's clear Sophia's feeling the pressure, too. She's scarcely slept for three nights, tending Erika. She's rallied them all.

Now she's standing there kind of swaying, with her long gray hair all wild about her shoulders like some mad Cassandra. It's obvious she sees no one. Whatever it is she's looking at, it's written in the ether.

Ondine looks around and sees it on every face – except Pearl's, of course. There's a kind of unspeakable desperation. They want *OUT* – even if they're being carried out on a stretcher to a hearse!

Heddi

"Well, Sophia, I hope you're right about... What?"

Sophia is suddenly motioning Heddi to be quiet. In an instant, a strange change has come over her. Her whole body is tensed, her eyes wide, as if her entire being were one big ear, listening. She brings her finger to her lips. They all freeze. She points toward the door and mouths, "Someone's out there."

Heddi feels the strangest sensation, a powerful electrical surge through her armpits, as if every pore has opened and is squirting sweat. There's a strange metallic taste back in her jaws and her breath is coming in short gasps. Her whole body, like Sophia's, suddenly knows that Death is lurking.

Now she can hear it, too. It's a faint, whispering scuttle of feet in the hall outside, and then silence. They sit staring at one another, eyes wide in alarm, watching Sophia from odd postures, as if frozen in a game of Statues.

Slowly, a kind of thaw comes over her. "It's okay," she mouths, "they're gone." And as a woman, they release a collective sigh of relief.

She creeps over, circling them in closer with a gesture of her arms.

"Something's happening. I don't know what. I feel it, though," she whispers. "The energy's definitely changing."

She looks around their bedraggled circle like a general marshalling her troops. "Now is the time of greatest danger. Anything can happen. You have to prepare yourselves."

She looks at each of them, in turn. No – not looks – *gazes*. Her eyes seem to go right through Heddi's into her brain, as if she could read her readiness for self-defense there – or for death.

"Things will happen fast, once they start. Very fast. If we're lucky, we'll be able to defend ourselves. Everything depends on keeping that machine barricading the door. If there's gunfire, that won't be easy. If there is, get down on the floor. Get into the corners, away from the door..."

X
=

When she comes back to herself, she is still lying on the floor and her screams have turned to sobs. The Brothers were right. She is no warrior – but for the first time, this brings her no shame.

She knows what they are doing, those cowards! She knows that the Brothers are tired of waiting for something to happen, for someone to pay attention to them. This is the thing they promised her that they would not do under any circumstances. And whom have they chosen to carry out their insane plan? Jamal! The kindest, gentlest, most poetic of them all. The one who will not resist.

And when he is gone *they* will still be alive, full of their conviction that they are brave warriors. They are sacrificing him on the altar of their own arrogance and cowardice.

And this is also retribution: Jamal and she love one another. The message is clear. There is no place for love in the warrior's world. The lover will be sacrificed. He is a useful example.

And how did they convince him? By lying! By telling him she was dead. So cowardly, these men who think themselves brave!

And suddenly, she realizes that they planned this from the beginning. Otherwise, how would there be the explosive vest? The work is so delicate; she should have been the one to make it. No, they made that thing without her knowledge because they always planned to do this. That is why they made the vest so it could not be removed. It is their revenge against her happiness; against her very existence among them.

Somehow, she finds the strength to pull herself up by the edge of the desk. Jamal was moving very quickly. He must be near his target now.

Her heart feels as if it will explode. She holds onto the chair to keep from collapsing and forces herself to look at the video screens, barely breathing as she scans them.

Please Allah-God! Please! Let that terrible vest fail! Please do not let Jamal be killed in this horrible way!

At last she finds him, crouching behind an airline counter very near the main entrance.

She looks at the clock. It is just five o'clock. She turns to the television and the news is just beginning...

Of course! That is how they have planned it! How stupid she is! The live news coverage of every major television station in America is focused on this building. The Brothers will give to them the explosive news for which they lust!

Now it is like a tennis match. She turns her head to see Jamal. She flips it back to see the newswoman, with her blonde hair blowing in the dry Los Angeles afternoon. She turns back to Jamal. Again and again. Everything seems to be happening in slow motion.

She sees him take something white from inside his vest.

She hears the reporter say, "Good evening from Los Angeles International Airport, where we are in the fourth day of a standoff with terrorists who are still holding an estimated 65 hostages..."

She sees Jamal stand from behind the counter and straighten the wadded white thing that is just a rectangle of white cloth.

She watches as the TV camera pans over the front of the terminal, the tanks, the hunched SWAT teams, the men in black jackets with *FBI* in big white letters on the back.

She sees Jamal begin to walk toward the doors.

She hears the newscaster say, "So far, there has been no sign of willingness to negotiate..."

She sees Jamal's hand touch the metal bar of the door handle.

She hears the woman say, "FBI officials at the scene..."

She strains to see his form as the doors swing open, as he becomes shadowy and vague through the glass and then disappears, as the door shuts.

She turns to the TV where the blonde has stopped in mid-sentence, her mouth hanging open. "Oh my God! This is amazing... Can we get a camera on that? Hurry! Ladies and gentlemen, someone has just emerged from the terminal, waving a white flag!"

A blurry image of a man all in black walks out from the shadows of the entrance, one arm raised and waving the white cloth.

Faintly, she can hear men yelling, "Down! Get down!" but the figure does not get down.

Slowly, he moves forward, still waving his flag, an isolated figure on the desolate plane of concrete, as alone and lost as a crash victim in the desert.

"He's ignoring the orders to get down, ladies and gentlemen! He seems to be moving almost in a trance..."

X leans toward the screen, straining to clarify the cloudy image.

"He seems to be shouting something! Can we pick that up on the mic? Ladies and gentlemen, this is the first big break in four days. This is apparently one of the terrorists and he seems to be trying to negotiate..."

And then X hears his voice. It is unmistakably Jamal's and, though distant and faint, she and the viewing audience of millions can hear his words distinctly. "We will wait no longer. We demand a plane and safe passage to Libya. Otherwise, in fifteen minutes, we will begin executing hostages..."

His words are cut off. A group of armored men rushes him and just as they tackle him, before her horrified eyes, Jamal simply disappears, with horrific noise, in a cloud of smoke.

Heddi

Suddenly there is the most terrifying explosion!

The entire floor rises under them like the back of a huge, shrugging beast and then subsides. Acoustic tiles rain down from the ceiling. The lights dim, brown out and go black. Thick dust fills the air, leaving Heddi choking for breath. All around her, she hears screams and wailing.

Then above the coughing and sobs, she's aware of an immense silence, as if the world has simply stopped turning – as if whatever it is that has happened has killed all life.

She raises her head and looks around.

Pitch blackness.

She hears bodies rustling, moaning, the scrape of grit and tinkling of broken glass.

Then miraculously, a light appears from over by the candy machine! She turns toward it, dazed by it like a moth. She can see nothing but it. It blinds her. But she feels a surge of life, of gratitude, as if it were an epiphany of God Himself.

Then there's a gravelly cackle, "I been luggin this ol flashlat round fer years, thinkin the day'd come when I'd surely need it, an it looks lak today's the day!"

The Brueghel! God love her!

Pearl shines her light around the room. The first one Heddi sees is Erika, half-blown off the couch, her left leg hanging to the floor, her body buried in acoustic tiles from which dust wafts like a cloud of smoke.

The light sweeps to the right and there's Betty, her head completely white, as if someone had upended a flour canister over her. Her eyes are so big and dark, she looks like an electrocuted owl. And mercifully, she seems to have been shocked into silence.

The beam sweeps on, toward the door where there's the most amazing sight – Sophia, with her entire body bent beneath the weight of the toppled drink machine that leans at an angle more prone than upright. Her eyes are about to pop out of her head from the strain.

"Quick!" Heddi shouts, without thinking of the noise. "Everyone help her!" She pushes herself up from the floor, feeling broken glass embed itself in the heel of her hand.

Her legs are gelatinous. She doesn't walk. She *wavers* towards the door. Other forms emerge from the darkness, weaving in the same direction.

Arms reach out. There are grunts. Someone says "Shit!" through gritted teeth. Slowly, ever so slowly, the machine rises, balances a second on its back edge, then rocks backward, slamming into the doorframe. The remaining glass cascades from its front window with a tinkle like wind chimes.

Sophia is breathing hard. She nods her head, mouths, "Thanks," too winded to speak. And then, Heddi sees her tense again...!

X
=

When the explosion comes, it is so huge and violent that X cannot believe what she is seeing. The floor buckles beneath her feet. The television and all the monitors go black. She is thrown violently to her right. The ceiling lights flicker, go brown and then blink out. She crashes to the floor, screaming to Allah to let the walls fall in and bury her.

Finally, she sees that a little light has come on over the door. It fills the room with an ugly red glow.

She does not know for how long she has been lying there. Her head aches terribly and when she puts her hand to the back of her skull, it comes away covered in blood that looks black in the lurid light.

She tries to sit up, but something is wrong. Then she sees that the monitors have all toppled to the floor, pinning her right leg. She cannot feel it and almost wishes it would hurt.

She lies back and tries to think.

So this is it! This is the glorious action of the Brothers – death, destruction, dust, terror, injury, despair. She knows from making bombs that this explosion is bigger than any she might have prepared. This is a concentration of C-4 of terrible force.

She wants to cry but no tears come. They are all expended. There are no tears left.

She sits again and begins to shove at the nearest monitor. As its weight slowly rocks backward across her leg, the pain follows. Suddenly, it bolts through her and she opens her mouth to scream but all that comes out is a groan – a terrible sound, barely human.

She cannot formulate a plan – her mind is too chaotic – but in some strange fashion, she knows what to do; what is her destiny. All she has to do is to get her stubborn animal body to cooperate.

Somehow, she manages to get to her feet in the chaos of ceiling tiles and monitors. In the red glow from the emergency light, it is a scene straight from the Christian's Hell.

She staggers through the wasted equipment. Wires are ripped from the wall and one is arcing quietly to itself, a greenish, jagged bolt of pure energy amid the jumble.

She has a secret and now it's time. If she had told the Brothers, they would have laughed at her – even Jamal.

With filthy, numbed fingers, she unbuttons her pants and drags them down around her thighs. Wrapped tightly around her waist, the secret is warm and fitted to her body like an embrace. She pulls at it blindly until an end falls loose and she begins to unwind it. It is wrapped around her twice.

She sets it aside, pulls up her pants and re-buttons them. Then she holds her prize up in the red light for inspection. It is the shawl her mother embroidered for her years ago, black and soft, with cross-stitch in red, green, and white, the Palestinian colors, making a wide geometric border. Red strawberries are strewn over the black field, like delicious hope sprinkled over a grave.

Her good luck piece.

She bends forward and wraps the shawl around her head like a woman wrapping wet hair in a towel, and winds the ends around and around until she can tie them in a knot.

It is her crown and she wishes she had a mirror. She wants it to be very impressive.

This is for you, Mama, and for my aunties and Cousin Sharona. This is for all the women in all the camps, wherever they are...for all their suffering, for all their patience, for all their love.

As she hobbles through the rubble searching for her assault rifle, she can feel the blood beginning to saturate the back of her crown.

Ondine

They are all staring at Sophia by the light of Pearl's flashlight. She's standing like a sibyl about to pronounce a prophecy.

And yet there's something animal-like about her, too. In Sophia's stance can be seen all the years of her wanderings in the woods, as her nerve-endings turned hypersensitive and she learned from the animals the arts of self-preservation.

Ondine has never witnessed such a transformation. It feels like Sophia might suddenly rise up on owl's wings or leap like a deer. She feels a slow creep of gooseflesh, just looking at her.

Sophia is like a dancer, poised on the balls of her feet, rocking slightly like a leaf lifted by wind. Her eyes are staring but not at anything in particular. Her entire body is like a tuning fork that's been struck and is vibrating. Her nostrils dilate, as her head rears back and she cocks her ear toward the door.

Sophia sweeps them all with her gaze and it seems as bright as a searchlight. Ondine thinks she sees an actual beam emitted from those eyes, piercing the curtains of dust.

"Down!" Sophia hisses. "Get down! Into the corners!"

They all start to move jerkily, strobe-like, through the curtains of dust.

Ondine collides with someone; Betty, by her doughy bulk. Her face is powdered white, her eyes huge, by the intermittent light of the flashlight's beam. Ondine grabs her by the elbow and drags her toward the corner at the end of the couch. She comes unresistingly, like a tired child.

She sees Heddi, bent double, mincing through the littered tiles toward Pearl and the candy machine.

"Turn out that light, Pearl!" comes Sophia's rough whisper.

The room goes black.

There's a heavy silence.

And then they hear it, too: the muted cadence of many feet.

They advance in a scurry, then stop.

Advance. Stop.

Advance. Stop.

They're drawing closer.

Who are they? Ondine knows without question that they're men. But terrorists? The SWAT team? There's no way to know. She feels her heart hammering as if it would break straight through her chest wall – hard enough that they must surely be able to hear it out in the corridor.

This is it, then. This is the moment of truth. And she thinks of Tante Collette, how she would likely reach over and take her hand and squeeze it at this moment, infusing her with her own courage.

Ondine can hear Betty muttering to herself, hysterically. In the dark, she gropes until she finds Betty's hand and follows it up her arm until she finds her shoulders. Then she reaches out and embraces her, with arms strong as a bear's.

Betty

"Oh God, I am humbly sorry that I have offended Thee. Please accept my apologies and preserve me, unharmed, through this nightmare. I've been a bad person, God, I admit it. A terrible person. I was lost. So lost! But now, I see the error of my ways. Now, I know that life is precious. I know that I should throw out all those plastic flowers. I know I should open my windows and let the air come through. I know I shouldn't have taken down my son's birdfeeder. I should never have told him birds were dirty. Oh my God! How could I have done that? My little boy, so eager and so kind, and me teaching him to hate and fear your Creation! And Serena and her hamsters! She thinks they're cute! She loves them. Probably more than she does me. And Larry! He always wanted to hold me in bed at night and I'd push him away and tell him to go to sleep. He didn't even want sex, God. He just wanted to be affectionate and I rejected him. I've been a witch, a wicked, wicked witch. And I thought I was so good. So filled with maternal goodness. And I was just a control freak. I strangled the life right out of every living impulse, God. I made the people around me so miserable! I stifled their lives. I'm so ashamed! I am so utterly ashamed. Oh, please forgive me. Oh! Forgive me, dear God. Dear angels in heaven. Forgive me, please!"

And then, out of the darkness come warm arms. Loving arms. Drawing her in, holding her tight. Radiating love.

"Oh God! Thank you! Thank you for sending one of your angels in my hour of need! I am so sorry, God. So very, very sorry. I've learned my lesson. I'm a changed person. I'll never act that way again. I promise. I promise you, dear God. Please have mercy on me, please..."

Pearl

That Heady gal come straight at Pearl, lak she was her salvation. Pearl seen rat away she's scairt spitless. Even by flashlat, she cain see her color is bleached as a boilt shirt.

Heady plunks hersef down next ta Pearl an Pearl cain feel her shiverin lak a dog shittin peach seeds. So Pearl jes reaches up an pulls her head down in her lap an strokes her hair an says, real quiet lak, "Shhhhh. Shhhhh. Everthin gonna be alrat now," jes lak she use ter do with her kids when Abel Johns was on a rampage.

Even her ol ears cain hear it now – the shufflin a boots out in the hallway.

Good Lord, you'd think after all Pearl's been through, that nothin short a God Hissef could scare her none. But she gots ta confess, she don't lak this one bit. It's lak all them times whar Abel Johns was a-huntin her an thar warn't nowhar ta run ta. That's the worst feelin in the world. Worse, almost, then when he finally done found her.

Pearl jes strokes an strokes on Heady, sayin, "Shhhhhh. Shhhhhh now. It's gonna be alrat."

Never fer one second believin one single word a it, hersef.

Erika

There's no pain now. She's swimming in a warm darkness where she can't tell up from down. Maybe this is how a baby feels in the womb.

There's a soft light over there. She kind of wafts over and...

Oh! It's my Daddy!

He's sitting under the streetlight like he always does on summer nights, hunched on a wooden crate, picking his guitar.

He looks up and smiles at her.

"Come over here, Little Girl. I'll play you a song my Momma taught me when I was no bigger than you."

She's so skinny she can fit in the crook of his elbow and he can still finger the strings. She leans into the warmth of his big ribcage, as it swells like bellows and he starts to sing,

> *"Way down yonder in the middle of a field,*
> *Angel workin' at a chariot wheel.*
> *Not so particular 'bout workin at the wheel,*
> *but I just want to see how the chariot feel.*
>
> *Now let me fly! Now let me fly!*
> *Now let me fly up to Mt. Zion, Lord, Lord..."*

Her body is both glued to the strength of his side and flying free, and so much weight seems to just drop away. And she feels it for the first time in her entire life: *I'm free!*

Sophia

Sophia knows this feeling. She's had it many times. It's the moment before the bombardment. The sweet suspension, while the shell hurtles toward earth. The time when you turn to the one you love and smile and say, "Bend over and let me kiss your sweet ass goodbye."

She doesn't know what she'll do when they come. She knows they're going to come. She knows beyond a shadow of a doubt that they're going to find them. Maybe they've always known they were here.

And there's no telling how that will come down. There's no telling, even, who they are. Are they friend or foe? Does she fight them with all the strength that's in her, or does she rip that machine out of the door and say, "What the hell took you so long?"

Where's her Little Voice when she really needs it?

All she knows is, she won't have to decide. The animal in her will know exactly what to do. Even now, it's not fear she's feeling. It's the pumping-up of every bodily reserve. All around her, the women are consumed by fear.

But Sophia – she's ready!

By some miracle, the barrel of her rifle is not bent, even though an avalanche of monitors has landed on it. She breaks it down and puts it back together again, just as she has been taught. It is a perfectly oiled instrument of death. She pumps a cartridge into the chamber and takes the safety off.

She takes a last look around this room that has been her prison. What a dreadful little cave! What kind of a person must Fat Guy have been to have expended his life force in such a place? Not a Warrior, certainly.

But she! She is a Warrior! She feels it now.

Now she understands that fear is a clinging to life by this weak body. She is disgusted to be attached to such a weak thing!

And she understands that the love for which the Brothers despised her and Jamal is not linked to this weak body, but to the soul – and is eternal.

She knows, too, that the Brothers' rejection of her was complete from the beginning. They never accepted her, but only planned how they might use her. Their words taunt her: "You are the unknown factor – so from now on, you will be called *X*."

But now, she says to them in her soul, *I am Najat! My name is Najat! I never will allow myself to be X-ed out again!*

She opens the door and steps into the corridor. She knows the way.

She does not do as Jamal has done, stooping and watching. She marches. Her feet seem to have minds of their own, like fine horses. Despite the limp dealt her by the monitors, they carry her along like the wind.

She would like to imagine that her mother is with her, or her aunties, or any of the women of the camps whose lives have been so mangled by the wars of men. But she knows that she is alone – just as she wished at the beginning. She is the sole woman. The duty is hers, alone.

She encounters no one in the corridors. It does not take long to reach the food court.

Her heart is beating wildly, but not with fear. It is swelling and beating with resolve, as she takes cover behind the edge of the wall.

Slowly, carefully, she peeks around. There are the Brothers. They have gathered the hostages into a tight bundle. She knows that, soon now, they will begin shooting them. She hears the voices of women, crying and pleading.

She raises her rifle and takes careful aim. For once, her stupid body is steady as a rock.

She squeezes the trigger.

The first of the Brothers falls.

She steps out from behind the wall.

She aims and fires again, and again.

Before they even know what has happened to them, Najat's Brothers have found their reward in Glory.

Ondine

When it finally comes, it's too chaotic to understand. It's all noise and shouting and crashing. Ondine holds onto Betty, as if she could keep them both from exploding from terror.

The drink machine topples inward and a rush of outside light spotlights Sophia, as the falling machine pushes her from her stand at the door. She's screaming, "Hold your fire! Hold your fire!"

She staggers backward to plunk down in the orange chair, as the invading force bursts in with an explosion of gunfire.

They come charging through the door, as if the machine were not even there. There are blinding lights and all Ondine can see are silhouettes surging through billows of shifting dust.

"Get down!" she screams at Sophia.

But Ondine doesn't know if she does because, suddenly, there is a huge man standing in front of her. He's got a headlamp on and it's shining right in her face and she hears herself shrieking, *"Don't shoot! Don't shoot! God! Please, don't shoot!"*

There is shouting and screaming all around her. She glances around in panic, but all she can see are standing walls of backlit dust and huge black figures careening through them, casting blue-white beams as they go.

It's a scene from Dante's *Inferno.* She lowers her head onto her knees and waits to die.

Betty

As they come through the door, the angel's arms hold her tighter.

Betty's screaming, "Oh God! Oh God! Oh God! Oh God! Oh God! Help us. *Please!"*

And wonder of wonders – she starts to laugh because she said "us" and not "me"!

Can you believe it?

It took all this to open her shell!

She thinks she's pooped her pants – like any new creature would.

She's about to die and she feels unaccountable joy!

Heddi

She's lying with her head in Matilda's lap and Matilda is crooning to her. She feels comforted. The dream is subsiding. Order is being restored.

No. That's not right.

She's on the floor and riot is going on all around her.

"*OW!*" Someone steps on her foot, hard.

Heddi sits up, enraged.

"You son of a *bitch!*" she shrieks. "Watch where you're stepping!"

And then, there's a blinding light in her eyes and someone is kneeling next to her; someone huge and padded, like a hockey player or a large beetle.

"Sorry, m'am," a baritone voice says. It sounds young and genuinely apologetic. "Are you okay?"

Heddi looks blindly into his headlamp, in the general vicinity of where she thinks his eyes should be and summons her most ironic and bitchiest tone.

"Oh! Never better!"

Pearl

Well, the Good Lord done give Pearl a long life an a passel a trouble. She's been round the Horn seven times, seen it rain, sleet an snow, been ta ten goat ropins an a hog-callin contest, but she ain't *never* seen the lak a this!

All hell and tarnation done sprung loose everwhar!

Theys all these big fellers trampin ever which way, raisin dust an flashin lights ta blind the dead.

That Heady, she's a feisty one. She's a-reamin out some young buck big as a buffalo an he's back peddlin, even though he's big enough ta squish her lak a ant.

Over thar, in t'other corner, theys the Onion, cradlin Betty lak a baby. An Pearl cain't believe these ol eyes a hers, but she thinks Betty's a-laughin!

Maybe her poor ol brain finally done tripped over the edge. None a this seems lak it cain really be happenin.

The only one calm is Sophia, which ain't no surprise. She's a-settin thar jes waitin fer the pandemonium ta die down. That thar is a gal ta be stranded on a desert island with, jes lak she says bout Pearl.

From what Pearl cain gather, they has jes done been rescued. These here fellers ain't the tearists. Theys the good guys.

Soons she cain catch her breath, she intends ta ax em what the hell took em so long.

Najat

They are treating her like a hero!

They have believed everything she has told them. It amazes her, how easily lies come to her lips. She, a good Moslem woman, and she speaks these things as if they were Allah's truth. How devious the mind and body of humankind are! Is there ever a bottom to their will to deception?

The women have helped her dress. They've hidden her black fatigues and guns. They are afraid that the SWAT team, when it comes, will shoot first and ask questions later.

They believe Najat when she tells them that she took clothing from a dead terrorist in order to do what she has done. They fuss over her because her head wound is still bleeding and she is feeling faint.

Now, she is not just a liar with a ravenous stomach and a weak bladder, but a murderer, too.

But she will not stop now. She knows, now, what is her mission.

Outside somewhere, very close, is the one who led them astray. They blamed Father Christopher and the Imam, but Najat alone knows the truth. That one in the FBI jacket who speaks on television as the leader – he is the one who planned this entire catastrophe.

She has no doubt that he is enjoying this event. He does not care about the lives that are lost or the damage that has been done to the living. He cares that his plan has succeeded. He cares that his pride is magnified. Maybe he cares that he has done the bidding of another, even higher than he.

She carries, now, a dead woman's purse. In it, she has her handgun.

She is not herself any longer. Jamal is dead and, with him, she has died, too. Now she is only the warrior-woman, Najat.

She will find that man. And she will kill him.

Heddi

The daylight, when they come out of the building, has faded to dusk – which is a good thing because even the low light is blinding after so long in the room. The electric blue dome of the sky seems immense and even the smoggy old Los Angeles air flows into Heddi's lungs like a freshet.

Her legs were so wobbly they wanted to put her in a wheelchair, but she refused. So here she is, emerging on the arm of the same young officer who almost crushed her ankle.

He can't apologize enough, but frankly if he'd cut the damned thing off, it would have been worth it.

She can't believe the nightmare's over!

Over to her left, there's a smoky crater where the bomb went off. Her escort – Curt is his name – says one of the terrorists did a suicide bombing. He says they don't know yet how many people are dead but probably quite a few FBI types and some news people. He's quite chatty, is Curt, once his testosterone subsides.

Heddi feels unaccountably gay and blithe.

Down at the end of the walk, she sees a mob of news people. There are lights and microphones and cameras – and they're all aimed at her.

At *them* – the others are hobbling out behind her.

Can you believe it – her fifteen seconds of fame and she looks like *this!* She smoothes her hair with a trembling hand.

Betty

Thank God they offered her a wheelchair so she can sit on this ooze, instead of having it run down her legs! She can smell herself and it's embarrassing.

But when they come out of the building, the smell of burning – what? Wood? Plastics? Flesh? Maybe all of the above – hits Betty hard. On her left, a smoking hole still has little fires burning in the bottom of it, like one of the pits of Hell. Firefighters are swarming all over it.

How could she even worry about her puny concerns? She's alive! And there are so many who aren't.

Up ahead, Heddi is limping along on the arm of one of the FBI's Hostage Rescue Team. They're chatting as if they were at a garden party. Even filthy, limping and disheveled, Heddi moves like a princess.

Betty guesses they teach you that early on in families like hers.

Families...will all their families be waiting? It's too much to imagine that Betty's will be.

Imagine the families of those who were killed today! They'll wait and wait and their loved ones will never come home. It's too terrible!

Heddi turns back toward her and calls gaily, "Smile, Betty, you're on Candid Camera!"

Up ahead there's a solid wall of media people. To Betty's exhausted eyes, they look like a medieval mob armed with pitchforks.

"Isn't there some way to avoid this?" she asks over her shoulder to the officer pushing the chair.

He doesn't even answer. Maybe he doesn't hear her. Maybe he just thinks that, in a free nation, victims must be re-victimized by the press. Maybe he's thinking about his dead comrades. Anyway, he keeps on pushing her inexorably toward the mob.

They're almost there when she hears a voice yelling, "Betty! *Betty!*"

She'd know that voice anywhere!

She scans the crowd up ahead. Suddenly, she sees him! He's pressed up against a low retaining wall that divides a ratty little garden of shrubs and grasses from a parking lot.

"*LARRY!*" she screams. But it's not really a scream – it's more like a great rosebud of sound unfurling from her, opening its petals like moist, welcoming arms.

He vaults over the wall and comes running down the walkway full bore, even though the officer walking with Heddi holds out a restraining arm. Larry just dodges around him and keeps running, shouting, "Betty! My *God*, Betty!" and he's close enough now that she can see he's streaming with tears.

And only then does she put her head down on her chest and sob for joy.

Ondine

The HRT officer is very nice and Ondine thinks he's still trailing along behind to make sure she doesn't collapse in a heap, but she wants to walk out of the terminal under her own steam.

She must look like a refugee from the Blitz.

The evening wind swirls around her, as she starts up the walk, lifting her auburn hair out around her in a Medusa's aura.

Has she reached the age when she actually can turn men to stone with a glance? If so, this is the moment to test it out.

A mash of media forms an impenetrable wall up ahead and Heddi and Betty are heading toward it, but Ondine just has to stop and look around.

There are some big bunches of grass waving in the wind, making a seething sound like water boiling. There's a deep hole on her left that's filled with shattered, completely unrecognizable debris that is still fluttering with weak flame despite the fire hoses aimed at it.

The sky is that brilliant, unearthly, Maxfield Parrish blue that comes sometimes on a fair evening after the heat of the day subsides.

She takes a deep breath and even though it's tainted with smoke and smog, the air tastes like champagne.

She feels completely ungrounded, as if her feet could lift off and she could soar away on the wind like Mary Poppins.

I'm alive! I lived!

God alone knows how or why.

But it's true.

The media frenzy up ahead doesn't faze her. She doesn't expect Kyle – or God forbid, Richard – to be here. But if they are, that's fine, too.

Her soul has already left the scene. It's gone on ahead and is already roaming Tante Collete's garden, pruning shears in hand, or sitting at the piano in the music room picking out a Chopin waltz, or bundled up, striding into the wild wind on the beach.

There is where her mallets are and her chisels, her pots of pigment and her sable brushes. The stone studio sits empty, like a temple awaiting its Muse.

The first thing she wants to do, though, is find whatever's blooming – Christmas rose, maybe, or even just holly berries – and place it at the foot of the fauntain at the *demoiselle's* doorstep.

She will never understand why she was spared when so many have died. All she knows is she's going to take her life in her arms and make love to it. She's going to paint it in all the colors of the rainbow, and sculpt it so that even when she's long gone, the evidence of her soul's passion for life will endure.

So help me God, I will never...NEVER...take this life for granted again!

Pearl

Well, *the Lord giveth an the Lord taketh away,* her Granny use ter say. *They ain't no accountin fer the ways a the Lord, He that dwelleth in Mystery an Mat.*

But this here, somehow, it jes don't seem fair. A body's got ter rail at the Almaty over this.

Thar she sets, upright as a post, stronger then three oxes.

Pearl cain't hardly look on her. But she's gotta cuz the others has done gone an went an Pearl's the only one left.

"Oh, Honey, I'm jes gonna pat yer hair inta place a bit. Wipe that blood from yer cheek.

"How beautiful you look...jes lak one a them statues out in front a the justice court.

"I wish it woulda been me. Hell! I'm older then dirt an meaner then a box a snakes. Ain't no reason, no how, that I should live an you not. The Lord's sent me many a mystery in this long life, but this here one is mysterious beyond all get-out.

"Theys sayin I gots ta go now, Honey. The others has done gone and went, and I sure hate ta have ta tell em what's befallen you. I sure hates ta leave you, but I don't suppose it'll be long fore we meet again. The Good Lord cain't be stern enough ta keep me here much longer. He's meant ta be a just God. A kind God, or so they say.

"They's out in the hall, the one what done it an his boss, an that poor kid's gettin the reamin-out a his lifetime! He's blubberin an sayin he thought you was a tearist cuz yer so big. He's cryin lak a baby, sayin it ain't natural, a woman being so large. Huh! What d'ya suppose *he* knows, anyways, bout what's natural in a woman?

"They's packin that colored gal off now. They say she's alive – an that's all yer doin. She'd be long gone, if'n it warn't fer you.

"Honey, you done nothin but give us all gifts an now, I'll be damned if'n you din't give me one more. I gots mah tears back. An from the feel a thins, they's back in Spades.

"The Lord bless you, Girl. Let a kiss from these poor, withered ol lips send you off ta Paradise whar the Lord knows you belong."

Sophia

It's a firefight. Automatic weapons fire on all sides, rattling off ammo in a steady chatter. A tree on her right is engulfed in flames and birds are screaming, as they flap chaotically out of the fire, their feathers burning.

Over the roar of battle, she can hear John's voice like a buoy clanging in a storm: "To me, men! This way! Take cover over here!" And she sees the men crouching toward him, firing as they go.

And so does she. She's drawn to his voice like iron filings to a magnet. In spite of bullets and mortars, it's the embodiment of warmth, the haven of her soul.

She crawls the last few yards, a hail of bullets whizzing over her like angry hornets. She can see him there, hunkered behind a fallen log.

He turns and sees her. A look of shock and joy convulses his face. He mouths, "What the *hell*...?" and Sophia grins. *Surprise!*

Their eyes lock, as she crawls the last few feet and then she's in his arms and he's holding her so tightly that she can barely breathe. And she sees with amazement that he has a bullet hole right through the center of his forehead, just like hers. She puts her finger up to it and touches it just to make sure.

"You, too?"

"Me, too."

His arms hold her tighter. She feels she could simply melt into him like butter into toast.

"What do we do now?" She's getting confused.

Everything is whirling around and even the ground underneath her is heaving, as if to throw them off.

"Let's blow this place. The party's getting rough," John says. "What d'ya say?" She looks up at him, trusting as a child.

Sophia nods dumbly, then whimpers, "But what about the enemy?"

"The enemy?" He looks at her with puzzlement.

"Yes. You know – the *enemy?* The *Cong?*"

"Oh," he says in dawning understanding. "Oh Honey... there's no *enemy*. It's just...just..." He waves his hand vaguely at the blaze of battle. "Just a bunch of men, fighting."

He stands and pulls her up after him. The entire jungle glade is a chaos of sound and fire and lethal projectiles. He points to their left. "Let's go that way."

And they walk away hand in hand, completely unscathed. Once they're in a quieter spot, he stops and pulls her to him. "God! I've missed you!"

And he kisses her and there is no end to it. They seem to just spiral out into space, locked together, their two hearts fusing like two pieces of molten metal.

"Where are we going?" she gasps when they come up for air.

"Where else, darlin'?" His eyes are full of mischief and he smiles that smile. "Let's go *home!*"

Acknowledgements

First & foremost, my thanks to Lou Aronica, publisher of the Fiction Studio imprint, whose vision & courage have made this book possible.

Also, thank you from my heart to:

My husband, David Roberson, the most multi-faceted, energetic & conscious person I know, who has loved, supported & encouraged me in more ways than I can count; my parents, Abram & Marjorie Still, for gifting me the mountain; Glenn Taylor, whose trust & belief have been transformative; poet Roxanne Williams, whose *A Gossamer Heart* is winging healing around the world, for the loan of Andrew the Book Angel; Reggie Kramer, whose creative fire lights up the darkest places; Fur Children Lilli, Sophia, Panda, Misha, Teddy, & Persephone, for taking me for my daily walks; Javier Aguirre for 30 years of dance, song, harassment, laughter & adventure – *no hay palabras*; the Dream Girls, Sandy Alarcon, Gael Amend, Debbie Dodge & Pam Marino, for demonstrating that a loving, supportive commune of women is possible; Greg Ford, for courage in honoring the Geneva Conventions even when his government didn't; James Hillman, whose archetypal understanding opens a view of patterns underlying life's seeming chaos; astrologer Laurence Hillman, for challenging me to create something solid that I could throw at him--this book is the result; Charles Ladley, who taught me the outhouse trick & shared his grandmother; Madniz, great captive spirit & poet, for demonstrating that *nothing* can destroy the power & sanctity of the human soul; Cheryl Fitzpatrick Keegan, who danced with the fairies--Godspeed, darling; Kathy Meyer, whose *How to Shit in the Woods* first showed me that a woman can succeed in writing; Susanne Nishino, who loves this Earth with such passion; Ralph Squire, President of the *Subtle*

Energy Research Institute (SERI), for his fearless quest into the space where religion & science meet; Melanie Stewart, for teaching this old dog new media tricks; Carolyn Takhar, my one, only & favorite sister, whose *Tibetan Life Spring* brings healing to the planet; Johanna Treichler, whose generosity will never be forgotten; John Van Dam, for his intelligence & his patience; Mary Christmas Van Winkle, one of the last to remember the old Miwuk ways & songs--fly with the spirits of the wind; Joan Wade, whose beauty, intelligence and chic are only surpassed by her steadfastness as a friend; Wang Kai, shining light in China; Hope Werness, companion in creative overload; & to Jean Ashford, Jack Avery, Barbara Baer, John & Tita Barnett, Vonna Breeze-Martin. Sylvie Carnot, Mary Clancy, Sarah Coehlo Webster, Ann Coyle, Carol Culpepper, Brian Fowlie, Dorothy Heron, Sister Mary Sean Hodges, Christie Holliday, Judie Kavanaugh, Carole & Amber Logue, Marcella Sirhandi & Kathleen & Sally – there's always a space in my heart for you; also, to Barbara Aronica Buck, who made the creation of this book's cover a joyful process; Meryl Moss of Meryl Moss Media Relations; M.J. Rose of Author Buzz; & award-winning photographer Robert White.

A Conversation with
Suzan Still

What was the inspiration for *Commune of Women*?

I've always been interested in women's issues, particularly in how women develop under the influence of, and often in spite of, patriarchy. I thought it would be interesting to isolate an extremely diverse group of women, to see how they might deport themselves when all the rules were theirs for the making. The title comes from the women in one of my dream groups, who joke about spending their later years together, in a commune of women.

Dreams are scattered throughout *Commune of Women*. Why have you given them such prominence?

I've run dream groups for over twenty-five years and I'm fascinated by how they develop into consciousness-raising groups – at the psyche's insistence. Dreams emerge that indicate the inner demand for transformation. Also, they clearly picture the inner and outer state of the dreamer and sometimes even foretell events, as Sophia's dream about standing in the middle of an intersection clearly foresees her collision with the terrorists. Dreams are the bucket that pulls our deepest knowing up from the well of the unconscious, and so, rather than being just a literary device, the dreams in *Commune of Women* promote character development because they indicate the true interior state of the character.

Why have you chosen to format *Commune of Women* as you have, with each character speaking separately?

My intention is to get as deeply into the inner workings of each character as possible, and for that, an omniscient point of view seemed too distanced, and so I use it sparingly. I've approached in intimate third person, so that the reader is pulled right inside the thought processes of each character. One of my favorite works of literature is Lawrence Durrell's *Alexandria Quartet*, in which four main characters share the same events but from completely different perspectives. That kind of psychological relativity is what I'm exploring in *Commune of Women*. Like a film, the narrative, within a very short time frame, flickers among multiple points of view. I think we've all wondered how we would respond in a truly life-threatening situation. The characters offer seven individual responses and the format is an attempt to understand those responses as intimately as possible.

Do you think *Commune of Women* will provoke some people, because of its show of sympathy for the individual terrorists?

It certainly might do so, although that is not my intention.

I think it's all too easy, these days, to scapegoat entire nations of people, without the smallest understanding of their cultural, economic, historic, religious or political circumstances. That's the point I hope to make – but I certainly have no intention of condoning terrorism!

Do you have a favorite character?

It would be hard to choose because I've lived so deeply into each of them and have such empathy for each one. If I were forced to decide, I suppose it would have to be Ondine, who seems to express a dilemma common in many women. Let's face it, American women have tremendous freedom of choice about their lives, compared to women in other parts of the world. Still, I find many women are for some reason afraid to be as big and glorious as they are able to be. Through Ondine I explore the kinds of brakes we all put on ourselves, in regard to living large. And besides, her character gave me an opportunity to live for a time at *Quatre Vents*, a place I am convinced actually exists and which I intend to locate, one day!

Pearl is such a unique character. Is she based on someone you know?

No, but I wish I did. I just love Pearl. She's actually a composite of several influences. My friend Charles had a grandmother as indomitable under difficult circumstances as Pearl is. She may be the gritty core around which the character of Pearl accreted. And then, from my years of working in a men's prison, I have come to love the cadences of black street slang and rap, which is poetic, rhythmic, vivid and blunt. Pearl's character also taps into experiences of my youth among the living remnants of California's Gold Rush and the migrants of the Dust Bowl, who were pretty pithy individuals – weather-beaten, marginalized, impoverished, honest, hardworking, and kind, once you breached their tough exteriors. Also, Pearl is a summation of the woes of womankind and she embodies the undefeated soul of the archetypal Feminine, with its wisdom, patience, faith, nurturance, endurance, hard work and humility.

What if you'd written *Commune of Men*, instead – how would it be different?

Oh my! What a question! Well, for one thing, I imagine the pace of the novel would be completely different – much more action-adventure oriented. I think it would be much more plot-driven–those guys would be inventing weapons out of materials at hand, sending out scouts, wrestling terrorists for their guns in the hallways and rescuing hostages. That kind of thing. Which is not to say that women can't be actively courageous – I think Najat and her entire lineage of Palestinian women demonstrate that. The women of *Commune of Women* are practicing a different kind of courage, distinguished by its patience and endurance, its willingness to cooperate, its self-restraint and focus on the needs of others.

I understand that the cover art for *Commune of Women* is yours?

Yes, even though writing is my main focus, I'm also an artist. As I was finishing *Commune of Women*, that particular image kept insisting that it wanted to be on the cover. I was so fortunate that Barb Buck, who did the cover design, felt the same way about it. That image, called *Three Graces in Paris*, is from a collage series I did that honors the strength and mystery of the feminine.

You have Sophia say that, in some ways, the Burning Times never stopped. What do you mean by that?

The term *the Burning Times* refers to the Inquisition, during which so-called witches were burned at the stake and in ovens. Deaths in this "Women's Holocaust" are estimated by scholars to have been between 60 to 110 thousand. My point is that the persecution of women persists today, long after the Inquisition. We see it in religious and legal repressions of women in various forms, in wholesale rape of women in politically unsettled areas, or in the booming business of sex slavery. The recent *60 Minutes* interview of the reporter, Lara Logan, in which she speaks of her harrowing attack in Egypt's Tahrir Square, during President Mubarek's fall, brings this observation right up to the minute. Her clothing was ripped off and she was sexually assaulted and nearly ripped apart by a mob of men for 25 minutes until an amazing thing happened: she landed in the lap of a woman covered head to toe in a black body veil. This woman embraced her, which slowed the mob long enough for help to arrive. Isn't it amazing how, in an instant, and between the most disparate types, a commune of women can form? The image of a battered, naked woman embraced on the lap of a mysterious feminine figure all in black is certainly a *Pietà* for our times!

What's next for you? Maybe a novel on the life of Tante Collette?

You know, I've thought of that. Tante Collette is ripe for the picking, isn't she? But she'll have to wait. I have several books in progress, lined up like a wagon train that extends from Kansas to California! Lead wagon is *Fiesta of Smoke*, a novel about the coming revolution in Mexico. It's a love story that extends over five turbulent decades – and in its center, there's a deep well that takes us back over nine hundred years into an ancient mystery. It's going to be a very long book – one to take on summer vacation or to read during the doldrums of winter. I hope to have it completed by year's end.

One last question: what did you learn from the women of *Commune of Women*?

They affirmed things that I've observed about women all my life. I know women have been the butt of endless jokes about everything from sex to driving a car to the shapes of our bodies. But when the chips are down, women can be tough. Steely. They can pull together, work to exhaustion, conquer unimaginable odds – and never lose their moral compass. Never sink to underhandedness or gratuitous violence, either physical or psychological. Each of the characters in *Commune of Women* is imperfect, flawed in some way. But through acceptance of one another's weaknesses and by working together, they prevail. When you look around the globe and see what women are enduring, you know there has to be something incredibly powerful inside that keeps us going against all odds. That's what I learned from the women of *Commune of Women*: we're *powerful*; united, we can, must, and will prevail.

Reading Group Questions

Commune of Women is composed of seven intertwining story lines: those of Erika, Heddi, Betty, Pearl, Sophia, Ondine and Najat. Discuss the structure and prose style of each narrative. Do you find the individual voices to be distinct? Did you enjoy the alternating of voices and time frames? What are the strengths and drawbacks of this format?

Which character did you prefer? Why? Is one voice more or less authentic than the others? If you could go out to lunch with only one of these characters, which one would you choose as most interesting to dine with? Did you consider Tante Collette, Madame Zola, Father Christopher, Matilda and Pearl's Granny when making your choice? Are they powerful enough as characters to warrant consideration as luncheon guests?

Discuss the ways in which interior and exterior spaces, houses, rooms and gardens define each character. Are you interested in such spaces, their aesthetic quality and distinctive characteristics? Recall the significant space of each character. Does any of these spaces become a character all its own? What kind of space most authentically defines you?

The use of dreams, the discussion of *demoiselles* and fairies, and Sophia's uncanny intuitive powers all introduce an element of the unknown into the narrative. How comfortable are you with these subjects? Did they "work" for you? Did they arouse your curiosity to know more? Have you ever experienced anything like this – precognitive dreams, visitations by Others, or deep intuitive knowing?

What are the major themes of *Commune of Women*? If you were to recommend this book to another reader, how would you summarize it?

What did you know about the political situation in Palestine – and Gaza and the Rafah Camp, in particular – before reading *Commune of Women*? Or in Rwanda, Iran, Bosnia, Chechnya, or Kurdistan? How did this book teach you about, or change your impression of, these important chapters in world history? Did it change your understanding of terrorism to read the individual histories of the terrorists? To what extent did the author take artistic liberties with this information?

What does the title, *Commune of Women*, mean to you? Did you associate it with communal living? With communication? With the taking of a sacrament? With communing with out-of-the-ordinary beings, including Pearl's Granny? Have you ever had an experience in which women worked together in difficult circumstances to accomplish something – especially basic survival? Do you feel that the women acted reasonably? What would you have done differently, in their situation?

How did you react to the underlying theme of government corruption? Do you trust your government always to do the right and legal thing? Do you feel that personal or corporate interests sometimes intervene in government operations and decisions? Have you ever had an experience of this, or can you cite instances in which you believe this has occurred?

How do you imagine the lives of the women, after the novel ends? What will their lives be like, what decisions will they make, and how have they been altered or transformed by their experience? Will any of the characters choose to forget or deny what has happened and the insights she has gained?

Is there a moral to *Commune of Women*? What have you learned about our world and about yourself, from reading the women's story?

To reach Suzan Still with questions or to arrange a personal or telephone visit with your reading group, contact her at SuzanStill@gmail.com.